PROMISES WE MEANT TO KEEP

NEW YORK TIMES BESTSELLING AUTHOR
MONICA MURPHY

Entangled Publishing, LLC
644 Shrewsbury Commons Ave., STE 181
Shrewsbury, PA 17361
rights@entangledpublishing.com

Amara is an imprint of Entangled Publishing, LLC.

Visit our website at www.entangledpublishing.com.

Edited by Rebecca Barney
Cover design by Emily Wittig
Stock art by vtorous/Depositphotos
Interior design by Toni Kerr

ISBN 9-781-64937-672-5

Manufactured in the United States of America

First Edition November 2023

10 9 8 7 6 5 4 3 2

ALSO BY MONICA MURPHY

THE LANCASTER PREP SERIES

Things I Wanted To Say
A Million Kisses in Your Lifetime
Promises We Meant to Keep
I'll Always Be With You
You Said I Was Your Favorite

FOR TEEN READERS

Pretty Dead Girls
Saving It
Daring the Bad Boy

At Entangled, we want our readers to be well-informed. If you would like to know if this book contains any elements that might be of concern for you, please check the back of the book for details.

PROLOGUE

SYLVIE

THE PAST

"Mommy!" My voice is a rasp, my throat raw and sore. I ache all over and I can't get comfortable in my bed, my blankets so heavy and hot, I kick them off in frustration.

"Sylvie, darling." My mother rushes into my bedroom, reaching for the duvet at the end of my bed and pulling it up so I'm completely covered once again. "Keep your blanket on. You're not well and you don't want to get sicker."

Frustration makes me want to scream but instead I close my eyes, concentrating on taking a deep breath without coughing. I've been home for the last couple of days, and I'm so bored. "I already have a cold."

A sigh leaves her. "Right. That's why you shouldn't go to school in the first place. You're always catching something." My eyes flash open when I hear her firm tone. "It's a cesspool full of germs at that place. Most expensive private school in the city, you'd think it wouldn't be this way."

"I love school." She threatens to take it away from me all the time, and I always cry and beg her to let me stay. I don't want to be home schooled. Just me and Mommy all day long. I like my teachers and my friends, though I don't have a lot of them. I'm never there long enough to get invited to sleepovers and birthday parties.

I'm always sick. I don't know what's wrong with me, or why I'm going to the doctor all the time. They can never seem to figure out what's wrong with me either.

"What time is it?" I ask her, wanting to change the subject. If she gets too fixated on school, she might try and do something. Like pull me out of it completely.

She's done that before. This is the third school I've attended since kindergarten, and I'm only in the third grade. Daddy says I need stability, but she always tells me when we're alone that he has no idea what he's talking about.

I guess I believe her.

"Almost nine. You need to take your medicine."

Sitting up in bed, I make a face when she turns away to grab the cough syrup that's on my dresser. I hate the way it tastes.

"Do I have to?" I whine.

"Yes." She turns to face me, pouring the thick, dark red syrup into the tiny cup before she hands it over to me. "Make sure you drink every drop."

I do as she says, grimacing after I choke it down. Cough syrup always tastes awful, but this stuff is worse than normal. There's a metal taste to it that I can't figure it out, and every time I ask her why it tastes like that, she says that's just the way it is.

"Good girl," she murmurs when I hand over the empty cup. "Thank you for always being so agreeable, darling."

I readjust my pillows before I make myself comfortable in bed, wishing I could leave my room and watch some TV or something. A movie maybe? But I know she won't let me. She'll tell me it's too late.

She always has an excuse.

"You should be sleeping. I'm sure you're exhausted." She tucks the comforter just beneath my face, leaning over to drop a kiss on my forehead. "My beautiful little darling girl. You need someone to take care of you, hmm?"

I ignore what she says, not liking how her words make me feel. "I'm not tired. I've been sleeping all day."

"You need to rest."

"I'm bored. Did you call my teacher and get my homework for me?" I want something to do. I don't have my learning packet for the week, and I need to work on my multiplication tables.

She rises to her full height, standing at the side of my bed. "You don't actually want to do homework, do you?"

Homework. She says it like it's a dirty word.

I shrug. "I like to learn."

"I can teach you so much more than whatever you learn at school. Practical things that you'll use later in life." She settles in on the edge of my bed, smiling at me. "We're different, you know. Our family. Our lifestyle. Some of those subjects they teach you…you'll never need."

She says that all the time. How we're different. Like we're better than everyone else. Sometimes I want to believe it and sometimes…

I feel bad for thinking that way.

"But I like school. I like my friends."

She frowns. "Don't you like your mommy?"

"I love you," I say without hesitation.

Her frown fades. "Then you should want to stay home all the time. With me."

But I don't. How do I say that to her without hurting her feelings?

There's a rapid-fire knock on my partially open door, startling us both. We turn to find my father standing in the doorway, his forehead lined with concern when his gaze finds mine.

"You okay, Sylvie-bug?" he asks, his voice gentle.

Before I can answer, my mother answers.

"Don't call her that. She's not a bug." Mommy's mouth screws up when she says bug. Like it's a bad word.

"I'm okay," I tell my dad, grabbing the stuffed unicorn he gave me a couple of years ago and hugging it close. "It's just a cold."

A cough escapes me as if to emphasize what I said.

His frown deepens and he glances over at Mommy. "She sounds terrible."

"We have a doctor's appointment tomorrow morning," Mom answers, her voice cool.

Disappointment fills me. I don't want to go to the doctor. I go there all the time. It's just a cold. It's no big deal.

"You always take her to the doctor, yet she never seems to get better." Daddy flashes me a quick smile before returning his attention to Mommy. "Why is that, you think?"

"What are you trying to say? That you doubt me? They're still trying to figure out what's wrong with her." She starts to leave my bedroom. "We'll be back, darling."

I watch them go, can hear them whispering furiously in the hallway, and when their voices rise, I close my eyes, letting my head sink into the pillow.

"Why don't you let me take care of her for once? Whatever you're doing, isn't working."

"How dare you say that? Like it's my fault she's ill. We don't know what's wrong with her! At least I'm doing something and trying to help her."

"I want to help, but you never let me. It's like you want to keep her all to yourself."

"Maybe I do. Maybe she's all I have. Not like you care what I need, or what she needs either."

My father goes quiet. I can practically feel his anger, and hers too.

They're always angry when they talk about me. She talks about him when she's alone with me too. Complaining about Daddy and how he doesn't love her anymore.

I don't like it. I don't want to hear it. Her words scare me. Sometimes...

She scares me.

Chapter One

SYLVIE

Three years ago

"Make a choice," Mother hisses as she roughly grabs my arm, her hold firm.

Bruising.

I jerk out of her grip, rubbing the spot where she touched me before I fix my glare on her. It has zero effect, as usual. "No. What you're asking of me is impossible."

A delicate brow arches. My mother is classically beautiful. Modernly preserved. Nary a wrinkle in sight, not that anyone cares. My father left her years ago. She has no man in her life. Nothing to focus her attention on.

Just me.

"Nothing is impossible, darling. You of all people should know this. Look at you. You're a living miracle."

White hot rage turns my blood to ice. The only reason I'm still alive is because I figured out what she was doing to me—convincing a team of doctors for years that something was wrong with me, when I was perfectly fine.

Perfectly healthy.

All while she poisoned me with unknown toxins. Deprived

me of healthy essentials. Kept me up so I could never sleep, making me look and act worse and worse.

I swear I have a faded memory of her holding a pillow over my face while I struggled to breathe. Did that actually happen? Or is it a figment of my overactive imagination?

I'm still not sure.

Despite my confronting her several times, calling her out for what she's done to me, she pretends those conversations never happened—and so do I. The winter of my junior year in high school, when I almost overdosed by my own hand versus whatever she was doing to me, she finally stopped with her charade. Her theatrics.

But she's given one hell of a performance throughout my life. Downright award-winning. Always the frantic, concerned mother unable to help her poor, sickly daughter. It took me some time, but I first suspected what she was doing around the age of eight.

Eight.

Then I immediately put the thought out of my head because no one ever wants to admit their mother would do something so horrible to them. I couldn't fathom her cruelty, until I had to finally face the fact that she wanted me dead.

But why? For attention? That's the only thing I could figure. My father neglected her. My brother avoided her and my sister pretended she didn't exist.

So she turned all of her diabolical focus on me. Her own life was complete chaos, and the only thing she could control was me.

Ironic that I nearly died because of my own choices, not hers. I was distraught back then, and I felt abandoned. I turned on my best friend and ruined that relationship. There was no point in going on. My entire life felt like a lie. Or so I thought.

Turns out, my mother still has plans for me—to send me to another sort of death.

"And I'm at least giving you options," she continues. Her smile is cold, her gaze calculating. "So go ahead. Make your choice."

We're in her study at the Manhattan penthouse, though we could be anywhere and still have this battle. We clash all the time, ever since I was little. It's as if this is the only way we know how to communicate—by tearing each other down.

My older brother Whit dismisses our mother so wholeheartedly that it takes her breath away every time he does it, which is often. My younger sister Carolina threw herself into studying ballet, so she wouldn't have to deal with our mother's controlling ways. She left home at thirteen and never came back.

That was years ago. And I always found it funny that she chose ballet, considering it's the most rigid, controlling form of dance there is, and Carolina still went to it in search of freedom. That's how domineering our mother is—when someone allows her to be.

That's me. The one with Mommy issues, the one who's constantly seeking her attention. Her approval. Her acceptance. Despite her almost killing me, I still want her love. Crave it, even.

Much to my eternal shame, I am the only one out of the three of us our mother can actually manipulate.

"Well?" Mother's sharp voice snaps me out of my reverie and I blink at her, momentarily confused. Within seconds though, it all comes flooding back.

My decision. My supposed choice. *Which man shall I marry, Mother? Perhaps Mr. Mid-Life Crisis? Or Mr. Older Than Dirt?*

I don't know which one is worse.

"Give me until tomorrow." I stand up straighter, lifting my chin, internally searching for strength, but coming up woefully empty. "I will give you my answer then."

"Giving you any amount of extra time is dangerous. You know this." Mother crosses her arms, her gaze sweeping over me, her disapproval obvious. "Don't try and run away from me, darling. I will find you. I always do."

"Oh, I know." I smile, but it feels forced, so I stop. "I don't plan on running away."

What's the point? She's right. She always finds me.

No one can save me now. Not even the boy who always swore he would run to my defense.

I think of that boy and can't help the small smile that curls my lips. Sweet, dumb Spencer Donato. He tolerates me like no other, which drives me mad. His father may have supposed mafia ties—that's the rumor, anyway—but Spence takes more after his sweet, loyal mother from the Midwest. He's always been the one I can count on to help me forget.

At least for a little while.

"Good." She takes a few steps, as if she's going to leave the room, but then stops directly in front of me instead. "You know I'm only watching out for you, Sylvie. You can't take care of yourself, not after everything that's happened. You need someone to guide you, and what better choice than an older, wiser man for your husband? To get with someone your own age could end up being a—mistake."

I say nothing. I've already come into one inheritance. The trust fund becomes mine, without stipulations, when I turn twenty-one, which is in less than two years. I assume she believes I would waste every last dollar, and there are hundreds of millions of them in that trust fund.

She doesn't trust me. She never has.

Which puts us on an even playing field, because I don't trust her either.

"Like that sweet teddy bear of yours. Spencer." I flinch at her saying his name out loud, and she catches it. Of course, she does. Many others would consider the smile that appears to be kind, but I know it's not. She dispatched her weapon, and it wounded me, just as she'd hoped. "He doesn't understand our world, darling. Not really. He's more like his simple-minded mother."

Sylvia Lancaster likes no one, respects no one. She believes she's above it all.

"His family is very rich—" I start, always trying to defend

him, but she cuts me off.

"Not like our wealth. Not even close. And besides, so much of his family's money is—tainted." She mock shudders. "It's best to cut him off. Don't you think? For all we know, he's working closely with his father now."

I don't bother responding. We don't know what he's doing. I don't ask him. We haven't spoken in months. His social media says he's a student at NYU, but is he really? I don't know.

If my mother has her way, I never will.

"You need someone who is solid. Established. Like the choices I gave you. They're both excellent, and no matter who you end up marrying, they'll take care of you, even with your—ailments."

My ailments. What a sweet little way to put how she fucked me up so hard mentally since I was a child. It's the same thing she's said to me for years. Since the first time she took me to a doctor's office in the hopes they could figure out what was wrong with me.

Everything's wrong with me, I've concluded. *I'm a mess. Who would want me?*

According to what my mother said earlier, Earl Wainwright the fourth has put in the highest bid for me, followed by another, much older gentleman whose name I've already forgotten.

Earl is near seventy. Divorced and lonely and looking for a pretty young thing to escort to social events.

He wants me. And she's offered me to him for a most tidy sum. Not quite sure how much, but I know she recently lost some money in a bad investment.

A shiver moves through me at the realization that I've been promised to someone.

When my heart belongs to someone else. It always has.

And always will.

• • •

knock so hard on the door it hurts my knuckles. I'm soothing them with my tongue, while clutching a chilled bottle of champagne in my other hand, when the door suddenly swings open.

Spencer is standing there, surprise etched all over his handsome face when he sees me on his doorstep, licking the back of my hand. "How did you get in the building?"

Pausing, I glare at him, dropping my injured hand to my side.

No, *hello, come in.*

No, *oh my God, I've missed you so much, Sylvie.*

None of that. He just wants to know how I snuck into the building.

"I gave the doorman a hand job." I push past him and enter the apartment, glancing around the clean, uncluttered space, doing my best to blink back the tears.

Now is not the time to be sad. I have a mission to complete.

"Aren't you glad to see me?" It's been months since we were last together, and he's grown tired of my games.

Those were the exact words he used, and at the time, they hurt. They still do, but I'm desperate to see him. Touch him.

Hold him one last time.

I turn to face Spence, lifting up the bottle of champagne, wishing I'd already downed some so I could feel that fizziness bubbling in my throat. Tickling in my stomach. Tingling across my skin.

He finishes locking the door before he slowly approaches me, wariness oozing from his every pore. I drink him in greedily, like this is the last time I'll ever see him, and for all I know, that could be the truth.

Spencer is unbearably handsome, even more so now that he's older and filled out completely. All dark eyes and dark hair, sinful decadence, like extra rich chocolate. Broad shoulders and wide chest and so, *so* tall, especially compared to me.

I'm tiny. Like a little sprite. That's what he called me one time, when we were both still at Lancaster Prep and I snuck him into my dorm room so he could have his wicked way with me.

We did that a lot back then. Sneaking around. I miss it.

I miss him.

Last time we saw each other though, we were in the city. Here at his apartment. I showed up unexpectedly, as I'm wont to do, and he tried to get me to leave. Like I interrupted him, when no one was here.

That I know of.

I might've yelled at him. I might've also told him I never wanted to see him again.

I lie. All the time. He knows this.

"I thought you hated me." His voice is flat, as is his gaze when he levels it on me, which fills my entire body with dread.

"Oh, I do hate you, Spencer. I shouldn't be here. This is a mistake, my showing up on your doorstep. You know it. I know it." I pause, noting the frustrated flare that lights up his eyes, which tells me he cares. At least a little bit. "Doesn't mean I don't want something from you, though."

He says nothing as I walk right up to him, grabbing hold of the front of his shirt and jerking on it so he has no choice but to dip his head. His mouth hovers above mine, full and ripe and tempting as sin. My lips find his, and I nibble on them for only a teasing moment before pulling away. "Let's get drunk."

"Sylvie..."

"I need to get drunk, Spencer. It's a special occasion tonight." My voice is hushed. Almost hoarse. I'm terrified he's going to say no.

"What's the occasion?" His gaze roves over my face, as if he's memorizing every tiny feature. The blemishes and the scars. He's the only one who sees me for who I really am. Yet he doesn't push me away. He doesn't try to change me either.

There is no one else like Spencer Donato.

No one.

"I need to get drunk, so I can work up the nerve to actually fuck you for once." I let go of his shirt and march into his kitchen, setting the bottle of champagne on the counter before I start pulling open each and every cabinet door until I finally find what I want.

Champagne glasses.

How I knew he would have some, I'm not sure, but I've spent plenty of time in his family's apartment in the past to know they're fully stocked with everything, especially when it comes to liquor.

He follows me into the kitchen, turning on the lights. I point at where I left the bottle on the counter. "Open it for me, please?"

He rolls up the sleeves of his dark blue button-down shirt and gets to work, eventually pulling the cork from the bottle, the loud pop startling me. I stare at his strong forearms as he grabs a glass and carefully pours the champagne inside before he hands it over to me, then pours one for himself.

I lift the glass toward him, my hand shaky. "Cheers."

"To what?" His voice is low. Calm.

Hearing his question, seeing the look on his face…

Destroys me.

I smile and lock my knees, my act in full force. Pretending that it's just me and him, when after tonight, there will be no more us. I'm promised to another, when I always meant to be promised to Spencer. "To the future."

He clinks his glass against mine and we each drink, our gazes locked on each other. He sips while I chug, draining the glass within seconds, then setting it on the counter. I grab the bottle and give myself a refill and turn to offer more to Spence, but he's barely touched his champagne.

Shrugging, I fill the glass too much, causing it to overflow. Laughing, I grab my glass, not caring that champagne is spilling everywhere. All over the counter. My coat. My neck. My lips. I drink and drink, growing hotter with every swallow.

"Why are you wearing a coat, Syl?" he asks, snatching the empty glass out of my hand before I can pour myself yet another one.

I've lost count of how many I've had, but I know it's not enough.

"Hey." I glare at him. "I want more."

"Take off your coat. Stay a while. We've got all night."

He doesn't understand. I don't have all night. I probably have a couple of hours, tops, before I must return home. Mother's doing God knows what, leaving me to my own devices, which was her first mistake. I took the opportunity to make my escape, knowing this was my last chance. My last night.

With Spencer.

"You want me to take off my coat?" It's constructed of thick black wool, with a faux fur collar and a belt cinched tightly at the waist, reminding everyone how horribly thin I am.

"Aren't you hot?" A dark brow shoots up as he contemplates me.

"Just you wait." I untie the belt and shrug the coat off of me, so it lands in a pile at my feet.

Revealing that I'm completely naked. An offering to the only man I can stand touching me.

His eyes go wide, and he shifts them up to mine, never breaking our stare. "Sylvie..."

I step toward him, slinging my arms around his neck, brushing my naked body against his. "Fuck me, Spence."

"What are you doing?" He keeps his gaze glued on my face, his hands resting lightly on my hips. As if he's afraid to touch me.

"I want you." I rise on tiptoe and press my mouth to his, my eyes tightly closed. He returns the kiss for only a second, then jerks his head back. I fall back onto my heels, my eyes opening to find his gaze full of concern as he studies me, and I hate it. I don't want him worried. I want him to fuck me. "Don't look at me like that."

"What happened? Tell me."

He's too smart. He can always figure me out.

"Nothing." I smile, reaching between us to settle my hand over his burgeoning erection. I can make him hard, just by looking at me.

"You're lying." His voice is irritatingly calm and I suddenly want to scream. Pull my hair out and ask why life has to be so damn unfair.

"I swear, you're the only man I know who would question a naked girl's motives. Don't you get it? I want to consummate our relationship, Spence. Haven't I teased you long enough?" I smile at him, my limbs growing languid, thanks to the alcohol mixing with the pills I took earlier. Though I need to be careful. I don't want to pass out and miss all the fun. "No other man would do this. They'd pick me up and take me straight to bed."

"I know how you are, Syl. You're worrying me."

"I'm fine." I clear my throat. "Really. Just fine."

Maybe if I say it enough, I'll start to believe it.

"Fine?"

"Yes." I stand taller, suddenly desperate to down more champagne. "Now take me to bed."

He snags my hand and pulls me even closer to him, his lips curled into a lecherous smile as he whispers, "Who says I want to fuck you in a bed?"

I blink up at him, trying to ignore the sudden throb between my legs. "I'm a young, virginal girl. You want to...what? Take me against a wall? Fuck me right here in the kitchen, maybe?" I pull out of his embrace and haul myself onto the kitchen counter, the marble cold beneath my butt. "Come here." I reach for him, but he's not close enough. "Let's test the height."

I slowly spread my legs as he approaches, allowing him to step between them. He settles his hands on the insides of my thighs, lightly caressing, little sparks igniting on my skin from his touch. "Young, virginal girl," he murmurs, his deep voice making gooseflesh rise. "There is nothing virginal about you, Sylvie."

"Except my intact hymen." I can't concentrate when he touches me like that, running his fingers back and forth, drawing closer and closer to my pussy, only to skitter away. He knows where I want him, and he won't give it to me. "My doctor just proved to my mother that I'm virginal in every way."

His lids lift, those dark brown eyes of his searing into mine. "You have the most fucked-up doctor—and mother—on the planet."

God, the truth hurts.

"It's not his fault. He only does what my mother asks," I say softly, sinking my teeth into my lower lip when his fingers lightly brush against my wetness. Testing me. Teasing me. "She's selling me off to the highest bidder."

His fingers pause in their exploration. "What do you mean?"

I reach for the front of his shirt and slowly start undoing the buttons, keeping my gaze on the task rather than look him in the eye when I say, "I'm to be engaged, Spencer. I'm sure the announcement will be made soon."

"To who?"

"You don't know him. He's an investment banker. Much, much older, and so worldly. He'll teach me things, I'm sure. Mother paid him off, so I'm not her problem anymore, since killing me with false illnesses didn't work." The words pour out of me, one after the other, as if I have no control over them.

A chuckle leaves him, and he resumes his search, his thumb pressing against my clit, making me hiss. "You're funny, Syl."

I didn't expect him to believe me. I've said this sort of shit before, but it's never come true. I haven't died. I haven't been shipped off to Australia, I haven't been committed to a mental facility, I haven't turned into a lesbian, I haven't gone to Harvard.

All things I swore to Spencer would happen, but didn't.

I am the consummate liar. The eccentric rich girl who does what she wants. Says what she wants. Buys whatever she desires.

That's what it looks like to the outside world, but here, right now? With this boy who's now a man?

I'm as real as I can get. And still, he doesn't believe me. I wish he could see through my façade. Most of the time he can, but lately, I'm not sure who the real me is anymore.

Pushing aside my melancholy, I concentrate on what's happening. How he's touching me. I need to chase after the feeling I experience only with Spencer. That's my goal tonight.

The only goal.

Leaning back, I prop my hands on the counter, my entire body trembling as he drifts his fingers across my sensitive skin. "I'm serious, Spence. The next chapter of my life starts with, 'Once upon a wedding…' Isn't that romantic?"

He ignores what I say, his gaze focused on where he strokes me. "You told me you would never get married."

"Guess I lied. Are you really that surprised?" When his gaze meets mine, I lift my brows. "That's what I thought."

"Did you take anything before you came here?" His fingers pause in their exploration and a frustrated whimper sounds from low in my throat.

"Of course not," I lie, spreading my legs wider. As wide as they can get. "Make me come, Spencer. I need it."

I start to move with his stroking fingers, undulating my hips. Biting my lower lip when those assured fingers slide inside me. He pumps them slowly, curling his fingers and nudging that mysterious spot that has me seeing stars.

"Look at you," he murmurs, his gaze on his hand as he strokes me. "Wet and naked on my kitchen counter. You're like a dream come true."

A dream that won't last, is what I want to say, but I don't.

Instead, I breathe out a sigh, arching my hips upward.

He doesn't let up. No, he makes everything worse when he leans over me, his tongue lashing across one hard nipple, then the other, leaving them wet and aching. I can't look away, my lips parted as he fucks me with his fingers and sucks at my nipples with his mouth. My normally buttoned-up Spence is sinfully sexy, with his shirt partially undone, showing off those rippling abs he always keeps under wraps.

Is it wrong that I only seek him out when I'm scared? When I know everything is about to fall apart? Habits are so very hard to break, and ever since I left Lancaster Prep, we've played it this way every single time. Getting each other off. Saying stupid shit that devolves into a raging argument that has me storming out, slamming the door behind me. Vowing to never see him again.

That's always a lie.

The problem is, lately, my stupid shit has become real.

Yet he thinks it's still a game.

This is what happens when you're young and rich, and seemingly don't have a care in the world. You pretend that life is one giant game and you're in it to win it.

Spence doesn't even realize that I've already lost. I'm taking one last thing just for me before I have to settle for my consolation prize.

"You ever have a girl show up on your doorstep, wearing just a coat and nothing else?" I lie back on my elbows, grateful for the long, wide counters in his kitchen, a gasp escaping me when he ducks down and puts his mouth on me.

I close my eyes on a moan and reach for his head, sinking my fingers into his thick, soft hair and holding him to me as he licks every inch of my pussy. He teases my hole with his tongue. Laps at my clit, circling it, flicking it.

Driving me out of my mind.

His hands settle on my hips, pulling me forward as he lifts away from me, my fingers slipping from his hair. "Can't say that I have."

I don't even know what he's talking about anymore, but it doesn't matter. When he returns his attention to my pussy, I revel in the rhythm of his tongue, his hands tugging on my hips, moving me with him. Blindly, I reach out, my hand accidentally slapping at one of the discarded champagne glasses and it rolls off the counter, falling onto the floor in a delicate tinkle of glass.

"Don't hurt yourself," I whisper, hoping the glass didn't hit him.

He doesn't say a word. Only murmurs against my flesh, the sensation driving me wild. I buck against his seeking mouth, rising up to grip his hair with both hands, staring down at him while he gazes up at me.

The look in his eyes is what does it for me. His mouth on my pussy, his fingers pressed deep. The wave rises, washing over me so suddenly, I shout his name, screaming my pleasure as I ride it out on his face.

His beautiful, beloved face.

When it's over, he gathers me in his arms and carries me out of the kitchen, sidestepping any glass. He takes me to his bedroom, depositing me in the center of the mattress. I lie there like a heap of bones, still breathless, my gaze never leaving him as he strips himself of his clothes. Until he's just as naked as me. Erect and huge.

All for me.

He approaches the bed, crawling on it from the bottom like a predatory animal, until he's right over me, caging me in. I stare up at him, curling my finger around the thin gold chain he always wears, tugging him down until his mouth is barely brushing mine. The rich, earthy scent of my pussy still clings to his mouth and chin, and I lick at his skin, savoring the taste.

"You're going to fuck me for real this time," I whisper. "Do you understand?"

I've always been the one who pushed him away at the last second, too afraid to go on. Once I got my period, Mother spoke of my virginity as a precious gift you give to the man you're to marry, and no one else.

Did I want to be a slut? She would ask me that question

often. *Did I want to spread my legs and give it up to every man who said I was pretty?*

No ma'am, I would always respond, my voice quivering.

I guarded my virginity with my very being, not that anyone wanted me like that. For the longest time, I wasn't in school enough for any boy to be interested in me.

Until Spencer. From the moment we locked eyes, I knew.

I *knew*.

I've done so many things. So many other things than actual sex with Spence. Oh, I've kissed a few other boys too. Let a couple of them feel me up even. But most every sexual encounter I've had has been with Spencer.

Except for this one thing.

When your mother has you go in for regular examinations to ensure your virginity is still provable, you do what she wants. I've never believed I've ever had an option. Despite my being an adult, I still have a difficult time leaving my mother. A small part of me needs her.

How twisted is that?

Marrying me off to someone she chose reminds me that I don't belong to myself. I never really have. My virginity is no longer mine to guard, and I'm giving it away, consequences be damned, despite me being promised to another.

And it's not this man who currently hovers over me, his thick cock resting against my belly, leaving a wet streak. Proof of his desire for me. With my other hand, I reach for him, my fingertips brushing against the head, making it twitch.

He exhales raggedly and hangs his head, breathing deep. As if he needs to regain some sort of control. "You don't really want this."

Now he's the one who pushes me away. I've had his cock in my mouth, his hands all over me. Yet he's rejecting me because he knows how much this—my precious virginity—means to me.

To my mother.

It's sick how involved she is in my life.

"I do want it. With you." I tug on the chain again, our mouths melting together, our tongues tangling. Stroking. Stoking the fire that always burns within me when I'm with this boy.

Man. He's a man now. And I'm an engaged woman.

About to fuck someone who is not my future husband.

I stroke his cock, and he slowly thrusts it against my palm, groaning into my mouth. My body feels empty, my inner walls clenching around nothing. For once, I just want to know what it's like. What *he* feels like inside of me. Fingers aren't enough. His mouth—while absolutely divine—isn't enough.

I need more.

"Let me grab a condom." He leans over me, reaching for the nightstand, pulling the drawer open. I try not to think of Spencer with other girls, but I can't help it.

He keeps condoms in his bedside table. How many girls has he brought to this apartment? How many girls has he fucked? We've never had a spoken commitment, yet we're continuously drawn to each other. We weave in and out of each other's lives constantly. I've gone months without seeing him.

I can have no expectations. No demands. It's not my right, despite how much I care about him.

Care is not a good enough word. I love Spencer. I do. I just can't work up the courage to say the word out loud.

"We don't need a condom. I'm on the pill." I'm testing him to see if he says he should wear one because he's been with others, but he doesn't say anything.

Not at first.

"What do you mean, you're on the pill?" His gaze is questioning when it finds mine.

"I thought it best to be prepared."

"And how long have you been prepared?"

I lift one shoulder, playing nonchalant. "Don't worry about it."

His gaze is steady—and too intense. I finally look away from him, swallowing hard. If he rejects me right now…

I don't know what I'll do.

But he doesn't. Of course, he doesn't. He has me spread open beneath him, ready and willing. He can't turn me away.

Instead, he shuts the drawer and resumes his position over me, rising up on his knees, his fingers wrapped around the base of his erection. He strokes himself, my mouth growing dry the longer I watch, and I realize I'm running out of time.

I need him to do this. Now.

Spreading my legs, I show him everything I have. His gaze drops, naturally. Zeroed in on glistening rose-colored flesh. I reach between my legs and stroke myself, the wet sounds making me wetter. "Please," I whisper.

I never beg. From the look on his face, he knows it.

"I want you inside me."

He strokes himself some more, his cock red. Almost angry looking.

"Please, Spence." I close my eyes, whimpering. "I need you."

Without hesitation, he looms over me, guiding his cock inside my willing body. I inhale the moment I feel him breach the entrance, my thighs stiffening, my entire body going rigid.

All willingness leaves me, fear replacing it completely.

"Relax," he whispers, his mouth against mine, just before he steals it for a long, tongue-filled kiss. The longer he does that, the easier it is for me to do as he says and relax. I begin to realize he's filling me, inch by unbearable inch, stealing my breath the farther he slips in, until his cock is fully inside my body.

My inner walls clench around him this time and it's like a jolt runs through me, electrifying my blood and my skin and my bones. There's a pinch. A sting as he starts to pull out, only for him to thrust inside again and this time…

This time, there's no pinch. No sting.

Spence moves and I do too, completely fascinated with every little thing he's doing. The way his hands are braced on the bed on either side of my head. The sway of his necklace as he pushes in and out of me. The sheen of sweat forming on his forehead and his chest. The curling dark hair in the center of his pecs, hair that wasn't really there when he was seventeen and we'd get naked, hidden away in my room at Lancaster Prep, so he could finger me, and I would jerk him off.

Oh, those were good days. When my worries had nothing to do with future husbands and babies and all of that horribly responsible adult-type shit. When I could just be with Spence without a care.

"Fuck, Sylvie," he grits out, sounding as if he's in pain. "You're so tight."

"Too tight?" I ask, like the virginal idiot I am.

He chuckles. "Never." Then dips his head for a kiss. "You're squeezing me so hard I'm going to come in minutes."

Good. I want him to come in minutes. We should hurry. This is my last shot to be with Spencer before I have to give him up forever.

He must sense when my muscles warm and loosen because, soon enough, he's fucking me in earnest. Fucking me hard. The slap of our skin connecting fills the room, as does the scent of sex. Despite the earlier orgasm I experienced, my body is fired up and ready to go, and I reach between us, my fingers finding my swollen clit as I begin to stroke.

Spence bats my hand away, his rough fingers drawing tinier and tinier circles around it, until I'm throwing my head back, unable to breathe as a second orgasm rockets through me, leaving me breathless.

Mindless.

"Fuck," he grits out, right as I feel that first splash of cum deep within me. Soon enough, I'm flooded, his thrusts never slowing as he rams himself inside me, a ragged groan sounding low in his throat.

I rub his back when he slumps on top of me. Up and down,

tracing along his smooth skin, breathing in the scent of his cologne. His shampoo. He's still embedded inside me, and I wonder if I'll always remember what this moment felt like when I think of Spence.

How he's become a part of me.

"I'm too heavy." He starts to pull away, but I grip him tighter, keeping him from leaving.

"No," I whisper, swallowing hard. Past the thick emotion coating my throat, making me want to cry. "Don't go. Not yet."

He lies there for a moment, giving in to my request, until he can't take it any longer. When he pulls out of me, semen gushes, wetting my thighs and the bed beneath me, and I feel hollow. Empty. I almost want to push his semen back inside, so I can take a piece of him with me when I leave, but I don't.

I don't want him to ask why.

"I should've worn a condom." He falls onto his side next to me, his hand reaching between my legs to gather up the cum.

I slap his hand away, then immediately regret it. "Leave it. I'm fine."

He rubs me, up and down, his fingers slow. Gentle. "There's blood." He holds up his fingers to show the streaks of blood mixed with his semen. "You really were a virgin."

"Did you ever doubt me?" My voice is small. Hurt.

"Not really," he says, his hand leaving me completely when I glare at him. "Come on, Syl. You tend to say a lot of crazy shit."

My glare softens. He's right.

"But you know you're the only one for me," he murmurs, the sincere glow in his gaze overwhelming.

"You'll say anything to get a girl into your bed," I tease, needing to lighten the moment.

The sincerity is replaced with pain, but I ignore it.

"Did you like it when I came inside you?" he asks, almost sounding…shy?

My sweet, sweet Spence. He's a romantic. A knight in shining armor. Always running to my rescue.

Nothing can save me now, though. Not even him.

I arch a brow. "Have you ever come inside a girl before? Bare? Without a condom?"

Slowly, he shakes his head, leaning in for another kiss. "Never."

"Promise?" Stopping him from kissing me, I rest my hand on his chest, right over his still rapidly pounding heart.

"Yes," he whispers against my lips, his tongue slipping between them as his fingers slip inside me once more. He toys with my pussy, his fingers finding my still sensitive clit, and my body responds like the whore it is for this man. "I want to make you come again."

"But I'm so tired." I roll away from his seeking fingers, hating that I'm pushing him away.

If I could, I would let him fuck me all night long, let him make me come again and again. But we can't do that.

We've run out of time.

He doesn't have to speak a word, but I can feel his frustration with me. It lingers on his skin, echoes in his voice when he insists, "Sylvie. Let me. You know you want it."

"No, I don't. I need to sleep." I glance over my shoulder at him, ignoring the pouty expression on his too handsome face. He is so hard to resist, but I have to. "That was my first time, Spencer. I'm sore."

I'm really not, but I need to get out of here.

"Aw. My poor baby." He doesn't argue with me anymore. Just pulls me to him, my back to his front, his muscular arms sliding around my torso, those big hands splayed across my stomach, holding me in place. I can feel his cock nudge my butt. He's still aroused. If I don't watch it, we could get carried away and he'd be inside me again. It would be so easy. It's always easy between Spence and me—until it's not. "Let me get a washcloth. I'll clean you up."

"No." I shake my head, my hair brushing against his face, and he pushes it away. "Just—let me lie here and close my eyes. It'll only be for a few minutes."

"Okay." He kisses my temple, his lips lingering. I feel him breathe me in, as if he's savoring my scent, and my heart, I swear to God, it cracks.

Wide open, spilling all of my pent-up emotions out. Everywhere. I could bleed out in this bed and die in this boy's arms, and no one would question it. Least of all me. He kills me in the absolute sweetest way. Eventually, I'm going to hurt him, and he's going to hate me. I'll have to live with myself for that, whether I like it or not.

We say nothing, the quietness of his apartment momentarily lulling me to sleep. Until I startle awake what feels like only minutes later, though I'm clueless to the time. The room is dark. I can hear the city noise outside in the distance. The honk of a horn. The wail of a siren.

I need to go.

Staying still, I hone in on Spence's steady breathing. It's slow and deep. He's fast asleep. He's always been able to fall asleep quickly.

I envy him that.

Carefully, so I don't disturb him, I slip out of bed, turning back to look at him one last time before I go.

He's lying on his side, the blanket drawn up to his waist, his eyes closed and his lips parted. He looks so peaceful. So beautiful. His dark brown hair tumbles across his forehead, and I long to push it back. Kiss his forehead. Breathe him in much like he did to me earlier.

Whisper that I love him.

I do none of that. I stare at him for a moment longer, trying to imprint this moment on my brain for future memories, and then I flee the bedroom, running down the hall naked, going into the kitchen in search of my coat. I snatch it up from the floor and slip it on, stepping right onto the glass I broke with a wince, biting my lip so I don't cry out.

There's no time for me to pull glass out of my foot, though I do brush at it quickly. I slip into my stiletto sandals, tie the coat belt tight around my waist once more, and check the pocket for my phone.

Pulling it out, I note the time on the screen, worry flashing through me. I've been gone longer than anticipated.

Mother might be in search of me.

Fear floods me and I ignore the notifications on my phone, shoving it back into my coat pocket. I scurry out of his apartment, slowly pulling the door closed. I take the elevator down to the ground floor, waving at the doorman I bribed earlier with his favorite cookies from a nearby bakery, exiting the building in a blur.

I've visited Spence enough over the years for the doorman to recognize me, but I always like to give him a little treat for never giving me any trouble.

Only when I'm in the back seat of my car and on my way home, do I feel brave enough to check my phone's notifications. There's a text from Mother.

Of course, there is.

Come home now.

I'm sure she knows where I've been, and who I've been with. She's tolerated my dalliances, as she calls them, with Spencer for years and mostly looked the other way.

But no more. Now she has a responsibility. To deliver to Earl Wainwright the perfect, little virgin bride.

An evil smile curls my lips.

Whoops.

Looks like I ruined that part of her plan.

CHAPTER TWO

SYLVIE

PRESENT DAY

I didn't mean to get drunk before my brother's wedding. Not really.

But when my new best friend Clifford Von Worth showed up at my Park Avenue apartment with a very large bottle of Clix vodka clutched in his hand, I knew immediately I was in trouble. Cliff held up the bottle as he entered the apartment, and I squinted at the label, my lips forming a shocked little O.

"Does that say *clit* vodka?" I ask.

Cliff chuckles, shutting the door behind him. "Please, Sylvie. As if I would purchase *clit* vodka. I don't even know what to do with one."

Cliff lives in the same building I moved into with my husband after we were first married. We became immediate best friends, especially with Earl always away, traveling for business. Oh, my husband wanted me to accompany him so he could show off his perfect little wife who's barely in her twenties. Arm candy personified, right? But I feigned illness—so easy, a role I was used to since I've been truly sick for years—and he allowed me to stay home.

With my sweet friend Cliff.

"Tell me the truth, Cliffy. You've never touched a woman's clit? Ever?" I ask as he follows me over to the bar that sits in the corner of the massive living room.

"I've never touched any woman in a sexual manner." I turn to face him once I'm behind the bar, just in time to see him mock shiver at the mere idea.

"You act as if it would be the most disgusting thing ever." I grab a couple of shot glasses while Cliff opens the bottle, then pours a drink for each of us.

"It would be. Vaginas are so messy." He holds up his shot glass, clinking it against mine before we both tip our heads back and finish it in one swallow. "Women aren't my thing. You know this."

"Penises are messy too. They drip everywhere. Shoot off at the most unexpected times." I lick the vodka from my lips and pour myself another glass. This is why I like spending so much time with Cliff. He's safe. He has zero expectations beyond friendship, and he doesn't want to be with a woman, so no sexual advances occur. Plus, we're never in competition with each other for anything. "I just figured you might've...I don't know...fingered a girl in high school during a heavy make-out session?"

The grimace on his face is almost comical. "Disgusting. I would never."

Laughing, I pour another shot for myself, ignoring the concerned look on Cliff's face when I tip my head back, the liquor smooth going down. "You know, you would really love my friend Monty."

"Monty who?" Cliff sets his glass down with a loud thunk, his eyes going wide. "Wait. Are you referring to Montgomery Michaels?"

Nodding, I take his glass and fill it yet again. "He's a dear family friend. And he'll be at the wedding."

"Oh my God, are you serious? Why didn't you tell me this sooner? Oh, he's stunning." Cliff shakes his head when I offer him his full shot glass. "I can't get drunk now. I need to keep my wits about me when I meet Monty for the first time."

I polish off his shot instead, smacking my lips together. "I'll introduce you to him."

"You'd better." He snatches the glass from my fingers. "Sylvie. Dearest. Please don't drink too much. You don't want to make a fool of yourself at your brother's wedding now, do you?"

"I don't really care. Everyone will expect me to act the fool anyway." I grab my own glass and refill it, drinking it before he can stop me. "Besides, will anyone be paying attention to me? Doubtful. After all, it is Whit and Summer's day. Everyone will be staring at the two of them. They're so beautiful together."

I stop talking, hating how I sound like a jealous shrew, which I suppose I am. And I have reason to be too.

Why does Whit get to marry the love of his life, while I had to marry the old man? I didn't even get to have a big wedding—Earl and I went to the courthouse and got married. A quick marriage ceremony for a bogus couple, I suppose.

Not that I wanted to have a big wedding with Earl. Talk about a wasted opportunity.

"How are you and Summer doing anyway?" Cliff's tone is somber. He knows everything about my past with Summer.

Well, mostly.

"We're okay." I shrug a shoulder and laugh, though it sounds hollow.

When it comes to my friendship with Summer, I still feel that way.

Hollow.

Will she ever be real with me again? We've healed our relationship somewhat after I betrayed her so long ago. When I was young and stupid and so heavily influenced by my mother. Full of insecurities and distrust.

I'm still that way, minus the heavily-influenced by my mother part.

Thank God.

"If you say so." The look on Cliff's face says otherwise. "And trust that everyone in attendance today will be paying attention to you at some point. It's your first public appearance after what happened, correct?"

"In an official capacity, yes." I don't really go out. Not anymore. I'm a little hermit, holed up in my fancy apartment, all by myself. I prefer it that way.

Going out, partying…leads to temptation. To things I shouldn't touch. Shouldn't do.

"Is that what you plan on wearing to the wedding?" Cliff's voice pulls me out of my thoughts.

I glance down at my severely cut jet-black dress that I found in my grandmother Lancaster's archives. Yes, my family archives clothes like they're museum pieces, but with our kind of money, it's a smart move. Most of the clothing we purchase goes on to become iconic. Historic even. "What's wrong with it?"

"It's black."

"I'm in mourning."

"Darling, you can't wear black to an afternoon wedding."

"Says who?"

Cliff ignores my question. "Definitely not a spring wedding. You'll look like a dark, little, dreary cloud."

"Everyone else will look like an Easter egg. I'm the only one who'll arrive with an ounce of sophistication beyond the bride." I drink more vodka, the alcohol buzzing through my veins pleasantly, making me feel warm. Loose. Languid. Like I could collapse on the floor and fall asleep at any moment. Cliff doesn't stop me from drinking either, though I see the judgment in his golden-brown gaze.

It's best that I ignore it.

"Hasn't it been long enough? Your mourning period?" The concern in my friend's gaze, in his voice, makes me pause.

A sigh leaves me and I rest my hands on top of the bar, curling my fingers around the edges of the marble countertop. "It will never be long enough."

"Mourning a man you didn't even love is pointless—"

"To you," I interrupt. "But to me, I must continue mourning him because I didn't love him, Cliff. I let him die. He deserves at least that bit of respect from me."

He doesn't acknowledge my *let him die* comment because Cliff doesn't believe it. More like he doesn't listen to me because if he did, for once, he'd realize that I'm telling the truth.

It's my fault Earl is dead. And he deserves more than my meager respect, but I am only one woman, and can only do so much.

"You can't wear black to your brother's wedding." Cliff says this with such finality, I'm momentarily taken aback.

And somewhat ready to agree with him.

"I still don't understand why you aren't a part of the wedding. He's your brother, and you're just a guest. At your family's estate." Cliff shakes his head. "It makes no sense."

"It makes sense to me," I say, my voice small. I didn't want to play even a small part in Whit and Summer's wedding because first of all, I don't really deserve to and second, I don't want to risk being forced to spend time with my mother. I expressed my feelings to my brother, and while he was upset that I didn't want to participate, he also understood my reasons.

She'll be there. The potential to run into her is unavoidable. I will do my best to ignore her and hope any interactions with her are quick and painless. People may talk about my lacking presence, but I don't care. I'm in self-preservation mode.

"Come on." He takes my hand and leads me away from the bar, from my beloved new friend, *Clit* Vodka. I trail after him as he drags me to the bedroom, the room that used to belong to Earl but is now mine.

It's dark inside, the blackout curtains drawn tight. Cliff lets go of my hand and marches over to the window, hitting a button so the shades pull back automatically, slowly and steadily revealing the sunshiny day. The cityscape laid out before us. The tall buildings, their windows glittering in the sun.

I throw up a hand, blocking my eyes and hissing. "Too bright."

"God, you're such a fucking vampire," he says drolly as he heads for the walk-in closet. I kept all of Earl's bedroom furniture, and the room still smells like him, which makes me think I need to get rid of it.

I need no reminders of my dead husband. I should probably sell this apartment, but where would I go? I don't want to move in with my father. I can't move in with my mother.

For now, this apartment will have to do.

The minute Earl was laid to rest, I hired someone to completely revamp the closet, donating all of his clothes to charity before I moved in my own extensive collection.

Oh, his children were pissed at me. I didn't even give them a chance to go through everything, but they wouldn't want it anyway. And what if they found something? A little clue tucked away in Earl's trousers or jacket.

I couldn't risk it.

Besides, his children just wanted to be angry with me, and I get why. I'm an easy target. The brand-new, much younger wife. Their mother is dead, and to them, I'm a pariah. Younger than all of them, which I'm sure disgusted them.

Whatever. The only thing they couldn't get me on was going after Earl's money. I paid them fair market value for the apartment. I let them fight over the money in his bank accounts, even though it was split evenly among the four of them, according to Earl's will. He may have married me, but he didn't add me to his will, so I had no real say in anything.

I didn't mind. I still don't.

"What are you doing?" I wander into the closet, my steps weaving. I slap my hand against the wall to brace myself. "Oh God, you're picking out something for me to wear, aren't you?"

"I have to, considering you'd rather show up in a dress that looks like something your granny would've worn in the fifties." The look of contempt on Cliff's face cannot be denied. "As if Christian Dior himself designed it in 1952."

I glance down at the Dior dress I'm wearing before my gaze finds his. "How did you know?"

"I am a fashion expert, darling. How dare you doubt me." He begins to flick through each garment hanging in my closet, dismissing them with a murmured insult. *Too pink. Too exposed. Too much. Too little.*

I say nothing, like I usually do. Instead, I rub at the front of my dress, along the placket of buttons that run down the center of the bodice. "My grandmother did so happen to wear this dress."

"Knew it." His voice is smug. "Was she as tiny as you?"

"Tinier. I don't think rich women in the fifties even ate." I tap at the belt around my waist.

"Too many barbiturates to take to keep you looking and feeling your best. God, I wish I would've lived during that time. I would've been a skinny queen who didn't eat a damn thing, spending every night with Andy Warhol at the Factory." The dreamy tone of Cliff's voice makes me laugh.

"That's more like the sixties," I remind him.

"Whatever." He pulls a hanger out, revealing a soft blue dress that's one shouldered with the occasional ruffle here and there. "Oooh, where did you get this?"

"At a tiny shop in the Hamptons a lifetime ago." I approach him, plucking the hanger from his fingers. "I bought it when Earl was still alive and we were out at his house for the summer, but I never got a chance to wear it."

Cliff glanced down at the dress, his frown apparent. "Hmmm."

"You don't like it?" I question.

"It's not that I don't like it." He puts the dress away and keeps looking before I can say anything in protest. "More that we need no memories of Earl tainting the day."

If he only knew. I don't actually mourn Earl, not really. More, I mourn the girl I was before him. Before I married a man I didn't love and lost the only one I actually care about.

Life is full of stupid choices and then you die. Someone said that to me when I had that brief stint at the mental facility a while ago. The one where my mother thought it would completely change me and solve all of my problems. I tried to fix myself.

I did.

Didn't take though. I'm still the same fucked-up Sylvie I've been for what feels like my entire life.

"He won't taint the day," I murmur. "He was never much a part of my life with my family. I think Whit met him once, and that was reluctantly, on my brother's part."

"Why only once? And why reluctantly?"

Because the marriage was fake. Because Whit knew that and had no desire to spend time with my husband, who's our father's age. Because everything in my life the last few years has been one giant performance, not an ounce of it real.

He knew what our mother did, and told her to her face he didn't approve, but she did it anyway. She doesn't care what anyone thinks.

Certainly not me. Especially not me.

"Whit was too wrapped up in Summer," is my answer, and close enough to the truth. "At the time I was getting engaged to Earl, Whit was in hot pursuit of Summer in Paris."

"Really." Cliff's voice is flat, the expression on his face, doubtful. He doesn't believe me.

I never said Cliff wasn't smart. I like surrounding myself with intelligent people. Then I feel smart too. But when they're too smart?

They become…dangerous.

"Find me a dress." I wave a hand at the racks of clothing, desperate to distract him. "Something beautiful and appropriate for a big wedding on a beautiful spring day."

"Something not so black?" His question is pointed as he resumes his search.

Surely I have something in my closet to wear to my brother's wedding. As a matter of fact, I know I do.

"Help me get out of this." I approach Cliff, turning my back to him so he can undo the zipper. He unzips it, giving me the freedom to shrug out of the well-constructed garment, and I shed it like a skin. I grab an empty hanger and slip it back on, smoothing out the skirt before I hang it on the door of my closet.

"It's a beautiful dress," Cliff says off-handedly.

"For a funeral," I add drolly.

Our gazes meet, just before we crack up.

CHAPTER THREE

SYLVIE

We arrive at my family's Long Island estate where the wedding is being held because, of course it is. The scene of the crime, so to speak, where Whit first fell madly in love with Summer during that one Thanksgiving break, when I brought her with me to be my support system. Instead, she fucked Whit every chance she got in secret, the two of them sneaking around for a week, much to my mother's disgust. Hooking up everywhere, the servants reporting their antics to her whenever she asked.

I don't blame them. They were compensated for their tattling. Mother needed as much evidence as she could gather to show that Summer was nothing but a common whore, just like her mother. Not that Whit cared. She scared Summer instead, and made her run away.

Again, who's laughing now? I can only imagine how disgusted Mother is, that Whit is marrying Summer. That she's the mother to the next generation of Lancasters, with their adorable baby boy August. I'm sure the ceremony being held at our estate is a way for Summer to rub it in Mother's face that she won.

I admire Summer's bravery, I really do.

"I knew you Lancasters were wealthy, but Jesus. This is something else," Cliff mutters as he leads me up the steps toward the entrance to the main house, my arm curled through his. "This house is a friggin' castle."

"It's been in the family for generations. We used to only summer here," I explain as I gather up more of my long skirt in my other hand. The dress Cliff found for me was hanging on the back of my closet door, forgotten. It had been delivered from the designer only last week, in the hopes I would wear it to the wedding and have my photo taken in it.

Lucky them, it's happening. I can feel the shutters clicking as we slowly trudge up the stairs, trailing after the other guests arriving for the wedding. Mother *would* hire paparazzi to take photos. She's always been more of the why fight them type when it comes to photographers.

Once upon a time, for a brief, shining moment, I was an it girl. A darling of the paparazzi—only because I gave them so much fodder to work with. Drinking and drugging and partying with pretty boys. I was every photographer's dream come true.

I became somewhat of an influencer too. Whatever I wore, carried on my arm, slipped around my wrist, sold out immediately upon my photo hitting the internet. It was a wild moment in my life that lasted far too briefly.

Mother helped squash it. She's not one to believe in bad publicity. It's good or nothing. Plus, she was probably terrified I'd open my mouth and tell my truth.

She trained me well, though. I've kept my mouth shut.

"You look to the manor born," Cliff says once we've reached the top of the stairs, his gaze admiring as he takes me in. A breeze causes my skirt to float and I tuck a stray strand of hair behind my ear. "Pretty as a painting."

Pleasure ripples through my veins at his compliment. The gown I'm wearing is absolutely gorgeous, I can't deny it. It's floor-length, white with a turquoise floral print, the tiny sleeves constructed of ruffled tulle. The skirt is a frothy delight of multiple layers of tulle beneath, the tiny belt tied in a permanent bow in the dead center of my waist.

I haven't felt this pretty in a long time. It helps that I'm a little drunk. Liquid courage and all that.

"Wait until you see the paintings in the house." I mock shudder as we walk through the open double doors. "Portraits of intimidating ancestors line the walls everywhere you look. When I was younger, I swore they were all watching me as I walked past."

"How creepy." Cliff sounds distracted as he takes everything in, his eyes wide. Clifford's family is rich, but not like us Lancasters.

There's hardly anyone like the Lancaster family. The original Augustus Lancaster was a ruthless son of a bitch who dabbled in a variety of things during The Industrial Revolution. He started out in shipping. Then he moved on to railroads, investing all the money he made selling his ships into the new frontier, in shipping goods. He invested well, but the later generations were smart and pulled out just before the Great Depression. At one point, Augustus and his sons even bought oil fields in Ohio, of all places.

Our family tree consists of a litany of innovators. Generations ago, it was as if we could foresee the future, and were always looking ahead. Some of the Lancasters are still this way, but while we have plenty of success stories, we also have the not so positive tales about various family members. Divorces. Mental illness. Cheating. There's even a hint of murder here and there. Deception and double crossing and revenge. Hostile takeovers of various businesses and bold moves that nearly destroyed the stock market. We're an adventurous bunch.

All in the Lancaster name.

We breeze through the house, heading for the open double doors that lead onto the terrace, where the reception will be held. I can hear a string quartet already playing, accompanied by the gentle conversations of people speaking all at once. There are guests clustered around, drinks in hand, all of the women in soft pastels, just as I predicted.

Looking like Easter eggs.

I go to the balustrade railing and glance out at the rolling green lawn, where the ceremony will take place. There's a gorgeous arbor laden with so many white flowers, I'm afraid it'll collapse under the weight. The aisle is white, lined with more lush white flowers and there is row after row of white chairs set up, a few people already seated in them.

"Shall we go down there and claim our seats?" Cliff stops right next to me, resting his forearms on the railing's edge.

"Don't worry, our seats are already claimed. We're in the first row, directly in front of Whit." I smile at him, my gaze momentarily catching on a familiar figure headed down the stairs that lead toward the lawn.

I freeze, my heart in my throat, making it hard to breathe. I recognize that dark head. The tall frame, how he moves. How he carries himself.

"Sylvie. Sylvie. Did you hear me?"

I ignore Cliff, my greedy gaze eating him up. The man walking onto the lawn clad in a black tuxedo, his inky hair gleaming under the sun. I swear he's taller. Broader even. He approaches another man I don't recognize, stopping to shake his hand, a faint, closed-mouth smile appearing on his face, and the sight of it is devastating.

Before, he only smiled like that at me. As if I was the only one who made him happy, and he did the same for me, no matter how temporary it felt. He was my respite. A way for me to forget.

Until I made myself forget him.

My heart races. Aches. I'm such an idiot. I should've known he'd be here. Was I that naive to think if I banished him from my life, my mind, my everything, that Whit would do the same?

Spence is one of his best friends. Of course, he wouldn't do that to him. My brother is far more loyal than I could ever be.

"Are you okay?" Cliff settles his hand on my forearm, bringing me back to the present, and I shake myself, offering him a brittle smile. "What happened just now? You look like you just saw a ghost."

"I'm fine." My gaze darts around, seeking out a server divvying out drinks. "Just a little thirsty."

The concern in Cliff's gaze is obvious. "I don't know if you should have anything else to drink before the ceremony, Syl."

I remember how Spencer would always call me Syl. When we were teenagers, I used to joke that we sounded like an old Hollywood couple. Spence and Syl.

Syl and Spence.

"It's so hot though." I fan myself with my fingers, panic racing through my veins, making me want to crawl out of my skin. "I need something to cool me down."

A sigh leaves him and he shakes his head. "I'll be right back." Cliff gives my arm a gentle squeeze before he takes off.

I stand there alone on the terrace of my own home, feeling like an outsider. No one approaches. No one says a word to me, though I can feel them watching. Talking about me in low tones. Curious as to my sudden appearance, when all the rumors claim I'm unhealthy and unable to function.

Anything horrible you can think of has already been said about me. Drugs. A complete mental breakdown. Flunking out of school, fucking a teacher, fucking my father's friend, my best friend's boyfriend. Whatever you can come up with, the rumor has been said. Some of them, I even started myself. When I was younger and didn't care, I told everyone I was fucking my brother's friend Chad, when really, I only had eyes for Spence.

It was enough to spur Spencer into action and he pursued me heavily, thinking I was with Chad. It worked so perfectly. My mother always said I was an excellent manipulator, which makes sense considering I learned from a master.

Closing my eyes, I grip the railing tight, the rough texture cutting into my soft palms. I don't know if I can make it through this day, knowing I'll have to watch him. Possibly even talk to him. Does he have someone else in his life now? He should. He's handsome and kind and smart. What woman wouldn't want him?

I cut off all ties between us after that one night where I gave him my virginity almost three years ago. I thought it best. The only way for me to move on was to eliminate him completely from my life, and he didn't approach me after that night either.

Within days of us being together, my engagement was announced, so I'm sure that was the biggest deterrent ever. Once that happened, once I married Earl, Spencer never made an appearance in my life again. He never even asked about me, and I would question Whit on occasion, curious about Spencer and what he might be doing.

But I never took it too far with my questioning, always protecting myself in the end. To find out certain details would hurt too much, and I was already in enough pain.

"Sylvie!"

My eyes fly open and I turn to find my aunt Louisa approaching me, beautiful in a coral-colored dress, a broad smile on her face.

"Aunt Louisa." I accept her hug and the kiss on each cheek, returning it with a coolness that indicates I have everything under control. I am a most excellent actress. "It's so good to see you."

"I'm so glad you're here. We've missed you at family functions." She pulls away, her hands clutching my upper arms lightly as she scans me from head to toe. "Oh, aren't you a delight. I *adore* your dress."

"Thank you." I smile at her, glancing around. "Where's Uncle Reggie?"

She's married to one of my father's younger brothers. The meanest one—Reginald. God, he's awful.

"He's with your father." The light fades from her eyes, her expression serious. "They're discussing business."

"On a Saturday? During my brother's wedding?" Truly, I'm

not surprised. When do they not talk about business and money and bullshit?

"You know how they are." She lets go of me, waving a dismissive hand, accompanied by a light laugh. "How are you doing?"

"I'm well." I stand up straighter, my back to the lawn and the man down there that still owns a piece of me. "Better than ever."

"You look well enough, considering all the trauma you've gone through in your life." Her smile is full of sympathy.

Oh, leave it to my aunt Louisa to offer a compliment wrapped in an insult.

"Is Charlotte here?" I ask, referring to my cousin and Louisa's only daughter.

"I don't believe she's arrived yet. She's coming with her husband, Perry." My aunt sounds proud, and I suppose she is. Perry and Charlotte are a golden couple. Rumor has it they started out as an arranged marriage that somehow worked out for them, which leaves me a bit envious.

Leave it to beautiful, quiet Charlotte to get the hot, young guy in an arranged marriage while my mother paired me with a decrepit old man.

"How about Crew?" I'm referring to Louisa's youngest son.

"They're already here. Not sure where, though." Louisa's smile remains pleasant, that glow coming back into her eyes. "She's lovely, Crew's fiancée, Wren."

I've met her. She is lovely. And Crew is completely smitten with her.

As if conjured up by magic, Crew and Wren appear. He's handsome in a gray suit, Wren beautiful in a pale pink sundress. They're both golden, as if they've been touched by the sun and their smiles match as they greet me with genuine happiness.

"Why are you both so tan?" I ask Crew after Wren hugs me.

She laughs as his arm comes around her waist, yanking her to his side in a possessive gesture. "We just came back from France."

"Cannes," Crew adds, his adoring gaze finding Wren's.

"What were you doing there?" I'm not just making polite conversation. I'm genuinely curious.

"Looking for art," Wren tells me, her green eyes dancing.

"It's her favorite hobby," Crew adds.

The four of us chat for a few minutes, mostly talking about family, my gaze going to the glass Louisa clutches, wishing I had my own. After a few minutes of chatting, I begin to feel a strange, prickling sensation in the center of my back. It makes my shoulders twitch and I lift them, giving a little shake. Wondering if a bug has landed on my skin.

Knowing my mother, she more than likely had pest control out in full force leading up to today, killing off every bug she could so they wouldn't bother the wedding guests.

"We should probably go to our seats," Louisa says to me after Wren and Crew leave us, headed for the lawn.

"I'm waiting for my date," I tell her. "He's getting me something to drink."

"Oh? Someone new in your life then?" Her eyes light up. She seems hopeful.

"Just a friend," I reassure her, touching her arm. "If you'd like to go down, please do. I don't mind waiting alone."

She gives me a quick hug and I watch her walk away, that odd sensation still lingering. Like someone is watching me. I glance over at the bar, the line mostly diminished, Cliff seemingly flirting with the attractive bartender behind the counter, two full glasses set out, waiting for him to bring one to me.

Turning away, I shake my head. It figures he'd flirt with the bartender. I never did spot Monty on the terrace. Is he already out on the lawn? I turn to look over the edge of the railing, bumping into something solid.

More like *someone* solid. A very tall, muscular someone.

"Oh." I back away, glancing up to find him standing directly in front of me, a glower on his dark face.

Spencer Donato.

CHAPTER FOUR

SYLVIE

I straighten my shoulders, my body trembling as his assessing gaze sweeps over me. I say nothing, afraid my voice might shake if I speak, and I don't want him to know how much he still rattles me.

"Mrs. Wainwright. It's been a while."

His deep, smooth voice washes over me, and I can't help but flinch at him calling me by my married name.

I never went by it. Not once. They would refer to me as Sylvie Lancaster Wainwright occasionally online, but legally, I never changed it.

I am forever a Lancaster, married or not.

"Spencer." My voice is level, and I'm proud of my apparent non-reaction to this boy. Man. Definitely a man. "What a surprise. I didn't expect to see you here."

I'm a liar. Deep down, I knew this would happen, though Whit hasn't brought up Spencer's name to me in a long time.

"I'm your brother's best man. He's one of my oldest, dearest friends." He tips his head toward me, his expression impassive. As if standing in front of me doesn't affect him whatsoever. "Whit didn't tell you?"

"No." I shake my head, pissed at myself. I didn't think to ask, but come on.

Subconsciously, I knew.

"I thought you weren't coming. When you weren't at the rehearsal dinner last night..." His voice drifts, a single brow arching.

"I stay away from my mother as much as possible," I admit, falling back into the old habit of admitting my truth only to this man. "We came to a compromise by my agreeing to attend the wedding."

He's quiet for a moment, letting that tidbit sink in. "Things still aren't—well between you and Sylvia?"

"They never will be," I say firmly. "I don't trust her."

The wary look Spencer shoots my way says he can't trust me either.

I suppose I can't blame him.

"Shouldn't you be with Whit?" I ask.

"I had to find the minister for him, so I could give him a message," Spence explains. "I saw you standing alone on the terrace and thought I would take a chance and approach."

His admission gives me hope, where there should be none. Over the years, I've done too much to him, and to us. I've destroyed whatever we could have. Whatever we could be. There was potential once upon a time, until I destroyed it completely. I don't deserve him, and I know it.

I'm sure he knows it too.

"You look great," I tell him, my voice low, my eyes only for him.

His gaze drifts over me again, lingering on the important bits, and he parts his lips, ready to say something.

"Sorry, Syl. I got caught up chatting with the bartender." Cliff suddenly reappears by my side, offering me a sweating glass of God knows what. I take it from him, barely looking at Spence as I sip from my drink, crushingly disappointed the second the liquid hits my tongue.

It's water.

"Who's this?" Cliff asks, sliding one arm around my waist and offering his right hand to Spence. "I'm Cliff."

"Spencer." He shakes Cliff's hand, his disbelieving gaze briefly meeting mine. "You work fast, Syl. Condolences in regards to your dead husband. Though it looks like you've moved on already."

Before I can say a word to clarify whatever he's thinking, Spencer is gone, striding toward the house without a backward glance.

Cliff loosens his hold on me, blinking at me in surprise before he glances in Spencer's retreating direction. "What the hell was that all about? He thinks we're dating? And what's up with him referring to your dead husband? That was all sorts of rude."

A sigh leaves me and I chug the water, fighting the disappointment that there's not a drop of liquor in the glass. "He's an old friend."

"Hmm. More like a pissed-off, old friend." Cliff's gaze meets mine once more, amusement flashing in his eyes. "He thought we were together, which is hilarious. Can't he tell I don't swing your way?"

I take in Cliff, trying to see him through Spencer's eyes. He's handsome as usual in a black suit with a crisp white shirt, no tie. He's tan and fit and his warm brown hair is perfectly cut so that it flops over his forehead in the most appealing way. "You're an attractive man, Clifford. Plus, you barged into the conversation like you owned me, so I guess he assumed we're together."

"Really? I didn't mean to act like that." He frowns. "Who is he to you, anyway? And don't say an old friend again. That doesn't explain anything and you know it. There's more to this."

"I'll tell you during the reception. Come on." I grab hold of his arm and steer him toward the stairwell that leads down to the lawn. We're one of the last of the guests to sit down, both of us settling in the front row, giving room to where my parents are going to sit, though my little sister Carolina is nowhere to be found. I glance around in search of her.

Anyone could pick her out of a crowd. Lina stands out. With her perfect posture and graceful moves. Her elegant neck and gleaming gold hair that she almost always wears up. I've heard Grace Kelly didn't just walk, she glided like a swan on water.

That's my sister. All those years in dance have molded her into a young woman who moves effortlessly. She still dances, is still a part of the London Dance Company, though she told me she's had the urge to come back to New York recently.

It would be nice, to have an ally on U.S. ground. Though I'm sure Mother would try to pit us against each other, like she did when we were younger.

The music starts, everyone in their seats swiveling to watch as people approach the aisle. First is Summer's stepfather, Howard, and her mother, Janine. They're beaming at everyone seated as they walk down the aisle together, and I can't help but smile in return.

It must burn my mother's bony ass that my father's ex-lover—the woman who broke up their marriage, once and for all—is at her son's wedding. That the woman's daughter is marrying her son. It's so juicy and scandalous.

More family walks down the aisle, including my own. My father, who struts down the aisle with Carolina on his arm. Monty walks down the aisle by himself to go stand on Summer's side, since he's her best man. He sends an interested look in my direction, his gaze flitting to Cliff before returning to me, and I know he's curious.

Perfect. That's exactly what I want.

Spencer and Whit escort my mother together, leading her to her chair, which is only two away from me. I try not to catch her eye, staring straight ahead, my heart beating wildly in my ears. In my head.

It's bad enough that she's sitting so close. Once I married Earl, once I did that one last thing for her, I've kept my distance, with the exception of that one last time. When she swooped in under the pretense that she was 'helping me'.

I don't like her type of help. It always comes with strings attached. And it's not up to me anymore to give her what she wants. I'm a grown woman now.

I owe her nothing.

When Summer appears and walks down the aisle by herself, the crowd is silent. Too caught up in her beauty, her obvious strength by choosing to walk alone. Admiration rises within me as I watch her, captivated by her gown, how it sparkles in the light. The way she walks straight toward Whit as if he's the only one she needs.

I glance over at my brother, catching the way he watches her, overwhelming love shining in his normally cold blue eyes. He is so completely smitten with her, even after all of these years.

My gaze shifts, meeting Spencer's, who's blatantly staring at me. He doesn't look away either when I catch him and neither do I. His expression turns downright defiant, his lip curled with disgust.

Yet his hot gaze is filled with unmistaken lust.

Uncomfortable, I shift in my seat, tearing my gaze from his, focusing on my brother and his almost-wife. The minister speaks in monotone about lasting love and promises made. Promises kept. I think of all the promises I made to Spence when we were younger. When I was foolish and believed he was the only one for me.

Back then, I believed it because I truly thought I would die before I turned eighteen. I glamorized the notion so much to ease my fear, and it was easier owning the realization that I was dying versus pretending nothing was wrong with me. Deep down, I was terrified of the thought of not living.

And here I am, barely surviving now.

Oh, I know what everyone thinks. Poor little rich girl, wah wah wah. I'm pathetic. I have all the money in the world, what do I have to complain about?

Many, many things. Money can't buy happiness. I'm lonely. I only have a few friends, and I've shut out most of my family. I'm scared to be honest with Summer because I'm afraid of her rejection. My brother tolerates me. Carolina doesn't speak to anyone unless she's forced to. My father is completely wrapped up in his latest girlfriend and my mother...

Cannot be trusted.

Like I can't help myself, my thoughts return to Spencer, my gaze lingering on his tall, broad form, handsome in his tuxedo. His expression solemn as he listens to the ceremony, his hands clasped behind his back, his legs slightly spread. A perfect specimen of masculine beauty.

I will him to look in my direction, to see that I'm watching him. I don't even care how hungry I may look, because I'm starved. Starved for this man's attention, his touch, his mouth.

But he doesn't look my way. Not once.

The ceremony goes on, with Whit and Summer sharing their own personal vows, making passionate declarations that leave the crowd swooning. I lean against Cliff, the heat from the afternoon sun getting to me. I didn't eat much today either, which doesn't help my situation, and I would give anything for a drink.

I should've shoved that giant bottle of clit vodka in a bag and brought it with me.

"Are you all right?" Cliff murmurs close to my ear.

My gaze remaining on Spence's back, I say, "No. I'm bored and I'm hungry."

Cliff chuckles. "It's almost over. Then you can introduce me to Monty."

"I will," I reassure him.

At least that's a promise I can keep.

"...you may now kiss the bride."

I nearly collapse with relief when the minister makes that declaration and a few people start to shout when Whit kisses

Summer with a ferocity that borders on indecent. I even hear my mother murmur, "Oh dear..." but I ignore her.

Everyone does.

Once Whit and Summer have walked down the aisle, everyone rises, including myself. My gaze never leaves Spencer's back as I start to approach him, stopping short when I see him offer his arm to my sister. Carolina rises to her feet in one fluid motion, curling her arm around Spence's before they turn onto the aisle and head for the house.

I watch them go, trying to ignore the nagging feeling in my gut when I see them together, their heads bent close as Carolina laughs at something Spence says. The way he smiles down at her, his eyes twinkling.

My stomach twists and I swallow hard, fighting the bile that threatens to rise up in my throat.

"Are those two together?" Cliff asks, meaning Spence and Carolina.

"If they are," I say as I watch the man who took my virginity escort my little sister into our family home, my voice deadly calm. "I will kill him."

CHAPTER FIVE

SPENCER

"Spencer Donato, tell me the truth. Are you trying to make my sister jealous?"

I do a double take, Carolina Lancaster smiling at me, appearing infinitely amused. Although she's the youngest of the Lancaster siblings, she's also the most composed.

And the hardest to read.

"What do you mean?" I ask carefully.

We're in the Lancaster ballroom, where my best friend's wedding reception is being held. The room is filled with the some of the country's—if not the world's—richest people. There are dignitaries and politicians in attendance. World leaders and plenty of royalty too. Supermodels and celebrities and I even hear Harry Styles is going to perform later, which wouldn't surprise me at all.

When the Lancasters do something, they go big.

"Escorting me after the ceremony. Standing next to me right now, while Sylvie pretends to not see us." A soft laugh escapes Carolina and I glance over at her, momentarily taken by the small smile playing upon her lips. She's grown into a beautiful woman, which is expected. The Lancasters have impeccable lineage and impossibly good looks. "You're playing with fire."

"She's burned me enough times already," I admit. And I have the scars to prove it.

"I thought you were in love with each other," Carolina continues. "I even believed you two would get married."

"Your mother would never approve."

"You think she approves of Whit's choice?" The laughter booms from Carolina, surprising me. She's always so quiet, so careful with her words. "My mother is infuriated right now. She just knows how to put on a brave face."

All the Lancasters can. It's in their blood.

"You were probably smart, not marrying Sylvie," Carolina muses.

"Why would you say that?" Am I not good enough? I know my lineage isn't as solid as the Lancasters, but damn. Whit just married his father's ex-lover's daughter. Janine is just a social climber who got a reputation for sleeping with very wealthy, very married men. Not that Summer is like her mother, but...

It doesn't look good, this marriage. Not that Whit gives a damn.

"You might've ended up dead within the first year, like Earl."

I send her a sharp look. "He died of old age."

Carolina shrugs. "If you say so."

I turn her words over in my mind as I glance about the room, hating the annoyance that grows within me and I tamp it down. It's a good day and nothing should get me down. My best friend is married, and that alone is worthy of a celebration. Whit hates everyone. If he allows you into his inner circle, you should feel honored. He doesn't open himself to others very often, if at all.

But I can't stop thinking of Sylvie and that old man she married. They didn't have a lavish ceremony like Whit and Summer. I don't think they had any kind of party at all, not even a reception. Almost as if they wanted to keep the marriage a secret, instead of showing it off, which makes no damn sense.

Earl Wainwright was connected. Revered. Rich as fuck.

And a total piece of shit.

"Lina. Spencer." Augustus Lancaster himself stops in front of us, smiling fondly at his youngest daughter before he tugs her into his arms and squeezes her tight. Carolina remains visibly rigid in his embrace, as if she can't stand the idea of him touching her and the memories come back to me.

Carolina doesn't like to be touched at all. She never really has. Even when I looped my arm through hers to lead her back into the house, she held herself away from me, our arms barely touching.

Once he's released Carolina, Augustus turns toward me, offering his hand. I shake it, giving him a firm grip, just the way he likes it. The Lancaster patriarch prefers a firm touch, a solid handshake, a manly hug with slaps on the back. He considers himself a man's man, unapologetic for his behavior even if it's misogynistic, homophobic, whatever. He's offensive, he smokes, he drinks, he gambles. Then he goes to church, confesses his sins and gains forgiveness.

Repeat, and repeat again. The man is a throwback to a different era. His children are nothing like him. Well, Whit is similar in some behaviors, which is what drew me to him. He flat out doesn't give a fuck what other people think about him, and that's easy to do when you're as rich as he is.

I wanted to be like that. Still do. As I've gotten older, I find myself not caring as much what people think of me.

With the exception of these damn Lancasters. For some reason, their opinions matter to me.

Too much.

"How are you, Spence? Heard you've been working closely with the old man." His grin is knowing. I think he even winks at me.

Ignoring it, I nod, shoving my hands into my pockets. "I've been working a lot lately, yes."

That's all I say. I can feel Carolina's curious gaze on me. She wouldn't know much about the Donato family business. She never paid much attention to me and she's a solid four years younger than I am. Besides, she's been out of the country for the most part, save that one year her parents forced her to come home and attend Lancaster Prep for her senior year.

Augustus chuckles. "Glad to hear it. Hard work is good for the soul."

Before I can respond, someone calls his name, distracting him completely. He smiles and waves, leaving us standing in his wake as he walks away.

"Typical," Carolina mutters, crossing her arms in front of herself.

I say nothing. Definitely don't argue with her because she's right. Plus, what the hell does Augustus Lancaster know about hard work? That man has never had to lift a finger his entire life. Everything's been handed to him.

While I come from wealth, the Donatos work. Hard. It's expected. It's tradition.

The party goes on around us while we watch, and I try to take it in as if I've never been here before. The black and white parquet floors that shine despite being over one hundred years old. Massive tapestries depict the Lancasters of long ago, as if they came from royalty. The giant chandeliers made of French-cut glass glitter down upon us, casting everyone in attendance in an ethereal glow. Laughing, chattering voices echo in the cavernous room, gentle music playing in the background as servers carry giant round trays laden with dishes. The first course of dinner is served, yet I'm not that hungry.

Not after seeing *her.*

I suppose I should be happy. I never thought this moment would actually happen. That Whit would actually find someone he truly loved, and who loved him in return. Growing up, we didn't believe in that shit. His parents divorced, as did mine. As I've already noted, our fathers weren't faithful—and neither was my mother. I have no idea what Sylvia was up to, but I know it wasn't anything good.

She fucked with her daughter's head and health, I do know that.

Pushing all thoughts of that evil woman out of my head, I refocus on the party, wondering if I should go find my seat and carry on as if nothing has happened. As if I wasn't rattled by seeing Sylvie again. Staring into her beautiful blue eyes, the way she looked at me, with reverence. Shock.

Adoration.

That last one, I'm sure I imagined.

The aroma of the food hits my nostrils, making my stomach growl. The food will be delicious, of that I have no doubt. The extravagance unfolding in front of me is nothing short of epic, but would anyone expect anything less from a Lancaster?

I think not.

The house is a monstrosity, built during the time when property tax didn't exist and the richest of the rich believed they were doing the local economy a favor by employing everyone to build their outrageous homes they only used for the summer.

Most of the homes were eventually donated to historical societies, since the families couldn't maintain the expenses on such a large estate. Not the Lancasters. They're still rich enough to afford everything the previous generations built.

Solid investors, every single one of them. Whit is on his way to being one as well. One day, he and Summer will own this house and fill it with all of their many children. Considering Summer is currently pregnant and they already have Augie, I assume they'll create a football team within the next ten years. Perhaps by then, they'll be in this house for good and filling every room with their family.

I'm sure the idea of that burns Sylvia Lancaster's ass. God, I hate that woman.

Her children? I like. One in particular, though she makes

me feel as if I'm losing my mind most of the time.

And it's not the woman currently standing beside me, amused that I'm using her to make her sister jealous. Because I am. It was that or drag Sylvie into a secret room—there are plenty of them in this house, I've dragged her into a few of them before, when we were younger and reckless and flat out didn't give a damn—and have my way with her.

But I'm still too pissed at her to even want to do that. Fuck her for getting married. I don't care if the man is dead—she married someone else, almost immediately after having sex with me. She gave herself to someone else—let an old bastard she didn't even know defile her beautiful body that belonged to me.

Every muscle in my body tightening, I clench my hands into fists. Fuck, I hate that so damn much. I watch her now, moving through the crowd in that dress that isn't what I would call sexy, but she looks damn beautiful wearing it.

So beautiful, she makes my heart ache. And my dick twitch.

She's talking to everyone, smiling and tipping her head back with laughter, as if she finds what they're saying so amusing. Though I know what she's doing.

Faking it. She's so good at that. Pretty sure I'm the only one she's ever been real with.

Or maybe I share that honor with her dead husband now. I don't know.

"You look ready to chew through nails."

I barely look in Carolina's direction, exhaling softly and trying my best to relax my muscles while I consider a response.

Instead, I remain quiet, my thoughts riotous. All of them involving the woman I can't tear my gaze off of.

She's so damn gorgeous in the sweet blue and white dress. Her blonde hair is loose and flowing, a smile frozen in place that I know is false.

I know her better than she will ever realize, which isn't reassuring. No matter how well I believe I know her, she always manages to surprise me.

"She's not the jealous type you know," Carolina continues, staring straight ahead. She could be talking to anyone, though of course, I know she's speaking to me. No one else is near us. "There's no reason for her to be jealous of anyone."

"Are you saying no one matters to her?" I rub the side of my jaw, tempted to undo the bow tie around my neck that suddenly feels as if it's strangling me. I wear a suit almost every damn day of my life, yet this one is somehow suffocating me.

"Sylvie is in her own little world. You know this. We all know this." We angle our heads toward each other, and Carolina sends me a look, one that tells me she sees all. "Our mother created that monster."

"You think Sylvie is a monster." My tone is flat, and I'm definitely not asking like it's a question. There are many ways I could consider Sylvie a monster, though I don't.

"We all are, in our own way. I tried to escape it, but they lured me back anyway." Carolina reaches out and pats my arm in a sisterly fashion before snatching it back, which I find shocking. She so rarely touches anyone willingly. "Looks like she lured you back as well. You're just as fucked as the rest of us."

A buzz sounds from Carolina's white Chanel bag, and she pulls her phone out, frowning at the text message she receives. Her gaze never straying from the screen, she murmurs, "I need to go."

Before I can say a word, she's walking away.

I watch as Carolina leaves me, as graceful as ever. Heads turn as she passes, her nose in the air, a serene expression on her face. As if nothing could ever bother her. Her sister has a similar attitude and expression, moving about the guests at the reception as if she's the hostess. Pausing at tables, greeting everyone with a smile and I'm sure a kind word.

Still hasn't come over to talk to me though.

Pushing away from the wall, I move through the room just

like Sylvie, going in the opposite direction of her. There are plenty of people I know who are in attendance. Kids I went to school with. All of them business associates now. I smile and nod as we pass each other. Even stop a couple of times to chat with some of them for a few minutes. All the while I can feel eyes on me, tracking my every movement. Icy blue and all-seeing.

Finally giving in to my urges, I glance over my shoulder to find Sylvie watching me while standing within a circle of people. The conversation is animated with plenty of hand gestures and laughter, but Sylvie doesn't react. Her expression is blank, her gaze heavy. She's too caught up in staring at me.

I look away, irritation making my blood run hot. I am not the same person I was the last time we were together. When she unexpectedly showed up at my apartment late at night, naked beneath her thick winter coat. Drinking way too much champagne before she fucked me and slipped away while I was sleeping. Never to be heard from again.

Her engagement was announced within days of that encounter. Her quickie wedding held soon after that. I realized then that the girl I'd known, the girl I loved for far too long…

Wasn't who I thought she was.

At all.

CHAPTER SIX

SYLVIE

"Why were you talking to Spence?" I ask Carolina, my voice purposely light.

Inside, I'm as dark and turbulent as a brewing winter storm, ready to unleash my fury if she says the wrong thing.

The amused expression on my sister's annoyingly beautiful face makes me want to slap her. Her delicate brows lift, a challenge in her gaze. "Jealous, Sylvie?"

"Never." My response is too quick and I take a brief moment to calm myself. "Why would I be jealous? He doesn't matter to me any longer. Did he ever?" The laugh that slips from me sounds so fake, I immediately clamp my lips together to silence it.

"Someone protests far too much." A sigh leaves Carolina as she glances about the room. The reception has been in full swing for almost two hours and we're currently sitting at a table with the family, finally eating the main entrée—steak or fish. I chose fish, though I don't have much of an appetite. The day has been far too stressful, starting with my worry over interacting with my mother. Then seeing Spence. Feeling his wrath.

It's my fault for not thinking he would be here—and that he would be angry with me.

Thank God, Mother is on the opposite end of the table, so I

feel relatively safe in being here, not having to talk to her.

Even if the conversation I'm engaging in with my sister is a tad uncomfortable.

"I was just catching up with him," Carolina says, as vague as ever. "It's been a while since I saw Spence."

It's been a hot minute since I last saw him too. The memories rush through my mind, one after the other. Arriving at his apartment that night, desperate and needy. Revealing my naked self beneath the coat. How he went down on me while I was sprawled across the kitchen counter, making me come with his perfect mouth before taking me to his bedroom and fucking me thoroughly. Just as I requested.

My intent when I went to his apartment was clear from the start. I had a task to complete, and nothing was going to stop me. I firmly believed my mother had sold my virginity to the highest bidder, and I was determined to get rid of it, thinking my lack of a hymen would completely ruin the wedding plan.

But Earl didn't want me. Not like that. He wanted the status my family name brought—and access to the Lancaster money, which he didn't always take, much to my confusion.

The money, the status, it didn't make him happy. Not much made my late husband happy.

"He's changed." When I shoot her a questioning look, she clarifies, "Your Spencer."

"He's not mine." Was he ever?

Yes, once upon a time. But no longer. I went and married someone else, and he's going to hold it against me forever.

I suppose I shouldn't be surprised. I was disloyal. In his eyes, he believes I gave myself to another man. Spence doesn't know it was in name only. And I'm sure he'll never give me the opportunity to explain myself either.

"He was," Carolina reminds me. "I've heard the stories."

"What stories?" I frown.

"Stories you told me, or did you forget? The two of you were very close when you were at Lancaster Prep." A haze of something clouds Carolina's eyes and I'm about to ask what's wrong, when our father shouts our names.

We turn to look at him, hating how my gaze snags on Mother, who's watching the conversation with curiosity lighting her eyes.

"Do either of you want to give a speech in honor of your brother and his new bride?" Our father smiles, looking rather pleased with his suggestion, his gaze never straying from Carolina. His favorite daughter.

Though he'd deny it until he took his last breath, I know it's true.

Augustus Lancaster is a handsome man, and only seems to grow more distinguished looking as he ages. I'm sure my mother hates him for it. She hates him for everything he does.

"I don't think they would approve if I gave a speech," I say hesitantly, imagining the look on Summer's face while I talk about love and promises kept. My abandonment still lingers in her mind, and yes, she already knows I was under the influence of my mother when it happened, but I don't know if that's a good enough answer.

I was only sixteen and highly impressionable. I couldn't think for myself—I really didn't know how. But I should've believed Summer, even though she hurt my feelings. I viewed her as the enemy once she abandoned me that week. I invited her to the house, not Whit. She was my friend, and Whit had no problem stealing her from me.

I suppose since I did it to him with Spence, he thought Summer was fair game. But look at the two of them now, madly in love and officially married. Spencer standing beside him as his best man.

Whit got everything, while I was left with nothing. Not even a scrap.

Typical.

Back then, when I was resentful and hurt, my mother ran my entire life. She had complete control of me, and I let her. I preferred it. I thought I was so strong, when I wasn't at all.

No, I was weak. Pathetic.

Well, no longer.

"I'm afraid I don't know Summer that well," Carolina adds.

"Monty is giving a speech. I thought it would be nice if one of you did too." The disappointment on my father's face is obvious when his gaze lands on me.

"Monty and Summer are very close," I remind him. "It makes sense, that he would give a toast."

"Spence is giving a speech as best man." Dad smiles. "I'm glad those two are still friends."

My father is clueless. He never knew that Spence and I had a thing, and we were so obvious, especially during that one Thanksgiving week, when I begged Spencer to come here and spend it with me.

"Where is your date anyway?" Carolina asks me.

"Talking with Monty over at the bar." We both glance over at where they're standing, their heads bent close together. "I'm playing matchmaker."

"That's the sweetest thing." Carolina's gaze returns to mine. "And what about Spence?"

I frown. "What about him?"

"Do you still care about him?"

I wave a hand. "That was a long time ago."

She arches a brow. "Not really."

"I've been married and widowed since I last spoke with him. He's moved on, surely." I've not heard much about his love life, but I haven't heard much about him in general since we were last together. He's always been a private person. Even a little secretive.

Maybe that's why I was always drawn to him. I love a good secret. After all, I'm an expert at keeping them.

"I suppose." The mysterious way Carolina just said that infuriates me.

"He has." My words, my tone, are insistent. I can't believe he would still give me another chance. Even if he did…

I wouldn't deserve it.

"Darling."

We lift our heads in tandem to find our mother hovering over the two of us, though her gaze is only for me.

"What?" I snap, irritated.

That fake pleasant look on her face disappears in an instant. "I was hoping we could speak." She glances over at Carolina. "Privately."

A sigh leaves Carolina and she rises to her feet. "Ignoring me as usual. Love how you haven't changed, Mother. You can have my chair."

She walks away before I can stop her, my gaze lingering on the back of Carolina's perfect blonde head as she abandons me.

Leaving me alone.

With our mother.

A woman who scares me to this day.

"Finally." Mother falls into Carolina's chair, her smile aimed right at me. She's impeccable in a vintage Oscar de la Renta dress. I only know this because I recognize it from her closet, which I always loved to go through when I was little. "You look well, Sylvie."

"Thank you." It's only because I'm out of her clutches. When I spend too much time with my mother, I end up skinny and frail. Sickly.

Always sick.

"There's color in your cheeks. And you're even a little...plump." Her gaze drops to my chest. My breasts.

My laugh sounds rough as it scrapes at my throat. "I am far from plump and you know it."

"You've definitely gained weight—"

"Stop trying to make me feel bad." I can tolerate her for only so long. "What do you want?"

"I miss you so much, Sylvie. My little twin." Mother leans forward, gathering my hands in hers and clutching them tight, her gaze never straying from mine. At least I didn't get her eyes. Otherwise, I could be her identical twin, born twenty-plus years later. "We used to do everything together, but once you got married, you tried to cut me out of your life."

My gaze drifts. It's hard to look at her. "I had to."

She doesn't ask what I mean by that because, deep down, she knows. And besides, she wormed her way back in eventually. Once my husband died and I needed someone, anyone to help me. "Sylvie, look at me." When my gaze finds hers once more, she keeps talking. "I just want to be there for you, darling. I'm so sorry for your loss, and what you've gone through at such a young age. You know I am. What happened to Earl was…unthinkable."

I remain quiet. There's no point in protesting her sympathy or her statement about Earl. What happened to him was definitely unthinkable. No one should die as he did.

"I know you suffered over Earl. You've suffered so much your entire life. It hasn't been easy. All the money in the world, and look at what you've dealt with." She squeezes my hands, like she's never going to let them go. "I'm sorry for what happened."

There are so many things she could be apologizing for. The list is endless. But I don't believe she's sincere. I don't think she's sorry for what she's done to me.

I'm not sure she even realizes exactly what she's done to me over the years. She pretends everything is fine between us whenever I see her, when it so clearly isn't.

Carefully, I pull my hands from her grip, ignoring the disappointment on her face when I withdraw them. "I appreciate the apology." Why I'm being kind to her, I don't know. "But it's too late."

She frowns. "Too late for what?"

I don't answer. Instead, I leave her, blindly walking away, my heartbeat pounding in my ears, in my blood. I push past people as they approach me with friendly smiles and a greeting on their tongue, ignoring them when they say my name. I don't stop until

I'm at the bar, ordering a whiskey neat, gulping it down the moment the bartender sets the glass in front of me.

"Well, well. Someone's traumatized."

That droll voice can belong to only one person.

Glancing to my right, I see Monty standing there, Cliff directly beside him. Two gorgeous, fashionable men who would make the perfect couple.

My matchmaking skills are on point, I swear.

"Sylvie. Sweetie. Are you all right?" Cliff frowns, taking a step toward me.

I request a refill from the bartender before I turn my attention to my date, who's ditched me. "I'm—recovering."

"From a conversation with Sylvia," Monty adds, earning a sharp look from me. "I saw the two of you at the table just now."

I take the refilled glass the bartender just set on the counter and sip from it, trying to control myself, but it's hard. My hands are literally shaking, and the temptation to down the whiskey is strong. "I don't know why I came to this wedding. I knew I would end up having to talk to her."

"He's your brother. Of course, you'd come. You love him. Would do anything for him," Monty says, his voice gentle. His gaze, kind. He's speaking the truth. I adore Whit. He's protected me my entire life from his jerk friends and anyone else who might've been a threat, with the exception of our mother. "Have you had a chance to speak to Summer yet?"

"Not really." I take another sip, hating how jittery I feel. Wishing I didn't have to worry about Summer and Spence and my mother. I'm sure there are other people at this party tonight who hate me. Who I burned with a careless remark or malicious gossip. I was the worst.

I'm still not much better.

"Oh." The disappointment in Monty's voice is clear, and I hate myself. I disappoint everyone.

It's as if I can't help it.

Inhaling deeply, I blow out a long, slow breath. "Has Summer said anything to you about me?"

"Not today. She's a little preoccupied," he reminds me. "Truthfully? She hasn't mentioned your name to me in a while."

I don't know if I should be bothered by that remark, or relieved. If she's not talking about me, maybe Summer has forgiven me.

Or she's not talking about me because I'm not worth her worry.

"It was a beautiful wedding, wasn't it?" Cliff smiles brightly. It's obvious he's trying to change the subject and the mood, which I can appreciate. "Whit Lancaster is delicious."

"Isn't he? Oh, the man is divine." Monty rests his hand on his chest as if he's overcome. He's always reacted this way toward my brother. His crush on Whit isn't a secret.

I roll my eyes and give in, downing the rest of the liquor in one swallow. It leaves a fiery trail burning down my throat, settling warm and tingly in my stomach. "Stop salivating over my brother. He's a married man now."

"Summer is such a lucky woman," Cliff says. "Look at how he watches her."

We all turn to observe Whit and Summer sitting at their table, completely engrossed in each other. Whit's gaze drops to Summer's lips and he touches the corner of her mouth with just his fingertips, and I tear my gaze away from them. I feel like an intruder on their intimate moment.

He's always looked at her like that. As if he's completely fascinated and can't quite figure her out.

"They're in love," Monty says with a wistful sigh. Have I ever heard him sound like that before? "They can't get enough of each other."

"It's a beautiful thing to witness," Cliff adds.

I turn away from them, requesting one more refill for the road from the bartender, who delivers it immediately. I leave my friends be, wandering the ballroom in search of a friendly face. There are a lot of Lancasters here, and plenty of distant relatives too—other branches of the family. Hundreds of people are in attendance, because when the oldest son of the oldest son gets married, you can bet that everyone who is anyone will be invited to the wedding.

On the other hand, my wedding was in a government building downtown on a cold and dreary winter day—a Wednesday. I wore a white tweed Chanel suit that belonged to my grandmother, and a funny little hat covered in white feathers, with white netting that hung over my eyes. My hair was pulled into a severe updo, not a strand out of place—I was trying to emulate my little sister now that I think back on it. I'm sure I looked ridiculous. I was also drunk and high on prescription pills—that was the only way I could go through with the ceremony.

I wouldn't mind a pill or five right now, if I'm being honest with myself. The alcohol can only work so much.

"Sylvie." Someone grabs my arm to stop me, and I turn to find my cousin Grant studying me, his gaze filled with concern. "How are you?"

He leans in and drops a kiss on each of my cheeks before he gives me a hug. He's much older than me, so we're not what I would call close, though I've always liked him. Tall and imposing, Grant is the oldest son of my uncle Reggie. And he's currently studying me as if he can tell I'm drunk and agitated, which I am.

"I'm wonderful," I tell him, my voice falsely bright. "I heard you recently got married."

"Six months ago now, yes." He rubs absently at the platinum band around his left ring finger.

"Congratulations. I'm sorry I wasn't able to make it to the wedding." I was still dealing with the aftermath of my husband's death and didn't feel it was right to be seen in public, celebrating when my husband was dead and gone.

"I was sorry to hear about your husband." His gaze and tone are somber, showing me respect.

He might be a mean and moody Lancaster male, but it feels like our generation has softened a bit. They're not as mean, not as fierce as our fathers.

"Thank you." I nod, trying to keep my expression solemn, but it's no use. I cave and finish off the whiskey.

"I knew your husband. Did he ever mention that to you?" He tilts his head, sending me a questioning look

I go still, staring at Grant. He has that same Lancaster look as the rest of us. The only exception is his hair is darker. "No, I don't recall him ever mentioning it."

"Finn and I handled a lot of his real estate transactions the last few years," Grant explains, referring to his younger brother. "Before we...lost him."

What a sweet way to put it. As if Earl is merely wandering around the city, confused and unable to find his way home.

"He didn't own much real estate that I know of."

"Only because he was selling off so much of it," Grant says, his brows knitting together. "Did he not tell you that? We unloaded a lot of properties for him the last three years or so. He made a lot of money too."

Interesting, considering he wasn't what I would consider liquid when he passed. I was even accused of hiding all of his assets at one point by his children, which was laughable. "I wouldn't know, since I wasn't in his will."

"Are you serious?"

"As if I need the money, Grant. We're Lancasters, remember?" I arch a brow.

He chuckles. "True. It's just—he told us repeatedly he needed cash. That's why he got rid of so much real estate. I didn't think anything of it in the moment. People do that sort of thing all the time, but now..."

"Now what?"

"If he didn't have much cash in the bank when he passed away, where did it all go?"

Hmm.

Good question.

CHAPTER SEVEN

SYLVIE

Oh, I'm really drunk. All those neat little whiskeys sent me right over the edge, to the point that I'm swaying by the side of the dance floor as I watch everyone lose themselves to the beat, the music flooding my veins.

Or is that the alcohol?

Harry Styles himself performed earlier, singing a slower version of "Adore You" while Summer swayed in Whit's arms, their gazes for each other and no one else. He's actually still here, out on the dance floor and surrounded by mostly women. Even Summer is dancing near him, laughing every time Whit glares at her.

Which is often.

Carolina is on the dance floor in our father's arms, elegant and graceful as she twirls and twirls. My father eyeing her as if he can't quite believe she is his daughter.

I mean, I get it. Sometimes it does feel like Carolina came to us her own little person, fully formed at birth and immensely talented from the get-go. She never seemed to fit in with the rest of us.

Do any of us fit into the supposed family ideal though? I'm starting to think no.

The song ends and my father approaches when another begins.

I start to shake my head, laughing when he catches my hand and drags me onto the dance floor. I'm not as smooth as my baby sister, but that's okay. He pulls me into his arms and we gently sway to the soft song, the mood shifting. Becoming quieter.

Summer and Whit are dancing on the floor together, too, staring into each other's eyes. I glance over at them with a wistful sigh, not trying to hide it as I usually would.

"I like her," Father says, the approval clear in his voice. "She's good for your brother."

"She doesn't put up with his shit," I say, feeling bold.

He chuckles, swinging me around. "You're right. She doesn't. And that's what he needs."

"Is that why you and Mother divorced? Because she always tolerated your antics?" We never talk about their divorce. It's still somewhat shrouded in mystery, what happened between them to end it for good.

I still believe it was our father who finally put his foot down and moved on. Mother clings—it's a bad habit of hers.

It can be a bad habit of mine, too, thanks to her.

His mood goes somber, just like that. "I did some things I'm not proud of."

"With Summer's mom?" My brows lift in question, even though I already know the answer.

He barely nods. His past makes for some awkward family moments when we're all together. "With other women too. It's no secret I was unfaithful. Your mother was too. We weren't a good fit."

"Much like me and Earl?"

His expression turns stern. "I hope you know I never approved. Your marriage to that man was all your mother's doing."

His words infuriate me. "Really? Why didn't you stop her?"

"You didn't give me a chance, and neither did she. Why do you think you were married so quickly? I was out of the country, remember? Your mother made her move because I was gone."

We're barely dancing anymore, too wrapped up in our conversation in the middle of the floor, couples shuffling past us. "He was older than *me,* Sylvie. Why would I want you to marry someone like that?"

"Because he could take care of me, when I couldn't take care of myself." That was one of the lines my mother fed me.

An irritated sound leaves him. "That's something your mother would say."

Now I'm the irritated one. All these years, my mother has been doing—things to me. Poisoning me. Convincing everyone I was sick. That I was dying. And my father never did a damn thing about it. He never interfered, never said a single word to stop her. To help me.

Ever.

"You've always got an excuse, don't you?" The annoyance is replaced with anger and I'm suddenly consumed with it. "I didn't give you a chance. My mother always prevented you from helping me. Whatever. You knew that something wasn't right, yet you didn't interfere. You didn't try to help. *Ever.* It's like you don't even care about me."

"My God, how can you say that?" His face falls, and I know I've upset him. "I care, Sylvie. I always have. I love you. My God, you're my child. How could I not—"

I shake my head, making him go quiet.

"No. You say you care. That you love me. You act like the doting father whenever you see fit, but for the most part, you've left me to the wolves my entire life."

The wolves. More like one singular wolf.

He stiffens, his eyes flaring with unmistakable anger. "I take offense to that."

"Good. You should. You also need to take a long look at your behavior over the years, and see if you've really come through for me. If you actually opened your eyes for once, you might realize how much you've disappointed me."

"Now wait a minute…"

I pull out of his arms, abandoning him right there on the dance floor, my anger too big to pretend anymore. My father faintly calls my name—barely loud enough for anyone to hear—but I ignore him.

Most of the wedding guests have already left for the evening, yet the massive room is suddenly stifling. I head for the doors that lead onto the terrace, taking a big, gulping breath of cool air the moment I'm outside.

I go to the spot where I stood earlier, before the ceremony began. The gorgeous arbor laden with flowers still stands outside, but the rows of white chairs are gone, as well as the white aisle runner. I lean heavily against the railing, an idea forming in my mind and, as usual, I give in to my impulses.

And run down the stairs, heading straight for the arbor.

The heady scent of roses greets me, and I breathe deep, noting the tang of salt in the air. The ocean rages just beyond the hedge of green in the distance, and I shiver when the breeze hits me. While it was a gorgeous spring day earlier, once the sun went down, the temperature plummeted.

Goosebumps line my arms, but I ignore them, reaching for a white rose, plucking it from the arrangement and tucking it behind my right ear. I find a piece of ribbon among the flowers and tie my hair back, then change it into a loose bun on top of my head, before I proceed to grab another rose. And another one.

Until they're all in my hair, surrounding the bun like a flower crown.

I start to spin around, the breeze catching my skirt, lifting it and exposing my legs. A giggle escapes me, the heavy flowers shifting in my hair and threatening to fall out. I reach up to hold them in place, pricking my finger with a leftover thorn on the stem.

"Ow." I check my wound, squinting into the twilight at the droplet of blood forming on my fingertip. I stick my finger into my mouth, sucking on it, the coppery taste on my tongue when I hear a voice.

A familiar male voice.

"Still always hurting yourself, I see."

My skin prickles with awareness and I slowly turn to find Spence in front of me, dashingly handsome in his tux. The bowtie is long gone, a few buttons undone on his shirt, revealing the strong column of his throat. He still has the jacket on, his hands tucked into his trouser pockets, his distinct scent mixed with the breeze, filling my nostrils.

Filling my head with melancholy and longing. No one smells as delicious as Spence.

Not a single person.

I drop my hand to my side, guilty. "You caught me."

"Stealing roses?" He glances above my head at the arbor behind me.

"I didn't think anyone would notice. There are so many." I shrug, feeling silly and immature.

I'm a grown woman. A widow, for the love of God. I shouldn't be dancing in the moonlight by myself, plucking roses out of the arbor and making a flower crown. Only children do things like this.

I am not even twenty-three. Regardless of what I've gone through, I'm still young. Even though I feel so incredibly old sometimes.

"I noticed." His gaze sears into me, making my skin feel as if it caught fire, and I go still, wondering what he means by that. "Did you get into an argument with your father?"

I frown. "What..."

"I saw the two of you inside. On the dance floor. You seemed mad. Then you walked away from him and I realized you were actually pissed." His voice is so low I take a step closer, so I can hear him. "What did he say to you?"

I'm not going to tell him. I don't necessarily trust Spence. Not yet. Or maybe not ever. My feelings are so conflicted. A riotous mess in my head. "It doesn't matter."

"Always so dismissive, our Syl." His smile isn't pleasant, and

I wonder if he hates me.

He probably does.

"Why did you follow me out here, Spence?" My voice is quiet. A whisper on the breeze, but he heard me. Even takes a step closer to me this time.

"I've never been able to resist your siren call, even when I know I should. Even when I'm so mad at you, I can't see straight." He says it all so matter-of-factly, as if he's been living with this wretched feeling his entire life.

Which, maybe he has. It feels like I've known Spencer Donato forever, but do I really know him?

No. Not anymore.

"Remember Halloween night? When you were sixteen?" he asks. "You dressed up as a dark angel."

Of course, I remember. It's a night that's burned forever on my brain, embedded deep into my memories. The pleasure. The humiliation. We took it so far, the two of us. Almost to the point of no return.

Until I pushed him away and he was so angry with me. Sexually frustrated. We got into an argument. We didn't speak for weeks after. Then I almost died.

Though that wasn't his fault, the almost dying part. That I can blame squarely on my mother.

"I still think about that night," he says, his voice distant, as is his gaze. "How you looked. So gorgeous in that costume. How carefree you were—and drunk. You were always locked up so tight most of the time when it was just the two of us. Only giving me pieces of yourself here and there, like stray little crumbs I couldn't help but gobble up."

"I was scared," I admit.

His gaze jerks to mine, surprise etched in his face. "Scared of what? Me?"

I shake my head. "Never you. Just of—the repercussions of you." Nothing good lasts. I learned that early on.

We don't look away from each other. It's like we can't.

"I gave you everything when I was younger." He removes his hands from his pockets, taking another step toward me. Until he's so close, I can feel his body heat reaching toward me, drawing me in. "Yet you pushed me away every single time."

"I was an idiot."

Spence shakes his head, his expression grim. "No. I was the idiot. Always there for you. Never turning you away, even though you rejected me constantly. I let you use me."

He reaches out, his fingers landing on my face. Tracing the line of my jaw slowly. So slow I close my eyes, my lips parting. God, I still savor his touch. His closeness. The very essence of him.

"I was young and stupid," I whisper, my eyes flashing open. I suck in a breath when he dares to touch the corner of my mouth. My entire body prickles with awareness, waiting for him to make a move, but nothing happens.

Much to my disappointment.

"I was too." His voice is harsh, slashing into my precarious emotions, shredding them to ribbons. "I'm not the same person I was back then. I'm stronger. Meaner."

My brows draw together. Meaner? I can't imagine Spencer ever being mean.

Especially to me.

His fingers drift down, until they're gently circling my throat, his thumb pressing into my skin. "You don't know what I've been through the last couple of years. How much I've changed."

He doesn't know what I've been through either, and how I've changed as well. Maybe we're too different now. We don't have anything in common anymore, and the realization...

Makes me sad.

"Pretty little fairy princess with the roses tucked in her gold-spun hair." His words are sweet, but his touch is crushing. His fingers tighten, making the air stall in my throat and my eyes flash open to find him watching me, his eyes glittering in the darkness.

There's a matching darkness that lies within him. I see it now. Can feel it surround me, holding me in its grasp, much like his fingers around my neck.

"You look like pure innocence, Syl. In that blue and white dress and the flowers in your hair. But I know the truth. You willingly married that man, and he was a pig." He jerks me forward, pulling me by the neck, and my body collides with his, my skin tingling upon impact. "How was it, fucking the old man? Did you enjoy it? Could he even get it up?"

I stare up at him, trying to find my voice. He doesn't know. He thinks I let Earl touch me, but my husband wasn't interested in me. Not like that.

And I never understood why. Never questioned it.

I preferred it. I didn't want him to touch me. The only person who's been inside me, is the very man whose fingers are currently around my neck.

"You've been tainted, you know that?" He presses against the underside of my chin, tilting my head back as he bends over me, his mouth hovering above mine. Tempting me to rear up and press our lips together. "Fucking ruined for life, Sylvie. I hope you enjoyed your time with that asshole, however brief it was. No one will want you now. Especially me."

He shoves me away from him before I can say a word, leaving me gasping for air. Bending forward, I rest my hands on my knees, swallowing hard as I try to catch my breath. The flowers fall out of my hair, one by one, landing on the ground with a soft plop. Yet he doesn't say another word.

Just walks away and leaves me there alone, fending for myself.

"You're a liar, Spencer! I know you still want me!" I call out to him, though he doesn't look back. Of course he doesn't.

I watch him walk away, anger and pain hitting me like a double punch to the heart. For the first time in my life, I feel utterly abandoned by Spencer Donato.

And it hurts far more than I ever thought it could.

CHAPTER EIGHT

SPENCER

THE PAST

It's Halloween, and I'm anxious.

Not that I let anyone see it. I play it cool as I wait out in front of the old, half-burned down building where the party is being held tonight. My best friend Whit planned the entire thing, and we ditched class so we could set up all afternoon, anticipating pretty much everyone he invited showing up. Considering he sent out a mass text to the entire junior and senior class, that's a lot of people.

Whit doesn't give a damn. His family owns Lancaster Prep—they have for generations. Centuries. He can do whatever the hell he wants, and no one is going to stop him. One of the perks of being close to a Lancaster.

What's that like, being so secure in your position you don't worry what anyone thinks? Personally, I have no clue, though I'm surrounded by the arrogance that makes up the Lancaster family. I choose to be too—I actually like the arrogant son of a bitch. Whit is one of my closest friends, and his little sister Sylvie is my...

Shit. I don't know what she is to me.

As I lean against the crumbling brick wall, the loud music pounding in my head, throbbing in my chest, I bring the bottle of beer to my lips and sip. My gaze is locked on the trail that leads to the building, waiting for my pretty little angel to make her appearance.

That's what I call her, when I have her in my arms, my lips on her neck, breathing in her delectable scent. She's an angel. Heaven sent. With a sweet mouth and flashing blue eyes and the evilest laugh. That's why it's fun to call her my angel.

Sylvie Lancaster is really the devil in disguise.

Of course, her brother dresses up as Satan for Halloween, because Whit is also the fucking devil. The only difference is, he owns it. He's currently got one of the hottest girls in our class on his lap, showing him all of her attention, though I can tell just from the look on his face that he's bored out of his skull. Caitlyn might be hot, but she's also not a challenge, and Whit loves a challenge.

Like Summer Savage. Not quite sure what's going on there, but there's something between the two of them. He's pretty tight-lipped about it, so I let it go. Sylvie fills me in on what she knows, and what she suspects, but she's as much in the dark as I am.

"About fucking time she shows up," Whit mutters when lights cut across our faces.

I glance up to find a golf cart headed in our direction, Sylvie behind the wheel. She's laughing, her hair streaming behind her in the wind, and I barely acknowledge the fact that Summer's sitting beside her on the bench seat.

My gaze is only for Sylvie.

She pulls up right in front of us and parks the golf cart, shouting, "The party has arrived, bitches!" before she throws her arms up in the air.

She's dressed as a dark angel with plenty of pale skin on display: black corset top that shows off her cleavage and black shorts that make her legs look impossibly long. Giant black wings loom behind her, covered in shiny black feathers that look real. Her eye makeup is dark, her lips a deep blood red, and she looks...

Fucking beautiful.

Her gaze darts from face to face, and I wonder if she's looking for me.

I bet she is.

I pull away from the crowd, taking a step toward the golf cart, saying the first thing that crosses my mind.

"Looking fine as hell tonight, Sylvie."

"Why thank you, prince of darkness." She hops out of the golf cart and approaches me eagerly, patting my chest as she smiles up at me before she glances over her shoulder. "Check out Summer."

My gaze shifts to Summer, my eyes widening as she climbs out of the golf cart. "Uh, holy shit."

If I thought Sylvie's costume was skimpy, she's got nothing on Summer. Ironically enough, she's dressed as a devil, just like Whit. A red-sequined tube top barely covers her chest, and I swear to God she's wearing skintight red panties, fishnet stockings on her legs.

Whit is either going to attack her when he sees her, or demand she put some clothes on.

Most likely the latter. He won't like seeing her on such display. He's so damn territorial all the time, which means if he has any interest in her, he won't want anyone even looking in her direction.

"Is it too much?" Summer stops directly in front of Sylvie and me, resting her hands on her hips in a provocative pose.

I'm trying to take her in, but I don't want to stare too hard. I can feel Sylvie watching me. "Does Whit know about this?"

Summer's expression turns annoyed and she pushes past us, shoulder checking me. "Fuck Whit Lancaster. I don't care what he thinks."

I turn to watch her go for a moment before I glance over at Sylvie, whose gaze is already on me. "She seems pissed."

"My brother is being an asshole." Sylvie slings her arms around my neck, tucking her hot little body against mine. "I like your costume."

I came as a vampire, right down to the fangs, which I temporarily glued to my teeth. I have fake blood trickling at the corners of my mouth, and even painted my face white. I dressed in all black and found a red-lined black cape online. "I like yours too. I didn't expect it," I tell her, letting my gaze linger on all of her exposed parts with approval.

Her expression is pleased. "I told you I was dressing up as an angel."

"Not a dark angel. I expected you to show up in a flowing white dress with a halo above your head."

She laughs, her eyes dancing. "That is so not my style. You know I'm not nice."

That's part of Sylvie's charm, that she acts like everyone hates her because she's rude like the rest of the family, but she's not. She's actually sweet. Thoughtful. Vulnerable. Broken.

So broken.

I'm a fixer. Maybe it's because my dad has been so obviously shitty to my mother my entire life, and I was always there to pick up the pieces. Offer her comfort when he wouldn't. When she finally got the balls to divorce his ass, I cheered her on. Dad didn't like that.

At all.

"Hey." Sylvie's soft voice cuts through my thoughts, her hand on my cheek bringing me back to the here and now. "You want to go dance?"

"I don't dance." I let my gaze rove over her, slowly. Taking in her beauty, how different she looks tonight. Big difference from the uniforms we're always wearing.

"Aw come on." She rubs herself against me, the soft press of her tits to my chest making my blood run hot. "Please?"

"I don't know…" I'd rather sneak off someplace with her alone, but what's the point of setting up all afternoon for a party only to ditch it before it's even started?

I'm going to stay. At least for a little while.

She pouts, those ruby red lips tempting as hell. "You won't do it for me?"

The slight tremor to her voice makes me immediately capitulate. "Okay."

Her smile of pleasure is a shot right to my dick. "Let's go!"

Sylvie grabs my hand and leads me into the fray, where the majority of party-goers are dancing, beer bottles or cups clutched in their hands. Almost everyone is in costume, and some people I don't even recognize.

But I can't worry about anyone else. Not when I have a beautiful blonde girl draping herself all over me, her lithe body moving while I stand there like an idiot and let her do whatever she wants.

"You're not dancing, Spencer," she chastises at one point, yelling over the loud music. We've been out here for at least twenty minutes, maybe longer, and she's not giving me any indication she's going to stop dancing or drinking.

"I told you I don't dance, Sylvie," I remind her stoically, making her smile.

"Always so serious." She shakes her hair back, the wings she's wearing quivering with the movement. "Don't you know how to cut loose and have fun?"

"I am having fun," I insist, making her laugh. I don't need to do anything else. Just get drunk and watch this girl. That's all I need tonight.

"You could at least touch me," she murmurs. I circle my arm around her slender waist and a purr of pleasure escapes her when my hand settles on her hip. "Everyone's always afraid to touch me."

"Really."

She nods, moving her body to the beat. She has a natural

grace, her limbs fluid. I know her little sister is the true dancer in the family, but Sylvie could've been just as good with the right training. "They think I'm going to break. You're the only one who treats me like I'm a normal human being, I swear."

Only because I refuse to believe all that nonsense she spouts about her mom trying to kill her. I want to believe her, but I also know Sylvie is melodramatic. Her brother has complained to me multiple times about how she carries on and says the craziest shit.

I've bore witness to her saying some crazy shit myself. I don't know where she comes up with it.

"You're stronger than everyone thinks," I tell her. I know she enjoys basking in my approval. No one gives her positive affirmations. The teachers and staff are all scared of her and don't question anything she says or does, for the most part. And her family treats her mostly like garbage. Yeah, Whit watches out for her, but he's hard on her too. Claims she needs it.

I think he's *too* hard on her. I also think her mom is a complete bitch. Her dad is neglectful. And everyone else who goes to this school is a goddamn coward, too afraid to even talk to her in fear they might cross the Lancaster heiress.

Sylvie doesn't scare me. Not in that way. My feelings for her though?

Sometimes, they creep up on me late at night when I can't sleep, making my chest ache.

"I like that you think I'm strong." Her smile is big, and she tips her head back, staring up at the stars since there's no roof over this part of the building. "You make me feel even stronger."

That's got to count for something, right? I want to lift her up, not keep her down. Though Whit would probably kick my ass if he knew all of the things I've done with his little sister. He barely tolerates me spending time with her, and he doesn't know the half of it.

I move my hand from her hip to cup her ass, pulling her closer to me. Not even a piece of paper could slip between us and she levels that icy blue gaze on me, her dark lips parted. "What are you doing?"

"You said I never touch you." I squeeze her plump cheek that fits perfectly in my hand. "So here I am. Touching you."

The music changes, the new song slower, with a sensual beat. She rocks her hips, her lower body brushing against mine, making me react.

Making me hard.

Her lips curve, as if she knows exactly what she's doing to me, and she slings her arms around my neck, her hold loose, her body swaying back and forth. "God, you're so sexy, Spence. Have I ever told you that before?"

"No." A guy from my history class walks by, a full cup of beer in his hand, and I swipe it from him, earning an irritated *hey* from him. "Thanks." I lift the cup up in a cheers' gesture before I take a drink. He shakes his head as he walks away, and I chuckle.

"You're mean," she whispers.

I send her a look. "You like it."

Her eyes flash. "You're right. I do. Because I'm mean too."

"You just think you're mean," I tease her.

Sylvie scowls. She hates it when I disagree with her. "I'll have you know, I'm the meanest bitch you'll ever meet." I'm about to polish off the beer I have clutched in my hand when she snags it from me, finishing it herself.

"Hey."

"Kiss me," she murmurs, just before she rises up and presses her wet mouth to mine. Her lips part, our tongues tangling, and I can taste the beer.

I tighten my hold on her, both hands on her ass now, controlling the way she moves. She clings to me, kissing me in the middle of the crowd, both of us ignoring the shouts and the oohs and the aahs.

We take it far in private, but never like this—out in the open, with everyone as witnesses. We don't want people to know we're together. Not really. I don't want to hear it from anyone we go to school with, especially Whit. I'm not ashamed of what we share, I just don't want to hear the gossip or deal with her brother.

And I think she feels the same way. We like having our little secret. Messing around in her room, just the two of us rolling around on her bed. My hand in her panties. Her fingers curved around my dick.

"Oh shit," Sylvie mutters, pulling away from me immediately.

I frown. "What's wrong?"

She tilts her head to the right. "Look at Summer."

I glance over to see Summer grinding on some asshole's junk, her cheeks flushed, her eyes dilated. It's clear the girl is drunk off her ass, and Bryan—that's the asshole—is currently leering at her.

"That won't end well," I tell Sylvie.

"If my brother sees her with that guy, he's going to freak."

Mild understatement.

"Oh God, I think he slipped his hands under her shorts." Sylvie sounds horrified.

This is the last thing I want to deal with. Drama. Fighting over a girl—whatever Whit says in protest, he's interested in Summer Savage, despite his constant denials.

"Come on. Let's get out of here," I suggest.

"No, wait." Sylvie is no longer dancing, even though the music is still playing. She's glaring in Summer's direction, trying to catch her attention when Summer finally looks over at us, offering a little wave as she starts to leave with Bryan.

"Summer, what the hell are you doing?" Sylvie asks.

"I'll be back," Summer says, pointing at the back of Bryan's head, mouthing, *he's cute* and giving her two thumbs up.

"Don't go outside with him!" Sylvie practically screams, but Summer ignores her. She sends me a pleading look instead. "We should do something."

I shrug. "What can we do? She's a big girl. She can handle herself."

"She's drunk. I need to talk to Whit." She starts to leave and I grab her hand, stopping her.

"Don't get in the middle of their business," I warn her, my voice low. The song changes yet again, this time a slow one. "Leave them alone, Sylvie."

Her lower lip trembles and I swear she's going to cry. "But she's my friend."

"And she knows what she's doing. Don't worry about her." I touch her cheek, letting my thumb streak over her lower lip. "Want to get out of here?"

The worry slowly dissipates from her gaze and she nods. "Go back to my room?"

"Yeah." I smile at her, pressing my thumb against her lips, making them part.

She nips at my skin before she turns away from me, snagging my hand and pulling me through the crowd until we're walking out of the ruins, heading straight for the golf cart that still sits out front.

"You drive," she says, and I settle in behind the steering wheel, waiting until she's seated before I take off. So fast, she squeals into the darkness, her laughter filling the air.

I get high off the sound, unable to stop sneaking looks at her. I swear this is the happiest I've ever seen her, though some of that might also be because she's drunk. She grips the side of the golf cart, her fingers curled around the bar as she leans to her right, the upper half of her body hanging over the cart and hovering over the path.

"Hey, get back in here," I tell her, but she just shakes her head. Still laughing. Still hanging over the ground. One wrong move, one slip of her fingers and she's tumbling out. She could get seriously hurt.

I let off the gas, slowing down. Until she's leaning all the way back into the cart once more, sending me a frustrated scowl.

"Why did you slow down?" She crosses her arms in front of

her chest, plumping up her tits as she leans against the back of the seat. Looking like an angry angel.

"I didn't want you to hurt yourself." I jerk the cart to the right, following the path that leads to the building where her suite is. She doesn't have a room with the rest of us in the dorms—she's a Lancaster.

They don't board with us commoners.

"You worry too much," she murmurs, tossing her hair back yet again. It's wild tonight. Wavy and flying everywhere. I'm tempted to grab hold of it and give her a tug. Pull her into me, kiss her until she stops complaining. Until she forgets all about her troubles, her worries. Her pain.

This girl carries so much pain within her. She won't come right out and say what it is, but I have my suspicions. I don't trust her parents.

Specifically, her mother.

"You don't get it," she accuses out of nowhere, and I send her a questioning glance. "Your life is so perfect. You don't have to worry about anything."

If she only knew. No one's life is perfect. Not hers, and definitely not mine.

I eventually stop the golf cart in front of the building, where both her and Whit's suites are, and she hops out, striding toward the front doors without a backward glance. I press the cart brake into place before I'm chasing after her, snagging her hand before she grabs the door and disappears forever.

Those doors lock the moment they shut. Knowing Sylvie, she'd walk right through them and not let me in.

"What?" She whirls on me. "What do you want from me, Spence?"

I frown, still confused by her attitude. "I could ask you the same thing, Syl. You're running hot and cold tonight. You want me. You want me to fuck off. Make up your mind."

Her chest rises and falls as she glares at me, her hands curling into fists at her sides. "You know what I really want? To have fun and not worry all the damn time. I want to feel good. Do you know how long it's been since I've felt good? Felt healthy? A long time, Spencer. A really fucking long time."

We stare at each other, Sylvie's harsh breathing after her outburst the only sound. I don't know where the hell this is coming from, and she can see the confusion on my face. In my eyes.

"I swore this school year would be better, but it's still all the same. All the time. She won't leave me alone. I don't feel normal. Ever. I don't even know what that means or what it's like. But being with you, and hanging out with Summer...you both help me forget who I really am." Her smile is small. Sad. "A broken little doll with nothing to live for."

"Aw, Sylvie—"

"Don't try to deny it. You know it's true. All my talk of dying sounds so dramatic, but it's my reality. Mine." She lifts her chin, the moon casting its gentle, silvery glow on her face and that's when I see the tears streaking down her cheeks. "She's killing me. Slowly but surely. I know it's all her fault. And no one wants to do anything about it. Not my dad. Not anyone."

I go to her, pulling her into my arms and holding her close, crushing the wings she's wearing beneath my grip. I don't even care about the damn wings anymore or the costume or the party.

I just want to take care of *my* Sylvie.

She's crying into my black shirt, her sobs quiet, her tears soaking the fabric. I run my hand over her hair, tangling my fingers in the soft strands, gripping it at the base, just as I imagined earlier.

Gently, I tug on her hair, pulling her head back so our mouths are perfectly aligned. "Come on, Syl. You're breaking my heart."

"I thought you didn't have one." She slides her hands across the front of my chest, her touch softening, her palm resting right in between my pecs. Her cheeks are tear-stained, her eyes rimmed with red, yet she's still so damn beautiful. "You told me that once. A long time ago."

When I would encourage her to leave me alone. Messing around with your best friend's little sister is one way of fucking your life up, especially when your best friend is Whit Lancaster. If he knew all the things I've done with Sylvie...

He'd kill me. Murder me with his bare hands.

"It's been a while since we've spent time together, Spencer." Her fingers curl into the fabric of my shirt, gently tugging. "I've missed you."

"You inviting me into your room for real this time?"

She nods, letting go of my shirt. "Come on."

I follow her into the building, the door slamming closed behind us, locking into place. It's quiet in here, and we're completely isolated. No staff checks on the Lancasters in this building past dark, if ever. Meaning we're all alone.

Just the two of us.

Once she's got her suite door unlocked, I'm pushing my way inside, crowding her, forcing her so her back is against the wall, where I pin her with my body, the black wings she's wearing getting crushed. That familiar urge rises up within me, the same one I only ever feel when I'm with her.

I'm a nice guy. Respectful. My mama taught me to have some manners. My father taught me to always remain quiet versus spilling your guts to every asshole you meet. Both have given me plenty of advice over the years. How to deal with other people. How to deal with girls. Women.

Yet I still don't understand this need I have for Sylvie every time I get her alone. She makes me feel edgy. Uneasy.

Like all I want to do is pounce. Jump her. Devour her.

Make her all mine.

It's like she can feel the energy I give off, and while she responds to it, she also pushes me away. Every single time. It's frustrating as shit, and I know I should be more patient, considering she's a virgin. But we've done so much already.

Why can't we get past that one last barrier?

"Spence." Her voice is a breathy whisper, more air than sound, and she tightens her grip on my shirt, yanking me close. I dip my head, my mouth landing on hers, her lips parting beneath mine, our tongues touching. Circling. A low sound comes from deep in my chest and I press my body to hers, wanting her to feel my need.

All of my need is for her. Only her.

She's taller with the heels on her feet, her tits crushed against my chest. I break away from her greedy lips, trailing my mouth down the length of her slender neck, licking and nibbling her pale skin. She trembles beneath me, a moan falling from her lips when I kiss across her chest. Along the top of her tits.

Lifting my head, I keep my gaze on hers as I tug down on the front of the corset she's wearing, her tits popping free, her pale pink nipples hard. I lick one, then the other, smiling when a jolt rocks through her, making her grab the back of my head, her fingers curling into my hair.

She holds me to her as I feast on her breasts, licking and sucking a nipple into my mouth, my hands finding her hips, holding her against the wall. She bucks against my grip, struggling as if she wants me to touch her even more, and I run my hands beneath the legs of her shorts, touching her thighs. I pull away slightly, staring at her as I slowly start to realize…

Damn, she's thin. Skinny legs and thighs, hip bones protruding. Tiny little waist, smallish tits, concave stomach. It's like the girl never eats. I've wondered before if she has an eating disorder…

"Hey." She settles her palm directly over my dick, quickly snatching my attention. I lift my head, my gaze locking with hers, and she studies me, her brows drawn together. "What are you doing?"

I can't tell her the truth. It'll ruin the mood, ruin the moment. She's always teetering on that edge, volatile as hell and not afraid to tell me to fuck off before she leaves me in the dust.

Can't risk it.

"What do you think I'm doing?" I run my hand across the front of her shorts, so I can cup her between her thighs. She's hot. Damp. I can smell her.

She catches her lower lip with her teeth, studying me. A fallen angel with crushed black wings still hanging from her back. Her lipstick is long gone, her eyes are extra dark and her tits are out. All-knowing, yet innocent too. "I want you to make me come," she demands.

I gently grind the heel of my palm against her pussy, making her breath catch. "Like that?"

"With your fingers," she urges in a whisper. "Inside of me."

I remove my hand. "Take your shorts off, Syl."

She does as I ask, her fingers fumbling as she curls them around the waistband and tugs them down. Until she's completely exposed, no panties on because that's how Sylvie operates. She wants me to see her like this, think of her like this. Experimental. Wild.

But she's also shy. Paranoid. A little scared.

"Leave them there," I tell her when the shorts fall to her knees. "Spread your legs."

Sylvie spreads them wider, allowing me a glimpse of glistening pink flesh. She doesn't have much pubic hair, and what she does have is a blonde little tangle that barely covers her pussy.

Fuck, she's a sight. If anyone could see her like this, they'd be shocked. This is not the act she puts on for anyone else.

Just me.

"Touch yourself," I suggest, feeling like a sadistic fuck. Knowing she gets off on this sort of thing.

Her hand automatically goes between her legs, the slick sounds of her busy fingers telling me she's already playing with her clit.

"You like it when I watch you do that?"

Our gazes clash, and I wonder where the hell we got this idea—to do it like this.

"Yes," she whispers, nodding. Her hair falls over her eyes, but she doesn't push it out of the way.

Her fingers are too preoccupied doing other things.

Impatience curls through me and I go to her, pushing her hand aside and replacing her fingers with my own. I sink them into her creamy flesh, stroking her, slipping a finger just inside her and she arches her head back, exposing her throat as she moans. I brush my mouth against her neck, licking and sucking, rubbing her clit over and over. Until her entire body is trembling and her breaths come faster. She's close to coming, I can tell, and at the last second, I remove my hand from her, taking a step back.

The glare on her face would slay dragons, and all I can do is smile at her.

"My turn," is all I say.

"This isn't a game, Spence."

"Ah, but it is, Syl. This is how you like it, remember?" I start to undo the buttons on my shirt, my heart rate increasing, my muscles tightening in anticipation. "Get on your knees."

She shakes her head, shrugging her shoulders to take off the fallen angel wings that are barely hanging on. She tosses them on the edge of her bed, black feathers fluttering everywhere, some of them landing on the bed or the floor. "Make me."

Everything in her life is so out of control. She's admitted that to me before. She's in freefall, constantly. Unsure and untrusting of everything and everyone.

Except with me. She prefers it when I tell her what to do. That way, she knows what to expect. What I want.

And I always give her what she wants in the end, so she has no complaints.

I whip off my shirt, and she falls to her knees, reaching for the front of my trousers. Her shaky fingers work the button and pull down the zipper. She presses her palm against the front of my boxer briefs, her fingers curling around my cock, giving me a firm squeeze.

"Harder," I grit out.

My pants fall, puddling around my ankles, and I kick them off, Sylvie leaning to the side when I send them flying. She rises up, her gaze finding mine as she leans in, her mouth pressing lightly against my cotton-covered dick.

Her breath is hot. Damp. She's panting, her lips parting, her tongue snaking out to lick. Just once. Just enough to earn a ragged groan from me.

"Take them off."

She curls her fingers around the waistband of my boxers and yanks them down, freeing my cock. She's downright eager as she grips the base, her mouth wrapping around the head and sucking me into her mouth.

"Fuck." I slide my fingers into her hair, watching in rapt attention as she slides my cock in and out of her mouth, her saliva making my hardened skin glisten. We've graduated from hand jobs and fingering to oral sex and her mouth is what I imagine heaven will feel like. Warm and wet and welcoming. With just the right amount of suction and a licking, eager tongue.

Cum drips on her tongue. I can feel it leaking out of me and I reach for her, curling my hand around her chin, making her stop. She pauses, her eyes wide, her mouth full of dick as she stares up at me.

"Slow down," I demand, my voice soft. "Lick it."

She runs her tongue up and down the length, teasing the flared head. Lightly tracing the slit, lapping up the precum. Her eyes shutter closed, a hum coming from deep in her throat that sends a vibration throughout my body.

My balls tighten, a warning that I'm going to come soon, which I don't want to do. I prefer to draw it out. But Sylvie has a way with her mouth. The sounds she makes. The way she looks at me.

Just thinking about her makes me want to blow.

Without warning, she removes me from her mouth, rising to her feet and rubbing the back of her hand against the corner of her lips. I'm left standing there like an idiot, my breathing erratic, my brain buzzing, my dick so fucking hard it hurts.

"You made me wait, I'm going to make you wait." Her smile is smug. Downright shitty.

I grab her, hauling her into me, her bare tits crushed against my chest. "You're a fucking tease."

"So are you." She shoves at my chest, but not very hard, and I can tell she enjoys it when we do this.

She always does.

"Get on the bed." I reach behind her, smacking her ass so hard she yelps. "Go."

Without hesitation, she does as I command, arranging herself on the bed so she's lying in the center of the mattress, her legs spread wide, showing off that pretty little pussy of hers. I shed the last of my clothing until I'm completely naked, and then I crawl onto the bed and am face to pussy, inhaling the sweet, slightly musky scent of her.

"Make me come with your mouth, Spence," she demands.

I study her, taking the moment in. She's lying in the middle of the mattress, black feathers scattered everywhere. A few small ones cling to her skin, reminding me of a tattered little dark angel who fell to earth, broken and confused.

Well, more like horny and needy. The impatience on her face is obvious, so I give her what she wants. What she needs.

Bending over her, I put my mouth on her pussy, my licks languid as I take my time and search every inch of her. She's so hot. Fucking soaked. I suck her clit between my lips, then let it go so I can tongue it. Flick it. Tease it.

Tease her.

"Yesssss." She thrusts her hands into my hair, holding my face to her and I devour her like I'm a starving man. She begins to tremble beneath me, her legs coming up, thighs pressing either side of my head, trapping me. I lick and suck her clit, never letting up as she cries out. Until she's shoving at my shoulders and I have no choice but to shift off her, leaning back on my haunches on the floor when she rolls onto her side.

"You should go." Her voice is muffled by the pillow she's got her face pressed into.

I frown. "Syl. Look at me."

She shakes her head, her messy blonde hair becoming even messier. "Go. Leave, Spence."

Glancing down at my still hard cock, I blow out a harsh breath. "You keep doing this."

"Doing what?"

"Pushing me away when we get closer."

She peeks at me, a single blue eye staring. "I do not."

"You do." I hesitate for only a moment. "And I'm sick of it."

Without warning, she hauls the pillow at me, and it smacks me in the head. "If you're so sick of me, get out!"

I stand, grabbing hold of my trousers and jerking them on before I throw the shirt over my shoulders, not bothering to button it. "I walk out that door right now, I might never come back in."

I mean it. I'm tired of the back and forth with this girl. Nothing is normal. Nothing is stable. I want to help her but…

Most of the time, she won't let me.

"Good. I don't want you to come back. Just go. Abandon me like everyone else does." Her voice is strained, like she might start crying at any moment, and for one second, I want to go to her.

Comfort her.

Instead, I slip on my shoes and leave, annoyance flaring through my blood, making it run hot.

I'm tired of being used by a Lancaster.

I'm not going to let it happen again.

CHAPTER NINE

SYLVIE

The call came out of the blue, as only the best calls can, and I'm at my lawyer's office the next day, anxious to know what he wanted to talk to me about. I decide there's no need for niceties or small conversation. The moment I settle into the chair across from his desk, I ask why he called me in.

Sterling Cavanaugh tries to hide the smile that barely curves his mouth when he ducks his head, flipping open the folder sitting before him on his desk. "Your husband's attorney got in touch with me yesterday morning."

Dread coats my stomach, making it churn. "What about?"

"It seems that he left you a little something no one else knew about." He pulls a sheet of paper from the folder and hands it over. I take it from him, frowning at the photo of the ocean view at the top. "A house."

"A house?" I study the other photos of the lodge-like structure nestled among the forest. "Where at?"

"California. Over one hundred acres on the Big Sur coast." When I glance up at Sterling, I find he's already watching me, a faint smile on his face. "It's a rare piece, Sylvie. Dense redwood forest and pristine coastline. There's nothing else like it. The house is over six thousand square feet, and was originally built in the 1920s."

My entire body vibrates with barely contained excitement. "Are you sure this belongs to me?"

"You weren't mentioned in the will at all, and I believe Earl realized it just before his death. That's why he put the house in your name. According to his attorney, it's been in his family for only a short amount of time. He picked it up a few years prior to your marriage," Sterling explains.

"Why don't his children want it?" I study the photos again, frowning when I take in the interior shots. It appears to have been remodeled, but not recently.

"They didn't know it existed."

"And once they find out, they'll come after me."

He shakes his head. "They can't. The house is untouchable by the estate. It wasn't even put into the estate. His children have no legal say in who it does or doesn't go to."

I'm frowning. This makes no sense. "Why not?"

"Because it was put into your name." Sterling hands over another document. A deed.

I snatch it from his fingers, my gaze roaming over the legal language, zeroing in on my name in black and white.

Sylvie Lancaster. He didn't even put it in my married name, not that I ever had it legally changed.

Hmm. The man did right by me for once.

"So this house is mine." I switch the papers, so I'm looking at the house images again.

"It is. And it is an interesting piece of property. Unique in size and scale. Like I said, plenty of dense forest and ocean coastline. There is nothing else like it on the market. Especially an estate so large," Sterling explains.

My excitement bubbles, threatening to overwhelm me. I don't want to get too overjoyed by this news, but an isolated property in California would provide an escape. From New York City. From my family. My mother.

My life.

I could start anew. Become a different person. Focus on different things. Maybe fall into some new-agey group and focus on wellness and self-worth. I'm sure California is full of those types of people.

Sterling opens a desk drawer and withdraws a yellow envelope, setting it on the desk and within reach. "The keys are inside. Along with the address and various instructions. The house doesn't come with a staff, though there is a groundskeeper. Not sure how he can manage to take care of the entire estate, considering how large it is. You might want to think about hiring more people to assist you."

I pick up the envelope and undo the clasp to peek inside. A variety of keys hang on a keychain that says Big Sur on it, along with an illustration of a sunset sinking into the ocean.

"You also might consider selling it," Sterling suggests. "There has been plenty of interest ever since it went off the market. There have even been inquiries into its availability lately, according to your late husband's lawyer."

"I'm not selling it." I seal the envelope back up, and stash it in my oversized black Valentino bag. The Roman studs make me feel tough. Strong. Like a gladiator.

Which is silly.

"As you wish," Sterling concedes, holding his hands out before clutching them together on his desk. "Merely something to consider for the future. California has never been your home base before. You don't know what it will be like, living there."

"Well, it might become my home base now, considering I'm a property owner." I grin, unable to hide my glee any longer. "This is wonderful news, Sterling."

"I figured you'd approve." His smile is warm. He's an older gentleman, younger than my dead husband but still old enough to be my father. I've always liked Sterling. He's happily married and has a son that's around my age who's a bit odd. Definitely not my type. Stodgy wannabe lawyers are boring.

But they always take care of you when you're in a pinch.

"I plan on going out there right away," I continue, my mind awhirl with plans. "I'll need to make arrangements with the family plane."

The Lancaster private plane is shared by the family. My father is the one who uses it the most, with Whit right behind him. I, on the other hand, rarely use it.

"I'm sure you'll have a lovely time there. The house and property included look spectacular." Ever the diplomat, my lawyer.

"You'll have to come visit me sometime, Sterling. Bring the family, especially your son," I offer, flashing him a toothy smile.

The nervous look that appears on Sterling's face can't be denied. The idea of me setting my sights on his son most likely terrifies him. "Ian is currently busy with law school."

I rise to my feet, slinging my bag over my shoulder. The weight of the world is light today, and I'm tempted to skip out of Sterling's office. "Such a shame. I'm sure he'd bore me to tears anyway."

Sterling clears his throat. "He has a girlfriend."

"Sure he does," I drawl, punctuating my words with a laugh. "Thank you for the good news, Sterling. You've made my entire year."

I skip right out of his office, just as I envisioned. By the time I've gone down the elevator and am out on the street in search of my hired car, I'm beaming from ear to ear, unable to contain the joy that is fizzing through my veins.

A house that's mine and no one else's. No other Lancaster attached to it but me. I can make my escape out of this dreadful city and never come back if I don't want to.

The idea of living on the coast of California by myself, surrounded by the forest and ocean, sounds like heaven. No father trying to make nice. No mother trying to slide back into my life, so she can control it. No brother casting his judgmental looks my way.

No chance of running into Spencer Donato ever again.

The last thought makes my heart pang, but I shove the thought aside. I can't worry about Spencer and what he thinks of me. He hates me. He made his feelings for me clear at Whit and Summer's wedding reception. I've ruined that relationship, once and for all, and have only myself to blame.

Maybe I can become a hermit. I'll hide away in my forest home with only the call of birds and the rustling of wild animals to keep me company. And the occasional groundskeeper, who'll call in and ask if I want the lawn mowed that week.

It sounds like a dream. Even better?

It's about to become my reality.

The moment I enter my apartment I freeze, sensing that someone is already here. When I'm the only one with access.

I pull my phone out of my bag, ready to dial the security desk in the lobby when my mother breezes out of the kitchen, humming a familiar tune. Like she belongs there. As if I gave her a key and told her she could stop by anytime she wanted.

"What are you doing here?" My voice is cold. Devoid of any emotion, though inside I'm trembling.

Her eyes widen with seeming surprise, and she rests her hand against her chest, her red-lacquered lips parting. "You startled me."

"This is my apartment," I stress. "How did you get inside?"

"I told the doorman I was your mother. He let me right in."

Of course, he did. To the outside world, Sylvia Lancaster is harmless.

"I want you to leave." I turn my back on her and march over

to the door, flipping the locks and opening it, pointing my finger at the open doorway. "Get out."

Her hand drops to her side, an amused curve to her lips. "Always so hostile toward me, Sylvie. I don't understand it."

I clench my fists at my sides, wishing I could smash her face in. Her blatant denial is infuriating. "You're gaslighting me."

She waves a hand, dismissing my accusation. "You young people and your terminology. Do you even understand what gaslighting means?"

"No, but here you go, gaslighting me again. As if I don't know what I'm talking about." I lift my chin, my hands still clenched. Armed and ready to fight. "This is my property, and you're not allowed on it. I'm asking you nicely to leave. If you don't, I'll call security."

"Security allowed me in. I had a personal escort and everything." She tilts her head to the side, contemplating me. "You're visibly shaking, Sylvie. Are you feeling all right?"

A roar leaves me unlike any sound I've ever made before. "Why are you like this?"

"I just want to talk." Her voice softens, full of concern. "Please. It's been so long. I don't like how you shut me out."

"I did it for my own protection."

"From me? What did I ever do to you?"

"You know." My voice drips with agony, making her frown. "You know exactly what you've done even though you pretend it never happened. I can't go on living like this, Mother. I just—I can't."

"Darling." She takes a step toward me, and I automatically shift back, needing the distance. "I'm concerned when you talk like that. Please tell me you're not contemplating suicide again."

This feels so familiar, it's downright eerie. We've already had this conversation. She's said these sorts of things to me before. Planting seeds and making me believe that I'm the one who wants to end my life.

Realizing that trying to get her to leave isn't going to work, I slam the door shut and wave a hand toward the couches in my living room. "You want to talk? Let's talk."

I settle onto the pristine white couch, keeping an eye on her as she sits on the pale blue chair directly across from me, resting her clutched hands in her lap. Her expression is pleasant, her eyebrows raised. As if she's waiting for me to tear into her while she sits like an angel, calm and reserved.

It's such a load of shit.

"I want to reestablish our relationship, Sylvie," she says, launching right into it. "I miss you. Seeing you at the wedding reminded me of how distant we've truly become, and it...hurts. We used to be so close, until you shut me completely out of your life."

The hypocrisy is real in this woman, I swear.

We stare at each other, each of us willing the other to break first, and like usual, I'm the one to do it.

"We can't have a relationship anymore, Mother. I just—you scare me," I admit, wanting her to think I'm feeling vulnerable.

Inside me, anger bubbles, hot and thick. She doesn't scare me. Not really. I just want her to think I'm weak.

"I would never hurt you. You know that, right?" She slides to the edge of her seat, poised and ready to bolt toward me if need be.

"You already have." I lift my chin, staring down my nose at her, taking in her features, which are so similar to mine. We look a lot alike, my mother and me. We basically share the same name. She'd hoped we'd be similar in every single way, and we're just not. She forgets that Lancaster blood flows through my veins, and it dominates. "Let's get it out in the open and talk about what you really did. How you took me to all of those doctors and convinced them I was sick, when I really wasn't. What exactly did you do to me, hmm? Poison me? Put me on so much medication I could barely function? Is that what happened? I can't remember. Things from my past are blurry, and I know why. It's all your fault."

I either want to forget, or whatever she did to me erased my memory.

"Watch what you say. Your accusations are dangerous." Her expression is smooth as glass, but I can hear the frustration in her words. The warning in her tone.

"They're especially dangerous because they're true." I shake my head again, and again when she tries to talk, effectively shutting her up. "Don't bother denying it or arguing with me. I know the truth. I lived through it. And that's why I don't want to be around you anymore. You're a threat to my life. You'd rather see me dead—or close enough to it."

She gapes at me, her mouth opening and closing like a dying fish. "That is the most—absurd thing I've ever heard. How dare you say that, Sylvie! How dare you."

I watch as she leaps to her feet, ever elegant as she heads for the door. She's going to leave without me having to kick her out, and that's so much easier.

"I refuse to sit here and let you say these sorts of things to me and expect me to just take it." She pauses at the door, her hand on the handle when she glances over her shoulder at me. "I've always wondered a few things about you."

That's all she says and, of course, she knew I'd ask what. So I do.

"What do you mean?"

Her eyes sparkle. "Your husband. His death was such a mystery. Did you have something to do with it?"

It's my turn to gape. To open and close my mouth, unable to form words. When my silence carries on, the triumph that alights my mother's eyes cannot be denied.

"That's what I thought." A sigh leaves her and she opens the door. "Such a shame. He was the one man I thought could tame you."

She shuts the door behind her before I can protest, and I

slump against the couch, gazing up at the ceiling as my breaths come faster and faster.

Does anyone else believe I killed Earl? His children have made thinly veiled comments that were digs, but they never came right out and said it.

No one ever has. Until my mother.

It figures.

CHAPTER TEN

SPENCER

I'm sitting at my desk in my office at Donato Enterprises when there's a knock on my door. Before I can ask who it is or wonder why my assistant didn't call with a warning first, the door swings open and Whit Lancaster strides inside, impatient as ever.

He comes to a stop in the middle of my office, resting his hands on his hips as he takes in the interior. Me sitting behind the grand desk that used to belong to my father. Until he bought a bigger, grander desk to sit behind and gave me the old one.

Whit grins. "What the fuck, Spence? Who are you now?"

I slam my laptop closed and lean back in my chair, contemplating him. "While you're off traveling the world for your month-long honeymoon, some of us have to work for a living."

"We were gone for three weeks." Chuckling, he wipes the smile off his face with his fingers, falling into one of the chairs that sits across from my desk. "This is unbelievable. You've really come up in the world."

I ignore his statement. "How was the honeymoon anyway?"

It's been well over a month since the wedding. Since I last saw Sylvie in the flesh. Moonlit and dancing with roses in her hair. Beautiful, infuriating Sylvie.

"Amazing. Exhausting."

"All the sex?" I arch a brow.

"My wife is pregnant," he says indignantly, like I offended him. "And we took August with us."

That was your first problem, is what I want to tell him, but they are a solid family unit and do everything together. It's not just Whit anymore. It's Whit and Summer—and August. Eventually, there will be another baby joining their ranks.

I can barely date the same woman twice in a row, and here's Whit, the most selfish asshole I ever knew, now a solid family man.

Life is wild.

"Sounds exhausting."

"Well, August kept us busy, I can't deny it." Whit grins. "But Summer is in her second trimester, so she's horny as fuck. Wants to jump me all the time."

"Spare me the details," I mutter.

He shrugs. "You're the one who asked."

True. My mistake.

"Why did you want to see me anyway?" I ask, changing the subject. Feeling impatient. It's a busy day—when is it not—and I don't have time to shoot the shit and catch up with my friend, despite my wanting to do so.

Whit frowns. "So formal. Can't I just want to talk to my old friend?"

"There is always a reason for an unexpected appearance," I remind him, knowing that Whit doesn't show up out of the blue just for kicks.

"I wanted to make an appointment, but you're booked. I even called your secretary."

"My assistant?" I check my watch. "I do have a meeting in ten minutes."

"Of course you do." He sounds irritated.

"Come on, Whit." My voice softens. "You get it. I know you do."

"Yeah, yeah, you're right. I do. I'll be quick." Whit leans

forward, amusement alighting his eyes. I'm sure he's tripping out that I'm the one with the upper hand in this particular situation, which is a rarity. "I need your help."

I lean back farther in my chair, angling it so I can look out the window at the cityscape spread out before me. The buildings' windows glitter in the sun, the towering Manhattan skyscrapers vast and seemingly never-ending. "Not sure I'm the one who can offer assistance."

"I didn't even say what I need help with," Whit points out.

My gaze returns to his, momentarily startled by the serious expression on his face. Guess he actually means business. "Donato Enterprises only assist others in…certain circumstances. You know this."

The family business is not quite on the up and up, and that's why Lancasters never get involved in business with Donatos. Oh, we have some legitimate avenues of income. Corporate holdings in various investments, including commodities trading, plus a global hedge fund. We're worth hundreds of millions and edging closer to the billion-dollar mark, which is my ultimate goal.

But we also dally in things that are…sketchy at best, absolutely criminal at worst.

"It's personal." The jovial façade drops, and Whit's eyes are now full of…is that worry? "It has to do with my sister."

"No." I shake my head. "Nope."

He rears back. I'm sure that's a word he doesn't hear too often. "Let me explain."

"If it has anything to do with Sylvie, I cannot be involved."

"What if it's about Carolina?"

"Still can't be involved." I won't touch either of those Lancaster sisters. To help Carolina would make Sylvie horribly jealous. And I can't help Sylvie. I just…

I can't.

This isn't about Carolina though. It's got Sylvie written all over it. I know it. That's why Whit came to me. I've always been the overeager puppy ready to do Sylvie's bidding.

Well, not anymore.

"Look, no one understands Sylvie like you do," he starts, but I interrupt him.

"I don't know about that. She married someone else. I'm sure he understood her far more than I ever could."

Whit barks out a laugh. "Not quite. You know that wasn't a marriage born out of love."

"Right." It doesn't matter what it was born out of. It happened. She ran off and married that fucker after having sex with me.

After giving her virginity to me. Like that's some sort of parting gift before she became someone else's wife.

Fucking weird if you ask me.

"Our mother paired her with that man. He wasn't Sylvie's choice." Whit sneers. "And he creeped me out. Something about him was off."

"I don't want to talk about Sylvie," I snap, earning a hard glare for my tone. I shrug. "If that's the only reason you came here, I'm sorry. I can't help you."

Whit slowly shakes his head, his disappointment palpable. "I never thought you'd turn me down when it came to Sylvie."

"The minute she took another man's name, it was done." A sigh leaves me and I sit up straighter, hating that little break of emotion.

"She's run away, you know," Whit admits softly.

"I don't care."

Curiosity blooms but I shove it aside. Fuck it.

I really do not care.

"No one knows where she's at."

"Not my problem." It's not.

"She planned it—even cashed out before she left. Took out a bunch of money before she disappeared. They have footage of her going to the bank and walking out twenty minutes later with a Chanel backpack stuffed full of cash."

Sounds like something Sylvie would do.

"Again, like I said, not my problem." I keep my expression as neutral as possible, refusing to react.

"Damn." Whit makes a disbelieving noise, rubbing at the side of his neck. "Summer warned me you might react this way, but I didn't believe her."

Point for Summer. She understands what it's like to come at a Lancaster from the other side. "Your sister isn't my problem anymore, Whit. She hasn't been for a long time. And what could I do for her in this situation, huh? Sounds like you need a private detective, not me."

"You're as good as one though, aren't you? When it comes to Sylvie at least? You two always know how to sniff each other out."

I hate the way that sounds. How he said that. Maybe we were like that when we were teenagers, but that was a long time ago. A lifetime ago.

"We're not on the same wavelength. We haven't been for years." I check my watch again, not caring if I seem rude. I don't want to talk about her anymore, though I can tell Whit isn't finished. "I need to prepare for my meeting, Whit. If you want, we could meet for drinks later this afternoon?"

Whit shakes his head, not budging from the chair. "I can't believe you're not going to help me."

"I can't believe you're trying to find her by asking for my help. You have more money than God, and you're telling me you don't know where she is? Maybe she doesn't want to be found."

Whit snorts. "Clearly. Look, I found Summer after she ran out on me. It wasn't easy, but I did it. I know you can do the same for Sylvie."

"The circumstances are different. You were in love with each other."

"And you're not in love with Sylvie now?" The doubt in his voice is strong.

I slowly shake my head. Fuck, I'm such a liar. "She's not in love with me either. It's been years, Whit. *Years*. We're older now. She married someone else. She's had lovers. So have I. We've both moved on."

"Such bullshit," Whit mutters as he rises to his feet. "You two drive me insane."

"Sorry to put you through it," I say, not sounding sorry at all.

"Fuck you," he spits out before his demeanor changes in an instant. "Come on. Help me out. I'm your best friend. She was your first love."

It's funny, hearing him speak of love. It's not something he's normally comfortable with, though that all changed once he had August.

"Right. My first love who fucked me over and got married without telling me." I don't tell him what she really did to me—coming over to my place naked, like some sort of offering that I didn't hesitate to take. That's our secret to keep, and none of his damn business.

"She didn't tell *anyone* she was getting married, you know. Like I already said, that was some sort of weird plan concocted by her and our mother."

"Well, maybe she concocted this plan with her mother as well," I point out.

"No." Whit shakes his head. "Our mother is freaking the fuck out. She called me and asked if I knew where she was. My father called too. No one knows where she ran off to."

"She probably took a little vacation."

"Sylvie's been missing for *weeks*. Packed her shit, turned off her phone and we haven't heard a word from her since. For all we know, she could be dead."

"Weeks?" The alarm that threatens to choke me is sudden. Nearly debilitating. Thank Christ I'm sitting down. "You didn't say she's been gone for weeks."

"Well, she has. Look, she's run away before, but not like this. Never like this." He leans forward, his expression earnest. "It's fucking scary, Spence. And nothing scares me, unless it has to do with my family. Sylvie and I have had our struggles before, but things have been good between us. She's been repairing her relationship with my wife, and she adores my son. She came to my wedding, which was the first family event she's been to in a while. She avoids them because of our mother, but she wanted to be there for me and Summer. It was a breakthrough. Then she just up and disappears. It's not normal. It's not right."

"This makes no damn sense."

"I know. So help me make sense of it. Help me find her." Whit swallows hard. "Please."

Now there's a word you don't hear a Lancaster say often.

Silence fills the room, and while it probably lasts no longer than thirty seconds, it feels longer. Like minutes. Hours.

Whit is waiting me out. Waiting for me to give in. And like the sucker he knows I am…

I do.

"I'll see what I can do," I say stiffly. "But I'm not making any promises."

"Right now, I'll take what I can get."

It's late, and I'm nursing a glass of scotch, scrolling on my laptop, bleary-eyed and exhausted. Still at the office, though everyone else is long gone.

I'm trying to think like Sylvie Lancaster, which is an odd headspace to be in. Where would she go, what would she do? What would make her run away like this? Did something happen?

Or is it more like someone?

The someone part rankles, but that's just my jealousy rearing its ugly head. I mentally tell myself to forget about it and focus on the clues.

There aren't many.

A vast amount of information pertaining to Sylvie is on the internet, but the majority of it is meaningless. Endless photos of her in the society pages, including a few of her with her old ass, dead husband. I scroll right past those, hating the anger that boils my blood when I see her smiling, standing next to an old man who she called her husband.

Did she actually have sex with that guy? How deep do her daddy issues go? Did I even really ever know her?

No, not really, is what I tell myself.

I do a little deeper digging. Pulling up her marriage license. Searching for other legal documents involving Earl Wainwright. There are plenty, including various lawsuits over the years, and the divorce with his first wife. He's bought and sold a lot of properties in Manhattan the last thirty years or so. And a single purchase in…California?

That's a one-off—and an odd purchase for him to make.

I open Google Maps and enter the address, startled to realize it's nothing but acres and acres of thick forest with a house nestled deep in the trees. It sits right next to the Pacific Ocean and he paid ten million for it.

What the hell was he going to do with a house on the California coast?

I search through deeds, first in New York, then in Monterey County in California, and that's when I find it. The clue I needed to find Sylvie.

Her husband switched the property into Sylvie's name a little over a year ago. I check the dates—the transaction occurred just prior to his death. Is that where she is? Holed away on the coast? Maybe she needed a change and decided to start over in California.

Or maybe she ran away and hoped I would pick up on the few legal bread crumbs left behind.

I shut my laptop and lean back in my desk chair, thrusting

my hands through my hair as a deep exhale leaves me. The temptation to follow after her is strong, even though there's no guarantee she's even there.

My senses are telling me she's in California. At that house. Hidden away so no one can find her.

I could take our private jet to Big Sur. There's an airport in Monterey and I could rent a car. If she's not there, I could detour to San Francisco and handle some business I have there. Or Los Angeles. Hell, I could visit both cities and get some work done.

Donato Enterprises has business partners on the West Coast. It wouldn't be a totally wasted trip.

Though I know deep down, I shouldn't go. It's what she wants, and I'm tired of always giving Sylvie exactly what she desires. She's a spoiled brat, and I've indulged her every whim ever since I first met her.

Despite it all, next thing I know, I'm on the phone, booking the plane for first thing tomorrow.

CHAPTER ELEVEN

SYLVIE

I am my own person. I am my own person.
I chant the mantra on repeat in my head, reminding myself that I am someone other than my family. I am not just Augustus Lancaster's daughter or Whit's sister or Sylvia's namesake.

Since I've been here, all alone on the other side of the country, it's been easier to believe. The more distance there is between my mother and me, the better I feel.

Though that's the hardest pill to swallow—being named after the woman who wants me dead. Of course, I was named after her. My mother is the biggest narcissist I know—and I know plenty. Family lore tells the tale of her first word being, 'Me'.

No surprises there.

My father thinks he picked her, but she told me the truth. I may have been young, but I hung on every word she spilled when she would drink too much and make her drunken confessions. His parents controlled the narrative, just like mine tried to. Sylvia Whittaker wasn't about to let her chance go at sinking her claws into the son of one of the richest families in the world. Once she married my father and gave him the prodigal firstborn son, she'd done her job. I was the girl she wished for. The child she was desperate to have.

The daughter she could name after herself in the hopes I'd grow up just like her.

When I was a little girl, she dressed me like her. Everyone said I resembled her when I was little, and I suppose I do.

But I have a hint of Lancaster in me too. The eyes. The blonde hair. I'm not all Sylvia.

Thank God.

I'm sure she hates that fact.

I am my own person. I am my own person.

That I have to remind myself of this is surely pathetic, but whatever it takes, right? I already feel better, being out here. In my own house—the house that belongs to me and no one else. I'm all by myself for the first time in my life, and I'm savoring it. Yes, the woods are scary and there are way too many noises among the trees, especially at night. Little forest creatures always watching as I walk past. Roland, the groundskeeper Earl hired after he bought the property, says if I'm going to live here year-round, I need a dog. Maybe two. There are already at least three cats on the property. They're not overly affectionate and they leave bloody little carcasses everywhere. Scattered feathers and a bird's head. Guts from the inside of some rodent. It's gross. Cats are ruthless. Sneaky. Cunning.

Like a Lancaster.

I do think Roland is right though. I need a pet—a dog. Something to watch over me.

The urge to flee New York City came to me in the middle of the night, a day after I met with my lawyer. I woke up from a dream where Earl was still alive, and he offered the house to me as a token of peace.

For all that I put you through, he told me.

A ten-million-dollar private hideaway is more than enough payment for what that man put me through, which wasn't much, considering he died fairly quickly after we were married. That I still feel responsible is a fact I don't like to dwell on for too long.

I may be my own person, but I'm not a good one.

I have dark thoughts. If I could murder my mother, I would. But I don't have the guts.

So I sit with my dark thoughts in my dark house late at night, all alone, while the walls and the ceiling and the roof creak and groan. It's been windy lately, and that makes the house shudder and moan and some nights, I can't take it. I pace the halls, unable to sleep, tears streaming down my face.

Thinking of chances lost.

Thinking of Spencer.

I exit the kitchen and walk out onto the deck that overlooks the thick forest. The hushed silence that greets me was eerie when I first arrived, but I'm getting used to it. The pine needles rustle with the constant breeze that blows through them, a sound that never stops.

That's what I learned after a few days of being out here. You think it's silent, but after a while, you can hear birds chirping. Animals calling to each other. The occasional burst of an ocean wave. The rev of a car's engine, hollow and distant out on the main road.

No voices though. Never voices. Unless Roland makes his appearance, which isn't often enough for me. The only voices I usually ever hear are in my head.

I've realized I don't like those voices sometimes. They're mostly full of doubt. And those voices in particular make me feel bad about myself.

I am my own person. I am my own person.

There is nothing more liberating than dumping your phone and everything attached to it. I shut down my social media profiles. I pulled out a lot of cash from the bank, so no one could track me down with credit card usage. I wanted to disappear. Go off the grid.

Become a ghost.

I'm also lonely. Hence the need for a dog. The cats that live on the property are mostly wild and want nothing to do with me. Except for one. She's silvery gray with long fur, though not too puffy. Her tail is straggly and her face is delicately shaped. She reminds me of a squirrel. So that's what I call her.

Squirrel acts like she doesn't like me, yet she follows after me every time I go outside, batting at my ankles when I walk, her claws lightly scratching, but never enough to actually hurt. I turn to try and pet her, and she dashes away every time. Yet never too far, always watching me.

Like she's interested, but cautious.

I feel her. I really do.

The flip phone I bought at a local Walmart in Monterey rings, and I yank it from my sweater pocket, frowning when I see Roland's number flash. He's the only one who has this number in the whole world, yet he's never called me.

"Hello," I answer.

"Miss Lancaster. I caught someone on the driveway."

I frown. "What do you mean?"

"A man in an Audi. Said he was looking for you."

Fear slithers icy cold fingers down my spine. "Did he mention my name?"

"Yes, he did. Said he knows you real well." I hear a deep voice speak in the background. "He won't give me his name though."

"Is he there with you?"

"Yes. I stopped him. Stood right out in front of his fancy car and wouldn't let him drive past me." Roland sounds frustrated. Protective. We've only known each other for a few weeks, and he's already taken me under his wing.

"I want to speak with him." I have no clue who this could be. One of my Lancaster relatives? There are plenty of male Lancasters with the brains to figure out where I might be. No one has taken my disappearance to the media, thank goodness. I assumed my mother would do exactly that to get me to come out and show myself.

It wouldn't have worked. I'd have stayed in hiding forever just to keep her out of my life forever.

"Here he is." Roland hands over the phone, and there's muffled conversation that sounds tense before a familiar male voice sounds in my ear.

"Syl. It's me."

My heart falls into my stomach. Deeper.

Spencer.

"Tell this man you know me and that I have your permission to come to your house," Spencer demands.

I clutch the cheap phone tighter, my heart racing. I can't believe he's here, in California. That he came for me despite everything. "I should tell him to kick you off my property."

An irritated sound leaves him. "You know you don't mean it. Come on, Syl. Call off your watchdog."

"Let me talk to Roland."

Spencer pauses for a moment. "You promise you'll tell him it's okay that I'm here?"

"Just let me talk to him."

A low growl escapes him and then Roland is back, his breathing accelerated, amplified as he exhales into the phone. "I'll kick his ass if you want me to, Miss Lancaster. Just say the word."

A laugh escapes me and I cover my lips with my fingers to contain it. "That won't be necessary, Roland. Go ahead and let him come to the house."

My groundskeeper grunts. I can tell he's not pleased with my answer. "I'm following him. And I'll stick around until he leaves."

"That won't be necessary," I start, but he interrupts me.

"I'm doin' it." The stubborn tone in Roland's voice is one I decide not to argue with.

"See you soon," I say cheerfully instead, and end the call.

Men. They go feral around me for some reason, and I don't understand it. There's nothing between Roland and me. He's more like an overprotective father—something I'm not familiar with.

A rasp of a laugh leaves me and I shake my head. It's like I can't help but insult a random family member every chance I get.

Realizing that Spencer will be here in a matter of minutes and I have no idea what I look like, I run into the house, ducking into the guest bathroom, so I can check out my reflection. I wrinkle my nose at what I see, hating how messy my hair is thanks to the ocean wind. I run my fingers through it, licking my lips. I have no makeup on—what's the point? My cheeks are pink, thanks to all the sun I've been getting lately. Plus, I'm not drinking.

I always look better when I lay off the alcohol.

I'm heavier than I've ever been, which isn't saying much. But I do look different. Some might even say healthier.

Not my mother though. She'd be disappointed she couldn't see my collarbones protruding. The hollows of my cheeks.

Mommy gets off on skinny, skeletal Sylvie.

I hear the gentle rumble of an expensive engine creeping up the drive and my heart is in my throat, making it hard to swallow. To breathe. Knowing that Spencer is here, that I'm about to see him again. I blink at myself in the mirror, my chest rising and falling rapidly, nervous excitement running through my veins.

He came, I remind myself. Spencer may have walked away from me that night after Whit and Summer were married, but he's here now.

That has to mean something.

Blowing out a harsh breath, I give myself a thumbs up and a grimace in the mirror, then march out of the bathroom, through the house and onto the front porch. Just in time to see Spencer roll up the driveway in his sleek black Audi, the engine purring. Roland is right behind him in his older model Ford truck, his blue ballcap pulled low, a grim look on his weathered face.

I wait anxiously, wringing my hands as Spencer cuts the

engine. Gathers his things. Taking his time.

Driving me slowly out of my mind.

Roland leaps out of his car as if his butt is on fire, striding toward me so fast he's directly in front of me in seconds. "Want me to call the police?"

"Absolutely not." I slowly shake my head, glancing around him to watch as Spencer finally opens the driver's side door of his vehicle. "It's not necessary."

Roland doesn't know my whole story, but he knows some of it. That I'm a widow in hiding from my family and friends. Trying to get away from the incessant noise that is my life, and that I'm searching for peace. He's been so good to me from the moment we met, and I appreciate how he checks up on me. Watches over me.

"Are you sure? That young man," Roland jerks his thumb over his shoulder, "is kind of an asshole."

I laugh, throwing back my head, letting the joy flow through me. No one could ever call Spencer an asshole. Not the Spence I knew. He was protective of me, watching over me.

Much like Roland does now.

A door slams and we both glance in Spencer's direction. He's wearing a black suit and a white button-up shirt, sans tie. Sunglasses cover his eyes and his dark hair appears freshly trimmed. Immaculate. His shoes are shiny and they make a clipped sound on the driveway as he makes his way toward us, a grim look on his too handsome, too beloved face.

There are no traces of the boy I first met and immediately crushed on. Not a single one. Spencer Donato is all man, and he is beautiful. Sexy. Confident. Faintly irritated—I can tell by the set of his jaw. The firm line of his lips.

I stand up straighter, bracing myself, waiting for him to say something horrible—why, I don't know. That's not his style. Or, for him to grab hold of my hand and drag me back to the car so he can fly me home and return me to my family like I'm a lost piece of luggage he finally found.

He does none of that. Instead, he stops directly in front of Roland and me, his expression unreadable. I can't even see his eyes, thanks to his sunglasses.

"What are you doing here?" My voice is sharp, unable to forget the last time we saw each other and how mean he was. His cruel words, how he so easily walked away from me.

Yet here he is, chasing after me like usual.

I think of the last words I said to him, how I called him a liar.

Looks like I was right.

"I've been looking for you," he finally says, his voice a seductive rumble coming from deep within his chest.

I tell myself I shouldn't give in, but when it comes to this man, I am weak. What makes it worse?

I know he's weak for me too.

"Looks like you found me," I tell him softly.

The air crackles between us, unseen sparks bouncing from me to Spencer as my body leans toward his despite my inherent resistance. I can't help but notice how Roland looks from me to Spencer, his graying eyebrows furrowed.

He can sense it too. The energy. The chemistry. It's probably how Spencer found me—that unseen thread between us that keeps us tethered. We've always been drawn to each other, despite everything that's happened over the years.

"Did you want to be found?" Spence asks, his voice as soft as mine.

I slowly shake my head. "Only by you."

His lips curve into the slightest smile. Barely there and gone in an instant. But I saw it. And in that moment, I know.

Nothing is ever going to be the same. For once, it's all going my way. This is what I want.

Me and Spence.

Spence and me.

CHAPTER TWELVE

SPENCER

Sylvie looks the best I've ever seen her—and I've seen so many versions of her throughout the years, the number feels infinite. I've seen her younger and older, and skinny and frail, and lush and brimming with health, and everything in between. Mostly the in between is the version of Sylvie I've witnessed the last couple of years.

Now she's the lush and brimming with health version. Her face is flushed and strands of untamed blonde hair waft across her face, thanks to the cool breeze coming from the unseen ocean. She keeps batting them away, her little scowl adorable.

She's wearing a white T-shirt covered by a deep brown, oversized cardigan and jeans. Not a lick of makeup is on her face. She's the plainest I've ever seen her.

And by far the most beautiful.

"I can't believe you found me." She keeps shaking her head, her eyes dancing with mischief. I think she fucking loves the fact that I found her. "How did you do it?"

I tap my temple with my index finger. "Used my brain."

"You've always had such a big one." Her tone, her smile is suggestive, and she laughs at my scowl. "Take off your sunglasses," she demands. "I want to see you."

I whip them off for her, slipping them into my jacket pocket. She stares at me for a long time, her gaze roving. Drinking me in. I don't move. I let her look her fill, until she takes a step forward and pats me gently on the chest.

"I've missed you," she murmurs.

I catch her hand, my fingers circling around her delicate wrist bones. It would take nothing to crush her, not that I would ever do that. She's so finely made, so easily crushable.

The flare in her bright blue eyes tells me she's stronger. This girl isn't going to let anyone push her around anymore.

Hopefully.

"I'm still mad at you," I admit, deciding to be truthful.

"I'm still mad at you too," she returns just as truthfully, and I'm taken aback.

"Why are you mad at me?"

"You were mean to me at the wedding."

She's right. I was.

"If you're so mad, then why are you here?"

"Whit asked me to find you."

The hurt in her gaze is unmistakable and she jerks her hand out of my grip, taking a step back. "So you're here for my brother. You found me at his request."

Only Sylvie would be insulted by her family being worried about her and coming to me for assistance.

"No." I shake my head. "I turned him down. I didn't want to be involved. He told me you've been missing for weeks and I said it wasn't my problem."

Sylvie lifts her chin, ever defiant. "Then why are you here?"

I could lie, but there's no point. I've always been truthful with Sylvie. She's the little liar in this relationship.

"Because I couldn't stop thinking about you and wondering where you were. I went on a deep internet search and eventually figured it out." I don't tell her I figured it out only last night. Or that I never told her brother I actually found her.

I wanted to see her for myself first.

She relaxes at my words, her lips curved in a barely-there smile. "And how did you find me?"

"I went through the various court documents that involved your husband." She flinches at the word husband, but otherwise, doesn't say a word. "Finally came across a few deeds on properties he owned in the city. Started digging for more and stumbled upon one in California that he transferred into your name."

I can tell by her expression that she's impressed.

"It was a surprise to me too," she admits. "I didn't know he even owned this house. Neither did his children. He never brought me here."

"Were they pissed?" I raise my brows.

"I asked my lawyer the same thing." She shakes her head. "I suppose not. They never knew about it, so it's hard to be mad over something you never thought belonged to you in the first place. I guess he owned it for a very short time. It's almost as if he planned for this to be here. For me. My own little sanctuary." She glances around, breathing deep. Her henchman still stands by her side, his arms crossed and his glaring dark eyes all for me. "I love it here."

"You'll have to show me around." I pause. "If you'll let me stay."

Sylvie contemplates me, tilting her head to the side, her blonde hair spilling over her shoulder. I'm filled with the urge to bury my hands in the silky softness. Press my face into her hair and breathe in her scent. My senses are buzzing, fully awake and attuned to this woman, and I understand completely why I came here. Why I sought her out.

I'm still in love with her. Like a complete dumbass.

"I'll let you stay for the day," she concedes. "I'll even give you a tour."

I incline my head toward her. "How generous of you."

She looks over at her groundskeeper. The guy had a fucking

shotgun clutched in his hand when he stopped me earlier from progressing any farther down the driveway. He's lucky I didn't pull out the handgun I tossed in the glove compartment box when I first slid into the car after renting it, and aim it at his fucking forehead. "You can go back to your house, Roland. I've got this."

"Who is he?" Roland flicks his chin in my direction, his arms crossed, legs spread wide in a bracing stance. Like I'm coming for him at any second and he's ready for it.

He's bold, I'll give him that. Asking her who I am. I've known her longer than him and he acts like he's her damn father.

"My first love." Her gaze seeks out mine. "The boy who first broke my heart."

I snicker. "More like you broke mine."

We stare at each other in silence until Roland breaks the trance with a snort.

"So it's like that then." Roland shakes his head with an exasperated sigh. "I'll leave you two be. But if you need anything, Miss Lancaster, anything at all, you give me a call, okay? It will take me less than two minutes to get here."

The threatening glare he sends in my direction almost makes me laugh.

"I will, Roland," she says. "I promise."

"I've known her for years, Roland," I tell him, my voice gruff. "Nothing is going to happen to her."

He points a gnarled finger in my direction. "You make sure of that, young man. You're too rich and fancy for my blood, but then again, so is Miss Lancaster. I'm guessing you two might be okay for each other."

Before either of us can say anything, he's striding off the porch, moving fairly fast for an older man. Maybe he's not as old as I thought.

Within minutes, Roland is back in his beat-up old Ford truck and driving away, kicking up dust once he comes off the circular driveway. We watch him go, the roar of the truck's engine growing more and more distant, until I can't hear it any longer.

With the vehicle gone, I realize it's unnervingly quiet here, surrounded by the lush, thick forest. The occasional chirp of a bird, or the pine branches gently swaying with the breeze are the only sounds. My gaze goes to the thicket of trees, staring at nothing. It feels as if someone is watching me in the hushed, thick forest and I glance over my shoulder.

But there's nothing there.

Sylvie is smiling when I return my attention to her, and for a moment, I savor that flash of teeth. The sparkle in her gaze. How good it feels to be in her presence once more.

Did she doubt I'd find her? Did she think of me at all? Probably not. She's selfish. Self-indulgent.

She doesn't even have to officially summon me, and here I am, just like anyone else who does the Lancaster bidding. Rushing to get to her without hesitation.

The logical side of my brain tells me I probably shouldn't have come. My gut warns it could be a mistake. My brain is reminding me of all the shitty things she's ever done to me.

Yet here I am, and she's so damn happy. I can see it in the sparkle of her blue eyes, the size of her smile. She gives up all earlier pretense of coolness and throws herself at me, her arms going around my neck as she presses that newly lush body against mine.

"I can't believe you came," she breathes, just before she settles her mouth on mine in the briefest, ripest kiss.

I've always thought her lips were like the most delectable fruit. Swollen and luscious. Sweet and tart.

My little angel who's really a devil in disguise. Aren't the fallen the ones who were the purest to start with? That's Sylvie. I'm surprised she's still not sprouting the black feathers she wore for her Halloween costume long ago.

I rest my hands lightly on her waist, keeping her still, so she doesn't come any closer. "You're not surprised, Syl. You knew eventually I'd show up."

She leans back, her eyes on mine, her lips parted. So many unspoken words rest on her tongue and they remain that way. Unsaid. She drives me out of my fucking mind.

I'm a glutton for punishment.

The sun shines upon her hair, spinning it into gold, and she reminds me of a wood sprite. An evil little fairy. She'd delight in giving me pleasure, as well as cutting me with the sharpest knife.

My body grows tight anticipating the pain she'll bring me.

The pleasure.

"What's going on in your head, hmm?" Her voice is like a hum, low and vibrating along my nerve endings and I shake my head slowly.

"You don't want to know." I set her away from me, proud of my strength. Resisting her is my greatest weakness. "You should make good on your promise and show me around."

Her gaze rakes over me, taking in my suit. I wear it like armor to protect me from her, and I'm already desperate to shed it. "I can't give you a tour while you're dressed like that."

"Show me the house first." I point toward the front door. "And after that, if you still want me to stick around, I can change and we can look around the property."

"Did you bring a suitcase?"

A giant one. I don't say that out loud though. "I came prepared."

"My smart, smart Spence." She laughs. "Okay, come on. Let me show you the house."

I follow her inside, immediately hit with her scent, mixed with woodsy pine. I blame the walls and the ceiling, which are mostly constructed with roughly hewn wood walls. The interior has seen better days, but it's rustic and charming, yet also somehow large and spacious. There are windows everywhere, some running floor to ceiling, showcasing the endless acres of trees.

"Where's the ocean?" I ask as we stop in front of the giant

windows that overlook the backyard and the forest beyond.

"Out there." She points. "Past the trees."

"You can access the beach from here?"

"Yes, just over the hill. There are trails everywhere, all over the property. It's like a park. My own little personal park."

I almost laugh at her using the word "little". There is nothing small about it. "This property is worth a tremendous amount of money," I observe. I did some research. He bought it for ten million, but it's worth all of fifteen now. Maybe even more.

"*I'm* worth a tremendous amount of money," she says, that Lancaster ego ringing through her words. "I won't sell this."

"I'm not suggesting you should."

A sigh leaves her and she angles her body toward mine. "When I found out Earl did this for me, that he bought me this, I knew immediately I had to come out here. And I didn't want to tell anyone. I didn't want them to know about it."

"Why not?" I want to hear her actual reasoning for once. Not a bunch of excuses or fanciful bullshit. "Be real with me, Syl."

She's quiet for a moment, the only sound the occasional chirping of a bird. The rustle of the trees. I'm not used to quiet like this. I prefer the city with all its noise and people yelling. Horns honking and loud music playing.

"I wanted to escape from my life." A sigh leaves her and she looks away. "From my mother."

I say nothing. I don't know all the details between them, but I want her to tell me eventually. When she's ready.

"From everyone, really." She returns her attention to me, her expression fierce. "The city. High society. I'm sick of being Sylvie Lancaster. I just wanted to be…me. Just Sylvie. Nothing else attached."

That's impossible, but I understand what she's trying to say.

"At first, I was scared living in this big house, all alone. Thank God for Roland." She laughs, and it's a soft, husky sound that settles in my gut. Stirs my dick. "I'm starting to get used to it though. It's so quiet. Nothing like the city."

"It's unnerving."

"Right?"

I nod, filled with the urge to reach out and touch her, but I quell it. I can't be weak. I'm here as a friend. Nothing more.

Ah, the lies we tell ourselves. It's almost embarrassing, how easily I believe myself when it's the furthest thing from the truth.

I can never just be Sylvie's friend. Not when I know the taste of her mouth. The feel of her naked body beneath mine. The way she looks when she comes. The snug sensation of her pussy wrapped around my cock.

There's too much history between us. It's painful and it's rough, but it runs deep. So deep, it's as if she throbs in my veins. In my blood.

In the depths of my very soul.

CHAPTER THIRTEEN

SYLVIE

I remind myself Spencer is only here because of my brother's concern, but I can't help but be giddy at his nearness. The way he smiles at me. How normal it all feels. The last time we were together, he was cruel. Punishing. The hatred in his eyes was obvious and I believed I'd lost any chance I could've had with him in that one moment.

Now, I have hope. I'm stupid to believe he could forgive me for marrying Earl without telling him, but I can't help it.

It's there, a tiny glimmer flickering deep in my heart. If anyone would've shown up out of the blue, I would've wanted it to be Spencer. No one else. Not even my brother or sister.

Especially not them. They would've eventually told our mother and she'd come right out here and try to drag me home. If she'd shown up when I first arrived, I might've let her. It was so scary, so quiet, so dark at night.

The darkness terrified me at first. What could be creeping out there? I had visions of people dressed in black slipping through the trees. Like a gang of ninjas sent on a mission to abduct me and bring me back to New York City against my will.

My imagination has always run totally wild. When I was young and under my mother's supposed care, my life was simple.

Boring. Locked up in a room, forced to remain in bed. Alone with my thoughts and imagination, which grew and grew.

I needed something to entertain myself.

Fortunately, no ninjas came out of the forest ready to abduct me and I grew more and more comfortable staying here. Living here on my own.

Sometimes it hits me, that this is *my* house. That it belongs to no one but me. I don't know what that's like, to own something that's only mine. Anywhere I've lived has belonged to the Lancaster family. Or when I married and moved in with Earl—that apartment I'm still in now may belong to me, but it was Earl's first.

Earl may have bought this, but he put it in my name before he died, and never came out here. It's basically untouched by anyone I know or am related to.

It's all mine.

And now I'm sharing it with Spencer.

I lead him through the house, not embarrassed in the least that it's seen better days. It has good bones, and eventually, I'll have it remodeled.

When I pull him into the elevator that will take us to the second floor, he finally breaks the cool façade.

"An elevator? For two stories?" He strokes his chin. "Kind of unnecessary, don't you think?"

"What if you're handicapped? In a wheelchair? This is so much easier. It's nice to have options," I remind him, bracing my hand against the wall when the elevator shudders before it starts its ascent. "It's not in the best condition though."

It halts at the second floor, giving another heaving shudder before the doors slide open.

"I'll say," Spencer drawls as he exits the elevator.

I follow behind him, dodging around him so I can continue showing off the house. I point out all the bedrooms, saving mine for last. It's at the end of the hall, and when we walk inside, he stops short at the wall of windows that greets him. The vivid green forest the sole view.

"It looks like you're sleeping in the trees," he says, his voice tinged with awe.

He described it perfectly. That's exactly what it feels like. The towering redwoods surround the window, the glass so clean it looks like you can reach out and touch them. The house sits on a hillside, and the second floor makes it feel like you're suspended in air. Among the trees.

I love it, and I've never been one who's drawn to nature. I grew up in the city after all.

I watch him stand in front of the windows, staring out at the scenery. He looks completely out of place, standing in this rundown house while clad in a ten-thousand-dollar suit. Immaculate and without a hair out of place, despite traveling over five hours in a plane to find me.

Most likely a private plane, so it wasn't too much of a hardship, but still.

"This is the best room in the house," he declares, glancing over his shoulder to look at me.

I nod my agreement. "The view is stunning."

"There are no curtains on the windows," he observes.

"I wake up to the view every morning." He turns away from me, staring out at the forest once more. "There's no point in covering it. The trees are so dense, the sun doesn't penetrate enough to be overly bright. And no one is out here. There's no need for privacy."

"I don't know if I could ever get used to this. Living out here," he says absently, almost to himself.

"It's amazing how quickly you can adapt."

Spencer turns once again, his expression neutral as he watches me. "That's how you survive. You've always been able to easily adapt to your surroundings."

I squirm under his observation, wishing to change the subject.

I've never liked the way he assessed me, always trying to figure me out, and most of the time, I want to tell him to kiss my ass.

Only because, most of the time, Spencer is correct in his assumptions—and it's infuriating.

He slowly scans the rest of my bedroom, stopping when he notices the cream-colored vase on top of the dresser, a bouquet of black feathers sticking out of it. It totally doesn't fit in with the rest of the décor in the room, but I found the odd arrangement at an antique store in Carmel and knew I had to have it.

"Nice feathers," he drawls, his gaze finding mine.

I smile. "They reminded me of...me."

"Still the fallen angel, Syl?"

"More like the black hearted angel who finally knows how to defend herself," I correct him.

He nods. "I like this version of you."

Pleasure courses through me and I tell myself to ignore it.

"Do you want to change out of your suit?" I ask.

"Am I deemed worthy enough to stay?"

"Do you want to stay?"

"I should probably head back."

Disappointment crashes through me, but I lift my chin, fighting against the emotion. "Then go back. Make your report and let my brother know I'm fine."

He lifts a brow. "You think I'm going to draw up a report on your current status for Whit?"

"That's why you're here, right?"

"I didn't tell Whit I was coming." He hesitates for only a moment. "He doesn't even know I found you."

Shock courses through me, rendering me still. "Really?" I squeak.

Spencer nods. "I told him I wasn't going to look for you, but then I couldn't help myself."

I love that confession—far too much. "Are you leaving today or not?"

"I should."

Irritation makes me snappy. "Answer me, Spence."

"I'll stay."

Relief makes my knees wobbly. "For how long?"

"Until I have to go back." His vagueness is irritating, but I don't acknowledge it.

"You should change then."

"You don't like me in the suit?" He glances down at himself.

I like him in the suit too damn much, not that I would ever tell him. "You can't make the hike in your fancy suit."

"I can do just about anything in this suit." He undoes the button, the jacket gaping open, showcasing the flat expanse of his stomach and how the crisp shirt is tucked into the waistband of his trousers perfectly.

"Not hike through the woods to the ocean. You don't want to ruin it."

"I suppose I don't. I'll grab my suitcase."

"So you did bring a suitcase."

"Just in case. Don't read too much into it." He strides toward me, pushing past me as he makes his way to the door. "I'm taking the room next to yours."

He doesn't ask, just tells me what he's going to do. Which isn't normal.

But I'm realizing younger, sweeter Spence is nowhere to be found. He's been replaced by older, fiercer Spencer, and I have to admit...

I kind of like it. This new version of him.

The sun shines down upon us, warm despite the chill in the wind that sweeps over us. The hill in front of us appears easy enough, but the ground is mostly sand, and we'll continuously fight to gain traction as we climb it.

Spence just doesn't know it yet.

I hid out in the kitchen when he dragged his suitcase to his bedroom, and I never said a word about the size of said suitcase either. It's large. Looks like he brought enough to move in. I thought I wanted to be alone here, but I know when he leaves, there's going to be a hole where he was, and I will never be able to fill it.

Perhaps it was a mistake that I allowed him to stay. It will be hard to recover from his visit. I'm only torturing myself.

But I don't tell him to leave. It's already too late. I need him here.

I just need him. Period.

He took his time upstairs while I puttered around the kitchen, picking up my dishes from breakfast earlier and rinsing them off, then stashing them in the dishwasher. I wipe the counters down and tidy up, marveling at the fact that I even know how to clean the kitchen in the first place. Every little thing has been done for me since birth. Servants everywhere to attend to my every whim. Enough money to buy whatever I want without a second thought.

I've never had to work for a single thing my entire life—except for Spencer.

Finally, he appeared, like a breath of fresh air clad in a NYU sweatshirt and dark jeans, ready for adventure. He didn't say a word when he caught me wiping down the counters, but I'm sure it threw him off. Sylvie Lancaster doesn't clean.

Well, guess now I do.

"This is a struggle." I wave a hand at the hill we stop in front of.

He squints into the sun. An attractive look for him, the wind ruffling through his dark hair, the creases at the corner of his eyes new from age. Tantalizing. "It's not that high."

"It's the sand." I wave a hand toward it. "It runs deep."

"I can handle it."

His confidence is appealing, but I glance at his feet, noting that they're clad in a pair of expensive Nikes. He should've worn boots.

"The sand will get in your shoes."

"I'm not worried about it." He points toward the trail. "Lead the way."

I do as he demands, marching up the hill, working hard to make my climb appear effortless. He's directly behind me, keeping pace, and the more I huff and puff, the more irritated I get.

We finally get to the top of the hill, the ocean spread out before us in the near distance, the wind whipping around us at a frantic pace. I shade my eyes, staring at the white-capped water, the expanse of flat, wet sand beckoning. It's still a ways till we actually get to the water, and I sort of want to hear Spencer groan in dread. I want him tired and panting, like me.

He's not even out of breath. And I'd bet money there's not a grain of sand in his shoes either.

Infuriating.

"The view is gorgeous."

I glance over at him to find he's watching me. "The ocean is beautiful. It's different on this coast. A little—wilder."

"I wasn't talking about the ocean, but you're right." His gaze drifts to the water, and I fight against the hot flush coating my skin. "It does look wilder. Let's go."

"The beach is farther than it looks."

He looks down at me, his lips curved in a faint smile. "Are you trying to scare me, Syl?"

"If I haven't already with everything you've had to deal with over the years, I don't think a laborious hike to the beach is going to do it," I tease, the realization hitting me as I say it.

I've tried to scare him away all these years. Yet he's still here. With me in California. The man deserves a medal. Or a stern talking to for being such a sucker.

We start down the hill and I let Spencer take the lead, my gaze snagging on the breadth of his shoulders. The elegant curve of his back. His perfect ass in the well-fitting jeans and those long, strong legs. He's tall, over six feet, and he walks with a confidence I don't remember him having when we were younger. Back when we were at Lancaster Prep and he supported me no matter what. He was always there for me when I needed him, and I took advantage of that. Of him.

God, I was awful then. So conniving. Everything I learned, I got from my mother.

By the time we make it to the beach, I'm exhausted. I find an outcropping of rocks and go to sit on one, Spencer continuing to walk along the water's edge. His silhouette gets smaller and smaller the farther he gets, until he's a sliver of a human in the distance, and I worry that he's going to keep on walking and never come back.

But eventually he returns, his form coming back into view until I can make out his every feature, and the relief I feel at his closeness threatens to overwhelm me. He joins me at the rocks, sitting on one that hovers above mine, so he looms over me. He's windblown and glorious, his dark hair sweeping over his forehead, his eyes squinting against the sun.

"Can I ask you a question?"

"Shoot," he says, though I hear the caution in his tone.

"Why were you always so nice to me, when I was nothing but awful to you?" It's a hard question, with an even harder answer, and I brace myself for the truth.

He doesn't say anything for a long time, the wind whipping his hair into his eyes, so he has to brush it away every few seconds. "I was in love with you."

My heart lurches in my chest and the air stutters in my throat. That was not the answer I expected.

"And you shit all over it. Continuously. It's like I couldn't help myself. But I suppose that's the way it always is, right? We can't stop the way we feel, even when we know it's wrong."

"Are you saying it was wrong to be in love with me?"

"I don't know. All I know is it hurt, being in love with you."

Misery courses through me. His confessions are like a punch in the gut. One blow after the other. "I was young and stupid back then. The only kind of love I was shown was always...conditional."

"I know."

We're both quiet. I bend my knees, wrapping my arms around my legs to ward off the cold that comes from his words. I didn't know what I had. I always counted on him returning and he always did. He still does, because here he is, on the beach with me on a sunny day in the middle of the week. There's still so much unsaid swirling between us, and the ocean and the wind and sun can't swallow it up. Our feelings need to be let out. Laid bare.

No matter how painful.

"I can't blame my treatment of you on my parents," I finally say. "I should've known better."

"Do you know better now?"

I have to be one hundred percent truthful with him. "I'm not sure."

That was a blow to him, I'm sure.

"I can't keep giving you a chance," he admits, his voice so low I lean in closer, wishing I was sitting next to him on the rock. Pressed against his warmth, my head on his shoulder. "The last time I did, you ditched me for another man."

I stiffen. I know what he's referring to. "I just wanted one more night with you."

"One more night so you could fuck me and leave me, then go on to marry someone else. Someone old enough to be your fucking dad." The venom in his voice has me leaning away from him, now glad I'm not sitting on the same rock as he is. "Why did you do it?"

"Like I said, I just wanted one more night—"

"No." He shakes his head. "I know why you came to my

apartment that night. I'm talking about you marrying that old ass man. Why, Sylvie? Why did you do it?"

Panic suffuses me and I climb off the rock, marching away from him, my feet making prints in the wet sand. Tears stream down my cheeks and I let them flow, not bothering to wipe them away.

I don't want to admit why I married Earl, when I barely understand it myself. My weak explanations won't make any sense to him because they don't make sense to me. I could've fought against it. Against her. But I didn't. I gave in and I did what she wanted, damn the consequences.

"Sylvie." His voice ripples on the wind, making me break out into a run, and soon enough, I hear him drawing closer, until he's practically on me, his long fingers encircling my upper arm and yanking, so I have no choice but to whip around and face him.

His expression is a steely mask and it drops the moment he sees my tears. Men are always weak when it comes to tears, even this one. Especially this one. "What the fuck? Why are you crying?"

"I don't know how to explain to you what happened," I admit, backing away from him.

He lurches toward me, grabbing hold of both of my arms so I don't run. "Just start with the beginning."

I gape at him, struggling to find the words, and he gives me a little shake. As if that's going to jump-start my explanation. "It was my mother's fault. She made me do it."

Doubt clouds his already stormy gaze and he shakes his head, his lips thinning into a straight line. "I don't buy that. You were an adult."

"Still under her care."

He barks out a laugh. "Under her *care?* By the way you always made it sound, she was out to get you every chance she got. I always believed she cared a little too much."

"You're right. She did." My throat is dry, my stomach roiling.

Like I might vomit at any second. I've never talked about this with anyone, not even her. "She cared about me, but not in the right way. More like she wanted to kill me. She tried to kill me for years."

His gaze scans mine, his expression turning to disbelief. "What are you saying?"

"All those years I was sick? That I said I was going to die? It was because of her. She wanted me sick. Dying. It got her attention, it got me attention, but it was all fake. None of it was real."

CHAPTER FOURTEEN

SPENCER

"Wait a minute." My grip loosens on her arms and she uses it to her advantage, slipping away from me and launching into a run, headed for the trail that leads back to her house. "Damn it, Sylvie!"

She doesn't turn around. Just keeps running, her blonde hair streaming behind her. I go after her, slower this time, trying to process everything she just said.

Could she be lying? It sounds like some sort of fucked-up fantasy. But her entire life sounds like one giant fucked-up fantasy, if I'm being real with myself. Ultra-rich parents who don't give a shit about her…

Well. That's not quite it. But how was I supposed to know her mother was making her sick on purpose for attention?

That's some straight-up, weird Netflix-type documentary shit right there.

I pick up the pace, chasing after her, slightly winded thanks to running against the stiffening breeze. But Sylvie isn't running very fast either and I catch up to her easily, until I'm jogging alongside her, as if it's just another normal day and we're out for a run on the beach.

Like she didn't just tell me her mom has been trying to kill her for years.

Anger churns low in my gut as the memories hit me. The weird things Sylvie would allude to. She spoke in mysterious terms, never coming right out and saying anything of substance in regards to her health. I always knew something was up with her relationship with her mother. I just didn't think it went that deep. That serious.

That messed-up.

"Sylvie…"

She shakes her head. "I don't want to talk about it anymore."

"We have to."

"No, we don't. I said it. You know. That's all I can say about it for now. Whatever else you want to know, has to wait."

"Until when?"

"I don't know!" She comes to a complete stop, throwing her arms up in the air. A cluster of seagulls go flying overhead, squawking their displeasure at her outburst, but I don't react at all. This is what I need, what I want to hear.

No matter how painful it might be.

"You're not…lying, are you? She really was trying to kill you?" I hate that I have to ask, but come on. I've heard some pretty fanciful tales come straight out of Sylvie's mouth.

Plenty of times.

"You really think I would make this up?" She's incredulous.

"Not at all. You have to admit it just sounds so fucking crazy. I know Sylvia Lancaster is a lot, but Syl. What you're accusing her of…" My voice drifts.

"Is the truth," she says quietly, her head dropping so she's speaking to the sand beneath our feet. "I was out of school all the time for being sick."

"I remember."

"Sometimes she'd have me so doped up on prescription medication, I didn't know what was happening to me, or how much time had passed. She'd keep me drugged for days. Even weeks. And I always felt nauseous. I threw up all the time. I think she was giving me something so I couldn't keep anything down. Couldn't even eat. My blood pressure would get so low, I could barely function. I would faint so easily. You saw me back then. You know how it was. At one point, I got pneumonia, and I couldn't shake it for the longest time. I was coughing and hacking for months. I really believed I was going to die."

Her words bring back all the memories of her at Lancaster Prep. Joking about death. Being so matter of fact about the subject too. She'd always tell me she was dying and she wanted to live life to the fullest, right in that very moment.

After a while, I thought it was horseshit. Just Sylvie being dramatic because that was her personality trait and she leaned into it heavily. I remember even asking Whit about it once, and he blew me off, saying it was just her way.

But maybe she was trying to tell all of us all along what her mother was doing to her, and we never believed her.

That's so messed-up.

"She's always had a hold on me," Sylvie continues. For someone who said she wasn't going to talk about it anymore, maybe the dam just broke. Now she appears ready to spill. "When I was younger, I could never break the bond. How could I? I lived with her. Even when I was at Lancaster Prep, she still pulled all the strings. She's controlled me since birth. Right up until I married Earl. When that happened, I felt—free. Like I finally got away from her for good."

Irritation sparks in my veins at the mention of her dead husband. I could've been the one to help her get away from her mother, but she never gave me the chance.

"And then he died. I was at a complete loss. You don't expect your husband to die when you're my age, even if he's much older than you. I didn't know what to do or where to go. His children were fighting with me over money. Money I didn't even want or need. It was a complete nightmare."

Is it wrong that I don't feel bad? God, I'm a callous dick. I hate that she suffered, but I could give a damn that her husband died. She should've never married that asshole in the first place. She should've married someone her own age.

Someone like me.

"My mother took over everything. She helped me with the funeral, with the meetings with the lawyers. All of it. She pulled me right back into her web, and like the weak person I am, I went willingly. She promised she would help me, and she did. At first. I thought she'd changed." Sylvie finally lifts her head, her watery eyes meeting mine. "Like an idiot I believed her. She was just so supportive. Incredibly sincere, making me all sorts of promises. Then about a month after Earl passed, I was staying at her apartment, and one night I woke up to her standing over my bed with a pillow in her hands like she was going to—smother me. That was it. That was the end. I hadn't seen her since, until Whit's wedding, and she tried to talk to me afterward, but I've mostly cut her off. It's just—it's better that way. Easier."

I'm still stuck on one tiny detail. "Wait a minute. You woke up to her standing over your bed with a pillow in her hands?"

She nods, her lower lip trembling. "I assume I woke up because I was gasping for air. She wanted to kill me that night, I think. It was right after the funeral."

There's a death that makes no damn sense. Earl was an old man, but he didn't die of old age. Something happened to him, something that's been kept hush hush ever since because I've never heard any details about it.

"It's a lot to process, I know." She says it as if she's trying to reassure me, when she's the one who should probably be getting all the reassurance. "Let's go back to the house. I'm starving."

Frowning, I fall into step with her like everything is perfectly normal, my mind going over all the details she just shared about her life, and how much she feared for it.

How her mother used to try to kill her.

I knew things weren't right between Sylvie and her mother when we were at Lancaster Prep. She would drop those hints and imply that she had only a short time left before she would die. After a while, I couldn't ignore what she said, but I was still just a kid. Maybe I didn't want to know what Sylvie was actually referring to.

Actually, I know I didn't. Easier to pretend she never said any of that shit.

Sylvie always had a flair for dramatics and she's lied plenty of times before. But if she says her mother was trying to kill her, I believe her. Putting together everything else she's said and done over the years, it makes sense, which is messed up.

Like seriously, what the fuck? What sort of sick bitch makes her child ill for attention? Who pulls her back in, only to try and smother her with a goddamn pillow?

Someone as demented as Sylvia Lancaster, that's who.

The walk back to the house is much shorter than the walk to the beach, but isn't that always the way? By the time we're entering the house, I'm grateful for the cooler temperature inside. Despite the chilly wind, the heat of the sun penetrated through my clothes, making me mildly miserable as we trudged back. I accept the cold bottle of water Sylvie pulls out of the massive fridge and hands over to me, taking a long pull from it before I wipe the back of my hand across my mouth.

She's washing her hands, all those earlier tears all dried up. Appearing unchanged, as if she didn't just drop a life-changing bomb on me only moments ago.

Typical.

What she said is most definitely life-changing. All of my protective feelings toward this woman are out in full force. I've always wanted to protect her, but now…

Now I know I can't let her out of my sight. We need to keep Sylvia Lancaster away from her at all costs.

"Do you want a sandwich?" she asks as she's drying her hands.

"Do you actually know how to make one?" I toss back at her, unable to help myself.

Her scowl is small, but it's there, and I almost want to laugh. "I wouldn't offer if I didn't know how."

"I'd love a sandwich."

"Turkey? It's all I have."

"Turkey works," I answer without hesitation. "Can I help you with anything?"

"No, go sit down. I'll make our lunch."

I watch as she bustles around the kitchen like she was born in one, which is the furthest thing from the fucking truth. This girl never lifted a finger her entire life, so to watch her act like a good little housewife is disconcerting.

And kind of hot, which makes me feel like a sexist male asshole. But come on. Sylvie is from one of the richest families in the entire world and she's making me a sandwich? I feel fucking special.

"You want cheese?"

"Sure."

"Swiss or provolone?"

This time I do chuckle. The moment feels so...normal, when our relationship, the circumstances that brought me here in the first place, is anything but. "Provolone."

"Mustard and mayo?"

"You own mayo?"

She glares at me.

"I'll take both," I say. "Light mayo though. Gotta watch my waistline."

I pat my stomach for emphasis.

Sylvie rolls her eyes but doesn't say a word as she puts together my sandwich, then hers. My stomach starts to rumble, and by the time she's setting the plate in front of me, I'm full-fledged starving.

"There you go." She smiles. "Want something to drink?"

"Another water if you've got it."

Within a few minutes, we're both seated at the table eating our lunch and sharing a bag of barbecue chips. The sandwich is fucking delicious, piled high with turkey and cheese and lettuce, even thinly sliced avocado and onion. I devour it in an embarrassingly small amount of bites and when I polish off the last of it, I glance up to find her watching me with amusement.

"Hungry?"

"More than I thought," I admit.

"This is so weird." She shakes her head. "I never believed this would happen."

I frown. "What would happen?"

"The two of us in a house I didn't even know existed until a few weeks ago. Sitting in my kitchen and sharing a meal together that *I* prepared." Her laughter is bright and unexpected. Full of joy despite the earlier dark confessions of the day. "A miracle has occurred."

"It was a damn good sandwich, Syl."

She wiggles in her chair, her smile unable to be contained. "I'm so glad you enjoyed it."

"I never imagined you could make me a meal either. You've always had servants for that," I continue.

A sigh leaves her and she pushes her plate away. "I was such a spoiled little shit."

"Yeah, you were," I agree, and she tosses her balled up napkin at me, missing me completely. "Though now I'm guessing you were just hiding a lot of pain."

Her somber gaze finds mine, never straying. "I was. Still doesn't excuse that I was so awful to you."

"I must've really liked you to put up with all that."

When I was a teenager, I was completely gone over this girl. I would've done anything she asked me.

"We made out a lot," she reminds me.

I chuckle, the memories hitting me, one after another. Plenty of secret moments, sneaking in kisses here and there. "You were insatiable."

"I don't think I was the only one who wanted to do it all the time."

"You were the one who almost always instigated it, though."

Her cheeks turn an adorable shade of pink. The widowed woman, embarrassed over teenage make-out memories. "True."

I eat a few chips, watching as she finishes her sandwich. "You've gained weight. I noticed it at the wedding too."

"Is that a bad thing?" She sounds vaguely defensive.

"Not at all. You were always so…" What can I say that won't offend her?

"Thin? Frail? Sickly?"

I press my lips together, not wanting to insult her.

A sigh leaves her. "I'm away from my mother. She's not poisoning me and keeping me deathly skinny anymore."

That she can say it so matter of fact, like it's no big deal, what her mother has been doing to her all these years. That she survived after everything is…amazing. Huge. "Do you hate her?"

"My mother?" When I nod, she shrugs. "I don't know. I should. Sometimes I do. Yet other times, I love her and miss her, because she's my mother, and at one point, she was all I had. My dad wasn't around much, and she always told me he didn't care about me. Not like she did."

I'm quiet, absorbing her words. She's been manipulated practically her entire life by her mother. Does she even see it?

"We shared some great moments together," Sylvie continues. "My memories with her, they're not all bad."

They've been tainted though, those moments. They have to be. I've been disappointed plenty of times by my parents over the years, but one of them never tried to *kill* me.

I don't know how you ever recover from that.

"What about your dad?"

"What about him?"

"He didn't—notice what Sylvia was doing?"

Sylvie laughs. Actually laughs, like I just told the most hilarious joke. "Augustus Lancaster only notices what's going on when it directly involves him. He's the most selfish Lancaster I know, and I know lots of them, trust me. But I love my father. I don't blame him for not noticing. He was too focused on Carolina back then. Besides, my parents' relationship has never been great, and he was living in his own world most of the time. I'm not surprised at all that he didn't realize what was going on. He was too wrapped up in his own bullshit."

I hate that he was oblivious. That we all were. Guilt fills me, threatens to pour out in a litany of words of meaningless apology, but I press my lips together, keeping them all inside.

Words are meaningless. Action is required in a situation like this.

"Are you feeling guilty?" When I meet her gaze, I find her peering at me with all-knowing eyes. "Don't, Spence. You didn't know. And you were just a kid. What could you have done?"

"I should've known. I should've believed you," I say fiercely, wishing I could fight all of her demons for her. Even after all these years, and all the disappointment and frustration and anger, I still want to defend her. Protect her.

I will always want to do that, even when she pushes me away.

I don't know if I can take much more of this kind of shit, but I also know I can't resist her. I'm loyal to a fault. My father always said that, making it sound like a character flaw when I'm just like him. Besides, my loyalty means I stand by his side no matter what, which is to his advantage.

"I tried to make light of it, like it was a joke. How could you believe me when you thought I was joking?" She shakes her head when I start to say something, cutting me off. "Stop with the guilt. I'm just glad you're here. If I wanted anyone to find me, it would be you."

Shocked pleasure courses through me at her words. "Really?"

"Yes," she whispers, leaning over to settle her small, pale hand over mine. "You're my favorite human in this world, Spencer. Even if I have a funny way of showing it, you mean more to me than anyone else."

I stare at her hand on my own, tempted to turn mine over and interlock our fingers. But I don't do it. Not yet. My feelings for Sylvie are...complicated. Being with her has brought them all roaring back, and I don't know what to do with them.

Giving in could be a mistake.

One I might never recover from.

CHAPTER FIFTEEN

SYLVIE

It's such a cliché, but after telling Spencer everything about my mother, I feel lighter. Like I just relieved myself of all my past burdens, and I'm finally free to just…live.

He took it all surprisingly well, but I know my Spencer. He digests information almost impassively, turning it over and over in his mind until the real emotions eventually build and grow, and if it makes him mad enough, he'll eventually blow up.

I expect that to happen. He'll become angry, and honestly?

I want to see that. I want him mad on my behalf. I want him to become my knight in shining armor and defend me against all the evils in the world. Even if those evils are related to me, I want him to show them no mercy.

Would he do that for me? Or have I ruined my chance?

Once we cleaned up after lunch, I told him I was going to take a nap, and he said he'd take a shower. I'm locked away in my massive bedroom, staring out the window at all the trees, not napping at all.

I can't sleep. I'm too attuned to the man who's staying in the room next to mine. I could hear the water running from his shower and my imagination went into overdrive. Spence naked, standing under the spray of water, the steam rising, obscuring him from view. His hair wet and slicked back, droplets clinging to his thick eyelashes.

My core throbs just thinking about it. It's been too long since I've been with a man. Far, far too long.

Longer than anyone would imagine, especially Spencer.

I may have purged most of my secrets, but he didn't say a damn thing about his own and I'm curious. What exactly is he doing, working for his family? What is he involved in? Why was it so easy for him to drop everything and come in search of me?

If he's still so angry with me, why did he even come here? Does he still care about me? Or is it more out of habit than anything else?

Does he have a girlfriend? Or a woman he's seeing? He didn't bring a date to Whit's wedding, so I'm assuming no, which is a tremendous relief. If I can't have him, I don't want anyone else to have him either.

Ah, my Lancaster tendencies always come out to play when it comes to wanting something. Or someone.

I hear the guest bathroom door creak open and I tell myself to resist, but it's like I can't. I slide off the bed and tiptoe over to the door, slowly opening it a sliver and peeking out. The guest bathroom is diagonal from my bedroom and I can see inside. Barely.

Steam billows out of the bathroom and I smile to myself. Spencer always did like an extremely hot shower. Guess some things haven't changed.

I can hear him move about the tiny space. The sound of a zipper—most likely his toiletry bag. The clink of something set on the tiled countertop. Water running. A brush gliding through hair. Yes, I'm that attuned to every little thing he's doing.

Without warning, he emerges from the bathroom, a white towel slung low around his hips, his shoulders and chest covered with water droplets. Men don't thoroughly dry themselves off after a shower and I've never understood why, but at this moment,

I'm not complaining.

Those drops slide down his skin. Through the tufts of dark hair at the center of his chest. Down the flat expanse of his belly. That towel hangs perilously from his lean hips, like it might fall off at any moment, and I wait breathlessly for it to do exactly that.

"Are you spying on me?" Spence asks, sounding amused.

My gaze meets his dark one through the crack of the open door and I jerk away, my entire body flushing with embarrassment. And something else.

Arousal.

I back away at the exact moment my bedroom door swings open, revealing Spencer standing in the doorframe, clad in a towel and nothing else. His dark hair slicked back just as I imagined. I swear I can see the outline of his cock beneath the towel and I stare at it for a moment, wishing I had see-through vision.

"Syl." His deep voice causes me to jump, my gaze finding his. His deep brown eyes are sparkling and his lips are curved in a knowing smirk.

I brush the hair away from my face, flustered. "Sorry, I just—"

"I thought you were taking a nap."

"I couldn't sleep," I confess.

We watch each other for a moment, the tension growing as per usual. It always does between us, making it near impossible to fight.

"You're staring," he finally murmurs.

"I can't help it. Look at you." I wave a helpless hand in his direction.

His smirk stays firmly in place. Damn him. And when he scratches his chest, my gaze tracks his fingers' every move. "You've seen it before."

"Not for a long time." I swallow, my gaze greedy. "You've changed."

He glances down at himself before returning his gaze to

mine, his brows furrowed. "How?"

"You're...bigger. Wider. There's more hair on your chest." That trail that leads from his navel and disappears into his towel is intriguing too. Far more intriguing than the hair between his pecs.

He chuckles. "I suppose. You've changed too."

"You haven't seen me naked yet." I lift my chin, fighting the trembling that wants to take over my body. I can smell his skin. Clean and fresh. A hint of sandalwood. I'm dying to press my face into his neck and inhale his scent.

"You haven't seen me naked yet either." One large hand settles on top of the towel knotted at his waist, his fingers curling around the thick white terrycloth, and I wait in breathless anticipation. "Though I think you want to."

"Spencer..." My voice is a warning. He can't tease me. We probably shouldn't do this. He'd be the first to say exactly that. Yet here he stands, about ready to whip his towel off and show me everything he's got.

Then he'd expect me to do the same, and God, I would. Despite feeling a little sticky with sweat and the salty ocean air still lingering on my skin, thanks to the hike we took earlier, I would strip myself bare for this man and let him run his hands and mouth and tongue all over me.

He is the only one I would do this for.

A sigh leaves him and his hand drops from the towel. "I don't know why we always do this."

I ignore the disappointment flooding my veins. "Do what?"

"Tease each other. Sexually."

"Maybe we still want each other. Even after all of these years."

"More like it's just old habits die hard, if you ask me."

The disappointment is replaced with frustration. How can he write us off like that? Tear down what we have and render it meaningless?

"Then get out," I say, my voice dripping with barely veiled

disdain. "Get dressed and leave."

He rests both hands on his hips, completely comfortable in just the towel. "Are you really going to pull that shit now, Syl? Even after everything you just told me?"

"You don't really want me." I sound like a hurt little girl, which I guess is the theme of my life.

"I have *always* wanted you. That's the problem." He takes a deep breath, his chest expanding with the movement. "If you really want me to leave, I'll go."

That is the very last thing I want. "More like you don't want to stay."

Anger flares in his gaze, dark and ominous. "Stop with your game playing, Sylvie. It doesn't become you anymore. It never really did."

He turns, his fingers flicking at the knot on his waist, the towel falling in a wet plop on my floor. I stare at his bare ass as he storms out of my room and I launch myself after him, following him into the guest bedroom.

He has the same view, though not as all-encompassing as my wall of windows, but he doesn't even notice. He's too focused on pulling clothes out of the suitcase that lies open on the queen-size bed, his face a mask of pure frustration. His dark hair hangs over his forehead, water droplets sliding down the side of his face.

Spencer is also completely naked.

My gaze goes to his cock. Even in its unaroused state, it's magnificent. Long and thick, with a flared head, nestled against dark pubic hair. As if it can feel my eyes on it, I swear it starts to harden. Lengthen.

"If you want it, get over here and suck it," he demands.

I'm startled.

Breathless.

Without thought, I cross the room, and he turns in my direction when I stop in front of him. I fall to my knees, in a trance as I nuzzle my cheek against his now hard cock.

We say nothing, the heavy beat of my heart loud in my ears. He threads his fingers in my hair, holding tight, as if he plans on keeping me in place in case I try to leave. Not that I'm going anywhere. My mouth drifts along his shaft, barely open as I breathe him in. He smells clean yet musky. Unmistakably Spencer. When my tongue sneaks out for a lick, he hisses out a breath, his fingers tugging, making me wince.

"Put me in your mouth." His tone is fierce. Angry.

I should run. I should tell him to fuck off. But I don't.

Instead, I do as he says, my lips enveloping the head of his cock, tongue tracing around it slowly, savoring every inch of his skin. He groans, his hips gently thrusting, pushing himself deeper into my mouth, and I relax the muscles in my throat, taking it.

Taking him.

We're still silent, the only sound my lips suctioning around his length. The wet drag of my tongue licking. Lapping. He's leaking pre-cum everywhere and when I pull away so I can tongue the slit, he growls, shoving his way back in between my lips.

"I'm going to fuck your mouth," he warns, and I nod, whimpering low in my throat just before he completely possesses me.

And I let him.

He shoves his cock as deep as he can get it inside my mouth, sliding in and out, fucking me steadily. Tears leak from my eyes as I moan around him, letting him use me, reveling in the way he's treating me. Brutal and mean and demanding. Not giving a damn about what I need or how I feel.

He's in it for himself.

His expression is fierce, his jaw tight, a vein throbbing along the side of his forehead. His focus is one hundred percent on my open mouth, my lips stretching in near pain as he continues fucking my mouth. My entire body throbs when his pace increases, my panties flooding with moisture, and I can't hold back the moan that comes from deep within me.

When I woke up this morning, I had no clue my day would end up like this. Me on my knees getting rugburn while Spencer Donato stands above me, his cock in my mouth as he fucks it until I can feel that first spurt of semen land on my tongue.

"Drink it." The words barely slip from his tight lips before he throws his head back, his entire body taut when he groans as the orgasm slams into him. His fingers tug my hair, holding me to him while he comes down my throat. I swallow it down, my gaze on him the entire time, fascinated by his body and the play of muscle as he strains and shudders.

Our encounter was quick. Not lasting even five minutes, but I'm completely changed. Transformed. I pull him out of my mouth, strings of saliva sticking to the tip, and I wipe away the connection. Then wipe at the corners of my mouth. My body aches, the need to be filled by him overwhelming me and when he pulls on my hair, I rise to my feet, my heart hammering in my chest when he thrusts his face in mine.

"You liked that."

I nod, alarmed by the dark tone of his voice. The matching glare in his gaze.

"You fell right back into your role as my little whore, didn't you?"

I blink at him, shocked by his coarse words.

Shocked further by my body's reaction to them. My hard nipples rub against my bra and I'm so wet between my thighs I swear my leggings are damp too.

"I told myself I wouldn't let this happen," he continues, his gaze dropping to my lips. "But then I catch you spying. Staring like you're starved for me and I cave." He wipes at the corner of my mouth, drawing his thumb across my bottom lip. "Now your lips are covered in my cum."

A moan sounds and I realize it's coming from me. "Spence…"

"Is this what you want? To give up all control? To be told what to do? You've lived your entire life like this. Everyone controlling you. You've never stood on your own until what? A few weeks ago? When you discovered this place was yours?"

I nod, hating the reality he's speaking of. Knowing that every word he says is true.

I've been controlled my entire life, but never like this.

"You need to learn how to manage your life instead of taking orders from someone else." He takes a single step backward, his hands falling away from me, and I whimper at the loss. "You need to figure out what you want. I refuse to let you use me. I know how you operate. You'll only abandon me again."

I part my lips, ready to protest, but he cuts me off.

"Don't bother denying it. You know it's true."

"Spencer. No. I need you." My entire body aches, especially my heart. I hate that I've hurt him. I can't erase what I've done, no matter how much I wish I could.

"For once in my life, I used you. I fucked your mouth for my own pleasure. I didn't give a damn whether you liked it or not. And the best thing is, you got off on it. I can tell. You're aroused. I bet if I slipped my fingers in your panties, I'd find that you're wet."

Spencer never, ever talked so boldly to me before. Not like this.

Swear to God, I'm more aroused because of it. My entire body aches, yearning for his touch.

"Are you? Wet?" He arches a brow.

I nod once, too choked up with desire to speak.

"Show me." When I frown, he rubs his hand across his jaw, the movement so wholly masculine, I nearly collapse to the floor. "Put your hands in your panties and prove it."

Again, there's no hesitation. I slip my hand into my panties, encountering creamy wetness. I coat my fingers with myself before pulling them out and showing him. They gleam with my juices and I swear a matching gleam lights up his eyes.

"Look at that." He grabs my wrist and pulls me toward him, lifting my hand to his mouth. "You are wet."

I gasp when he pulls my fingers into his mouth, sucking them. Licking them. His gaze never strays from mine, and I am overwhelmed with emotion, my body drawing tighter and tighter at the thought of him putting that magical mouth on other places.

Like between my legs.

"If we have nothing else, Syl, we always have this," he murmurs, his gaze growing even darker, I swear. "Take off your clothes."

I pull my hand out of his grip and shed my clothing as if my skin is set on fire. Until I'm trembling and naked in front of him, my nipples so hard they hurt.

He barely looks at me. Just points at the bed. "Lie down."

"We should go to my bedroom—"

"No." He shakes his head. "Lie down. Now."

I do as he says, positioning myself so I'm sprawled across the middle of the bed, my legs spread, open and waiting. The air touches the sensitive skin of my pussy, making me suck in a sharp breath, and when he studies me there, I swear I can feel myself grow even wetter.

How that's possible, I have no idea.

"Touch yourself," he demands. "Touch your tits."

I cup them. Squeeze them. Curl my fingers around my nipples and tug on them until they're hard, aching points. He watches, downright impassive as I cup them in my palms, holding them to him like an offering.

But he doesn't take me up on it. He doesn't do anything but tell me what to do.

"Finger yourself. Show me how you like it."

I glide my hand down my belly until my fingers are right there, dipping the middle one in, swiping it across my distended clit. God, I'm so aroused. It will take nothing to get myself off, if that's what he wants to watch me do. I'll put on a show for him. I'm not embarrassed. If anything, I'm more comfortable doing something like this with Spencer than any other man out there.

I stroke myself, the wet sounds filling the room, urging me on.

His breathing accelerates, I can tell by the rapid rise and fall of his glorious chest, and I go faster, bringing my legs up so my feet are flat on the mattress, my thighs still spread wide. Showing off.

Showing him what he's missing.

"Stroke your clit," he whispers, and my fingers find it, rubbing. Circling.

I bite my lower lip, my orgasm building. Looming just out of reach. It feels so good, better than usual, and I know it's because he's in the room. Watching me. His presence, his gaze heavy on my skin.

A shuddery breath leaves me and I curl my toes into the comforter, anchoring myself. My thighs shaking, my fingers growing tired and I'm straining toward it. Oh, it's going to be big.

Without warning, he's there, pushing my hand out of the way, thrusting two thick fingers inside me at the same time his mouth finds my clit. He sucks and licks, my thighs clamping around his head, a keening cry falling from my lips.

I'm coming, wave after delicious wave washing over me. Spencer holds me down, his hands at my hips, his mouth latched onto my pussy, never decreasing the intensity as I come and come. I thrust my fingers into his still damp hair, pressing his face against me and he lets me. Until I'm the one pushing him away, completely overwhelmed. Unable to take it—him and that wonderful, filthy mouth—any longer.

I collapse in a boneless heap on the bed, staring up at the ceiling, my breathing harsh, my heart racing. Chest aching. I feel him turn his head, wiping his mouth against the inside of my thigh before he kisses me there. Softly. Sweetly.

The gesture makes me want to cry. Tears actually spring to my eyes, but I squeeze them closed, fighting them off.

"Damn" is what he finally says and I have the oddest reaction to what he said.

I laugh.

And so does he.

CHAPTER SIXTEEN

SYLVIE

The previous afternoon's incident is seemingly forgotten by the next day. As if it never happened. We treat each other like we're old friends hanging out at an Airbnb or something. Like we planned this trip together.

We went to our separate bedrooms last night early, both of us too exhausted to keep our eyes open much past sundown. I woke up to the sound of him downstairs in the kitchen, the clatter of a fork whisking in a bowl, a clue that he was making breakfast.

I enter the kitchen to find he's making eggs and toast, the coffee already brewing, a scowling Roland standing outside on the wraparound porch, glaring through one of the windows.

"Your guard dog is here," is how Spencer greets me, his attention only for the iron frying pan on the stove as he pushes the eggs around with a spatula.

"I see that," I say as I wrap my robe tighter around my naked body.

Yes, I'd planned on greeting Spencer by whipping off said robe and asking him to feast on me instead, desperate to experience what we shared yesterday. Thank God I spotted Roland first.

"You should probably talk to him." Spencer turns off the burner before facing me. "I don't think he's happy to still see me here."

"He's just…being overprotective."

"Considering I've known you far longer, I'm wondering if I should be the one who's overprotective of you in regards to him." The smile Spence flashes me is more like a sneer and I almost want to giggle.

Is he actually…jealous of Roland?

"I'll talk to him," I tell Spencer, heading for the door that leads outside. Flashing him a quick smile, I go onto the deck, startled by the cool air that greets me. The fog hangs low this morning, wispy tendrils of it lingering in the trees, and I regret my nakedness beneath the thin robe almost immediately.

"Miss Lancaster." Roland whips off his hat, clutching it between his fingers. Almost crushing it. "I'm sorry to disturb you. I know you have your guest here."

"It's okay. Is everything all right?" I frown, hating how concerned he seems.

"Everything's fine. I just—are you okay? I've been thinking about you all night. Had to come check on you." His gaze goes to the window, and I can tell he's watching Spencer in the kitchen. His eyes narrow, as if he doesn't like what he sees, and I'm almost amused. I might've even laughed if my teeth weren't chattering from the cold.

"I'm all right," I say, my voice soft. "I've known Spencer a long time. He's my brother's best friend. We have—history."

That's such a simple way to put it. History.

"I don't like 'em."

Now I do laugh, shaking my head. "Why not? What did he ever do to you?"

"It's more what he did to you. Showing up here without a warning. You were shocked. I saw it all over your face. And you don't need trouble sniffing around here when you're just trying to live peacefully by yourself. Because I can tell that's what he is, Miss Lancaster. Trouble," Roland mutters, sniffing loudly.

"I didn't tell anyone where I would be. I don't have my old phone, so no one can reach me. How could he warn me that he was arriving?" I smile, trying to ease my sweet-yet-sour-when-only-Spencer-is-around caretaker who's far too invested in my personal well-being. Though I do appreciate his protectiveness, I also want to be alone with Spencer.

Especially after what happened yesterday.

"How did he even find you, hmm? When you didn't want to be found?"

"Breakfast is ready."

We both turn to find Spencer standing there, half hanging out the open door. His expression is grim, his eyes dark and aimed straight at Roland, who glares at him in return.

"Sylvie, it's cold out here." Spencer's voice is extra deep. "Come inside."

He doesn't ask. He's telling me.

"We can talk later," I tell Roland, offering him a quick smile before I turn and walk back into the house, Spencer following close behind me. He shuts and locks the door and I turn to face him, noting the determined look on his face.

"You're jealous of Roland."

"I'm not jealous. I just don't want him convincing you that my intentions are bad," he says, returning to the stove and plating our breakfast. "He doesn't know you. Not like I do."

"You *are* jealous," I murmur as I sit at the table, reaching for the cup of coffee waiting for me. I bring it to my lips and take a sip, pleased to find it's exactly as I like it. "You're the one I was on my knees for yesterday. Don't forget that."

He sets the plate down almost violently in front of me, the toast nearly falling off from the forceful impact. "I haven't forgotten."

I remain quiet, sipping my coffee, watching him play house, much like I did yesterday at lunch. We are quite the pair. What's real, what's fake? I don't even know anymore.

That I can't define us is almost comforting. It's what I'm used to with Spencer. We've never been able to fully define what's happening between us, and that's mostly my fault. I'm the one who's always been sketchy, who can't commit. Who was forced to marry another man when that was the last thing I wanted to do.

We should discuss what's happening between us, but I can't muster up the courage. Not yet. I'm enjoying spending time with Spencer too much to ruin it with a serious conversation, despite his wavering moods toward me.

I like it best when it's just the two of us, Roland is our only distraction, and he's not much of one. There have always been other forces working against us. My mother. My brother. School. His friends. Me. His family.

My husband.

My loveless, pointless marriage to Earl ruined things between us, especially when I ran off and married someone else immediately after having sex with Spencer. But then again, I was the one with his dick in my mouth yesterday, so I guess I win in the end.

Bonus, him giving me that spectacular orgasm. I'm still tingly over it. Hence the reason I wore my robe and nothing else.

But is it really about winning and losing between us? It's not a game, what we share. My feelings for Spencer are real and they run deep. He feels something for me too. He has to. Why else would he come across the country to make sure I'm all right?

We eat in silence, and I marvel at the delicious eggs he prepared. They're light and fluffy, with just the right amount of salt. The toast is cooked to perfection, buttery and crisp. Don't even get me started on the coffee.

That he made this for me makes it all taste that much better.

I'm taking my last bite of eggs when Spencer finally speaks, and I nearly choke on my food at what he says.

"I think we need to start over."

I begin coughing, my fist in front of my mouth, the eggs stuck in my throat. Taking a necessary sip of my coffee, so I can choke them down, I can finally speak.

"What do you mean?"

"I mean exactly what I said. That we need to start over. You and me." He wipes his mouth with a napkin before crumpling it up and dropping it on his empty plate. "Yesterday probably shouldn't have happened."

Disappointment floods me, setting in my stomach and making it churn.

"I'm not saying I regret it," he continues. "But we do everything out of order, Syl. We always have."

I keep my head bent, not wanting to look him in the eyes. I might start tearing up, because what he's saying right now isn't necessarily what I want to hear. Though it's not bad either. Not at all. It's just...

I don't know how to feel, starting over. I'm finally being given a real chance with Spencer, without any outside influences for once, and this is his solution?

"I don't want to start over," I admit, my voice barely audible. He leans across the table with a frown, trying to hear me. "Why can't we start from this point? There's too much history between us, don't you think?"

He studies me, his dark brows drawn together, lips parted. His gaze wanders over my face as if he's trying to figure me out and I know that's...

Impossible.

"I don't know how to move forward with you after this point," he admits. "I have to go back to New York, somewhere you don't want to be. We're living two different lives, and I don't see how we'll be able to make this work if you're here and I'm not. Plus, all of the history we share is...painful."

"It wasn't all bad, was it? What we shared?" My voice is scratchy, my throat raw from holding back the tears that want to come.

"No." He shakes his head, hesitating for only a moment before he says, "But a lot of it was."

I rise to my feet as if I have no control of myself and storm out of the kitchen, irritated he would say such a thing.

Irritated more because I know, deep down, what he says is the truth. Our relationship was fraught with bullshit, most of it my fault. I kept too many things from him.

Like my feelings.

What would he say if he discovered he's the only one I've ever really been with sexually? There were a few boys here and there when I was younger. Before I became completely fucked up over Spencer. Before I was forced to marry Earl. Spencer is the only boy I've ever loved. I still love him.

I could never admit that to him, especially now. He would laugh in my face.

I go outside because I don't know what else to do, and he follows me. Of course, he does. I'm leaning against the railing of the wraparound deck, the chilly air sinking into my skin, settling in my bones, and then there's nothing but heat pressing against my back. Strong arms wrapping around my middle and I lean back into him as if I can't help myself.

Which I can't.

"I'm an asshole," he murmurs against my temple before kissing it.

"A truthful one," I admit.

I relax against him, and I swear I feel his cock press against my ass. "I don't know what to do anymore."

I don't either, but I can't admit that out loud. When I don't speak, I think he understands that I feel the same way.

His hand sneaks into the front of my robe, beneath the fabric to find my bare breast. He cups it, his thumb slowly brushing against my nipple, and I close my eyes, savoring the touch. Realizing this is most likely the last time I'll ever experience this. With Spencer.

"You frustrate me," he admits against my cheek, his lips on my skin. "But I've never wanted a woman like I want you, Sylvie."

I rub my butt against his erection, making him groan, his grip on my breast tightening. Both hands are on me now, pulling my robe apart, exposing my upper body to the cool air. I gasp at the shock of it, squeal when he turns me around in his arms, a low moan sounding deep in my throat when he bends down, his hot mouth seeking and finding my nipple.

He sucks and licks and I clutch him close, my fingers in his hair, my gaze locked on his busy mouth. My breathing is already erratic, my body tingling everywhere, and when he slips his hand into the parted fabric of my robe, his fingers tickling the inside of my thigh, I spread my legs, eager for him.

His assault on my chest continues as his fingers begin to stroke. My legs tremble when he thrusts a finger inside me. Then another. Finger-fucking me on the deck, ruining this space for me forever. I will always think of this moment, I tell myself as I tip my head back, my gaze catching on the redwoods that soar above us. I could live here for the rest of my life and the memory would still be vivid in my head. Of me and Spencer, out here on the deck, letting him take me.

I go easily when he hooks his hands beneath my thighs and lifts. I curl my legs around his hips, helping him shove his sweatpants down so his hard cock springs free, our movements awkward, hands fumbling. Splinters cut into my bare ass when he presses me against the railing, making me wince. The pain immediately forgotten when he slides inside me, filling me up.

I wrap my arms around his shoulders, holding on for dear life as he fucks me brutally. The cold air long forgotten thanks to the heat our bodies create, his cock sliding in and out of me, Spence grunting with every thrust. My eyes fall closed when he tears the robe off of my body and I'm completely naked, an offering to nature.

An offering to the beast inside him.

He fucks and fucks as if he could do it forever, his cock nudging a spot deep inside that has me seeing stars. I bite his earlobe, hissing when he hits that spot, and I firmly squeeze my inner walls, strangling his dick.

"Fuck," he groans, his hands shifting, fingers sliding over my ass, teasing the seam. "I missed you so much, Syl. I'm going to come if you keep that up."

I do it again, crushing my breasts against his chest, wanting him to feel me. To know it's me and no one else. His fingers trail lower, until he's teasing the ridged skin of my asshole, and I part my lips on a silent scream, my pussy gripping him tight.

"You like that?" The tip of his finger barely slips in and I gasp, going completely still, as does he. The only movement the throbbing of his cock. "I'd fuck you here if you let me."

"I'd let you," I say without hesitation, my hips lifting as I try to ride his cock on my own. But my position makes it difficult and he helps me, shifting me up and down. God, it feels so good.

It always does with Spence. He understands me. Knows my body and what I like. I don't have to worry or feel self-conscious when I'm with him.

"You going to come?" he whispers in my ear, his finger pushing into my ass, his cock sliding deeper inside my pussy. "I'm close."

I turn my head, my mouth resting on the strong column of his throat as I breathe in his scent. "Me too."

Within minutes, I'm shaking, milking him, wrenching his orgasm out of him. He comes with a shout, his face in my hair, his finger slipping out of my ass as he grips me against the railing. I don't notice the splinters, the scratches. I don't notice anything else but the sensation of his semen filling me up, and the dread that consumes me at the realization.

I'm not on birth control. I haven't been for a long time. He didn't wear a condom.

"Get off me." I bat at his shoulders, and he rears up, studying me with a frown. "Put me down."

He does as I ask and I take off, headed into the house, cum coating the inside of my thighs. I'm in the bathroom in seconds, turning on the shower, diving under the steady stream of water the moment it's hot enough. My fingers are scooping out as much semen as possible, but I know it's not enough. I know what I'm doing is futile.

The shower door opens, revealing Spence. He steps inside, completely naked, nudging me away from the water, so it will hit him instead, and I scowl.

"What are you doing?" He runs his fingers through his dampening hair, his voice calm. The complete opposite of what I'm feeling.

The panic is still streaking through me, my mind calculating the last day I had my period. I use one of those apps to keep track though, lately, social media tells us not to. Not that it matters, considering I got rid of my smart phone before I left and have a cheap flip phone instead.

I seriously think I'm ovulating right now, which would be... such a mistake. There is no way I can be a mother. I can't even take care of myself, let alone a helpless baby. And what if I'm just like my mother? What if I'm horrible and controlling and I'll eventually want to hurt my child, all for the attention it'll get me?

I press my forehead against the tile wall, closing my eyes. I can hardly bear the thought.

"Syl?" A warm hand cups my shoulder, turning me toward him, and I open my eyes to find him watching me. "Are you all right?"

I slowly shake my head, finally letting the tears I've been holding back all morning break free. I've cried more since Spence showed up than I have in a long time. I don't even think I cried this much when my husband died.

Considering it's my fault Earl is dead, you'd think I would've shed more tears out of pure guilt.

CHAPTER SEVENTEEN

SPENCER

It's hard to leave a crying woman, so I don't. After I fucked her out on the deck and chased after her to the shower, Sylvie turned on the waterworks and hasn't stopped. We're currently lying on her bed, her in my arms, her face nestled against my bare chest, her leg draped over both of mine. She's naked too, our skin and hair still damp from the shower. My chest extra damp, thanks to her tears.

I don't know what to do or what to say, so I try and offer her comfort in the best way I can. By holding her and remaining silent. We've done this a lot over the years, and I'm used to it.

For once, I'd like to see us go through a period of time together with Sylvie not shedding any tears. Jesus.

"I'm sorry," she finally says, lifting away from my chest, so she can stare into my eyes. Hers are still watery and red-rimmed, her lips puffy. Despite all the crying, she's still beautiful. Maybe even more so.

This is where I admit to myself that I've always gotten off on a sad Sylvie. What does that even say about me?

"It's fine." I run my hand along the side of her head, my fingers tangling briefly in the wet strands of her hair before I pull away. "I fucked up."

I'm referring to us having sex without a condom. A stupid, idiotic thing. Our relationship isn't even close to stable. If I got her pregnant? That would be a giant mistake.

Huge.

Even her laughter is sad. "Yeah, you did. But I fucked up too."

"I didn't mean to do that."

"You didn't mean to have sex with me? Or you didn't mean to forget the condom?"

"Both," I admit truthfully.

Pain flickers in her gaze, and I feel like a shit. "I'm not on any kind of birth control."

Of course, she's not. "I figured."

That's why she panicked and tried to...wash my semen out of her. I'm sure she got a few sperm cells out, but come on. I came inside her. Deep inside her.

A shiver moves through me at the memory. It had felt good too. Skin on skin, no condom acting as a barrier. I didn't even think of putting on a rubber. I was just in the moment, enjoying it.

Now there are consequences I don't even want to have to consider.

"What if something—happens?" Her voice is hesitant. A little shaky.

"What if you get pregnant?" I clarify.

She nods, her lips pressed together.

"We'll deal with it then." I stare up at the ceiling, my thoughts drifting. I'm tired. Sex always makes me sleepy.

"I'd get an abortion," she says without hesitation.

Alarm slams into me, making me pull away from her. "What do you mean?"

"I mean what I say. I can't be a mom. First, I'm too young. Second, what if I end up just like...her?" She whispers the last word, referring to her mother.

"You're nothing like her," I say quickly.

"I'm exactly like her," she counters, sending me a look that says come the fuck on. "I'm manipulative and demanding. Selfish. Vain. All of her bad traits, I have. That's why I can never be a mother. I'll do everything to my child that she's done to me. Maybe even worse."

That's her own panic and worry talking. She's been through so much, she would never do that to her child. I just don't believe Sylvie has it in her.

"You would never." I tug on her arm, pulling her back to me, and she comes willingly, her face buried against my shoulder, as if she can't look at me. "I know you, Syl. You don't have a mean bone in your body."

She lifts her head, the incredulous look on her face clear. "That's not true and you know it. I am horrible. I'm mean. You always said I looked like an angel, but I'm the devil in disguise. Or a fallen angel. I don't know what's worse. Pretty sure they're one and the same."

"I was just teasing you—"

"No." She shakes her head. "Don't bother arguing with me. It's true. My soul is black. My wings are black too. That Halloween costume is the perfect representation of who I am."

"You wore it when you were sixteen. You're not like that at—"

"Stop." Her voice is firm, shutting me up. "Don't make excuses for me when you've said those very things to me before."

We're quiet for a moment, analyzing each other. Memories flit through my mind, one after the other, and I'm sure the same thing is happening to her.

"You're panicking." I reach for her, cupping her face, forcing her to look at me. "You're not going to get pregnant."

"I need the morning after pill," she whispers, her voice pleading. "God, why does this house have to be so far from civilization."

"You're not going to have a baby. You're just freaking out."

"With reason."

Right. And, sometimes, there's no reasoning with her.

"I wouldn't want you take a morning after pill anyway," I murmur, my grip easing, fingers streaking across her soft cheek.

"Why the hell not?"

"If we made a baby? Me and you?" I can't handle the thought of her destroying the one good thing that could possibly come out of this union.

"That's just you being a chauvinistic male." She circles her fingers around my wrists, pulling away from my touch before she rolls out of bed. "Wanting to plant your seed in every woman you desire."

"Plant my *seed*?" I start to laugh, watching as she marches across the bedroom to the dresser on the other side, her perfect ass on display. She's definitely gained weight since the last time I was with her like this, and it's a good look for her. "In *every* woman?"

She yanks a drawer open, pulling out a pair of lacy, sheer panties. "I'm sure there are plenty of women you've desired throughout the years."

I was not a saint over the nearly three years without her, I can't lie. But we don't need to discuss that either. "I don't want to plant my seed in any woman."

Except you.

The two unspoken words ring throughout the room, but she pretends not to hear them. She's too focused trying to get the panties on, yanking them up over her slender thighs, covering up her delectable pussy.

My cock stirs and I immediately want her again.

"You still want to start over with me?" She turns toward the bed, her hands on her hips, clad in the skimpy white panties and nothing else. Her hair is drying into a wild tumble of blonde around her head and her skin is literally glowing, I swear. She is the picture of health. Gorgeous.

Sexy.

All mine if I want her.

I sit up, yanking the comforter over me and covering my growing dick. "I think we're too far out to start over."

"Told you." She throws her hands up in the air. "The back and forth is a pain in the ass."

"I agree."

"I don't want to return to New York."

A sigh leaves me and I rub the back of my neck. "I knew you would say that."

"But I would return to New York if it meant we were actually together." She bites her lip, looking so scared, all I want to do is comfort her.

I'm surprised by her confession. This is big for her. Sylvie doesn't make sacrifices for just anyone.

"You'd do that for me?" My voice is gentle, like I'm dealing with a wild animal and I'm worried she'll bolt if I say the wrong thing.

She nods, her eyes wide and unblinking. "If you'll still have me."

If I'll still have her. That's hilarious.

She's all I ever wanted.

"I need you to listen to me." My tone turns fierce. Sincere. I'm going to be real with her right now, and I hope it doesn't bite me in the ass. "I have been in love with you for so long, I don't know how to stop. I will do whatever it takes to make this work. Even give you another chance, despite how you shit all over me the last time we were together. I should've turned you away then and banished you from my life. But it's like I can't, and you know it.

"Seeing you at Whit's wedding threw me. You looked so damn beautiful, were so vulnerable and open. All those old feelings came flooding back. I probably shouldn't have come after you now, but I can't help it. I can't stop the way I feel about you. And I think you feel the same way too."

She stares at me, to the point that it's difficult to stare back, and I let my gaze drop, focusing on her perfect tits. Her pale pink nipples are hard. Tempting. I'm on edge, dreading what she might say because, for once in my life, I told Sylvie how I actually feel about her, and I'm thinking she's going to tell me to fuck right off.

I suppose I deserve it, but so does she.

"I'm tired of the round and round we put ourselves through Syl," I admit, my voice low. "This endless cycle we can't seem to break."

Now is the time to break it. Either we try to make this work or we walk away from each other.

Forever.

"You really love me?" she asks, her voice small.

That would be the one thing she focused on out of everything. She is starved for love. She always has been. All of the Lancasters are. "I've never stopped loving you."

Despite my telling her I love her, she still looks...worried. Unsure. "I didn't know you loved me in the first place."

"I don't recall ever telling you how I felt. I assumed you just... knew."

She rolls her eyes, the sass returning in full force. "Typical Spence."

"Typical Syl," I return to her before I throw back the comforter, revealing my hard dick. "Come over here." I pat the empty spot beside me.

She's wary, but her gaze snags on my erection, and she slowly makes her way back over to the bed. When she's within touching distance, I grab her hand and pull her onto the mattress, making her shriek. I roll over, so I'm on top of her, my face in hers, and she spreads her legs, allowing me to settle in between them.

"If I have to stay here with you for the next few weeks, I will," I tell her, giving her a kiss when she tries to speak. "I'm not budging from your side until we know for sure if you're pregnant or not."

Her brows draw together. "What are you, a caveman? That's

so archaic, Spence."

"I don't care. If I have to lock you away in a room for the next nine fucking months, I will. If you're pregnant, that baby is just as much mine as it is yours."

"But I'm the one who'll have to carry it," she reminds me.

"I'll be there with you every step of the way."

She makes a face. "I don't even like babies."

"I'm not too fond of them either."

Sylvie makes an exasperated noise. "Then why would we have one?"

"Because we'd like ours. We might even love it. Her. Him."

Her eyes widen. I'm not saying what she wants to hear. "I'll get fat."

"You've always been too thin." I draw my hand down her side, settling on the gentle curve of her hip. "Though you're definitely not too thin now."

"I will turn into a raging shrew."

"You already are." I kiss her again before she gets too angry, my tongue seeking, finding hers before I break away. "You'll have to come back to New York with me."

She slowly shakes her head. "I don't know if I can."

"What do you mean, you don't know?" I thrust my hips against hers, my cock dipping just inside her. "You just said you would."

"I'm—scared." She's shaking her head faster, her hair rustling against the pillow. "*She'll* be there. She'll find out I'm back. And she'll want to see me."

Her fucking mother ruins everything. "I will protect you no matter what. I won't let her get near you."

"You can't keep guard over me all the time." She arches against me, sending my cock deeper, both of us groaning at the sensation of me sinking inside her.

"Watch me," I murmur before I race my lips down the length of her elegant neck, tonguing the spot where her pulse beats erratically. "I will do anything to protect what's mine."

We're quiet for a moment, moving and shifting. Fucking without actually doing it? I don't know how to describe it, but it feels fucking phenomenal.

"I don't know." She undulates beneath me, her body lighting up, responding to mine. I shift my hips, sending myself deeper, just before I pull back. "Maybe I'll go with you."

I pause, staring into her eyes. "You will."

She rests her hand on my cheek, sincerity glowing in her bright blue eyes. "You're right. I will do just about anything to have another chance with you. Even go back to New York and face all of my demons. Like my mother."

I press my forehead against hers, thrusting deep and pulling almost all the way out before pushing back in. "I've got you. Don't worry about her."

"So easy for you to say." She runs her hands over my shoulders, her head falling back, eyes slowly closing. "God, that feels good. Keep doing what you're doing."

The rhythm is steady. In and out. Back and forth inside her wet, suctioning heat. She's got the tightest, sweetest pussy and I'm addicted to it. To her.

I can't get enough.

Without warning I pull out of her and she cries out, confusion on her beautiful face. Ignoring her protests, I grab her hips and flip her over so she's on her stomach.

"Get on your hands and knees, Syl," I command.

She doesn't hesitate, scrambling into position, wagging her ass at me, her pink pussy glistening. I loom above her on my knees, grabbing her hip with one hand, slipping a finger deep inside of her with the other.

"Oh." The sound falls from her lips when I add another finger, my gaze never straying as I push them in and out of her cunt. My fingers are coated with her juices and I pull them out, gently drifting them across the ridged skin of her ass.

A low moan falls from her lips and I test her back there,

slipping just the tip of my finger inside of her. She stiffens, going completely still, her breaths heavy.

My finger sinks deeper, only by a centimeter or so and she spreads her knees wider, pushing back against my touch.

Sending me a little deeper still.

"Oh. My. God," she bites out as I barely move my fingers in and out of her ass. "That feels…amazing."

"About to feel even better," I say before I guide my cock inside of her welcoming pussy.

I thrust hard, again and again, my fingers slipping out of her ass when I feel the need to grip her hips tight, keeping her in position. She moans with my every deep thrust, her fingers clawing at the sheets as if she's completely out of control. I pound my way inside of her, concentrating on the rhythm, watching my cock slide in out of her, over and over, and that's all it takes.

I'm coming. Fucking hard. So hard, my vision grows blurry as the shudders take over me. Her inner walls have me in a chokehold, strangling the orgasm right out of me and her name leaves me on a groan.

Fuck me.

When it's over and we collapse onto the mattress, she crawls her way into my arms, her head nestled beneath my chin, her soft hair brushing against my jaw.

"Sometimes I worry I might die, it feels so good being with you," she admits, her voice so soft I almost don't hear her.

I slip my arm around her shoulders, pressing my lips to her forehead. "You're never going to die on my watch."

She strokes my chest, her light touch making goosebumps break out on my skin. "Promise?"

"Always."

CHAPTER EIGHTEEN

SYLVIE

THE PAST

My brother brought home a special Christmas present just for me, though he had no clue. The moment he walked into the house, the cavernous mansion we've spent every Christmas at since I could remember, all the air left my lungs when I first saw the dark-haired boy standing beside Whit.

His best friend, he announced. Spencer. Fourteen and incredibly tall, with ruddy cheeks and braces on his teeth. Hands in his pockets, trying to play it cool, though I could see the way he tipped his head back, taking in the monstrosity called our home that's been in the Lancaster family for generations.

He was impressed. Who isn't? Our family wealth is unlike anyone else I know—we are truly the one percent.

Whit introduced us, and all I could offer was a soft hi and an awkward wave, which made Spencer smile.

I immediately wanted to see that smile again.

The first couple of days, I followed them as much as possible, spying on my brother and his friend wherever I could. I was bored, with no one to spend time with. Carolina was participating in the annual production of *The Nutcracker* at the dance academy she attends, and we never saw her.

Typical.

Whit warned me off at one point, about two days into Spencer's stay. He caught me spying on them in one of the hallways and yanked me into my bedroom, slamming the door behind him so Spencer wouldn't witness the tear down.

"Stay the fuck away from us," Whit had growled, his eyes glowing with anger, his finger thrust in my face.

He'd been angry for a while. At least the last year or so, and I truly didn't understand why.

"I'm bored," I'd whined. "And your friend seems nice."

"He hates you," Whit told me, making me flinch. "He said so."

"Out loud?" I found it hard to believe. How could a boy who didn't even know me hate me?

"He's not interested in little girls." Whit sneered. "You're only thirteen, Sylvie. Quit lusting after him."

Those words hurt. So much, that I immediately stopped following them everywhere and spying on them. That's my brother—he knew just what to say to cut you deep. His words were harsh, and they're only getting worse.

Two days before Christmas, Spencer found me sitting in the library that overlooked the expansive back lawn. I was in the deep blue velvet chair next to the Christmas tree that stood in the window, magnificent with its sparkling white lights and silver ribbon threaded throughout the lush green branches. It was one of the only real Christmas trees in the house, and therefore, it was my favorite.

Plus, no one came in here. Not really. It was a way for me to get away from my mother's stifling behavior, at least for a little bit.

"Why are you in here alone?"

I startled at the sound of the unfamiliar voice, glancing over my shoulder to find Spencer standing in the open doorway of the library, his dark brow furrowed in...what? Confusion? Concern?

He doesn't even know me. And supposedly he doesn't like

me. The reminder hurts, making my chest ache, and I return my focus to the tree, not looking at Spence as I say, "Go away."

Clearly, he doesn't listen, because he steps farther into the room, until he's standing on the other side of the tree, his gaze on me. I feel it and I want to squirm where I sit, but my mother raised a lady and so I don't move an inch.

"Why are all you Lancasters so mean?"

My gaze flits to his, wondering if he's mocking me, but I see the earnestness in his gaze and realize it's a genuine question.

"You're the one who didn't like me first." Oh, I sound so young. I wish I would've never said that.

"Who told you that?" Before I can answer, Spencer answers his own question. "Whit."

I nod, curling deeper into the soft chair. I bend my legs, holding them to my chest as I contemplate him. "I didn't mean to follow you guys around like that. I just wanted to hang out with you both."

"You should've said something. I would've let you." He shrugs, and like the greedy girl I am, I let my gaze wander all over him, eating him up. The longing I suddenly feel deep within me is unlike anything I've ever experienced before, and I have a thought.

I want him. All to myself.

"I never said I didn't like you," Spencer says, his voice breaking through my thoughts. "I think it's more that you were irritating Whit."

"Everything irritates Whit," I mutter, unable to hold back.

Spence smiles. "I've noticed."

"Why do you put up with him then?" I am curious. We have to deal with Whit because he's blood. Why do people actually *choose* to spend time with him?

"He's a good friend. Loyal. He's funny. And he's got access to some really good weed." Spencer laughs at my shocked expression. "What, it's true."

"You smoke weed?" My voice is a rasp. I'm just—shocked. I snuck a few sips of alcohol here and there, but I've never done drugs. Of course, I go to a very sheltered, all-girls' private school, so we're not exposed to much. This is my last year though. Once I finish the eighth grade, it's off to Lancaster Prep I go. Where Whit is.

And Spence.

I was never excited about going to Lancaster Prep but now... I totally am.

"I do." Spencer tilts his head toward me. "Have you?"

I shake my head furiously, practically making myself dizzy. "Never."

"Want to?"

"With you?" I gape at him. "Where's my brother?"

"Talking to your dad. They got into a fight earlier. God knows how long that discussion is going to last." Spencer glances over his shoulder quickly before he reaches into the front pocket of his jeans and pulls out a little baggy of green stuff. "Know somewhere we can smoke this?"

This is how I came to have my first experience smoking weed with Spencer Donato.

I led him outside and over to the garden shed, which no one really uses in the winter. We enter the small, dark shack, our gazes adjusting to the dimmed light, and I lean against the wall, watching in utter fascination as Spencer uses the potting table to lay out his paraphernalia. He has the baggie of weed, plus a glass pipe that's actually quite beautiful. A swirl of various colors formed into a delicate shape. He packs the tip of it with the marijuana, pulls a lighter out of his pocket and sparks it up before taking a slow, deep inhale.

"You gotta hold it in your lungs for a minute if you wanna feel it," he says, his voice strained before he exhales all the smoke in my direction, making me wrinkle my nose.

"Maybe I don't want to feel it."

"I think you do." He takes another puff, not holding this one in as long. "That's why you came in here with me."

"I think you wanted me to come in here with you because you can go back to school and brag to all your friends you got Sylvie Lancaster high for the first time."

He chuckles. "No one knows who you are."

I'm offended by his comment, but he's probably right. Why would they know me? I'm just Whit Lancaster's little sister.

"Come here." He waves the pipe at me. "Let's do this."

I take cautious steps toward him, still keeping my distance while watching him prepare the pipe for me. "I don't know..."

"Just don't inhale as deep as me."

Panic zips through my veins. I think of my mother. My health problems. I've been feeling good since arriving at the house once winter break started. Mother has been preoccupied with holiday preparations, giving me some much-appreciated freedom, and it's so weird, how when I'm not around her as much, I always feel better.

Sometimes I think she's just bringing me down. Her moods. Her drinking, which has increased lately. She complains about Daddy a lot, and I think they're having problems.

"I don't have the best lungs," I admit, noting the irritated look on Spencer's face. He must think I'm so young and scared.

Well, if that's the case, he's right. I am.

"How about we shotgun?" He raises a brow.

"What's that?"

"I'll inhale, and then breathe it out into your mouth," he explains. "It's like the ultimate contact high."

My entire body tingles at the thought of Spencer's mouth close to mine. Is he for real? "I don't know..."

"I'll go easy the first time." He tilts his head to the side, his lips curling into a small smile. "Come on."

I walk forward as if in a trance, shocked when he takes my hand and pulls me closer. That skin-on-skin contact sends electricity racing through my veins, making me shake, and when he lets go of my hand, I can still feel his touch, as if he imprinted on me. "What do I do?" I ask shakily.

"Stay right where you're at. After I inhale, open your mouth and inhale too. Ready?"

I nod, silent, my heart beating so hard I'm afraid something is wrong with me. He takes a hit off the pipe, his lips slamming shut, and I shift forward on instinct, parting my lips just as he leans in close, his mouth opening, allowing all of the smoke to flow from him to me.

I inhale softly, my lungs tickling, my gaze stuck on his lips. They're perfect. Equally full on the top and bottom and I wonder what it would feel like to kiss him.

"Wasn't close enough," he says when we're finished. "But did you feel it?"

"Yes." I'm not sure if it's the marijuana or if it's him, but I feel giddy. A little shaky.

"Want to try again?"

"Yes," I repeat without hesitation, making him laugh.

But it doesn't feel like he's laughing at me. More like he thinks I'm funny. Maybe I'm too eager. Perhaps I should be playing it cooler, but I don't want to.

We repeat the process, and this time, he yanks me close, our lips brushing when he exhales into my mouth at the exact moment I inhale. This time, I take a lungful that makes me cough, and he looks pleased.

"You'll feel that for sure," he murmurs, nodding. "One more time?"

"Okay," I say weakly, not doing it for the high the weed might give me.

No, I'm doing it for the chance to brush lips with Spencer again. I've never kissed a boy before. This is as close as I've gotten and I want more.

"Or do you want to say fuck it and just kiss for a while?"

I blink at him, taken aback by his words. At the sudden gleam in his eyes that wasn't there before. Is he living inside my head or what?

"What did you just say?"

"I know you're a pretty, rich girl and you've probably kissed a bunch of boys already, but I thought I'd shoot my shot." He shrugs. "If you're not interested, it's cool."

He starts to back away and I grab his sleeve, pulling him back to me. "I'm interested."

His smile is warm, and it makes my stomach twist and tumble over itself. "Is that why you were following us everywhere?"

"Don't flatter yourself," I say, channeling my inner Whit by acting like a snot. "Is that why you suggested we get high together?"

"I just wanted to get high, and found you in the library so you lucked out."

"You're saying it's my lucky day, that I get to kiss you in the garden shed?" I raise my brow.

"Well, it was kind of hot, sharing smoke with you. Not gonna lie." He rubs the back of his neck, a little uncomfortable, which is adorable. "I probably shouldn't do this with you. You're my best friend's sister."

"It can be our little secret," I whisper, my gaze falling to his perfect mouth yet again. "I won't tell Whit if you don't."

"Okay," he readily agrees, and the next thing I know, I'm in Spencer's arms.

And he's got me pressed up against the rough wooden wall, crowding me.

His body is warm. And firm. I tilt my head back to find he's already watching me and when his head descends, and his mouth brushes against mine…

I melt. Until I'm nothing but complete goo, rendered useless by Spencer's perfectly shaped lips and flickering tongue. I follow his lead, not sure what to do with myself. With my hands or the rest of my body. When I finally settle my palms against his chest, he deepens the kiss, his searching tongue sending all sorts of foreign sensations coursing through my body.

When he finally pulls away, breaking the kiss first, I press the back of my head against the wall, my eyes still closed as I try to catch my breath. I can feel him fumbling around and I realize he's searching for his phone. I hear him open it. The distinct sound of his fingers tapping out a text response. The swooshing noise of it being sent.

"Whit's looking for me."

I open my eyes to find him watching me.

"I have to go."

Unable to find my voice, I nod, the movement slow. I feel... weird. And I don't think it's just from the kisses we shared.

He's laughing. "You high, Syl?"

No one calls me Syl. Not really. I'm Sylvie. That's it.

"Maybe," I offer, my voice weak.

"We should do this again." He kisses me, a brush of lips so soft, I could almost imagine it didn't actually happen. "Tomorrow?"

"It's Christmas Eve tomorrow," I protest.

"Even better reason to do it then. We'll need to be high to get through the family shit," he mutters.

I frown, his words making me ask the question. "Why aren't you with your family for the holidays?"

"They'd rather go off by themselves and try to fix their fucked-up marriage." He rubs a hand across his mouth. "Sorry. Brutal but it's the truth."

"I think my parents aren't doing well either," I admit softly.

"Your brother said they'll probably get a divorce soon." And with that shocking statement, Spencer heads for the door. "Wait a few minutes before you come back into the house."

"Okay," I say to his retreating form, but I'm not sure if he even heard my response.

The door shut behind him the moment the word left my mouth.

I think about what he said the entire walk back to the house. Turning his words over and over in my mind. The kiss was amazing, and yes, I'm probably a little high, thanks to the shotgunning or whatever you call it, but I can't stop thinking about the offhand statement he made about my parents.

And how they're going to get a divorce, according to my brother.

I can't wrap my head around it. Worse, I hate how scared it makes me feel.

If my mother doesn't have my father to focus on anymore, that means she's going to focus all of her attention on...

Me.

CHAPTER NINETEEN

SYLVIE

My eyes pop open, slowly adjusting to the darkness of the night. I turn my head, checking the alarm clock that was left behind by the previous owner. All of the furnishings in this house came from them, and while they're not necessarily my taste, they work in the moment.

The red numbers on the clock screen read 3:22.

Blindly I reach out, my hand hitting a solid, warm body lying next to me. Spencer. We had sex before we fell asleep, and it was…

It was so good. As usual.

"Why are you awake?" he murmurs into his pillow, his voice muffled.

"I had a dream. More like a memory." I hesitate, wondering if I should tell him.

"What about?" he asks when I remain silent.

"The first time we met."

He rolls over and hauls me into him, our bare skin colliding. He's warmer than me, like a furnace, and I snuggle up close. Taking advantage of this moment, though it always feels like something bad is coming, just on the horizon.

I hate that feeling. Why can't I ever just enjoy the moment?

"You dragged me into that shed and had your way with me,"

he says against my temple.

I shove at his bare chest, marveling at how firm he is. "I was a year younger than you and you're the one who corrupted me, getting me high for the first time."

"And then you kissed me."

"No." I shake my head. "You're the one who suggested we should kiss. That wasn't my idea."

"I remember it differently—"

"Nope, you're wrong. It stuck with me, how you said earlier that I was the one who dragged you off somewhere, so we could make out, but the first time we kissed, it was all you."

He's quiet for a moment, his fingers sliding up and down my arm, making my skin tingle. This is so…nice. Just lying with him in my bed, talking. Sharing a moment about nothing serious.

"You're right," he finally says. "But after that first time, it was all you."

I rest my head against his chest, listening to the steady beat of his heart for a moment before I ask, "Why did you do that?"

"Do what?"

"Get me high and kiss me."

"I saw you sitting there by the tree and you looked so…sad. And bored. Bored out of your mind. I wanted to show you how to loosen up."

"You were only fourteen."

"And you were only thirteen."

"You really wanted to show me how to loosen up?"

A sigh leaves him. "Fine. I wanted to get you alone, and I didn't know how else to do it."

I lift up on my elbow so I can stare down at him, shocked. "You did?"

He nods, reaching toward me, his fingers drifting across my cheek. "Pretty little blonde Sylvie Lancaster. You reminded me of a doll the first time I saw you."

"A blow-up doll?"

Spencer chuckles. "No. One of those pretty little dolls kept on a shelf. Look but you can't touch. That's what I thought of when I first saw you. I can look, but no way can I touch. Whit told me I couldn't."

My mouth drops open. "What?"

"He warned me off you. Said I couldn't come near you or he'd chop off my balls. I took the risk anyway. And once it happened, once you started to chase after me, he knew there wasn't much he could do about it."

I blink at him repeatedly, trying to process what he's saying. "But we were so young."

"And I was horny. All fourteen-year-olds are."

"I was a baby."

"A baby with sweet tits and big blue eyes who studied my every move. We were babies together, Syl."

I think about that winter break when Spencer stayed the entire two weeks. The pretense of getting high together only happened twice. By the third time we found each other in an empty hallway of a forgotten wing of the house, he was yanking me into a dark corner, his mouth landing on mine easily. We kissed for what felt like hours, never coming up for breath until he was getting yet another text from Whit asking where he was.

I remember he told Whit he had stomach issues and he was always in the bathroom, which is so gross, but it kept Whit away from us. At least for a little bit.

"You went back to Lancaster Prep and forgot all about me," I say, my voice brittle. I didn't hear from him for the rest of the school year. Not a single peep, and we even exchanged phone numbers.

The jerk.

"I didn't. I swear."

"What happened?" I know what happened.

I just want to hear him say it.

"I got a girlfriend," he admits. "But you know this."

I do. I'm just a glutton for punishment.

"She was blonde. With blue eyes." He touches my hair, his fingers tangling deep. "And she wasn't as good a kisser as you."

"Please." I roll my eyes.

"It's true." He tugs on my hair, keeping me in place. "We were a natural fit back then."

"We still are."

Spence lets go of my hair and I readjust myself, sprawling across the top of him, thrusting my face in his. I can feel every inch of him beneath me growing tense, including his cock, and just like that, I want him again. I lower my hips, dragging my pussy against his erection, and he rests his hands on my hips, stopping me.

"I have to ask you a question." His voice is deadly serious. "And I don't want you distracting me with sex when I try."

"I'm distracting you with sex before you try." I reach down, my fingers searching for his balls and he grabs my wrist.

"What happened between you and Earl? Why did you marry him? Did he treat you well? What happened when he died?"

"That's four questions," I tell him, vaguely offended.

There's the scary thing I felt sitting on the horizon, just out of reach. Now it's here, resting between us, and he's not going to let me avoid it any longer.

"I need more information, Syl. If we're really going to make a go of this, I have to know…everything." His grip on my wrist loosens, his thumb stroking the spot where my pulse beats rapidly. "You fucked me up so bad when you married him. I was fucking broken."

My heart cracks at his admission. Spencer bottles most of his feelings up inside. He doesn't like to talk about them. Like me.

But he's being real with me right now, which means I need to do the same.

"I'm sorry," I whisper. "I didn't mean to hurt you. I know what I did was wrong, and selfish. I just wanted one last chance with you. One last chance at us.”

"You knew you were going to marry him when you came to me that night, huh.” His voice is flat, tinged with devastation, and God, I am the worst human alive.

I'm quiet for a moment, the single word getting stuck in my throat before I'm finally able to croak it out.

“Yes.”

He doesn't shove me away, and I'm grateful, I cling to him. I curl my hands around his shoulders and lie there on top of him, matching my breathing to his, savoring the feel of his bare skin against mine. He's silent for so long, I start to think that's it. He's not going to say anything else about it, but I was wrong.

“Your mother made you marry him. Why?”

“She didn't want me with you.”

“What the fuck, Syl? Are you serious?” He's shouting so loud that, if we were outside, he'd send about a dozen birds flying from the trees from startling them so badly.

“She wanted me with someone of her choosing. Whit gave her the big fuck you by falling in love with Summer, and Carolina ran away to London, so no one could control her but dance, and that left me. Always me. I did what she wanted, because I was scared to go against her.” I feel like I'm repeating myself. “You already know this.”

“What was your marriage like? Did he fuck you?”

I press my lips together and close my eyes, knowing he won't believe me. “No.”

“Bullshit.”

“He didn't.”

“Right. You're just trying to save my feelings. Well listen to this. I fucked other women. I've been fucking other women since the moment I met you. That girlfriend I got after winter break with you my freshman year? She was my first. I fucked her in my dorm room. I was her first too. She looked like you. One time, I called her Sylvie, and she got so pissed, she broke up with me.”

I wince at his words. I know he's just trying to hurt me.

"And I've fucked plenty of others too, so you can go ahead and tell me the truth. I can take it," he says irritably.

Can he though? Really?

"I've never fucked anyone else." I rise up, so I can stare him straight in the eyes. "Only you, Spence."

His hands find my hips, pressing into my skin. "Give me a break."

"It's true."

"What about that asshole you took to Whit's wedding?"

"Cliff?"

"Cliff?" He mimics my voice, high-pitched and girly, and I almost laugh, but I'm afraid it would piss him off even more. "Yes. Cliff. He looked like a pretentious asshole. Just your type."

"Are you calling yourself a pretentious asshole? Because you're definitely my type." I roll my hips, letting him feel me, and he inhales deeply when I brush my pussy against him.

"You know what I'm saying. That guy was so territorial."

"That guy is gay and he's been on a couple of dates with Monty," I say.

Spence goes still, his brows drawing together. "Serious?"

Nodding, I lean in, pressing my mouth to the side of Spencer's jaw. "Serious."

I continue kissing along his jawline, Spence staring off into the distance. "I'm an idiot."

"Yes, you are." I kiss his chin.

"I'm sorry I said all of that shit about being with other women. I was exaggerating."

Relief makes my heart grow light. "Good."

"Though you didn't answer the most difficult question of all."

I pause in my exploration of his face with my mouth. "What question is that?"

"What was your marriage like with Earl? What happened when he died? How did he die? Those details were never shared from what I could find."

My heart bottoms out, and I choose to ignore it. "Can't I answer that tomorrow?"

"No." He slides one hand down, until he's cupping my ass. "Stop trying to distract me and give me an answer."

He's being so bossy, and like the good little girl I've always been, I automatically answer him.

"Our marriage wasn't much of one. We were wed only a little over a year when he died."

"And how exactly did he die?"

A sigh leaves me. It's difficult to explain, without offering up a few details first.

"He had a secret life," I admit.

"What do you mean?"

"I mean what I say. Earl Wainwright was living a double life for years. It's why his first wife left him. He paid her a lot of money to keep her mouth shut in the divorce settlement. I had to sign an NDA, once I discovered his dirty little secret. He tried to keep it from me, but of course, I found out."

"And what the fuck was it?" Impatience fills his tone, and I hate it. I don't want him angry with me.

I don't want to give him any reason to leave.

A sigh leaves me and I rest my head on his chest once more, my cheek pressed against his hot skin. "He liked little boys."

"*What?*" Spencer stiffens beneath me, and not in the good way.

"Not little. That's the wrong word choice. He liked them young. Eighteen. Sometimes they were younger, though he always swore he asked before he attempted anything with them. But trust me, he didn't usually ask." A sigh leaves me and I shut my eyes. "His first wife found out and was destroyed. Told him he had to change or she wanted a divorce, and he couldn't change. I mean, he did cheat on her throughout their marriage. I can't blame her for divorcing him."

Spencer is quiet for a moment, digesting the information, no doubt. "So he was gay?"

"He didn't like to call himself that, didn't appreciate the stigma that was attached to it, which I always thought was silly. But he comes from a different generation, you know? It would be his family's shame, to realize that he was gay. But it was more than that. He wasn't interested in a relationship with a man his own age. He didn't want any sort of steady relationship at all, beyond a fake marriage to a pretty wife who could be his beard. What Earl liked, was hooking up with men who were barely old enough to vote. As many as he could."

"Oh."

"Yeah, oh." I lift my head, studying Spencer's face. "When I found out, he told me that he chose me because he knew I had a lot of gay friends. Young gay friends."

Spence grimaces. "He used you."

I nod. "And I let him."

He doesn't say anything, and I eventually settle my head against his chest again, savoring the quiet, going over my relationship with Earl in my mind. How kind he was. Really, he wasn't so bad. He had a thing for younger men, but how many guys Earl's age have a thing for younger women and no one bats an eyelash?

It's not fair. A total double standard.

"Your mother knew all of this?" Spencer asks out of nowhere.

"No," I say immediately, "she wouldn't have paired him with me if she did."

"You so sure about that?"

I nod, trying to ignore the unease coursing through me. "When she found out, she was horrified. Extremely apologetic."

"And when did she find out?"

"After Earl died." I hesitate. "She really did feel bad. She thought she was making a proper match."

"You keep telling yourself that."

Irritation flits through my veins and I try to ignore it. "It's my fault he died, you know."

Spencer goes completely still beneath me, and I realize I've shocked him. Good. He's being a little flippant right now.

"Why would you say that?" he asks warily.

"I was the one who paired him with the guy he was with when he…passed." I sniff, fighting the wave of sadness that wants to overtake me. "I'm responsible for his death."

CHAPTER TWENTY

SPENCER

"Hey." I reach for the side of Sylvie's face, tilting her head back so her gaze meets mine. "You're not responsible for his dying. Were you there?"

She slowly shakes her head, her big blue eyes full of sadness. Regret. "No. If I had been, maybe I could've saved him."

"What the hell happened?"

Sylvie's expression turns pained. "It's really weird."

I cup her cheek. "Tell me."

"Earl was into…some kinky shit. He was at his apartment in midtown with this guy, a casual friend of mine I met at a party once. He was a friend of Cliff's."

Cliff. The dude I thought she was with, who is also gay. I was so jealous of him the day of Whit's wedding.

"Anyway, they were together, and Earl put on a nude-colored latex suit that covered him literally from head to toe. They were doing…whatever, and it's believed that Earl started having a panic attack. Those suits are hot, and they cover you everywhere. I'm sure he felt restricted."

She's quiet for a moment and I finally tell her, "Go on."

"Sorry. So he's freaking out, and according to the guy he was with, he's freaking out too. Trying to get the suit off of Earl.

But he's sweating so badly, the guy is having a hard time and eventually—Earl went into cardiac arrest and died."

"Seriously?"

"Would I lie about that?" She shakes her head, my hand dropping away from her face. "It was…a lot. To protect him, we kept the story quiet. Said he was at the apartment alone and had a heart attack. Everyone believed us. His team of lawyers spoke with the EMTs who were first on scene and I think they even paid them off not to say anything. He was a very prominent businessman. The gossip sites and society pages would've had a field day discussing the kinky sex life of Earl Wainwright."

She's right. Scandalous headlines would've been everywhere, discussing his death in a latex suit. It would've turned into an epic shitshow.

"What about his kids?"

"They don't know," she admits. "We kept it from them too. You're the only person I've told. Well, besides my mother."

Probably not the best idea, to give Sylvia Lancaster that kind of information. Knowing her, she'll use it against Sylvie eventually.

I tug Sylvie close to me, rolling over so she's on her back and I'm on my side, hovering next to her. God, she's so young. All I want to do is protect her from all the shit she's been through. Mostly at the hands of her mother.

What the fuck is wrong with that woman? Why does she continue to put Sylvie through so much? All in the name of loving her?

What a crock of shit.

"I hate what your mother has done to you." I pull Sylvie in, pressing my mouth to her forehead in the lightest kiss. I feel her melt against me, her soft, naked body brushing against mine and just like that, I want her.

I always want her.

"I'm still here though, right? I'm sure she resents me for it."

The bitterness in Sylvie's voice is telling.

"She really wants to kill you." It's not a question. I just need her to confirm it again.

"*Yes*. I told you the last time we were together alone, I caught her standing over my bed with a pillow in her hands, Spence. A pillow. She wanted to smother me and end it. End me." Her voice turns shaky. "What did I ever do to her to make her feel that way toward me? I don't get it. I don't get her."

I slip my fingers beneath her chin to tilt her face up to mine, spotting the tears streaking down her cheeks, which breaks my heart. I hate that she's crying tears over someone who doesn't deserve them.

"I will protect you from her if it's the last thing I do for you," I vow, my tone fierce. I want Sylvie to realize I mean it, because I do.

"I won't willingly put myself around her anymore, so you don't have to worry about that," she says, trying to smile.

I dip my head, kissing her. Tasting the saltiness of her tears, which only incites me further. "Fuck her. I mean it, Syl. She does something, she even says something to you, looks at you, and I will be the one ending her."

"But...she's my mother."

"Your mother, who wants to kill you," I remind her. "I will never let her get near you. Never."

She stares at me, her eyes shining, her lips curling into an actual smile this time around. "Are you saying what I think you are?"

"What do you think I'm trying to say?"

"That you want to be with me," she whispers.

"I already told you I did," I remind her.

I wonder how long she wants to hide away in the woods when I have to go home. My father called me earlier today, demanding that I come back to the office, but I put him off. That's going to work for only so long. I'm needed at Donato Enterprises. I have work to do. Things to attend to.

But I love this woman. I want her with me, and for once in her goddamn life, she seems to want me too. For real this time.

"Oh. Right," she says softly.

"I've always wanted to be with you," I confess. "You're the one who pushed me away."

"I was an idiot."

I crack a smile. "Yeah, you were."

She scowls. "I've changed my ways."

"Not completely I hope."

"Oh. So you want me to push you away again?"

"Hell no," I practically growl, grabbing her by the waist and rolling onto my back, so she's now lying on top of me. "You're not going anywhere."

She laughs and the sound is so joyful, so unexpectedly Sylvie, my heart pangs at the sound. This woman hasn't known enough happiness in her life.

Maybe I can be the one to give it to her. I want to give her everything.

Every single little thing that could make her life better, I want to be the one who makes it happen.

"You have to leave soon though, don't you?" A soft sigh leaves her before I can answer. "I'm going to miss you."

"You said you would come back with me."

"I don't know…" The fear in her voice is obvious.

"You really want to stay out here by yourself? With Roland to keep you company?"

"And the cats," she says at the same moment I lean in and press my mouth to her slender throat. She trembles at the first touch of my lips on her skin. "I'll be okay without you."

"Liar." I glance up to find her watching me. "It's okay to admit you don't want me to leave."

"I don't want you to leave," she automatically says.

"And I don't want you to stay here." I slide my hand down her side. Around her hip. Until I'm gently cupping her pussy. She's warm and wet and I'm suddenly dying to sink myself into all that tight heat. "Come home with me."

I keep having to repeat myself, but I've always had to coax Sylvie. I'm used to it.

And I've gotten better at it, too.

She frowns despite rocking her hips, leaning in to my touch. I part her lower lips, searching her, thrusting a single finger inside her body. She hisses in a breath. "I want to, but..."

"I'll do this to you every night. Imagine it." I withdraw my finger before plunging it back in, and she rocks with me, a soft moan sounding when I crook my finger, hitting that sensitive spot. "The two of us in my bed. Fucking all night."

"Spence," she whispers when I increase my pace, my thumb nudging against her clit. "That sounds like a dream."

"I could make it a reality for you. For us. Just say the word." I make her come with ease, noting the way her inner walls squeeze around my finger, her entire body shuddering, a soft exhale leaving her as the orgasm washes over her. It's soft and subtle and the most beautiful thing I've ever witnessed.

"Where would I live? At my apartment?" she asks, once the orgasm has passed and she's sprawled all over me.

I run a hand through her hair, breathing in her delectable scent. "Hell no. Sell that apartment. You don't want it anyway. And I want you to live with me."

"My parents won't like that," she admits, her lips brushing against my neck.

I shiver. "Fuck your parents. Like they give a damn about you."

She slides down my body slowly, her mouth blazing a hot, damp path across my skin. "No one gives a damn about me like you, Spence."

"Don't ever forget it." I sink my fingers into her hair, holding her to me when she takes my dick into her mouth and starts to suck. "Fuck, Sylvie. That feels so good."

She takes me deep, her tongue swirling, her fingers curling around the base. I lift my hips, thrusting between her lips. Withdrawing. Thrusting again. She lifts her gaze, her eyes meeting mine, her mouth full of my cock and from the familiar tingling sensation I feel at the base of my spine, in the depths of my balls, I know it's not going to be long until I'm coming. Filling her mouth.

"I could do this to you every night," she says at one point when she withdraws, her lips wet and shiny, her chest rising and falling with her labored breaths.

I'm panting. Dying for her to continue.

Dying to get inside her even more.

I grab hold of her, rolling us over so she's on her back and I'm rising above her. I grab a condom from the pile she left on her nightstand earlier and tear it open, sheathing myself before I plunge inside her, pushing deep again and again, fucking her fiercely until she's coming with a shriek, her hands grappling at my back, nails sinking into my skin, making me hiss.

Making me come so fucking hard I almost black out.

We cling to each other, our bodies shaking, our breaths harsh, the scent of sex filling the room, pungent and sweet. I turn my head into her neck, inhaling sharply, her fragrance overwhelming me. Floral and distinctly Sylvie.

"You're coming home with me for sure," I tell her firmly, not wanting her to argue.

"You promise?" She giggles when I deliver soft, quick kisses to her throat.

"Yeah. And I'm keeping that promise too." I lift up, my gaze finding hers. "No more broken promises between us, Syl. When we talk, we mean what we say."

Her gaze is solemn as she slowly nods. We're still connected, my cock still inside her body, and this moment, the last few days, feel...huge.

Important.

"I'll go home with you," she whispers. "As long as you promise to take care of me."

"You can take care of your—"

She cuts me off by settling her fingers over my lips, silencing me. "Promise me. I need you."

I nod, her hand falling away.

"I'll take care of you." I kiss her once. Then again, before I confess, "I love you, Sylvie."

The fucked-up thing is she doesn't say it back.

She says nothing.

Not a single word.

CHAPTER TWENTY-ONE

SYLVIE

"I don't want to do this," I admit, not surprised at all that Spencer grabs my hand and grips it tight while we walk along the sidewalk, headed for the restaurant. As if he's afraid I might run away again.

I'm half tempted to do exactly that. Facing my family after I ran out on everyone without a word was cowardly on my part, and I know it. How do I explain to them why I did it? Will they even want an explanation, or will they act like this is just another night where we get together and have dinner? I'm not sure. I never know what to expect when it comes to them.

We may share a lot of the same traits and memories, but no one else in my family understands what it's like, being me. What I suffered through at the hands of my mother. I fight a lot of demons, and they visit me often in my sleep.

And all of my demons have my mother's face on them.

"It's going to be okay." He stops walking and so do I, watching him as he brings our linked hands up to his mouth and drops a quick kiss on my knuckles. "You ready?"

I shake my head, deciding to be truthful. "Not at all."

He chuckles. "Too late. We're here."

We're meeting my dad and Whit and Summer for dinner.

We've been back in New York for only a few days, and Spencer has been telling me since we returned that I need to face them. I let him know I would have this meeting only if we were in a public place where no one could throw a fit, and he agreed. I was referring to my father being the one who would possibly throw a fit, but really?

I was also referring to myself.

Being in public is the only way to ensure I'll be on my best behavior.

Spencer holds the door open for me once we get to the restaurant and I walk inside first, my heart leaping to my throat when I spot my father, my brother and his wife at a nearby table. I make eye contact with Father first, and the relief I see in his gaze when he spots me is...reassuring.

Like maybe he was actually worried about me after all.

The hostess escorts us to their table and my father is already out of his chair, hauling me into him the moment I get close, hugging me tight. I cling to him, breathing in his familiar scent, my eyes falling closed as past memories of the two of us together hit me, one after another.

Not enough memories between us though. I hit a certain point years ago where it felt like he gave up on me, but maybe it was never that.

Maybe my mother pushed him away. She always did want me to herself, pulling me out of school and taking me to one doctor's appointment after another. Perhaps that's why he tried to cling to Carolina, though she eventually ditched him for dance and ran away to London. She ditched all of us. Yet she somehow gets away with it because she has some sort of purpose, thanks to her being such a beautiful dancer.

Ugh I need to get over my envy over Carolina's situation. At least they all leave her alone mostly. I'm just jealous, that's all.

"I was so worried when we didn't know where you were," Father says before pulling away from me, his hands still gripping my upper arms as he studies me carefully. "We all were."

I don't need a guilt trip. I feel bad enough already.

"You look good," he continues, his concerned gaze scanning me from head to toe. "You have some color in your face. And have you gained weight?"

"Yes." I nod. "I finally have my appetite back."

His smile is small, but genuine. "I'm glad."

Notice how he doesn't ask why I didn't have an appetite in the first place. Sometimes I think he'd rather pretend nothing is wrong with me.

It's easier that way.

We settle into our chairs, my father sitting at the head of the table, Whit and Summer directly across from us. I haven't seen them since the wedding, and they are golden from the sun that I'm sure they soaked up during their honeymoon. Whit has his arm slung around the back of Summer's chair, his fingers skimming her arm. Across her back. Along her shoulder. Every chance he gets, he's touching her, and it's noticeable.

An affectionate Lancaster is not normal. I know Whit loves her, and it's become so obvious over the years. It's nice to see.

I sneak a glance in Spencer's direction to find him already looking at me and I turn away, embarrassed to be caught. I can only hope we have a relationship like theirs. Where he can't stop staring at me. Touching me. Maybe I'll be all he thinks about. I'll consume him just as much as he consumes me.

A girl can dream.

"Tell us what happened," Whit says, getting right to the point once the server has taken my and Spencer's drink order. "Where exactly did you go?"

Spencer sends me a knowing look. He already told Whit where I was, but my father was never informed. I didn't trust that he wouldn't blurt it out to Mother if she contacted him. Whit is acting like he didn't know either to save my father from having his feelings hurt, which is kind of…sweet.

And trust that I would never describe my big brother as sweet.

I launch into my explanation, letting them know Earl left me the sizeable property and house in California, and how beautiful Big Sur is. Summer listens with rapt attention as I describe it, her lips curling into a smile when I go on about how much I love the house, the thick redwoods and the ocean. Only when I pause to take a drink of water is she able to finally say something.

"You seem really happy, Sylvie," she offers. "Maybe California is good for you."

"I think it is definitely good for me," I say in agreement. "I want to spend more time out there for sure."

"Harumph." That's my father's response.

Guess he doesn't like thinking of me being so far away.

"More like the asshole sitting next to her is what's really good for her," Whit drawls, making Father laugh.

Irritation flashes in Spencer's eyes and his hand drops to the top of my thigh, sliding over until his fingers rest between my legs. "Shut the hell up."

"Now, now don't act like we're back in high school," Summer chastises. "Don't call your friend names, Whit."

"I'll quit, but only for you." He leans in to give his wife a kiss, Spencer making a retching noise when their lips connect.

"Stop," I admonish, just as he dips his head and kisses my cheek.

"Your brother loves it," he whispers close to my ear. "He's just trying to pretend he wasn't worried sick over you these last few weeks."

"It's true," Whit says, his stern expression back in place. "I don't like how you ran off and didn't tell anyone, Sylvie. That was straight up bullshit."

"Whit, don't curse at your sister," Father says.

I almost laugh.

"I didn't like it either," Father adds, his expression identical to Whit's, his gaze all for me. "I know you're an adult, but we worry when we don't hear from you. When we have no idea where you even are. If you plan on taking a trip, the considerate thing to do is to let us know where you're going."

"I'm sorry," I say, my voice soft. "I just—I really needed to get away for a little while. Everything can get to be too much sometimes, you know?"

The men in my life stare at me with blank expressions on their faces, even Spencer, and my heart dips.

"I get it," Summer says and I glance over at her, our gazes meeting. I see nothing but understanding shining in her eyes. "Sometimes with everything I have going on, I feel...overwhelmed."

I nod, grateful for her input, even though she deals with so much more than I do. She's a mother and a wife, and I'm just me, but I do appreciate her saying she understands me. We've been mending our relationship for quite a while, and I've worked extra hard to gain her trust back. I can only hope it's working.

In this moment right now, it feels like it is.

"If she does decide to leave again, we all have to agree that we won't tell Sylvia where she's at if she asks," Spencer says. Like my mother would ever reach out to him. She has to know he wouldn't tell her even if he was aware of my whereabouts—which he so would now, considering the positive shift in our relationship. "That's Sylvie's biggest fear."

"And the biggest reason she needs to get away sometimes, I'm sure," Summer adds.

I remain quiet, shocked Spence would just throw that out there for my brother and father to deal with. We tiptoe around my issues with my mother. Very rarely do we face them head on.

"Of course, of course. I know not to tell Sylvia much of anything whenever she reaches out." My father is blustery, and I can only guess he's offended Spencer would have to make the reminder.

"If Mother ever gives you any shit, you understand that you can reach out to me at any time, right?" Whit's voice is firm, as is his expression when he stares me down.

I nod, grateful for the reassuring squeeze Spencer gives my thigh. "I know."

The server shows up, asking if we're ready to order and my father starts asking him about the various entrees they have, which is typical. Whit starts whispering to Summer, making her giggle and I watch them, lost in thought.

"We've all got your back," Spencer says, startling me. I turn to find him watching me. "When it comes to your mother. To anything. Every single one of us sitting at this table will protect you. Your sister will too. You realize that, right?"

I nod slowly. "Yes, I do."

The words slip from my lips without much thought, but I don't know if I actually believe them. It's felt like I've moved through most of my life without any sort of protection.

Sometimes, it's still hard to believe they all actually care.

CHAPTER TWENTY-TWO

SPENCER

"I want to have a party," Sylvie announces when I walk through the door, her eyes sparkling, her behavior downright giddy.

We've been back in Manhattan for not even a week, and she already wants to have a party?

"Hello to you too," I say in greeting, approaching her so I can give her a kiss.

Her face is already turned toward mine, her lips slightly pursed, and I give her a deep, tongue-filled kiss before I pull away, smiling at the dazed look filling her eyes.

"That was nice," she murmurs.

"More where that came from," I say as I walk away from her, headed to my—our—bedroom, working at the tie around my neck until it's coming undone. I toss it on the bed as I stride into the walk-in closet, eager to get out of this suit and relax for the evening.

"Did you even hear what I said?" she calls out to me.

I quickly strip and throw on a T-shirt, exiting the closet with a pair of joggers in my hand, which I hurriedly put on while she watches. "You want to have a party."

She nods and smiles, clasping her hands in front of her expectantly. Giving me younger Sylvie vibes, giddy like a teenager. "Great idea, right?"

"I don't know."

Her expression falls and she drops her hands at her sides. "What do you mean? Why not?"

"You want to put yourself in that kind of position, inviting people over? It's a lot, Syl." I'm just watching out for her, wanting to protect, like I promised her I would. I hope she sees that.

From the scowl appearing on her face, I'm guessing not.

"I'm ready for a lot. I'm bored, sitting in this apartment all day, Spence. I want to announce my return to the city." She throws her arms up in the air, a big grin on her face reappearing. "It'll be an intimate party for just friends and certain members of my family."

"Certain members? Like who?"

"Whit and Summer. Carolina. She's home for the summer, you know."

"I didn't know." I settle on the edge of the bed, grabbing her hand and pulling her close, so she's standing in front of me.

"I just found out. She called me earlier. I guess she hurt herself dancing. She's out for a month. She works too hard, she told me. And now she's climbing the walls, desperate to do something to fill her time. We're going to meet for lunch soon."

"Your mom's not in on this lunch, is she?"

Sylvie shakes her head, her gaze finding mine. "I told Lina I don't want to see our mother. She knows how I feel."

"Just checking." I tug on her hand and she dips her head, our lips brushing. It's been nonstop sex between us since she's come back here to live with me. We have plans to return to California in a couple of months. She's currently looking for someone to renovate the house, and she's put a deadline on herself, so when we return, she'll meet with people and discuss her plans. She's not about to give up that house, and I don't blame her. It's the only thing in the world that is solely hers.

Well, my heart is all hers too, but she doesn't seem as excited about that.

Fuck, I love torturing myself sometimes, I swear.

Earl's old apartment is already up for sale at my urging. We don't need the reminder of him lingering in our relationship and she agreed. She even offered the apartment to Earl's children at a bargain price, but they weren't interested. Looks like they have no interest in harassing Sylvie any longer either.

Lucky for them, because I would make their life a living hell if they ever came for her.

"How was your day?"

"Good." I kiss her again before hooking my arm around her waist and pulling her to me so we fall backward on the bed, our legs tangled. I kiss her again, my tongue sliding against hers until she breaks away to catch her breath, her hands on my shoulders.

"You never tell me what you do during the day," she protests.

"You don't care. Trust me," I murmur, kissing her again.

How can I tell her that I went with some of my father's men and we met with someone who hasn't repaid a loan we extended him six months ago? That I had to threaten him and then watch while they roughed him up some? That sounds like some criminal shit because guess what?

It *is* criminal, what we're doing. We bribe and steal and smuggle—that's our business. My father is always up to no good, and I've already fallen directly into his footsteps. Like I'm the fallen angel in this situation, giving in to my father's demands only because we're bound by blood.

Deep down though, there's a part of me that...likes what I do. Working with my father, handling all of the accounting for the business, amongst other things. I'm the chief financial officer of one of the biggest smuggling operations in the city, not that I can show the title off.

I also hate what I do, specifically in this moment. What will Sylvie think when she finds out everything? Will she hate me? Think less of me? Push me away? Will she believe me when I say that I tried, but I can't fight it? That I was born to do this?

I can't escape my life. The only way I could leave is if I fled to another country and changed my identity. And I can't do that to my dad.

He needs me.

"But I do care." She shoves at my chest, making me pull away from her. "I don't want any secrets between us."

"It's not a secret, what I do." Shame washes over me at the thought of telling her, of watching her expression slowly but surely turn more and more horrified with every word I said.

No. I can't risk it.

"It is to me." She dodges my seeking lips, her hands curling into the fabric of my T-shirt and giving me a gentle shake. "Tell me."

An aggravated sigh leaves me and I deposit her onto the bed, rising to my feet. "No."

I march out of the bedroom, headed for the kitchen, feeling like a complete shit. Damn it, I'm not proud of what I do for my father. I knew this moment was coming, that Sylvie would want to know, but I don't want to tell her.

Not now. Not when I'm her hero. Once she finds out the truth, she won't look at me the same.

I know I don't look at me the same, that's for damn sure.

I'm pouring myself a glass of whiskey when she enters the kitchen, bringing her fury with her. Her face is flushed and her eyes are wild, her entire body practically vibrating with anger.

"You can't walk away from me like that," she admonishes, her tone haughty.

"I just did." I take a gulp of the whiskey, finishing it off in two swallows before I pour myself another. "Want a drink?"

"Only if I can throw it in your face," she retorts.

"No whiskey for you then." I sip from my second pour, taking it slow so I don't get drunk too fast and say something I might regret.

Too late, I think.

She scoffs, positively scandalized. "Sometimes you're so sweet, like the Spence I used to know, and then you turn into a complete dick, like how you're acting right now."

"I'm just...protecting you."

Sylvie rolls her eyes, reaching out to grip the edge of the counter. "From who? You?"

I swallow thickly, shoving the glass across the counter. "Sometimes I do...not so nice things in the name of my father's business."

"Like what? Off someone? Are you in the mob or what?"

I say nothing, just stare at her, and the longer the silence grows, the wider her eyes get.

"You're full of shit," she whispers.

I grab the glass, taking another big gulp, still remaining silent.

"Spencer. Tell me the truth." Her voice rises, giving me serious mom vibes, which is a vibe I've never gotten from Syl before. "Are you in. The. Mob?"

"My father kind of is." Fuck. I can't come straight out and say it.

"Which makes you what...a member by default?"

"I help him out. Sometimes helping him out involves violence. If you're a Donato, it comes with the territory." I shrug, not wanting to give her too many details.

She's gaping at me, seemingly at a loss for words, and I almost want to laugh, though the moment isn't funny. Not even close. "I always thought the mob talk surrounding your family was nothing but rumors."

"Rumors are usually based on truth, you know." I grab an empty glass and pour some whiskey into it before pushing the glass toward her, but she doesn't pick it up. "Look, Syl. I've done some things I'm not proud of."

"Me too," she admits, her voice soft. "But I always thought you'd be truthful with *me*, Spencer. This feels like you've been living a lie."

I stare at her, her words like arrows piercing my heart, one after the other. "I was trying to protect you."

Another scoff. "Please."

I decide to be one hundred percent real with her. "I didn't want you thinking less of me."

"Come on, Spencer. Don't you know me well enough by now? That I would never think less of you, no matter what you do?"

"You still surprise me on occasion," I admit, reaching for her, but she steps away before I can get my hands on her.

"I'm disappointed in you." She grabs the glass and tosses back the alcohol in one long swallow, and fuck, if that wasn't sexy as hell.

"How can I make it up to you?" My tone is dark. Suggestive. I'd rather fuck than talk.

She settles the glass onto the countertop with a loud clank, then runs her hand over the smooth marble. "Did you ever think of me on this counter? Remember what we did?"

My skin tightens. "I remember every second of that night."

"I was drunk and high, showing up like I did only wearing a trench coat."

"Hot as fuck in just the coat and nothing else," I murmur.

Her eyes lift, meeting mine. "I was scared I would never see you again. I took a chance, coming here in the middle of the night. It could've ended ugly, you know."

"I would've never turned you away."

"Exactly, and I would never turn you away, no matter what you've done. I need you to be real with me, Spencer. Truthful. Always. We can't have secrets between us anymore. Secrets destroy a relationship. A marriage. Secrets destroy everything, and I've dealt with enough over the years." Her gaze is pleading. "Please don't keep any more secrets from me. I don't know if I can take it."

I round the counter and go to her, yanking her into my arms

and holding her close. "I'm sorry," I murmur into her hair, closing my eyes and saying a silent prayer of thanks when she doesn't pull away. "I didn't mean to hurt you."

I still don't want to talk about it, but I know that I'll have to, eventually. It's just the way of the world, the way of our world. Our relationship.

Keeping secrets never work. They grow and fester, eventually tainting everything they touch. And I can't taint what Sylvie and I have, now that we're together.

"Does Whit know?" she asks.

"He knows some things, but not all of them."

"So even my brother knows this about you, but I don't." She tries to pull away from me, but I tighten my hold.

"That's not fair. He's my best friend. He figured it out on his own, I never told him about it." I pause, stroking her hair. "Besides, we haven't been in actual contact with each other for a couple of years. I'm not going to lead with that information."

Sylvie giggles, her mood switching quick as lightning, as usual. "Why not? Could've made the conversation between us extra stimulating."

"We can do other, extra stimulating things," I tease, trying to keep the moment light.

It's easier than facing my truth and sharing it with the woman I love.

She tilts her head back, and I can see the battle in her gaze. She wants to be mad at me, but can't be. I know exactly what that feels like. "Promise me you'll never hurt me."

I frown, shocked by her demand. "Of course, I'll never hurt you."

"Promise me," she insists. "Say it out loud."

"I'll never hurt you. I promise." I lean in, giving her a quick kiss. "You know I'm only keeping this from you to protect you."

"Oh please. Spare me." She pats my chest. "You're going to have to tell me everything soon. I mean it, Spencer."

"I will." I don't ever want to admit to her what I do. It's hard for me to admit to myself what I come from.

"Good." Her smile is wide. "Your punishment is that you have to come to my party, whether you want to or not."

Like that's a hardship. "You're really set on having this party, huh?"

"Absolutely. Just a few friends and relatives, like I said earlier. We'll have it here on a Saturday afternoon. A little tea party perhaps? All the ladies can wear pink."

"Whatever you want." I will indulge this woman's every whim, just to ensure she's happy. That she'll never leave me.

I've done things that could make her leave. I will continue to do them too. I can't stop. Besides...

My father won't let me.

CHAPTER TWENTY-THREE

SYLVIE

I glide into the restaurant with my head held high, ignoring the whispers that follow me as I walk past the crowded tables. It's lunchtime at one of the most popular eateries frequented by those I grew up with. Went to school with. Gossiped with and talked shit about, they're all here.

Well, not all of them but quite a few.

I spot a girl who I graduated with that's now a mom. Considering I'm currently on my period and not worried about that particular sans condom moment between Spence and me any longer, it's perfectly fine for me to feel a tug of longing as I walk past her, noting her abnormally large breasts. I'm guessing they're full of milk and the longing leaves me, just like that.

The idea of being a mom and having a greedy baby gnawing on my nipple does not appeal. I don't care if it's a little boy who looks just like his daddy.

Fuck that.

For now.

I light up the moment I see him sitting at the table, his gaze on his phone, his lips pursed in seeming disgust. I settle into the chair across from him, silent and sneaky, and he barely glances up, doing a double take when he sees it's me.

"Darling. You're positively radiant." Monty smiles, and I smile in return before I reach across the table and take his hand. "You're getting fucked on the regular, aren't you?"

I nod, quietly beaming as I squeeze his hand.

"And not by that decrepit old man either. Not that I ever believed you had a normal relationship with him." He studies me, and I swear I see the cogs turning in his head as he contemplates what he's going to say next. "I always heard he didn't like women."

Again, I say nothing. How can I respond to his very-close-to-the-truth allegation? "It's kind of difficult to get fucked by the dead."

Monty laughs. "Please. The dead fuck all of us on a constant basis. I could give a list of things my dead relatives have done to my family that have fucked us for eternity."

I release my grip on his hand, thinking of past Lancasters and what they've done to our family name. "You're so right."

"Forget our dead relatives. You need to tell me who your lucky man is. Or is it a woman? You know me, I don't judge. I'd love it if you joined our team." Monty sends me a shrewd look.

My smile is small. Devilish. "I'm with Spencer now."

"Donato? God, he's a gorgeous piece. Has a mysterious edge of danger to him that intrigues me." Monty sighs and shakes his head. "I bet he fucks like a beast."

"Monty," I admonish, though there's not much emotion in my voice. "So dirty."

"You like it." He glances around the crowded room before his gaze returns to me. "Where's Summer?"

"She should be here soon." Nerves bubble up, making it hard to speak. I'm both excited and worried to see her. I know she'll be fine, and so will I, but the guilt I still carry over the way I treated her so long ago is ever present, and taxing.

I'm the one who put this luncheon together in the first place. I know her and Monty are extremely close, and he's always been a good friend to me as well. Considering I've never had a large number of friends, I've always cherished him.

It seemed only right, to have lunch with the two of them. He could be a good mediator between Summer and me, if we needed one.

I send him a look. "I hear you and Cliff are getting cozy."

Monty turns immediately coy. "Oh, it's nothing."

"Not according to Clifford." I've been in constant contact with my friend since I returned to the city. He's sad I moved out of his building, but he's happy that I'm with Spencer.

He's your soulmate, he tells me.

I suppose he's right. It's been Spence and me since I was thirteen.

Monty drops the pretense. "Fine. He's a doll. So cute. Very attentive. Great kisser. Interesting conversationalist."

"Wow. Looks like he checks all of your boxes."

"I know. Praise be, a miracle has occurred." Monty's smile is wry. "I wouldn't call myself in love though."

"It hasn't been very long."

"A few months."

I blink at him. "Really? Already?"

Monty nods, reaching out to grab his drink, and takes a sip. "Time flies when you're having fun."

"Or when you're supposed to be in mourning," I add.

"Please. If jumping on Spencer Donato every chance you get is called mourning, then sign me up." Monty waves a dismissive hand. "Tell me how you two got back together."

"We ran into each other at Whit's wedding, and it sort of sprouted from there," I say truthfully.

"I hear he's got you holed up in that gorgeous apartment his father purchased with blood money and he won't let you out of his sight." Monty glances around the restaurant once again, a little more exaggerated this time. "Is he here? Spying on us? Making sure I don't try anything on you?"

I roll my eyes. "Stop. You're being silly. He lets me out of his sight."

Barely.

"If he keeps you naked in his bed, I'm sure you're not complaining."

"I'm not." I point at the drink he's still clutching. It's pink and frothy and looks delicious. "I want one of those, please."

"Whatever the princess requests, she gets. Oh waiter!" Monty raises his arm, snapping his fingers, and I make a sheesh face because oh my God, so rude.

The server comes running right over. He's young and gorgeous and staring at Monty with stars in his eyes. "Can I help you, sir?"

"Another one of these for me and one for the lady." He inclines his head toward me. "Should we order one for Summer?"

"She's pregnant," I remind him.

"Such a shame. Just two please." He bats his eyelashes at the waiter, who sends him a sexy smirk in return. "And hurry."

The moment the server is gone, I'm slapping Monty's arm. "You're naughty."

"He's cute. I can't miss my opportunity to flirt." Monty drains the last of his drink. "Just because I'm seeing Cliff doesn't mean I'm dead."

"True." My gaze catches on a dark-haired pregnant woman, making her way toward our table, and my heart leaps to my throat. "Summer's here."

"Gorgeous mama!" Monty exclaims, leaping to his feet and wrapping her up in a big hug. "God, it's so good to see you."

"Monty." Summer returns the hug with the same enthusiasm, tilting her head back as she clutches him close. "I've missed you."

I rise to my feet, afraid she might not hug me. Would she reject me? I'd deserve it. I know we're on better terms, but sometimes it feels like there's still a hint of animosity between us. "Hi, Summer."

She turns to me, her cheeks glowing, her smile large. Genuine. "Sylvie. You look…"

"Ravishing, right?" Monty adds.

"I was going to say beautiful, but ravishing is more appropriate." Summer hugs me and I squeeze her tight, closing my eyes, all the air escaping my lungs. This feels real. Almost too real, and tears threaten to spill. "I'm sorry we didn't get to talk much at the reception."

"It's okay." My smile is so big it hurts as it stretches my mouth, and I fall into my seat, watching as she settles in next to me.

"I'm so glad we could do lunch," Monty says, clapping his hands together.

Summer sends him a look, and he drops his hands in his lap. "You would suggest the most public location to meet."

"If we can't help spread the gossip that we make by choosing a very public spot to meet, then what's the point of lunch?" Monty lifts his brows. "Besides, you both agreed. It's just as much your fault as mine."

I shake my head, sharing a conspiratorial glance with Summer. "I didn't choose this place, that's for sure."

"Please, you used to put your business on the front page of every gossip site, just to get a rise out of your mama," Monty says drolly.

"I don't bother with her anymore." I wave a hand. "Our relationship is over."

"For real this time?" Summer asks quietly.

My gaze catches on hers, and I nod slowly. "I can't be alone with her. Ever again."

Monty glances from me to Summer, then back to me again. "I feel as if I'm missing something here."

"You're missing nothing. Sylvia Lancaster is a toxic human, that's all," Summer says firmly, and I'm grateful for her answer.

"Aren't most of the Lancasters?" Monty laughs when we both shoot him a dirty look. "I mean it with love! Our generation is much better than the previous one, my family included. Though you have to admit, all of those Lancaster brothers that came before us are a bunch of real pricks."

"Augustus isn't so bad," Summer counters.

I snort laugh. My father even has Summer in his sway.

"I hear Reginald is a nightmare." Monty mock shudders. "Mean to the very bone. Treats all of his children like shit."

"Especially my cousin Charlotte," I add.

"Well, she's fine now, married to that blond hunk Perry Constantine." Monty's eyes glitter. "He's gorgeous."

"You think every man is gorgeous," Summer says with a laugh.

"I can't help that the Lancasters have impeccable taste. Or impeccable looks. I do think the only uncle of yours that has any sense is George, Sylvie. His only fault is he can't keep his dick in his pants."

I burst out laughing. Uncle George has five children with a variety of women, so Monty's description is spot on.

We gossip about everything and nothing while sipping on our drinks, Summer sticking with berry-infused water. We order salads for lunch and listen to Summer talk about her honeymoon with my brother, leaving out all of the sexual bits despite Monty whining how he wants all the details.

"I do not want to hear her describe what my brother does to her in bed," I say.

"You don't have to! She can describe what he does to her against a wall. Or in the shower," Monty argues.

The very last thing I want to know.

"You're hopeless," I tell him.

"You love it," he counters.

When he excuses himself to use the bathroom after sucking down three alcoholic drinks in quick succession, Summer starts the real conversation.

"Tell me how you and Spencer got back together," she demands, her eyes dancing.

I explain the situation, being truthful with her, but not going into too much detail since Monty will return to the table at any second. When I'm done, she's watching me with a glow in her gaze and her lips curved upward.

"You two were always perfect for each other."

"Like you and my brother?"

"Not nearly as toxic, but yes." Summer waves a dismissive hand.

"I don't know. I've treated him terribly for years." I remember catching Whit referring to Summer as his whore once, and how appalled I was by that.

Then I recall how Spencer called me his whore at the house in California, and everything inside me goes warm and tingly.

"I think it's the way Lancasters show they care about someone," Summer admits, her voice soft. "You verbally abuse and push away those you love the most."

I think of my mother, and her sort of abuse. She didn't want to just push me away. She wanted me out of her life completely, which makes no sense when you think about it.

How was she going to get all of the attention my so-called illnesses got her if I was dead? Though she could play up the grieving mother part, that would've lasted her only so long...

"Whit told me he spoke with Spencer a few days ago, and that Spence seems the happiest he's ever seen him," Summer continues. "I'm sure that's because of you."

My heart feels as if it just expanded. "That's sweet."

"Are you happy with him? Truly?" She leans in closer, her assessing gaze snagging on mine. "I worry about you sometimes."

"What do you mean?" I ask with a frown.

"That you might be searching for something that's impossible to find." Her smile is regal, her gaze lifting, and I realize Monty is approaching the table. "You took forever."

"I had to piss for five minutes straight." Monty settles into his chair, dumping his napkin in his lap. "Did the server come back? I want to order another one."

"Please tell me you didn't drive here," I say.

"I don't *drive*. I have a *driver*," Monty stresses. "God, get it together, Sylvie. You know how I live. How you live."

"I envy the both of you being able to drink." Summer runs her hand over her swelling belly. "Little miss here won't let me do anything."

"A girl," I say with a sigh. "I love that. Do you have a name picked out yet?"

Summer slowly shakes her head, her gaze on her stomach and nowhere else. "Too many options. I can't make up my mind, and Whit is no help. He tells me it doesn't matter what we name her, as long as I'm happy with it."

"My brother actually said that?" I'm stunned. His favorite thing is getting his way.

"Well, yeah, after I let him come all over my face." Summer slaps her hand over her mouth, her eyes wide with shock as I gape at her. "God, I'm so sorry, Sylvie! I should've never said that out loud!"

Monty is laughing uproariously, clutching his stomach. I'm afraid he's going to roll onto the floor if he doesn't watch it.

"Nice visual," I say with a grimace. "I hate that you just said that."

"This is the best conversation, ever," Monty gasps between laughs.

"I hate you both," I tell them. "Now I'm tempted to talk about my sex life and freak you both out."

"Do tell." Monty sits up straight, all laughter gone as he props his chin on top of his fist, studying me. Summer mocks his position, the two of them focused on me. "Does he have a big cock?"

My cheeks go hot. "I am not sharing that."

Monty turns to Summer. "He does." He refocuses on me. "And does he know how to use it?"

"Very well," I say without hesitation, giving my audience what they want. "He's talented with his fingers and mouth too."

"Dreamy." Monty sighs. "You're a lucky girl, Sylvie."

"I know. I think we're all pretty lucky." Summer and Monty nod their agreement. They're happy. Carefree. I'm happy too.

So why is there a constant feeling of dread coursing through me? As if everything's going to collapse into ruin at any second?

"I'm having a little get-together," I announce, my gaze landing on them both. They perk up at my words. "Something small. Intimate. Two weeks from now, on a Saturday afternoon."

"Sounds fun," Summer says.

"Tell me there's a theme," Monty adds.

"There is. A tea party."

"High tea? Oh, that sounds glorious. I'll wear a special suit and a hat, and I'll also be as pretentious as fuck."

"You're coming as yourself then," Summer observes, the two of us laughing when he gives us the finger.

"Jealous girls. You wish you were as cultured as me." He looks down his nose at us, his gaze snagging on me. "You're perhaps even more cultured than I am."

"I probably am." I shrug. All that good breeding has to amount to something.

"Guess I'll just have to step it up a notch." He contemplates me. "Who else is coming to high tea?"

"I'm inviting other Lancasters. A few cousins. My sister. My father and his flavor of the month. You and Whit, of course."

"Of course." Summer nods.

"A few friends," I add. "Only the very closest ones."

"Meaning everyone else will be dying for an invite. My favorite kind of party." Monty rubs his hands together.

"Spencer will be there?" Summer asks.

"Definitely."

"What about your mother? I do love a catty Sylvia. She always brings a certain *je ne sais quoi* to every occasion she's at," Monty says.

I stiffen at the casual use of my mother's name. "She definitely won't be there."

"Such a shame." Monty waves a hand. "We'll have fun without her."

Summer and I share a look. She doesn't even know half of what my mother did to me, yet she understands. I've never shared with Monty any of those things. He only knows about the usual complaints—how controlling she is. Rude. A complete snob. All traits he finds admirable.

Would he find her attempted-murderer status admirable?

I'm hoping not.

By the time our lunch date is over, it's well past three o'clock. Monty is three sheets to the wind, and Summer is ready for a nap.

And I'm eager to return home and prepare for my boyfriend's arrival from work. Work he won't really discuss with me, which only makes it all the more intriguing. My secretive Spencer. I can't judge, though.

I'm just as secretive. Though not so much anymore. I opened up to him, and I'm hoping as time goes by, I can get him to open up to me.

Maybe.

CHAPTER TWENTY-FOUR

SYLVIE

THE PAST

I'm lying in my bed, Spence next to me. He's long and lanky and so incredibly warm. Despite the furnace-like heat radiating from him, I'm shivering, yanking the covers up to my chin to ward off the chill, but it's no use.

I'm cold to the very bone.

"Hey." He slings an arm around me, his sleepy voice lighting me up inside. "You're shaking."

"C-cold," I admit, snuggling closer to him.

Late at night, he comes to my room at Lancaster Prep, and we lie in bed and hold each other and talk. In between all the kissing, that is. Can't forget the kissing.

He's trying to get it to progress further and there's a part of me that wants that. That wants him.

And then there's that other part of me that's terrified to take it beyond kissing. To do so means we're getting closer, and when you get closer to someone, you shouldn't have any secrets.

I have a ton of them. Every one of them would have him running away from me. And I wouldn't blame him.

That's why I keep my secrets to myself. And why I won't let

him take what we have any further. It's scary.

He scares me.

No, my feelings for Spencer scare me. I have never cared for someone beyond family members, and most of the time, I can barely tolerate them.

"Part of your problem is you're so skinny," he admonishes, making me feel terrible. "You're not eating, are you?"

I cling to him, my eyes sliding closed when he wraps me up in his arms. "I'm never hungry."

"Have you told the doctor this?" He knows all about my doctor visits with my mother. Though I don't think he realizes just how many times I go, or how many I see.

"Yes," I lie, my voice muffled against the solid wall of his chest. Every part of Spencer is solid. Real. Grounding. There is no one else who makes me feel safe. Not a single person in this world but Spence.

"I'm worried about you." He runs his fingers through my hair, and I note the concern in his voice. He cares. Probably too much.

It doesn't matter. I'll take whatever bit of concern and feeling he has for me and savor it always. I'm not sure how much longer I'll be in this world, and I'm afraid these moments are drying up. Soon I'll be gone.

And Spencer will move on.

The idea is too painful to contemplate, so I shove it from my mind.

"Can I admit something to you?" I ask him, my voice hushed in the quiet stillness of the room.

He rolls us both over so we're lying on our sides, facing each other. "Tell me."

I take a deep breath, wishing I could spill all of my real secrets.

My mother hates me.

Controls me.

Pretty sure she's trying to kill me.

Instead, I say something else. Something inane and expected of the flighty, reckless Sylvie Lancaster.

"When I get married, I want to wear a red dress."

I can feel him smile. That's my favorite thing about Spence. When he's happy, he lets the whole world know it. He doesn't hide his emotions like I do.

"I don't think your mother will approve."

"That's the point." I lift my head, so I can look into his dark eyes. "I'd wear red to make her angry."

"How about black?" He lifts a brow.

I shake my head. "She'd expect that. She'd probably even pretend to like it. Red though? She'd hate it. It's one of her least favorite colors."

"I never see you wear red."

"Because of my mother."

"She controls what you wear?"

She controls every single aspect of my life.

I don't say that.

"I stumbled upon a photo one day on the internet. This beautiful blonde woman sitting on a chair surrounded by a group of debonair men all in morning dress. Proper coats and top hats and silver cravats. She was wearing a gorgeous, vivid red dress with a matching red veil. Clutching red roses and green ivy. Red roses in her hair. God, it was stunning." I clamp my lips together to shut myself up. I'm rambling. And he doesn't care. Not about stuff like this.

Especially wedding stuff. He's sixteen. I'm fifteen. We are never getting married. I don't even think I'll make it to twenty.

"Who was the woman?" he asks after I remain quiet for at least a minute. "Getting married?"

"Some British woman who married a pop star in the mid-eighties. It doesn't really matter who it was, it's just—that dress. Someday, I'm going to get married, and I'm going to wear a replica of that gown," I say fiercely.

"Even if your mother hates it?"

"Especially if she hates it."

His fingers slip beneath my chin, tilting my face up so his mouth can settle on mine. The kiss steals my breath. Not because of its intensity, though that is unmistakably delicious.

There's emotion there. A depth I don't think I've ever felt before. The kiss is like a branding. An imprint on my soul. Dramatic and perfect and sweet and wonderful.

I could die happily after a kiss like this.

Spencer pulls away first, slowly. Almost reluctantly. He touches the corner of my mouth, his thumb a gentle brush against my skin, and I open my eyes to find him watching me, his dark gaze burning.

We're young. I know we are, but I feel so much when he looks at me like that. As if I'm his everything.

"If we were to get married, I'd want you to wear a red dress."

I laugh, needing to break the seriousness of the conversation. "We're not going to get married."

He's quiet.

"I'll be dead before I graduate."

His thumb presses against the seam of my lips, effectively shutting me up. "Stop saying shit like that. You're not dying, Syl."

"Believe what you want." I know the truth, is what I want to add, but I don't.

"We're all dying, but that's a long way out. You're only fifteen."

"And here you are, lying in bed with me, trying to feel me up." I'm teasing, desperate to change the direction of our conversation.

His mouth lifts in a crooked smile. "You like it."

"Too much," I readily agree, leaning into him, my mouth on his, but he presses his hand on my shoulder, stopping me.

"Just—don't talk about the dying stuff all the time. Freaks me out," he says, his voice soft.

I stare at him, hating that he wants to take that away from me. It's the only thing that gets me through it. Making light of my situation. It's either I joke about it or drown in my worries every time I'm alone, which is far too often.

"You're not dying," he continues, repeating himself. "I know you're not. The doctors will figure out what's wrong with you and they'll fix the problem. Your mom is trying her best."

I want to laugh. Trying her best, indeed.

To kill me.

There's no more laughing or arguing or protesting. Instead, I kiss him, drowning in his taste, the stroke of his tongue, the sensation of his hands sliding up and down my body. I lose myself in him, knowing that I'll find myself soon enough.

And I'll be miserable all over again.

CHAPTER TWENTY-FIVE

SPENCER

"T his is very…" I glance around at the terrace off my apartment, at a loss of words to describe how completely Sylvie transformed the space.

"Feminine? Elegant?" Sylvie supplies hopefully.

"Pink," I say lamely, earning an eye roll from my…

Girlfriend? Is that what I should call Sylvie? That feels too informal, too simple. She's not just my girlfriend. She's the woman I love. The woman I want to protect from everyone else in the world, though she's not as hopeless as she used to be when she was a teenager.

Though was she ever hopeless? Or was all of that an act?

"Pink and beautiful." She scans the terrace, her eyes lighting up with pleasure. There's a long table in the center of the space, set to perfection with delicate floral plates and matching teacups and saucers. Lush flowers and greenery line the center of the table, and each plate is covered with a strip of pink velvet ribbon engraved with a guest's name. There's another table off to the side, laden with a variety of desserts too beautiful to eat, and there's a makeshift bar set close to the balcony, two men standing behind it as they catalogue what liquor they've brought.

"I thought this was a tea party," I say as my gaze settles on the bar.

"With alcohol, of course." She sends me a look. "Monty wouldn't come unless I promised there would be liquor."

"Is that a smart idea?" I lift my brows.

"It's a small party. Hardly anyone is invited. I don't want trouble. Just my friends and the family that I love. No one else."

"Is your father coming?"

Sylvie nods, her blue eyes wide. "I couldn't not invite him."

"You didn't invite your mother," I point out.

"Don't need another attempted murder to ruin the vibe." Her smile is light and carefree, but her eyes turn dark. Turbulent.

"As long as your father won't be a problem." I take her hand, holding it up so I can study what she's wearing. The dress is long and floral printed, reminding me of the dress she wore to Whit's wedding. Though this one is lighter. Airier. It nips in at the waist, making her look so small. Waifish. Her hair is up, revealing her elegant neck, and she's wearing a simple gold chain around it, with no other jewelry. Her lips are slicked with a light pink that matches the tone of her dress, her skin glowing with health. The sun bathes her in golden light, her gilded cheeks sharp. A Lancaster through and through.

She's beautiful. Regal. And all mine. I'm filled with the sudden urge to fall to one knee and ask her to marry me. I don't have a ring. I don't have anything to offer her but myself and my love. And my name. I don't want her to be a Lancaster any longer.

I want her to be a Donato. Like me.

More than that, I want her to belong to me. So I can tell the world that this beautiful woman is all mine.

"He won't be a problem," she says, her sweet voice confusing me for a moment.

Oh, right. She's talking about her father.

"He doesn't want anything to do with her, just like me," she continues as she glides about the terrace, stopping at the outdoor couch and fluffing the already-fluffed pillows. "Do you think it looks good out here?"

I go to her. "It looks beautiful." Slipping my arms around her waist, I pull her into me, pressing my mouth to hers briefly. "Almost as beautiful as you."

Her cheeks turn the faintest pink and she gently shoves me away. "Flattery will get you everywhere."

"I only speak the truth."

Her gaze snags on me and we stare at each other for a long, heavy moment, emotions swirling between us. "I feel like this is some sort of coming out."

"For you? You never did go the debutante route."

She slowly shakes her head. "I was a disaster waiting to explode. No way would my mother allow me to debut."

Her expression is pained, and I know it's because she mentioned her mother. I hate how that woman pops up in conversation all the time.

Sylvie has no clue, but I've had an extensive background check done on Sylvia Lancaster, and most of what I've discovered only makes me hate the woman even more. She's a nightmare. No wonder Augustus had multiple affairs. Yes, he's a philanderer, but he was only trying to escape Sylvia's clutches.

It's like everyone in her immediate family did exactly that. Whit defied her every chance he got. Carolina ran away at an early age. Only Sylvie stuck around, and I think that's because she believed she had no other choice.

"The party starts in what…in thirty minutes?" I ask, whipping my phone out of my pants pocket. "Make that twenty."

"Oh God." She starts rushing around, her movements frantic. "I need to go talk to the caterers."

She dashes into the apartment before I have a chance to say anything, headed for the kitchen. I follow after her, answering the door when I hear a knock, to find Whit and Summer standing in front of me, Summer wearing a pink dress similar to Sylvie's.

"Is there a dress code?" I ask as they enter the apartment.

"She asked that we wear pink." Summer points at her husband. "He didn't follow orders."

"I never do. Where's the fun in that?" He undoes the button of his jacket, revealing his pristine white shirt beneath. "Where's your suit?"

I'm in a polo shirt and jeans. "I was helping set up."

Whit's gaze is sharp. "You better change then."

"And we're wearing suits on a Saturday because why?" I shake my head, though I'm definitely going to indulge my woman. If she wants us clad in suits and the ladies in dresses, then that's what she'll get.

"Because it's fun!" Summer calls after me as I head for the bedroom, and I can hear Whit mutter something rude.

By the time I've changed into the proper attire fit for a tea party/luncheon, more people have arrived. The terrace is full, and I spot Monty standing at the bar, wearing a pink velvet suit, that tall guy who was Sylvie's date at Whit and Summer's wedding standing beside him.

I head outside and straight for Monty and Cliff, nodding and smiling at people as I pass by them, noting how Sylvie is the queen holding court, sitting in a chair and clutching a delicate umbrella to ward off the warm sun.

"Spencer Donato, aren't you a delight?"

I let my gaze wander along the length of Monty and all of that pink velvet. "And aren't you a sight."

He grabs his fresh drink from the bartender, curling his arm through Cliff's. "Have you met my date?"

"Not properly." I thrust my hand in Cliff's direction. "Spencer Donato. Nice to meet you."

"Cliff Von Worth." He shakes my hand, Monty smirking throughout the entire interaction. "Our last run-in wasn't... pleasant."

"Do tell," Monty encourages.

"I thought he was with Sylvie." I release Cliff's hand,

embarrassed at admitting my assumption.

"That's hilarious," Monty deadpans. "Sylvie isn't his type."

"I know that now. Are you two an item?" I send them each a questioning look.

"Sort of," Monty says at the same time that Cliff answers, "Yes."

We chat for a few more minutes, the tension ratcheting between them until I excuse myself and allow them some privacy to have a lovers' spat.

The drama never stops. Glad I'm not involved in it this time.

I stop and talk to Crew Lancaster and his fiancée Wren. He's a few years younger than us, and one of the more decent Lancasters out there. His fiancée is beautiful. Dark hair and green eyes, she can't stop sending adoring glances in Crew's direction.

"My two favorites!" Sylvie exclaims, appearing by my side before she pulls them each into a hug. "Where's your sister?"

"Out of the country with her husband," Crew answers, slinging his arm around Wren's shoulder. She too, is wearing a pretty pink dress, though hers isn't a floral print. It's a pink and white check with a deep V neckline.

"You know my boyfriend?" Sylvie leans against me, her smile so bright it's almost blinding. "I had no idea you two were acquainted."

"Boyfriend, huh?" Crew's brows shoot up. "Good to see you so happy, Sylvie."

"Thank you," she says her voice turning shy. "For once, right?"

Augustus Lancaster chooses that moment to arrive and it's like his presence sucks all of the oxygen out of the air, drawing all of the attention toward him. Not necessarily a bad thing, as the man definitely knows how to command a room. He expects all eyes on him at all times.

Soon, there's a crowd surrounding him, Sylvie standing right at his side, her gaze admiring as he tells a tall tale. Carolina is on his other side, seemingly bored. I stand off to the side with Whit and Crew, the three of us watching the women flutter around Augustus, a sneer on both Whit and Crew's faces.

"Annoyed?" I ask my best friend.

Whit lets forth an aggravated sigh. "He always does this. He revels in female attention."

"Every Lancaster seems to," Crew adds.

"True," Whit agrees. "Even my sisters are into it. Well, Carolina looks like she wants to take a nap."

"I only like one female in particular," Crew says, his gaze zeroing in on Wren, his lips parting.

Do I look like that when I'm staring at Sylvie? Like a love-starved fool?

God, I hope not.

I probably do though. I feel that way when I catch myself staring at her for too long. Like she's the only thing that matters to me—and she is. She's a distraction, one I didn't think was worth the heartache at one point, but now I can admit…

I don't know how I'll live without her if she ever chooses to leave me. Because trust that I'm going nowhere. That woman is a part of me, and I can't give up on her. Not now. Not ever.

After Augustus has regaled everyone with one entertaining story after another, it's time to eat. We all settle in at the extra-long table, me sitting to the right of Sylvie, Whit directly across from me. The lunch is delicious and the alcohol is flowing. My gaze keeps finding Sylvie, entranced by how happy she seems as she laughs about something with Carolina. My girl is completely in her element, laughing and talking nonstop.

I don't think I've ever seen her look so…alive. So beautiful and sparkling and effervescent. She was close to this when I went after her in California. When she was alone and finding herself. Coming into herself.

Her gaze catches mine at one point and she leans in, her voice low when she murmurs, "Is everything okay?"

"Everything is perfect," I answer without hesitation, pressing a quick kiss to her cheek. "I think your tea party is a raging success."

She looks pleased as she slowly pulls away. "Thank you. I think everyone is having a nice time."

"And you're beautiful." I kiss her again because I can, right on the lips, and her cheeks flush with pleasure.

"Thank you for letting me have the party here," she murmurs.

"I will give you whatever you want." I touch her cheek, streaking my fingers across her soft skin." All you have to do is ask."

Sylvie stares at me, the party happening all around us. Conversations and laughter and carrying on, but we're lost in our own little world for a moment, studying each other. I don't let my gaze stray because I want her to know how serious I am. I mean what I say.

I will give her whatever she wants, whenever she wants it.

"Spencer," she whispers, swallowing hard, "I lo—"

"Well, well, would you look at this!" a familiar voice screeches from the door that opens out onto the terrace.

We both turn to find Sylvia Lancaster standing there, clad in a bright pink suit, her gaze zeroed in on Sylvie and sparking with barely contained fury.

Dread and anger fill me and I rise to my feet, my hands clutched into fists at my sides.

"What are you doing here?" I ask, my voice deadly calm.

Sylvia barely pays any attention to me. "Coming to see my family. I think I have every right to be here."

"Now the party has really started," I hear Monty say drolly, and I glance over my shoulder, sending him a ferocious glare.

He blinks, leaning back in his chair, his lips snapping shut.

If he invited Sylvia, there will be hell to pay.

I guarantee it.

CHAPTER TWENTY-SIX

SYLVIE

My heart pumps furiously when I see my mother standing on the terrace as if she belongs here, wearing one of her beautiful pink tweed Chanel suits. It's warm outside and I'm sweating, yet there's not even a sheen to my mother's face. Her makeup is perfection, her hair coiffed into the standard Sylvia Lancaster style. That severe blonde bob that looks like a weapon when she swings her head. Sharp and cutting.

Much like the words she says.

I glance around the table, the shocked expressions on my friends' and families' faces, and I wonder which one of them betrayed me.

My heart cracks at the realization.

Mother walks out onto the terrace, stopping one of the servers with a gentle hand on his arm. "Can you set an extra place at the table for me, young man?"

"Of course." He dutifully nods and heads into the house, closing the door behind him.

Only moments ago, we were talking. Laughing. Now it's dead silent, everyone sending secret looks to each other, the air growing more and more uncomfortable the longer nothing is said.

Straightening my spine, I march over to my mother, curling

my fingers around her elbow and steering her toward the door. "Let's talk inside."

Before she can say anything, I drag her into the apartment, shutting the door behind us. My gaze catches on Spencer, who's watching us both, his expression impassive, though I see heat in his gaze. Anger.

That man will burst in here and save me if he has to. All I need to do is give the signal.

"Why are you here?" I ask, letting her arm go immediately. I don't want any connection with her. I can't even believe she showed her face at Spencer's apartment. Somewhere she wasn't invited. Talk about rude. This goes against all of those decorum lectures she used to give us as children.

She huffs, tugging on the hem of her jacket, straightening it. "My entire family is here, yet somehow my invitation was lost in the mail."

I decide to be truthful. "You weren't invited."

Her lips part, a soft exhale escaping her. "It has always been the Lancaster way for all of us to be present at family events. Holidays. Your father and I made sure that happened once the divorce proceedings started. We may not want to be together any longer, but we still want to be a family."

"I don't want to be a family with you," I tell her. She noticeably flinches, and there's a part of me deep inside that feels terrible for saying such a thing, but she needs to hear the truth. And it has to come from me. "Not after everything you've put me through."

"Darling, that should be all the reason for us to become closer." She takes a step forward, and it's my turn to flinch. "We have been through so much together, and look at us. We came out of it alive. Thriving."

"No thanks to you," I retort, glancing over at the server who walks past us, a new table setting clutched in his hands. "Don't bother," I tell him. "She's not going to eat."

He stops, his gaze sliding between me and my mother. "Uh…"

"Set it," Mother says firmly. "I'm staying."

"You're not," I return. "You need to go."

"Sylvie! You're being ridiculous. I'm staying," she stresses. "Go set the table."

Mother waves a dismissive hand at the guy and he takes off, most likely freaked out by our power struggle.

I can't blame him. I'm freaked out too. I'm shaking, and my stomach roils, threatening to send back up the lovely lunch I just ate.

Taking a deep, fortifying breath, I turn to my mother once again, hating the triumphant expression on her face. She believes she's got me cornered. That I'll give in to her like I always do.

"You can't just show up to places you're not invited. You know better than that." God, I sound just like her, but it's the truth. "We don't have a relationship anymore, Mother. I don't want to be around you."

She blinks at me, shock in her gaze. On her face. "Why in the world not?"

Is she that oblivious? That delusional?

I glance around before I speak, lowering my voice. "Because you hurt me."

She rests a hand on her chest, scandalized. "I did nothing of the sort. I would never hurt you. You're my child! Your health issues were brought on by...hysteria. Thankfully, you weren't as sick as we thought you were. Was I a little overprotective in my quest to heal you? Probably, but I don't see how anyone can fault me for wanting my child to be well."

Yes. She's completely delusional. It's clear.

"The last time we were together, I woke up to you holding a pillow over my head," I remind her, my voice turning into a whisper. "You were trying to smother me."

"Not at all. I was checking on you because I knew how distraught you were, and I brought a pillow with me for your comfort," she says, changing the narrative. "You were going through such a tough time after Earl passed. I was trying to be there for you."

"Please. For whatever reason, you were trying to *end* me. You've always tried to end me, ever since I was a little girl. At the very least, you tried to control me. Smothering me with your constant attention, when all I wanted was for someone else to notice me, especially my father. Anyone, really."

Her expression is somber. "It's amazing, how similar we are."

I flinch at her words. I hate hearing her say that. "We're *nothing* alike. For one, I don't try to destroy the people I love."

"Oh darling." She makes a tsking noise. "Look at what you've done to Spencer over the years."

Rage floods me, making my head feel like it's going to pop off. "Keep his name out of your mouth."

A sigh leaves her and she slowly shakes her head. "Why do you always say the worst things about me, when I only wanted the best for you? You were a sickly child. Don't you remember?"

"Only because you made me sick. There was nothing wrong with me. It all came out of nowhere. The sudden visits to the emergency room in the middle of the night. The endless consultations and tests. I remember thinking you enjoyed telling the doctors what was wrong with me, and how you fought for my well-being like you were some sort of saint. You always said you were my greatest advocate."

Her chest seems to puff out with pride.

"But you were more like my greatest detriment," I add.

She deflates like a balloon at my words.

"I can't be around you," I tell her, my voice small. I'm sad. I don't know how many times I have to say this to her. When will she finally get it? "If you keep coming around uninvited, I'll have to file a restraining order against you."

"You would never," she breathes.

"I would." I nod, glancing over my shoulder to find Spencer still watching us on the other side of the window. The moment our gazes connect, he's marching toward the door. Walking inside the apartment until he's standing right beside me.

"Is everything okay here?" he asks, his voice firm, his gaze on my mother.

"This is private family business," Mother starts, but I cut her off.

"I want him here. I consider him a part of my family."

She presses her lips together, contemplating the two of us, her upper lip lifting in a slight sneer. "It's like that now, hmm? You two are together?"

Spencer slips his arm around my shoulders, and I almost want to faint in relief at his nearness. "We are," he says.

Her gaze is filled with fury when it settles on me. "Did your father put you up to this?"

"Why would he have anything to do with my relationship with Spencer?" I'm incredulous.

"He knows how I feel about the Donato boy." She speaks of Spencer as if he's not even standing in front of her. "I never approved of the two of you spending time together. I didn't like how close your brother got to him either."

"I'd watch what you say if I were you," he says, his tone clipped. "You're standing in my house."

"Paid for with mob money." Mother turns her wrath on Spence. "Your father is a criminal. I assume you're one too."

"Get out," Spencer says between clenched teeth, his nostrils flaring. "Leave my house now before I have you escorted out."

"By some of your goons? How charming." Mother lifts her chin, returning her attention to me. "When you finally have enough of his criminal lifestyle, I'm sure you'll come crying back to me, begging me to take you in, though I won't. You need to learn a lesson. The only one who's ever been there for you is me. Not your father. Not your brother or your sister. And certainly not this man, who probably busts kneecaps for a living. Me. I'm the only one who truly loves you."

I stare at her, visibly shaking. Thank God Spence still has his arm around my shoulders, stabilizing me. "Shut up," I whisper.

My words only seem to egg her on and make her talk even more.

"You can't go it alone, Sylvie. You've never been able to. You need someone to guide you. To take care of you. You're a pathetic little creature who can't stand on her own two feet, and I want to help you. I really do. But it's so terribly hard to help those who can't help themselves." With a little sigh, she shakes her head and turns, heading for the door. "I don't need to be escorted out. I hope you come to your senses soon, Sylvie. Before it's too late."

The door closes seconds later and my entire body seems to turn into liquid as I lean into Spencer. He steers me out of the living room until we're in his bedroom, the door closed behind us, me crying into Spencer's shirt. He holds me close, running his hand up and down my back in a soothing gesture, murmuring comforting words I can barely hear.

I hate that she said all of those cruel things. Worse?

I hate that I believe what she said.

Maybe I can't go it alone. I am a pathetic creature who needs guidance. Help. She made me that way. She raised me to not believe in myself. To think she's the only one who can actually take care of me, and I hate her for that.

I hate her so much.

"We figured out how she knew about your party," Spencer says at one point in the midst of my crying.

I pull away from him, so I can look at his face. "How?"

I brace myself, waiting to hear who betrayed me by telling my mother about this.

"Social media. Cliff posted a story on IG and tagged you. Your father did too." Spencer winces. "He feels terrible about it. They both do."

"How did she know that the party was being hosted by us?" I wipe at the corner of my eyes, trying to catch a few stray tears.

"Cliff tagged you and noted his location. In your father's video he posted, you can see all of us in the background. You and me. Carolina. Whit and Summer."

I press my forehead against his chest, closing my eyes. "She's been stalking me on social media, I assume."

"Stalking everyone it looks like," he agrees, just as he slips his fingers beneath my chin and tilts my face up. "No one told her about the party. She just made her own assumptions."

"I worried someone said something," I admit. "I thought maybe Monty would want to create a little chaos, not knowing how bad it really is between my mother and me."

"He did nothing, though he did admit he got a little excited when your mother first appeared. He didn't realize your relationship with your mother was basically destroyed. No one told him the real reason either," Spencer reassures.

"I don't want it getting out. The gossip will be unbearable."

His jaw firms, and I can tell he's clenching his teeth. "Why are you protecting her? She tried to *kill* you, Sylvie. You said so yourself."

"Based on my own assumptions. I don't know it as fact," I say.

"Don't fall for her lies. She's trying to convince you that your assumptions are wrong, when they're not. You should try to see some of those doctors she used to take you to. Look at your medical files. You have every right to request to see your medical records from when you were a kid."

"I visited so many doctors and specialists, and went to so many clinics. All over the state, the country. We even went to a few places internationally. Not a single one of them knew what was wrong with me. I'm sure my records are filled with an endless list of symptoms and no solutions."

"Don't give up on yourself." He grips me by my shoulders, giving me a gentle shake. "You deserve to know what she did to you."

"Her evil deeds aren't documented, Spence. My mother isn't

stupid." I hang my head, staring at my sandal-clad feet. They're a nude color and strappy, and my toenails are painted the same shade of pink as my dress. I put so much planning and thought into this afternoon, and it's all been ruined by my mother's appearance.

If I'm not doing the ruining, she is.

"Maybe you should file a restraining order against her," Spencer says quietly.

I lift my head. "That's just so...final."

"You need to do something. She's a threat to you, Syl. It's like she gets off on making you uncomfortable. She knows she rattles you." He snaps his lips shut, exhaling through his nostrils. Oh, he looks angry on my behalf, and a part of me loves that. "I hate that she spooks you so badly."

"It's more than spooking me," I admit. "She...terrifies me. Even when we're with a bunch of people. Even when we're in the middle of a wedding with hundreds of guests. I never know what she's going to do or say to devastate me. And that's just with her words. The fact that she's a physical threat to me is...horrifying. She wants to hurt me, Spence"

The last words come out of me in a harsh whisper, my throat closing up. Knowing you can't trust the woman who brought you into the world is agonizing.

Heartbreaking.

"You can never be alone with her again," he says vehemently.

I can't help but smile. "Don't worry. I try my hardest not to be around her at all."

"Yet she still comes around." He shakes his head. "She shows up here again, I'm calling the cops."

"You'd call the police for me, despite what you—do?" I'm referring to the mob stuff. His father's business. The blood money, Mom accusing him of being a criminal. Everyone talks about it, but I don't see it.

I kind of want to see it.

"I would do anything to keep her away from you." He yanks me back into his arms, holding me so tight, it's like I can't breathe.

"Sometimes I wish she would just...disappear," I admit, resting my cheek against the lapel of his jacket.

He's quiet for a moment before he says, "That can be arranged."

I don't respond, unsure if he's serious or not but...

I'm kind of thinking he might be.

CHAPTER TWENTY-SEVEN

SYLVIE

After Spencer calms me down, we walk back out into the living area to find everyone waiting for us, somber expressions on their faces, most of them clutching glasses filled with alcohol. It's been a stressful afternoon, not just for me but for them too, and I feel terrible.

Carolina greets me first, tugging me into a hug. "Are you okay?" she murmurs close to my ear.

I nod, squeezing her in return before I let go of her. "She... unsettles me."

"Me too," she whispers.

"Complete understatement of the century," Monty says before he takes a swig of his drink, like he needs it. "I didn't realize it was so awful between the two of you."

"I'm sorry I posted your party on social media," Cliff says, appearing contrite. He can barely look me in the eye and I go to him, giving him a quick hug as my sign of forgiveness.

Not that there is anything to forgive him for. He didn't know his posts would start such a shit storm.

"I posted something too, and I'm so sorry, Sylvie-bug. I didn't mean to start any trouble." My father is suddenly in front of me, pulling me in for a bone crushing hug. I can't remember the last time I've been hugged so much and I have to admit...

It's nice.

"It's okay, Daddy." He hasn't called me that nickname in so long. Mother always hated it, but not me.

I loved it.

My father pulls away, smiling down at me as he cups my cheek. I lean into his palm, smiling at him in return and something unspoken passes between us. Like he just asked for forgiveness and I gave it to him.

"We should meet for dinner soon," he says, his head lifting so he can scan the room. "All of us."

He means all of his children.

"Call my assistant and set up a time," Whit says gruffly and I roll my eyes at my father. Such a typical Whit response.

I have to appreciate his consistency though.

Spencer never leaves my side as our guests leave one by one. We remain by the door, thanking everyone for coming as they exit. I try to apologize for what happened but none of them will hear it.

"It's not your fault," Summer tells me, her sincere gaze never straying from mine. "Unwanted guests always have a way of ruining the party."

That made me laugh. But only for a minute.

I'm still to shaken up by what happened with my mother. How her mere presence rattles me. She holds a different kind of power over me now and I despise it.

I despise her. I do.

Once everyone is gone and the house is cleared of the catering staff, Spencer leads me into the massive bathroom connected to his bedroom and practically demands I take a bath. He even starts the water for me, adding some fragrant bath salts. I let him take care of me, barely moving when he unzips my dress. Lifting my arms when he tells me to do so to take it off. When I'm standing in front of him in just a pair of lacy pale pink panties, staring off into space, he kisses me. A lip-smacking loud kiss that pulls me from my stupor.

"It's going to be okay," he murmurs, his mouth right at my ear. "I promise."

I watch him go, and the moment the door closes, I'm so incredibly lonely, I'm tempted to call him back into the room. Strip him naked and have him bathe with me.

We'd do more than bathe. We can't be near each other with our clothes off without something happening. I'm surprised he used such restraint and walked away from me when I was basically naked.

He's never really done that before.

My gaze drifts around the giant bathroom, spotting my phone on the sleek marble counter. I grab it, spotting the notifications on the screen and I tap the iMessage one.

A text from my mother.

I miss you so much. I wish you wouldn't turn me away from you. Setting your watchdog on me won't work forever. Nothing can keep us apart, darling. I'm as much a part of you as you are of me.

A chill ripples down my spine at her words. At the ominous tone within them.

Another text appears, my phone vibrating when it arrives, making me jolt.

It hurts, seeing my family together and not including me. I don't know what else to do to fix your problem with me. I said I was sorry. What more do you want?

Glancing up, I catch my reflection in the mirror, and slowly, I drop my arms at my sides, fascinated with what I see.

A normal-sized woman. Average really. Not gangly and sickly and awkward, like I used to be. Not pale and gaunt and barely able to stand. With clear lungs and a clear head and rosy cheeks. Silky blonde hair where it was once brittle. Clear blue eyes where they were once clouded and rimmed with red.

I lift my chin and take a step closer to the counter, bracing my hands on the edge of the marble. Once upon a time, I had been a timid little girl who was scared of her own shadow. Who pretended she was fine, when she was anything but.

A girl who listened to every word her mother said, and believed her. Who then turned on her family and friends because she didn't know any better.

Who almost lost the man she loved, yet somehow, here I am, living with him. He takes care of me. Spencer loves me.

And I love him.

I was about to tell him that too, when she showed up and ruined everything.

Typical.

The phone buzzes again, and I check my messages to see it's just the same one she sent before. I'm tempted to answer her. I even open my phone and go into the text thread, my fingers poised and ready to tap out a scathing response.

Instead, I carefully set the phone back on the counter and back away from it. The phone sounds again, the vibration sending it rumbling on the counter, and without thought, I run to it, scoop it up in my hands and go to the window. It cracks open in an instant, too easily really, and I'm tossing the phone out. Off the thirty-sixth floor. The whoosh of the phone being caught by the air before it plummets to the ground makes me take a step back before I rise on tiptoe and try to peak through the barely-opened window, but I can't see anything.

It's as if it's been swallowed up by the sky. Gone.

Gone.

Then I remember I got a new phone, with a new number, and I wonder how she got a hold of me. Who gave her that number? Who?

I slam the window closed and flee the bathroom, in search of Spencer, who I find standing at the kitchen counter, a tumbler full of rich brown liquid clutched in his fingers as he's about to bring it to his lips. He pauses when he sees me, and I'm sure I'm a sight. Clad in just the panties that are completely see-through and my eyes wild. I feel wild.

Feral.

"Who gave my phone number to my mother?"

He carefully sets the glass on the counter. "I don't know."

"I got a new phone before I went to Big Sur. I didn't give that number to anyone but Roland."

"You gave your number to people when you returned here, didn't you?"

I nod, glancing about the kitchen, wishing I had a drink too. "What is that?" I flick my chin at the glass in front of him.

"Scotch."

I make a face. "Gross."

"It's an acquired taste."

"I need a beer. Or vodka. Maybe tequila." I go to the refrigerator and open the freezer door, the blast of cold air making goosebumps dot my skin. "You don't have any vodka? What kind of mobster are you?"

"Not the Russian kind, that's for damn sure." He shuts the door for me, angling his body between the fridge and me, his warmth seeping into my nakedness. "What are you doing?"

"I'm pissed."

"I can see that." His hot gaze rakes over me, making me shiver. "Did you turn off the water?"

"What? Oh. No."

"You want to flood out our bathroom?" He arches a brow.

It's my turn to let my gaze roam the length of him. He removed the suit jacket and tie long ago, the white shirt unbuttoned at the neck, exposing the tanned column of his throat. His shirtsleeves are rolled up, showing off his muscular forearms, and everything inside me goes liquid.

Hot.

"No." I slowly shake my head, my fingers brushing against his right arm. Bare skin that's hot. A body that'll help me forget. "I threw my phone out the window."

"We're on the thirty-sixth floor, Syl."

"I know. My mom wouldn't stop texting me."

It takes everything for him to remain calm. I can see the internal struggle happening in his turbulent gaze. "What did she say?"

"Nothing important." I push her words aside. I don't want to think about them. I don't want to think about her.

"Important enough to piss you off and have you stomping in here after tossing your phone out the window."

"I can buy another one," I say with a little shrug. "I can buy a hundred new ones. And I bet she'd eventually figure out my new phone number and know how to get in contact with me."

He tilts his head to the side, studying me with those dark, assessing eyes. "What else aren't you telling me?"

"I was trying to tell you something earlier. Before she came in." I form my lips into a little pout before I dance away from him, going over to the counter and hopping onto it, so I'm sitting on the edge, my legs dangling. "Do you remember?"

He comes closer, crowding me, his hands braced on either side of the counter, his arms boxing me in. His scent fills my head, making me dizzy, and I lean forward, until my face is directly in his. "I remember," he murmurs.

"Should I say it now?" I brush his mouth with mine. Featherlight. A complete tease. "Or wait?"

"Should I go turn off that water?" When I smile, his expression turns stern. "I'm serious. You're going to flood the apartment if we don't watch it."

"That tub is massive."

"And it doesn't take long to fill it up." He's about to walk away when I grab hold of his shirt front, keeping him with me. "Come on, Syl. Let me—"

"I love you," I announce, interrupting him.

He goes still, his gaze settling on mine. Hot and burning

bright. "Yeah?"

I nod, slowly undoing each button of his shirt, exposing the strong expanse of his chest. "Yes. I love you. I never say it. It's a scary statement to make, that you love someone that's not a member of your family. And even then, us Lancasters don't make declarations of love often. We keep our feelings tucked away inside, where they're safe."

He doesn't say a word as I work at removing his shirt. When it's nothing but a discarded scrap of fabric on the floor, I reach for his belt, slowly undoing it.

"You don't have anything to say?"

"I figured you weren't finished."

The moment his trousers are undone, I'm sliding my hand inside, curling my fingers around his erection. He's fully hard and throbbing against my palm, and I feel an answering throb between my thighs. "You are the only person in this entire world who makes me feel safe, Spence. Only you."

He leans in, nuzzling my cheek, his mouth at my ear. "I would destroy this entire world if it meant keeping you safe."

I dive my hand beneath his boxer briefs, encountering velvety, hot skin. "You mean it?"

"With my whole heart." He nips at my ear, making me shiver. "Which you own, by the way."

"Spencer," I whisper, suddenly overcome. To the point that my eyes are damp and my throat is thick. "I've been in love with you for what feels like forever."

"Even when you were married to someone else?" He thrusts his cock into my hand, and I squeeze him hard, making him groan.

"Especially when I was married to someone else." He keeps bringing it up, and I hate that, but I suppose I can't blame him.

"You want me to fuck you on this counter?"

I nod, stroking him, my breaths accelerating. His cock grows in my hand, I swear. Thicker. Longer. Harder. "Please."

"Gonna need to check the water first." He scoops me up without warning, making me squeal, and then he basically throws me over his shoulder, so I'm hanging upside down. I pound at his back, letting forth a frustrated growl.

He merely smacks my ass in response, the crack of his palm hitting my skin loud in the quiet apartment.

"You spanked me!" I'm shocked. Heat spreads where his large hand made contact with my flesh, leaving me flustered.

Jittery.

"You deserved it." He does it again, and this time, I scream.

Oh God, my panties are wet. Who knew that a smack on the butt could feel so good?

He strides into the bedroom with me, tossing me onto the bed like a blanket he's discarding before he makes his way to the bathroom. I hear him curse under his breath as he turns off the water, but otherwise, he says nothing else.

I nibble on my bottom lip, hoping he's not mad at me for flooding his precious bathroom.

When he reappears, he remains in the open doorway, the bathroom light gilding the outline of him, so it's as if he's glowing. He's shirtless, his pants hanging half undone, his shoes gone somewhere along the way. His gaze remains on me as he reaches for the front of his trousers, shoving them down along with his boxer briefs and kicking them off, so he's standing in front of me with only gray socks on his feet.

I rest my hand over my mouth, stifling a giggle.

He cracks a smile. "You think it's funny, huh?"

I shake my head, a tiny trickle of fear and a heavy amount of desire coursing through my blood as he stalks toward the bed. I scoot backward, as if I'm going to run away, but he clamps his fingers around my ankle, yanking me toward him. Dragging me down the mattress until my legs are dangling over the edge.

He slides his hands up until they're between my thighs, and he spreads them wide open, his gaze dropping to my lace-covered pussy. He stares for so long I start to squirm, and when he finally touches me there, a gentle brush of his fingers over the lace, I sigh with longing.

"More," I whisper.

He doesn't give me what I want. Instead, he removes his hand from me completely, bracing his hands on the edge of the bed while he toes off his socks. Not the sexiest move I've seen from Spencer, but right now, everything he does leaves me breathless. Primed and ready for him.

"You're stalling."

"You deserve it." He leans over me, thrusting his face in mine. "You left a mess in the bathroom."

"It flooded?" I frown.

He nods slowly, dipping his head to nip at my lower lip. "Yeah. I'm never leaving you alone with a bath again."

"I almost asked you to join me."

"You should've." He kisses my jaw, nibbling the skin. "I would've made sure to turn off the water in time."

I brace my hands on his chest, his heat burning against my palms. "You're not really mad, are you?"

His brows draw together as he pulls away, so he can look into my eyes. "No. Not at all."

Relief makes my shoulders sag. "Good."

"I'm trying to distract you." His mouth lands on my neck, sliding down until he's raining kisses across my chest. Then farther, until he's breathing on my nipple, just before he envelops it with his mouth.

"It's working," I murmur, thrusting my fingers in his hair and praying he doesn't leave. "Oh God, don't stop."

He works his magic on my breasts. Sucking and nibbling and licking. Drawing a nipple into his mouth so tightly, I gasp. When his hand slides back down, landing between my legs, I whimper. And when he slips those fingers beneath the lace to touch my hot, wet skin, I moan.

"Fuck," I bite out when he strokes my clit. It's swollen. Hot and achy to the touch and my hips begin to work when he rubs tiny circles over it. "You're going to make me come."

"That's the goal, Syl." He lifts away from my chest and I can feel him watching me, his gaze heavy. Intimidating.

I'm so close, and the moment feels so...intimate. After everything that happened today, I'm raw. Vulnerable. Angry and aroused and so in love with this man. I tilt my head back, a moan sounding deep in my throat when he thrusts two fingers inside my body and begins to pump.

"Open your eyes, baby."

They flash open as if I have no control over them, surprised by him calling me baby. He's never done that before. Not that I can remember.

His dark gaze meets mine, and he doesn't look away as he continues to fuck me with his fingers. "I love you."

A shiver moves through me at his declaration. That this big, handsome man could love me. That he's loved me since we were teens. Kids.

"Say it." His fingers pause, buried deep inside me, his thumb pressing against my clit. "Tell me you love me, Sylvie."

I'm breathing deep, taking fortifying gulps, my entire body buzzing with the need to come. I can feel it, just hovering on the edge, ready to sweep over me, but he keeps me hanging there. My clit is electrified, throbbing beneath the pressure of his thumb, and I shift beneath him, needing more of that friction.

"Say it." He presses harder, his fingers sliding deeper, until it feels like an invasion. "I won't let you come until you say it."

Why is it so hard? I said it once already. But the words are stalled in my throat, until it feels like I'm choking on them.

He kneels down in front of me, his other hand finding my hip, yanking me closer. His mouth is just above my pussy, I can feel his breath waft over my sensitive skin, and I press my lips together, closing my eyes.

"Look at me," he demands, and I do. I can't help but do everything he tells me to. "I love you, Syl. So fucking much, I would do whatever it takes to keep you safe. To make you feel protected. To make you happy. All I want is for the two of us to be together forever. And I don't take that shit lightly. I'm not like the rest of my family. When I care about someone, I love them hard."

My entire body is trembling at his words.

"And I've been fucking obsessed with you since I was fourteen. The poor little rich girl who was always sick. That's how you portrayed yourself to the rest of the world, but never to me."

"Spencer..."

"You say you love me again and I'm never going to let you go. It doesn't matter what happens. I'm by your side until the day I die." He dips his head, his tongue lightly tracing along the side of my clit.

"I love you," I breathe, my gaze staying on his as he puts his mouth on my pussy. "I love you so much. You know it's only ever been you."

"Promise?" He lifts his brows, his thumb doing slow circles on my clit once more.

I nod, my hips moving with him as his fingers slide in and out of me. Faster and faster.

"Say it."

"I promise to love you forever. You're the only one for me. The only one who's ever been inside me," I declare.

"Fuck that's hot." He rises above me, hands braced on either side of my head, his cock sliding into my body unassisted. I arch into him, my clit nudging against the base of his erection and that's all it takes.

I'm coming, my inner walls milking him, clenching tight around his shaft. He fucks me hard, grunting with every thrust, no condom necessary since I went on the pill the minute I came back to New York.

No babies. I'm not ready for them like my brother. I'd be a terrible mother.

I know this is true.

He fucks me steadily, grunting with every thrust, making me come again, sweat dripping down his face. His chest. I rise up, rubbing my cheek against his skin, absorbing the tangy saltiness of his sweat, wanting him to mark me everywhere.

An idea forms in my head and I push against his chest, making him stop. "What?"

"Come on me."

He frowns. "Really?"

"Yes. Pull out and come all over me." I run my hand down my front. "Here."

He resumes thrusting, pounding his body into mine, and I can tell he's close. The tension in his shoulders, the sounds he makes deep in his throat. I know all of his tells already, and when the orgasm is almost upon him, he rips himself away from me, grips the base of his cock and…

Spurts cum all over me.

I smile as I watch him, reaching for the spot on my stomach, dragging my fingers through the sticky liquid. He's on his haunches between my spread legs, his head tilted back, his eyes closed as he breathes raggedly. He shivers, another tiny spurt of creamy liquid dripping from his cock, and I reach for him, tracing the slit. Scooping up what remnants I can before I bring my fingers to my lips and taste.

"Jesus, Syl."

"I know." My smile grows. "That was the best distraction ever."

CHAPTER TWENTY-EIGHT

SPENCER

I am a man in love. And I don't give a damn who knows it.

I stroll into the Donato headquarters first thing Monday morning, whistling like a damn fool, which was my first mistake. The second one was me smiling at everyone I walked past as I strode through the office, which caused pretty much every single one of them to report this tiny fact to my father. Most of the time, when I come into work, I'm a grouchy ass motherfucker who won't even speak until I've had at least one cup of coffee in me. Maybe two. And none of that sweet Starbucks dessert crap either.

I take my coffee black. No cream, no sugar.

I'm sitting at my desk with my feet propped on the edge, contemplating if I should send Sylvie a text or not to wake her up when my office door bangs open, my father marching his way inside.

"What the fuck is wrong with you?"

I drop my feet to the ground and sit up straight in my chair, tossing my phone on my desk. She doesn't even have a new phone yet. It's coming later today, so there's no point in trying to text her. She wouldn't get it. "Well, good morning to you too."

Victor Donato stops to stand behind a chair, reaching out to grip it so tightly, his knuckles turn white. "Do you have anything to tell me?"

"Not anything in particular." I brace myself for bad news. Maybe we lost a shipment over the weekend. Or someone slipped in and bought out that building downtown we've been trying to acquire for the last six months. It could be a myriad of things to set my father off.

"People have been reporting in. About you." He loosens his grip on the chair. "They say you're too damn cheerful for your own good."

"So?" I shrug a shoulder, trying to play it off. Keep it cool.

My father is always looking for a reaction and I've learned over the years not to give him one. It's a talent I've honed since I was a teen.

"You're like me. You're *never* cheerful. What's gotten into you?" His gaze never strays from mine and I swear I want to squirm in my chair like I'm eight and just got caught busting out a window with a baseball. I hate it when he looks at me like that. As if he could read my every thought. I see the realization dawn in his eyes before he declares, "You've met a woman."

"I've known her for years," I say calmly.

Chased her for years.

Loved her for years.

Don't admit those facts out loud.

"Sylvie Lancaster?"

I nod, keeping my expression impassive. I know what he's going to say in three, two, one...

"A woman is a weakness. Why else do you think I left your mother? She was so needy. Always wanting me around. Making demands I could never meet. My enemies knew of her existence and threatened her pretty little head on a constant basis. She had no clue." He waves a hand, as if he could make her disappear that easily. Which he, sort of, did. "Trust me that this one will be the same for you."

"She's already living with me." I hadn't planned on telling

him that little fact just yet, but it's like I couldn't stop the words from leaving my mouth.

"Really."

I nod again, remaining silent.

"For how long?" His brows shoot up.

"Weeks."

"Jesus, son." He falls heavily into the chair he was just gripping, rubbing a hand along his jaw. "What if she's not the one for you?"

"She's always been the one for me," I correct, needing him to know how serious I am about her. "I'm going to marry her."

"A Lancaster?" He drops his hand. "I suppose you could do worse."

"This isn't a business merger," I start, but he holds up his hand, silencing me.

"All marriages are business mergers. You don't think I'm aware of that wedding between the Constantine kid and that other Lancaster girl? Talk about a power move." He sounds impressed. "You could do the same thing. A Donato and a Lancaster coming together. You could build a new dynasty between the two of you."

"I'm in love with her."

"Bah." Another dismissive wave. "Love is a weakness."

"Not to me." I clear my throat. "Not to us."

He leans his big body back in the chair, slouching a bit. Looking more like my father and less like the powerful businessman he is when he's in the office. "You can find good quality pussy anywhere, Spence. You don't have to marry it."

"Don't talk about her like that," I snap.

He grins, the fucker. "Ah, so it *is* serious. No one can talk about the precious pussy, just you."

"You really shouldn't say such things," I bite out between clenched teeth. "She's going to be your daughter-in-law."

"We'll see. Once you put a ring on it, then we'll talk about weddings and all the bullshit that comes with them." He leans forward, resting his elbows on the chair arms. "You take her to meet your mom yet?"

I slowly shake my head. I didn't even want to tell him about Sylvie. I knew he'd react like this. He most likely wants me to dump her, while my mother will ask why I haven't married her already.

"When you do that, then I'll know you're serious." He rises to his feet with a grunt, pointing at me. "I know you don't want to hear it, but a woman is a liability, son. Your enemies will figure out your weak spot and they'll come in for the kill."

I sit up straighter, anger making my blood run cold. "No one will touch a hair on her head."

"You'll need bodyguards."

I raise my brows. "I don't remember any bodyguards around when I was growing up."

"Because you didn't notice them. Didn't see them for a reason. I hired trained assassins to guard my family. I never fucked around. If you want to keep her safe, don't fuck around."

And with that last blistering statement, my father strides out of my office, leaving behind the scent of his overpowering cologne in his wake.

A sigh leaves me and I prop my feet on the edge of the desk once more, my phone clutched in my hand. I bring up the phone number and make the call, grateful when he answers on the second ring.

"It's too early for you to be calling," Whit growls into my ear.

"You have children now. Aren't you up at the crack of dawn every morning?"

"My wife is a genius. She somehow trained Augie to sleep in, which we should enjoy because that baby of ours is coming soon." I hear the murmur of a voice in the background, and I assume it's Summer. "Call me later."

"Meet me for lunch later this afternoon and then I won't have to call," I counter.

"Done. Text me where and when." He ends the call before I can respond.

The grouchy asshole.

I enter the restaurant a little past one, spotting Whit sitting at a table waiting for me. He glares when our gazes meet, and I can't help it.

I'm grinning the entire time I walk toward him, which only makes his scowl deepen. By the time I'm settled in the chair across from him, he's in full-on disgusted mode.

"God, you're cheerful. I can only assume you're getting laid on the regular."

"I'm in love," I declare, unafraid to say it. For once in my life. "With your sister."

Whit's hand immediately shoots up in the air, waving at a nearby waiter. "Going to need a stiff drink for this conversation."

We order drinks, and once the server is gone, Whit leans back in his chair, studying me carefully with those always assessing eyes.

"I don't like what happened at your apartment Saturday."

"I don't either," I agree.

"My mother oversteps her boundaries. She doesn't understand why no one wants to be around her. Specifically, Sylvie, who was her little puppet her entire life." Whit leans forward, resting his forearms on the edge of the table. "I don't understand it either. What happened between the two of them? Do you know?"

I shift uncomfortably in my chair. "It's not my place to tell. You should talk to Sylvie."

"I've tried. She dodges the question every chance she gets."

"She might not anymore. If you tell her you spoke to me, she could open up a bit."

"Did she try to hurt her? My mother," he clarifies when I frown. "When Sylvie was sick all the time, was that because of—our mother's doing?"

I don't want to reveal what isn't my story, but I offer him a curt nod in response.

A ragged sigh leaves Whit, and he stares off into the distance, his jaw working. "I hate that."

"I do too."

"Summer gave me bits and pieces of her conversations with Sylvie when we were all in high school, and we came to our own conclusions, though it was hard for me to fathom. Why would our mother try to hurt her? Why would she purposely keep my sister sick? Then Summer started sending me links to articles about Munchausen by proxy, and after reading them, I realized that sounded a lot like my mother's relationship with Sylvie," Whit explains, his voice low.

"It's child abuse." I did my own research, and what I read disgusted me. "Your mother is an abuser."

"I never noticed. Not when I was younger. Not really." He stares off into the distance. "I should've known. I should've done something."

"We were kids. What could you have done?"

"I don't know. I should've talked to my father. I should've helped my sister." He shakes his head. "I feel guilty."

"Don't. She doesn't blame you for anything. This is your mother's fault, and no one else's."

"It's why we don't let her spend any time alone with August." Whit's expression slightly pales. "I could never forgive myself if something happened to him while in her care."

"I think that's best," I agree.

The server appears with our drinks and takes our lunch order. Once he's gone and we've downed a few sips, I decide to be completely truthful with my best friend.

"I want to marry Sylvie."

Whit barely hides the smile curling his lips. "I assumed that would be the case."

"I want to ask her to marry me soon, but I don't know if I'm rushing things." I feel like an idiot for even admitting that to him.

"You two have been dancing around this for years. I don't think you're rushing anything." His words dismiss my worry in an instant.

Mostly.

"She's still a widow in the public eye," I remind him. "We have to consider that."

"Please. That marriage barely happened. And she was forced to do it."

"By your mother."

Another sigh leaves my friend and he slowly shakes his head. "My mother needs help. Something is wrong with her, and she doesn't seem to be getting any better."

"She's obsessed with Sylvie." I saw the text messages from her mom on the old phone—we were able to look up the messages on her iCloud. They weren't normal. Not even close. "In an unhealthy manner."

"That's a polite way of phrasing that our mother has lost her damn mind." Whit grabs his glass and drains it. "I'll speak to her."

"Really?" I arch a brow.

He nods. "I don't know any other way to broach the subject besides being upfront with it. The woman needs to face facts— what she's done to Sylvie throughout the years isn't right. My mother has always basked in attention, and my father rarely gave it to her. As if he knew she thrived on it, and he didn't want to see her thrive."

Their marriage was a wreck, but I don't bother saying it. Whit already knows.

"I'm wondering if she used Sylvie's so-called illness as a way to gain attention. From my father, the family, doctors. I don't know. Clearly, she needs help. A therapist. A licensed psychiatrist, whatever. Perhaps she needs to be put on medication."

"All of that should be considered," I say.

"I agree." He studies me for a moment. "And what about Sylvie? Is she all fucked up over this still? Does she need to see a therapist? Be put on medication?"

"Probably," I say. "Though I don't want to answer for her."

"Something to talk over with her. I know she's been in therapy before. And she's also taken gobs of pills throughout the years. A variety of medications that never seemed to help."

"I don't think it's easy, being Sylvie Lancaster," I point out. "She struggles with that most of all."

The wistful expression on Whit's face is reassuring. It means he cares about his sister. "I know. It's not easy being a Lancaster in general."

"The rich have problems too," I say, lifting my glass in his direction.

He lifts his empty glass, clinking it against mine. "Indeed."

CHAPTER TWENTY-NINE

SYLVIE

It's been weeks since the tea party. Since my mother appeared uninvited and scared the crap out of me. I've been hiding out in Spencer's apartment ever since, only accompanying him when we go out for meals, and even then, we usually get takeout and end up staying home. If someone wants to see me, they have to come to the apartment.

I don't trust going out on my own. She knows where I'm at. She could be lingering, hiding nearby as I leave the building, anxious to pounce the moment I'm far enough from the doormen and anyone else who could potentially rescue me.

It's weird, not trusting the person you used to depend on the most. I thought I'd already processed my feelings about it, but I guess I haven't fully. I've made an appointment with a new therapist, and I hope it works out. It's hard to find someone you can click with, who you feel comfortable enough to share all the vulnerable feelings you rarely discuss with anyone else.

The one person I trust more than anyone else is Spencer. He's stayed true throughout all the years. By my side, loyal and supportive. He gives his love to me unconditionally, and I don't know what I'd do without him.

I'm starting to become too dependent, but I don't care. I'm

in love with him. He's in love with me.

Nothing can keep us apart.

The sex is phenomenal too. Not that I can compare it to anyone else, since he's basically the only man I've ever been with, but it's so good. He knows exactly what I want, when I want it. He can be tender and sweet, or growly and a little rough. Those are my favorite moments, when he acts out of control and does things to me that I never expected.

We're lying in bed after a particularly passionate moment together, the two of us flat on our backs, panting as we stare up at the ceiling. It's hot outside, summer having showed up and made everything outside muggy and miserable.

Inside, I'm muggy right now, though I'm definitely not miserable. But my bare skin is sticky with sweat and my hair is clinging to the back of my neck. Fingers trail down my arm, light enough to make me shiver, and when I glance to my left, I find Spencer already watching me.

"You all right?"

I nod, frowning at him. "Why do you ask?"

"You're extra quiet." He curls his fingers around mine.

"And you were extra ferocious."

"In a bad way?"

I roll over so I can wrap my body around his, absorbing his strength, his warmth. "Never in a bad way."

"Good." He wraps his arm around my shoulders, tucking me close. "I'm tired."

We're both quiet for a moment, and I can feel his body slowly relaxing. He's falling asleep, and I blurt out the one thing I keep thinking about off and on lately.

"I want a cat."

His arm tightens around my shoulder. "A cat?"

His voice is deep and rumbly. A little sleepy sounding. I love these moments when it's just the two of us in bed, naked and wrapped up in each other.

"Yes. A cat," I admit.

"What kind? Do you have a special breed in mind?"

"I think a certain kind of cat, yes. Very specific." I'm being vague on purpose because I know what I'm asking for is…silly.

But I want it. Her.

"Well, we know money is no object." Spencer kisses my forehead. "Why don't you go ahead and get the cat you want?"

"She's, um…a little wild."

He takes a while to respond. I'm sure he's absorbing what I just said. "What cat are you talking about exactly?"

"Squirrel."

"You want a squirrel? That's just a glorified rat, Syl. No one wants a pet squirrel."

"No, no. I don't want a *squirrel*. I want the cat I called Squirrel. She was so cute. Totally wild. Followed me everywhere I went." I glance up at him. "The gray cat that hung around the house in Big Sur. I want her."

"You want to take her out of the only home she's ever known and bring her here to the city?" He's frowning, and it's adorable. "She's not a city cat. She wants to be wild and free. On the coast of California."

"I think I can convince her to be happy here. I'm kind of wild, and so is she. I think we're kindred spirits, Squirrel and me." I press my face against his chest, a little embarrassed. I sound silly. I'm sure he'll say yes, just to humor me, and I'm grateful for that. I am.

But I also want to prove to him that this cat will be good for me, and I'll be good for her.

"I say get what you want. If you want to bring Squirrel here, bring her." His voice turns stern. "If she fucks with my furniture, I'm kicking her out."

"You are not." I poke his side with my index finger, making him grunt. "You'll love her. She'll sit in your lap and purr for your attention."

"Like you do?" He rolls me over, so I'm on sprawled on top of his naked body, my face in his. "I know how to make you purr."

I roll my eyes. "You do not."

He grins, his hand sliding over my butt cheek. "Oh, but I do."

"Stop trying to distract me." I bite at his bottom lip, so hard he yelps. "I'm calling Roland in the morning and asking him to catch her for me. I'll make all the arrangements and fly her here."

"Will he want to send the cat here?"

"He'll do anything to help me. He already told me so."

Spencer's careful gaze settles on my face, his hand drifting up and down my ass. "How is it you end up with every man you know wrapped around your finger?"

I shrug. "It's a gift."

"I'll say." He spanks me, making me jolt.

Making me wet.

"You are very naughty," I murmur against his lips before I kiss him.

"Wait until you see me at my filthiest."

"I haven't yet?" My brows shoot up.

He smirks. "Not even close."

I arrive at Summer and Whit's building in the car my brother sent over. He reassured me that our mother wouldn't know I was coming over.

"She's in Ibiza," he told me on the phone a few days ago. "A little solo vacation. Though I hear she's over there to have some work done."

"Really? In Ibiza?" I'm shocked.

"Yes. She's done this before. A lot of people do, including Summer's mom. They claim they're going on vacation, but really, they're getting a tweak here and there. I hear our mother is going for a face lift."

"Who told you this?"

"Dad."

She would tell him everything. Still desperate to get him back in her clutches, though he never falls for it.

I don't fall for it anymore either.

The driver escorts me inside the building, handing me off to the security guard, who leads me to the penthouse elevator. Lots of protection, thanks to my brother, which is reassuring.

Between him and Spencer, I feel safe.

Loved.

The moment the elevator opens, Summer is standing there in front of me, gloriously pregnant and with my nephew, August, on her hip. She's wearing a pale blue, flowing dress, and I swear she's glowing with vitality.

"Down! Put me down!" Augie shouts the moment he sees me, squirming in his mother's arms. "Auntie!"

"Aw." I kneel down as soon as Summer sets him on his feet, and he runs toward me, tackling me so hard I almost teeter backward and land on my butt. "Augie. I've missed you so much."

"Auntie." His sweet little baby voice is so cute. We've been talking on FaceTime lately, and Summer is always reminding him that I'm his auntie. His father's little sister, just like he's going to be the big brother to a little sister soon too.

He probably doesn't get it now, but he will eventually. There's going to be someone in his life he'll need to watch over for the rest of his life.

"Come on, August. Let's go in the kitchen and get a snack," Summer suggests.

Augie places his sweaty hands on my face, smiling at me in absolute glee. "You want a snack?"

"Please," I tell him, grinning when he leans in and presses a sticky kiss to my cheek. I rise to my feet and take his hand. "Let's go."

Summer leads us into the kitchen and prepares her son a snack along with something to drink.

"Let's go talk in the study," Summer tells me when Augie's nanny shows up to take over with his care. "You want some lemonade?"

"Please," I tell her, watching as she glides about the kitchen, the domestic goddess she is pouring us glasses of lemonade.

I envy her ease at performing domestic chores in her multi-million-dollar apartment. Pregnant with her second baby. Married and happy with my brother, who is one of the unhappiest individuals I've ever known, besides myself.

Until he met Summer. Once she came into his life—and he allowed himself to admit his feelings for her—he became a changed man. Still a cruel asshole, who barely tolerates the human race, but he does love and adore his wife and son, and soon-to-be baby girl.

A wistful sigh leaves me when I think of me and Spencer. I'm only happy when I'm with him. All of my problems seem to fall away, disappearing completely, when I'm in his presence. When I let him love me.

And I'm not talking about sex either. He shows he loves me in a variety of ways. He takes care of me. Listens to me. Is willing to fight my battles, but backs down when I say I can handle them myself.

His support is what I've craved my entire life. My father is too self-absorbed to understand my needs. Or he was too focused on Carolina. Whit. Never me. Sometimes I wonder if he even cares about what's going on in my world. And my mother...

She's too obsessed with me. It sounds arrogant, even in my own thoughts, but it's true.

"Let's go," Summer says, and I take the crystal glass of lemonade from her, falling into step behind her as we head for the study.

The interior is warm and inviting, with a giant window that

overlooks the city. It's crystal clear this afternoon, not a cloud in the sky, and the sun blazes high. A typical early summer day in Manhattan, and it makes me want to leave. Makes me yearn to go to the house on Long Island and spend my days by the ocean.

"How are you?" Summer asks once we're settled in chairs across from each other. "And be real with me."

I take a sip of my lemonade, the sweet yet tart taste bursting on my tongue. "I'm great. Really."

"You and Spencer are doing well?"

"The best we ever have," I admit truthfully.

Her smile is slow. "I love that."

"Me too." I hesitate for only a moment. "I love him."

"That's so sweet. Does he know this?"

I nod, my cheeks going warm. It's still embarrassing to me, being truthful with my feelings.

"You two have been living together for weeks."

"Actually, a couple of months," I correct.

Summer leans back in her overstuffed chair with a sigh, patting her belly. "Time drags, yet also flies by. I'm going to have this baby in less than a month, and I still can't believe it."

"I can't believe it either, but I'm so excited." I smile, watching as Summer gazes down at her protruding stomach. "Do you have a name picked yet?"

"It's so difficult. I wanted to choose an old Lancaster family name for her, but so many of them are extremely old-fashioned. Whit shoots down every single one of them I suggest," Summer explains.

"Figures." I roll my eyes, making her laugh.

"We should get together sometime soon, before the baby arrives. You could come over for dinner. Or we could go out," Summer suggests.

"I would love that," I admit softly.

I need a friend right now. I can't unload all of my troubles on Spencer all the time, though he never seems to mind. He's supportive no matter what, but I don't want to push him away with my constant neediness.

He doesn't complain, but I know I can be intolerable sometimes.

Most of the time.

"I'm glad we're seeing more of you," Summer says. "We were worried we lost you completely once you married Earl. And then he died, and your mother monopolized you completely, though we believed she was truly helping you. Then you completely locked yourself away in his apartment and rarely saw the family anymore. Truth be told, I was surprised you went to our wedding."

"Whit had to convince me," I admit.

"He told me." Summer takes a long sip of her drink, and I wonder if she's searching for the right thing to say. "We're concerned, Sylvie. About your mother, and the relationship you two have."

I'm silent, absorbing her words, trying to ignore the incessant throb starting at my temples.

This is stressful, being called out. Exposing the secret that I've held so close for so long. It's easy to tell Spencer because he feels like a witness to most of it. Summer saw things too. More than anything, I told her so much back in high school. More than I'd ever told another soul, minus Spencer, and then I shit all over our friendship and ruined everything.

"We don't have a relationship any longer," I finally say.

"According to you. According to Sylvia, you two are fine. You're just working some things out. That's what she told Whit when he called her."

I frown. "When did he call her?"

"Yesterday. She just returned from Ibiza. He and Spencer went to lunch a few weeks ago and were sharing their concerns about you and your mother." Her brows drag together when I assume she sees the confusion on my face. "You knew they met up, didn't you? That Spencer came to him and let him know he was worried about Sylvia."

"No." I shake my head. "He never told me."

"Oh." Guilt flashes in Summer's eyes. "I'm not trying to cause any trouble between the two of you. He said something because he hoped Whit would have some advice. Considering none of us were fully aware of the extent your mother went in harming you, it was a difficult bit of information for Whit to digest."

"And I suppose that's my fault, not saying anything." I press my lips together, leaning over to set the glass of lemonade on the nearby table with shaky fingers. I can't help but get defensive when it comes to my mother.

"I'm not accusing you of anything," Summer says gently. "It's just—we didn't know. I mean, I assumed some things, but you never told me everything. You didn't tell Whit anything either."

"It's very—difficult to say your mother is trying to kill you without worrying that people will think you're a liar."

"I never thought you were a liar. You would allude to things here and there. Concerning details that left me confused, but at the time, I was too young to be of much help. Plus, I didn't know if you were possibly…lying."

"I suppose I warranted your distrust of me. I wasn't the most loyal, and yes, sometimes I exaggerated things. I'm not proud of my behavior back then." I lift my chin, trying to keep it together.

"I'm not accusing you of anything, or looking for an apology. We've already discussed this, and everything is forgiven between the both of us. Just know that I'm definitely not proud of my behavior back then either. I've done some stupid things in my life. So have you. Back then, we were both young, and you were heavily influenced by your mother," Summer says.

Everything she says is right. I know it. But it's still hard for me to deal with how I treated her when I was her only friend—and she was mine. How I shut her out because I was jealous. I felt used that time when I brought her home for Thanksgiving break. She didn't come for me. She went to spend time with my brother, and that hurt.

Even though she was there for me whenever I needed her. Eventually, so was Spence. I invited him over that week too, and abandoned her like she abandoned me. Kept Spencer in the dark to all of the problems, and eventually ratted Summer and Whit out to Mother.

Ultimately, I just wanted her approval and I would do anything to get it.

Including betray one of my only real friends.

Tears are suddenly leaking from my eyes and I close them for a moment, taking a deep breath. But it's no use.

I'm crying.

"Sylvie…" Her voice is soft and she appears ready to leap out of her chair, but I hold up my hand, stopping her.

"I'm sorry for everything I did back then. I know it was a long time ago, and you've told me you forgive me, but it hangs over me still. Like a dark cloud I can never escape. I betrayed you in the worst way possible, and took sides. The wrong one." I'm full-on sobbing now, and Summer propels herself out of the chair, grabbing a box of tissues from a nearby console table. She waddles toward me, holding out the box, and I take a few tissues from her.

Fuck it. I take the entire box from her.

She's quiet, letting me cry. Letting me get it all out. She returns to her chair, settling in it heavily, and when I wipe my eyes one final time and blow my nose, she finally speaks up.

"You need to let it go."

I dab at the corner of my eyes, confused. "Let what go?"

"The guilt. That was years ago. I've told you before I've forgiven you, and I mean it. Whit has forgiven you as well."

"I didn't realize he was angry at me," I say drolly, blowing my nose yet again.

"He didn't like you for a while. You have to admit, the things you were doing once you left high school were pretty unlikeable.

You drove everyone important in your life away from you."

Summer is right. I need to let everything that's happened go for good. What's done is done. I can't change the past.

But I can work on myself for the future.

"I take responsibility for my actions, but my mother had a hand in that too." She was always so careful, isolating me when she felt outside influences were creeping too close. Letting me go away to school was tough on her. Witnessing me making friends, seeing how other people acted and lived probably scared her. She wanted us to have our own little world.

Just me and her.

Spencer showed up and made things worse, I can see it now. His influence was the strongest yet. I wanted him. I thought of him and no one else. And she hated that.

So much.

Losing control of me made her do desperate things. Dangerous. I'm lucky I'm alive.

I realize that now. More than ever.

"I know. We both know. She's returned to the city, though I guess I already mentioned that, right? Whit saw her. Says she looks ten years younger. To the point that it's kind of freaky." Summer breaks out into a smile, then tries to hide it with her fingers.

I can't help but smile too. It's always fun, when Whit picks on our mother.

"Is it bad?" I can imagine a botched facelift. Or maybe her skin is too tight, her lips too plump.

"No, it's good. Too good. She looks so young." She goes quiet for a moment, and I see an internal struggle there. As if she wants to tell me something, but she's not sure if she should. "She actually looks just like…you."

CHAPTER THIRTY

SPENCER

"I'm nervous."

I glance over at Sylvie to see that she is indeed visibly nervous. She's shuffling her feet from side to side, shaking out her hands every few seconds, like she's got sweaty palms.

I'm guessing she does.

I grab one of her hands, noting the clammy palm, and give it a squeeze. "It's just my mother."

We're in the elevator on our way up to her penthouse at this very moment.

"Do you realize I've never met her? Not even once? Whit has. He said she's a dragon lady." The worry in my woman's gaze is almost comical. Whit's description of my mother even more so.

"He lied to you." I lift her hand to my lips, dropping a kiss on the top of it. "She's not a dragon lady. She's sweet. My father is the one to watch out for."

"That makes me feel so much better." Her smile is weak and she startles when the elevator jolts to a stop, the doors sliding open. "Oh God."

I give her hand a squeeze and lead her out of the elevator, stopping in front of the single door in the short hallway. Before I even get a chance to knock, the door swings open and my mother is standing there, a welcoming smile on her face.

"Spencer!" Her gaze cuts to Sylvie, curious. Vaguely assessing. "And you must be Sylvie."

"Yes." Sylvie's voice is shaky and she lets go of my hand, a soft "oh" falling from her lips when my mother yanks her into her arms and gives her a fierce hug. "It's nice to meet you."

"Aren't you a precious little doll?" Mom holds Sylvie at arms' length, studying her. "Oh Spencer, she's lovely."

"Mom, she's standing right in front of you. Don't talk about her like she's not here."

"Sorry, sorry. Come in." Mom lets go of Sylvie and we follow her inside. I shut the door behind us, turning the lock. Valerie Donato is big on safety. Locks and security alarms and cameras. Her building is one of the most secure in all of Manhattan and she chose it for a reason. The wrath of her ex-husband's enemies terrifies her, and I don't blame her.

Though they're not interested in her any longer thanks to my father not being interested in her either. Like he told me, women are a liability. Problem is, I can't live without the one standing next to me, so I'm willing to take the chance.

"You kids want something to drink?" Mom calls as she heads for the kitchen.

Sylvie sends me a look, her lips curved into a faint smile.

"Got any beer?" I ask her.

"Spencer, I am not serving you beer. It's lunch time. Have some iced tea," she chastises as she opens the refrigerator.

Sylvie and I stand at the kitchen counter, and I roll my eyes, making Syl giggle. "We're not kids anymore. I can legally drink. So can Sylvie."

"I'll just have iced tea," Sylvie says, eager to please.

Mom grabs a glass and fills it with ice before pouring the tea in, the ice crackling at first contact. "Here you go, sweetheart."

Then she pours me a glass too.

"I made a nice lasagna." Mom isn't the one with Italian roots in the family, but living with my father all those years honed her Italian cooking skills. "It'll be ready in thirty minutes."

"I knew I smelled something cooking when we first walked in." Sylvie takes a sip of her drink. "I can't wait. I'm starved."

"Me too." Mom is a good cook. That's about as far as her parenting skills took her.

I shouldn't be so tough on her. Living and dealing with my father had to be rough. He's demanding and volatile, and he took a lot of frustration with his work out on my mother. It was difficult to witness as a kid. After a while, I was grateful they sent me away to school. It was easier that way. They were so wrapped up in making each other miserable, and a lot of the time, I was miserable too.

Now they're much happier without each other, and my relationship with both of them is better. Mom and I are still a work in progress though. I don't see her Monday through Friday like I do my dad.

The moment I called her and said I wanted her to meet my girlfriend—still don't love that description for Sylvie, feels cheap to me—I know Mom went and told my dad. Which was my plan all along. He said I wasn't serious until I brought Sylvie around my mother so here you go, Dad. Proving to you that I'm dead ass serious.

Maybe that'll get him to stop saying shitty things about my future wife. He opens his mouth again and utters something crude about her, there's no telling what I might do to him.

"Sit, sit. I have appetizers." Mom brings over an antipasto plate, and I grab a couple of slices of salami, fortifying myself for the onslaught of questions she's about to ask Sylvie. "Spencer says you two have known each other a long time."

"We have," Sylvie admits, plucking a green olive from the plate and popping it into her mouth.

"Since high school?"

"I met him when I was in the eighth grade and he was a

freshman at Lancaster," Sylvie says after she swallows the olive. "He's my brother's best friend."

"Right, Whit Lancaster." Mom shakes her head, her lips curved in a barely-there smile. "I have a feeling those two were up to no good back then."

The smile on Sylvie's face falters and I silently curse my mother's comment.

"He's a married man now, Ma." I haven't called her Ma in years. She used to hate that shit and the irritation in her eyes tells me she still feels the same way. "And a dad."

"You're close to your brother?" Mom asks Sylvie.

"I am. I also have a younger sister," Sylvie says.

"That's nice. And what about your parents? Are you close to them? How about your mother? I always did want a daughter. A sweet little girl to dress up, a shopping buddy, you know? Instead, I got this guy." Mom reaches out and ruffles my hair, and I duck away after a few seconds.

"My parents…" Sylvie's voice drifts and she shakes her head. "I'm not as close to them as I used to be."

Close enough to the truth.

"Aw, that's a shame." Mom is funny. She always talks about family, and how important it is. What a difference it makes in the way a person is raised, and how they act. Yet she wasn't the most attentive mother during my growing up years, and she knows it. Her theories don't make much sense, but I don't bother questioning her.

"It's okay. I've learned to deal with it. My father and I are working on repairing our relationship." Sylvie's gaze finds mine and I send her a reassuring smile. She's handling this first meeting with my mother really well, not that I was worried about it. Not like she was.

"And how about your mother?"

"I don't know if that relationship can ever be repaired," Sylvie admits, her voice soft.

The look Mom sends me tells me she wishes she would've never opened her mouth and asked that question.

Yeah. I feel the same way.

"Well, tell me more about you and Spencer!" Mom says brightly, not realizing she's opening another can of worms. "You two make such a nice couple."

"It's more than that." I decide to be forthright. "I'm in love with her, Ma."

She blinks at me. I've never brought a girl around before, and definitely never said I was in love with any of them either. "I guess you two aren't wasting any time then?"

"We've wasted enough time already." I slide my arm around Sylvie's shoulders, tugging her close to my side. "We're living together."

"Oh." Mom blinks some more. "Well, that's certainly your business, though you know how I feel about that sort of thing."

I try not to roll my eyes because come on. She's really not that old fashioned. "Don't worry. I'm going to make everything right between us eventually."

"And you're in love with Spencer?" Mom asks Sylvie.

That is still a sensitive subject with her, confessing her feelings. I get it. She's used to living in a house where people didn't say *I love you* on a constant basis.

I didn't much either, but when it comes to this woman, I'm afraid I want to declare my love for her almost too much.

"Mom—"

"I can answer for myself," Sylvie interrupts, sending me a serene smile before turning it onto my mother. "I am *madly* in love with him, Mrs. Donato. I've been in love with him for years, though to be perfectly honest with you, I married someone else a couple of years ago."

Well shit. Leave it to Sylvie to throw everything out on the table, so to speak.

"You've already been married?" Mom's voice squeaks.

Sylvie nods. "Yes. It was a major mistake though. I was young, and I was sort of—forced into the matter. Plus, he was so much older than me, and unfortunately, he died a little over a year after we were married. Thank goodness Spencer and I reconnected though. My feelings for him have never faded."

"Oh. Well. Yes, that's so nice," Mom says faintly. I can tell from the dazed look on her face that her mind is trying to process everything Sylvie just told her. "If Spencer is bringing you here to meet me, then he must be very serious about you. And I'm happy for you bo—"

The oven timer sounds, snapping Mom into go-mode.

"Lasagna's done," I tell her.

"And I still haven't finished prepping the salad." Mom rushes to the oven, turning off the timer and opening the door to peek inside. "I should let it rest for a few minutes anyway. It's going to be piping hot."

Mom bustles around the kitchen, refusing our help and I offer to show Sylvie my bedroom, which is really a replica of the one I used to have in our old apartment. Mom moved everything over and kept my room almost exactly how I left it when I moved out a few years ago. Like it's a museum piece or something.

"I'd love to see it," Sylvie says, relief shining in her eyes.

The moment we're walking down the hall headed for my bedroom, Sylvie is tugging on my hand, urging me to stop.

"You okay?" I ask her.

"Do you think she likes me?" Sylvie chews on her lower lip. "I probably shouldn't have told her about Earl."

"I think it was the right move. She would've found out eventually." I pull her in close, pressing a kiss on her forehead. "She likes you."

"We barely talked. I just—I'm so nervous." She slumps against the wall, like she needs it to hold her up. "I've never met a mother before."

"I know."

"It's nerve-wracking. She seems nice, but I just want her approval. I want her happy with her son's choice. You're her only son. This is kind of a big deal."

"It's not like we're getting *married*, Syl. It's all gonna be okay." I smirk, waiting for her outburst, which comes in seconds.

"What the hell, Spence, are you serious? You said—"

I cut her off with my lips, kissing her until she's clinging to the front of my shirt, a low whimper sounding in the back of her throat. "I'm just teasing," I murmur against her mouth, nibbling on her upper lip. "I'm going to make an honest woman of you someday. Just wait. It's going to happen."

She swats at my chest, her eyes sparkling. A few weeks ago, I would've never been able to tease her like this. She's come a long way, my Syl.

Then again, so have I.

"Spencer! Sylvie! Lunch is ready!" Mom calls from the kitchen.

Sylvie's gaze finds mine once more, her lips curved into a faint smile. "I've never had a mother make me lunch before."

"Her homemade lasagna is out of this world. My father still talks about it," I tell her, leaning in to steal another kiss. She pushes at my shoulders, laughing.

"Come on." She pulls away from me, taking my hand and leading me back to the kitchen. "I'm starved."

"We didn't get a chance to check out my room," I protest as she drags me down the hall.

"We can do that after lunch," Sylvie says, glancing over her shoulder at me. "Maybe I'll even let you kiss me in your room."

"If I can only be so lucky," I tease her, loving this light and airy version of Sylvie.

I do need to make an honest woman of her.

Soon.

CHAPTER THIRTY-ONE

SYLVIE

"I want to go to the family house in Newport," I tell Spencer later that night, when we're in bed and the apartment is dark and quiet.

Too quiet.

I've been amped up ever since my visit with Summer, and then the lunch with Spencer's mother. It's almost like I'm…manic. I haven't felt this way since Earl died. Full of nervous energy mixed with a healthy dose of uncertainty. Always unsure of what could possibly happen to me next. There are no more visible threats, not really. I have Spencer with me, and he swore he would protect me no matter what.

Even from my mother.

So why the uneasiness? Why is there constant dread swirling in my stomach, making it tough for me to eat? To think? To sleep?

I've dealt with this feeling pretty much my entire life, and I hate it.

I want it gone.

The only way I believe that'll happen is if my mother is truly out of my life. I may have banished her out of it as much as I can, but her energy is still out there, filling up the city. It's as if I knew she'd returned. I could feel her spiritual pressure or whatever you want to call it. When she went out of the country, I was totally free.

But I'm not free any longer, and it's the worst feeling in the world.

"You want a cat. You want to go to the Newport house. Next, you'll want to go back to California." The amusement in Spencer's voice is obvious.

"Yes. I'll probably want to do that next week," I tease, sitting up in bed so I can look down at him. He's lying flat on his back, his arms propped behind his head, biceps bulging. I can barely see him, but the city lights from the cracks in the curtain shine through, illuminating him in an orangey glow.

He's so stupidly handsome, I want to grab my pillow and whack him on the head with it.

Then I think of my mother and her clutching that pillow, eager to press it to my face in the hopes to end my life, and I forget all about it.

"Why do you want to go to Newport? That house is enormous."

"And blessedly private."

"With a thousand servants to indulge your every whim."

"Not a thousand," I tease. There are quite a few though. "Knowing they're there makes me feel safe. My mother won't try anything with a bunch of servants in residence."

I've thought about this. There is nowhere nearby I can escape to but that house. People will be watching me constantly. She doesn't go there anymore. Not really. Not since we've all become adults and moved on.

"Whatever. You want to go there, you should go there."

"I want you to go with me. We could spend the weekend there. It'll be fun. The weather is better. The food is delicious. We could sit by the pool and bake ourselves in the sun." Another idea comes to me, better than the first. "Maybe we should go on vacation. I know Europe is extra hot right now, but the Italian coast has been calling to me lately. God, it's so beautiful there."

"I've never been," he says, his eyes slowly closing.

"What? You've never been to Italy?" My mouth pops open in shock. "You're *Italian*, Spence."

"I never said I haven't been to Italy. I have been, plenty of times." His eyes crack back open, his lips curling in a sexy smirk. "We just never made it over to the coast."

"Oh. Well, that's just…shameful. You must go. We need to plan a trip now. We can go by the end of the summer. Maybe even September, when it's still warm but not overly so. I can put everything together—I have a travel agent who's amazing. Has inside connections with all of the luxury hotels on the Amalfi coast. We could take a couple of weeks away. Just the two of us." I practically throw myself at him, landing on his chest and making him grunt. His arms spring away from his head and automatically go around me, and I snuggle in close, almost purring in contentment.

I got what I wanted. My man holding me.

"I can't leave until later in the fall. Too much going on with work right now." When he speaks, his mouth brushes my temple, making me shiver.

"You always have to work." I'm pouting.

"You're right. I do."

I contemplate what I want to say to him and wonder if he'd consider it rude.

Forget it—I'm saying it. He knows how I can be and I haven't scared him away yet.

"I have a lot of money." I lift my head to find him already watching me. "I could take care of us for the rest of our lives and still have a ton of money left over."

"I don't want your money, Syl." His expression is serious, as is his tone.

"Is this some sort of macho thing, where you won't take my money and you want to stand on your own two feet?" I roll my eyes when his head barely moves in a nod. "That's incredibly archaic. My trust fund is so huge it would take generations to spend it all."

"Leave it for your children then," he says.

My heart stalls in my chest. "My children? Or *our* children?"

"Our children." He pauses. "Though now I'm remembering you said you didn't want kids."

"Yet," I emphasize.

The more time I spend with Spencer, the more I want to have his children. I can envision it now. They'd all be dark-haired and dark-eyed, and we'd break the fair-haired and blue-eyed curse of the Lancasters.

My children wouldn't even be Lancasters. They would be Donatos, and I like that idea.

A lot.

"All right then, yes. *Our* children. Eventually," he tacks on to make me happy.

My blood pumps hot and fast at his words. The soft glow in his eyes as he watches me. He reaches out, his fingers sifting through my hair and my body goes liquid.

"Are you implying that you're going to ask me to marry you?" My heart trips over itself at the thought, and for one terrifying moment, I'm afraid I overspoke.

It gets worse when Spencer gently dumps me onto the mattress before he's climbing out of bed. I watch him go, sitting up once more, clutching the sheet to my chest. I am naked and vulnerable and scared he's going to say we're moving too fast. That I need to slow down.

He does none of that. I watch as he walks over to his dresser and pulls open a drawer, withdrawing something small from within before he shuts it. He ambles back over to the bed, completely naked and one hundred percent casual about it, leaning over to flick on the lamp before he takes my hand.

And proceeds to get on one knee.

"What are you doing?" I squeak.

"Listen to me." He squeezes my hand and I go completely still. Utterly quiet. "I love you, Sylvie. So damn much. I barely remember a time when I didn't love you. I'm probably rushing this, but fuck it. I bought you a ring." He holds it out to me with his other hand, and I gasp.

It's a giant, deep red ruby flanked by diamonds on either side. It's bold and outrageous and exactly what I've always wanted.

"Will you marry me?" he asks as I stare at the ring, too overwhelmed to speak. I lift my gaze to his, noting the nervousness I see there.

I throw myself at him again, making him fall backward onto the floor, the ring dropping as well. I rain kisses all over his face, murmuring "I love you" over and over again, until he's laughing and trying to get away from me.

"You didn't answer my question," he's finally able to say when I stop kissing him everywhere.

"Yes." I straddle him, his thickening cock nestled between my legs. I thrust my hips forward, hissing out a breath when I feel him nudge against me. "Yes, I'll marry you."

He glances around, his brows furrowed. "Where's the ring?"

I look around too, until I spot it to my right, lying on the carpet just out of reach. I lean over him, my tits in his face as I grapple for the ring, and a jolt runs through me when he draws a nipple into his mouth, sucking it deep.

"Spencer," I chastise, though my voice is weak.

I don't really mean it. It feels too good, his lips on my skin. Tugging and pulling, his tongue lashing. I clutch the ring in my fist, my eyes falling closed when he switches to my other nipple, and I tilt my head down, watching him.

He eventually releases my nipple with an audible pop, his heated gaze locked on mine. "Where is it?"

I hold it between my fingers in front of his face. He snatches it from me. "Give me your hand."

I do as he asks, holding my breath when he slowly slides the ring on my finger.

It's a perfect fit.

"I saw it, and immediately knew it was yours," he admits.

I stare at my hand, at the deep red ruby that's so large it practically covers my whole knuckle. "I love it."

"I love you."

The depth of emotion in his voice threatens to send me into tears. I kiss him instead, clutching his beloved face with my hands, my tongue delving deep, searching his mouth. We kiss and kiss, rubbing against each other, our skin heated, our bodies ready.

Eventually, I readjust myself, sliding down his thick cock until he fills me completely. We lie there, his body throbbing inside mine, our gazes catching. He kisses me before he shifts up into a sitting position, me on his lap, my legs winding around his waist, his erection still embedded inside me.

"You belong to me," he whispers in my ear, his hands on my hips guiding me. "There is nothing I won't do for you, Syl. Not a single thing. You're my everything."

I wind my arms around his neck, my mouth finding his, devouring him. I love how protective he is of me. How safe I feel when we're together. I don't want anyone else.

Just him.

"I love you," I whisper against his lips. "I can't wait to be your wife. But I need something from you."

"Anything." He pulls me down, his cock going as deep as it can get, making me moan.

Making me forget for the briefest moment what I want from him.

But I can't forget. I need this one last thing.

"Be truthful with me." He tries to kiss me, but I dodge his seeking lips. "Tell me what you do. For your father. For the family business. I deserve to know the truth, Spence."

He goes still and I do too, my gaze never straying from his. I want him to know I'm not scared. He can tell me anything and

I won't run.

"Whatever it is, I'm not leaving. You won't lose me. I'm not afraid. Not of you," I say when he still hasn't spoken. "Please, Spence."

"Syl—"

"Don't give me an excuse. Tell me, Spencer. I need to know. I deserve to know."

Leaning in, he presses his forehead to mine, blowing out a harsh breath. "It's a lot."

"I have witnessed so many things over the years, had so much happen to me, I can handle it. I'm not afraid." I swallow hard. "Tell me."

"Right now? Don't we have better things to do?" He thrusts upward, gripping my hips and keeping me in place as he slowly fucks me. "We can talk about this later."

"You always say that, and it's never later. I hate that you won't talk to me about this. It's like you're keeping this from me on purpose."

"I am," he says without hesitation. "There are some things better left unsaid."

Irritation fills me. "If you won't tell me, I don't know if I want to marry you—"

He clamps his hand over my mouth, silencing me. His cheeks are red, his eyes blazing with barely-contained anger. "No. You don't get to play that game. You love me, I love you. We're getting married."

I stare at him, shocked by his ferocity. I don't bother speaking since his hand is still covering my face.

"Besides, it's too late. You can't back out now." He slowly lowers his hand from my face, his mouth brushing against mine. "You're mine. Forever."

He kisses me, his body moving in mine, trying to make me forget, but his words are on repeat in my head.

You're mine. Forever.

They make me feel safe, but they also leave me a little...

Scared.

CHAPTER THIRTY-TWO

SPENCER

I enter my father's office and settle into the chair across from his desk, quiet while he's on the phone. I pull mine out of my pocket to check if I have any messages, but there are none.

Impatient, I shove my phone away, stewing as I listen to my father smooth talk some sucker into giving him money. Extorting another small business owner to smuggle drugs—the life of a mobster.

We're on the fringe, linked to one of the most powerful mafia families in the country, if not the world. We're protected by them, unless we cross them in any way.

If that ever happens, we're dead. My father first, me next.

I used to be the heavy. The one who would meet with those who owed us money, who stole drugs from the shipment and sold them on their own. The squirrely ones, the sneaky ones. The men who would piss their pants when we showed up, threatening their lives, their family's lives.

I hated it. Only did that for little over a year before I went to my father and demanded to do something else. I couldn't take it anymore. I'm smart, I'm good with numbers, so I started cooking the books next. We have an accountant team and even a CFO, but I've got an entire set of books and countless spreadsheets that sing a different tune. Siphoning money here and there, so we don't have to pay taxes, so we can put that money into our pockets, and our employees' pockets too.

What we do is illegal. I'm putting myself on the line every day I go into the office, but what can I do? This is my world, and it always has been.

There are some advantages to this lifestyle though, and I take advantage of them whenever I can.

Like now.

The moment my father ends his call, I'm talking.

"Did you find out any of the information I asked for?" I lift my brows, waiting for his answer.

My father leans forward, resting his forearms on the edge of his desk. "You like chasing after rich old ladies now or what?"

Irritation flits through my blood, and I mentally tell myself to cool down. I knew he'd say something like this. It's just his way. "I'm looking out for my fiancée."

His brows shoot up practically to his hairline. "Your fiancée now, is it? You never bothered to tell me about this. Though I heard you took her to meet your mother. Guess you mean business after all."

"Don't think you much care who I'm marrying anyway," I retort. "Besides, you knew I was with a Lancaster. You even expressed your approval."

"Not sure if I completely approve. The Lancaster name does bring a different kind of exposure."

I can't deny that, but I also need to make one thing clear before this conversation goes further.

"No more insults about her. You can't call her a liability either. Do you understand?" I lift my brows, waiting for him to challenge me.

A soft chuckle leaves him. "Look at you. Manning up. I like to see it."

I don't say anything in response. Maybe he's right. I've been shuffling along, just living life. Now that I've got something—someone—to protect, I am manning up, as he calls it.

"Just watch it with that family. Don't give anyone too many details about what you do, even your girl. That family could blow us up and put a spotlight on our business."

"I'm not scared. We've always stayed in the shadows. And I'm thinking about getting out of this anyway."

He snort-laughs. "It's not that easy, son. You really believe I'm going to just let you walk away and let your new rich wifey take care of you? I don't think so."

I think of Sylvie saying her money could take care of us for life, and I realize my protests weren't in vain. There's no way my father will let me escape from the business. No matter how hard I try.

"Tell me what you found out about Sylvia Lancaster," I say, changing the subject.

I asked my father to have his best private investigator do a little digging into Sylvia Lancaster's background, see if he could come up with anything that's been kept quiet. Any information I can use against her, I'll take straight to her and blackmail her ass straight out of Sylvie's life, once and for all.

Dad sighs, leaning back in his chair. "Not much. Most of what she does is public knowledge. Except for her recent facelift. She was photographed at the airport, arriving in Ibiza, but she was never caught leaving that place. They did that shit in secret, so no one would see her with bandages."

"Already knew about that." I jiggle my foot, anxious for something juicy. "Anything else?"

He snags a manilla envelope from the bottom of the pile of paperwork on his desk and drops it on top, flipping the file open. He scans over the information and I marvel at the fact that he's so damn old-fashioned he couldn't have the info sent to him via email.

"Paper. Really?" I ask.

"Easier to get rid of compared to an electronic file, which leaves a trail."

"And paper doesn't?"

He lifts his gaze to mine. "It was put together on a typewriter. My guy doesn't like to take any risks."

I almost laugh, but when I see the look on his face, I remain quiet.

"Looks like she was questioned by a team of doctors about six years ago or so," Dad says offhandedly as he continues reading.

That has me sitting up straighter.

"Really? What about?" I keep my tone nonchalant, but my interest is definitely piqued.

This could be exactly what I'm looking for.

"Something about filling false prescriptions at a variety of pharmacies?" Dad's brows draw together as he continues to read the report. "Yeah, she was accused of gaming pharmacies and using fake prescriptions to obtain medication for her kid."

For Sylvie.

"The child wasn't named because she was a minor." He glances up at me. "Your fiancée?"

I nod, clenching my jaw. "Yes."

"Uh huh. Well, I'm sure this was all kept very hush hush, because of who she is. Never brought before any type of official medical board or even the police. A team of doctors that she'd been taking her child to got together, compared notes and eventually questioned her. Sounds like she was outraged and claimed it must've been some sort of mistake. I'm thinking she most likely paid them off and then it was done. She was off the hook and the allegations disappeared."

Such bullshit. Money is most definitely power. Money buys you everything you could ever want. Even when you get caught trying to poison your child, you're able to pay off a team of doctors—people who are supposed to protect the ill and the hurt—and take care of things with a few quiet payments. Sweeping everything under the rug, never to be mentioned again.

My father continues skimming the documents and I let him. I'm too angry to try and read at the moment. My hands are curled into fists and I pound one on the edge of the chair over and over. Harder and harder. Until it starts to hurt.

The woman should pay for what she's done to her daughter. Sylvie is a fucked-up mess, thanks to her mother. I know she'll eventually heal. That everything will be okay because I'm going to take care of her.

But I will never rest, knowing that woman merely exists. Living in the same city as us. No wonder Sylvie wanted to leave.

Maybe we should both leave. Go to her house in California and hide away in the forest. I could make something work. My father won't want me to leave, but I could figure something out.

Eventually.

"That's about the most scandalous thing I can find here," Dad says as he flips through the papers. "The divorce looks like a doozy. He paid her a lot of money. Alimony and child support, which is hilarious, considering none of those kids lived with her. They were all away at school. The child support eventually stopped, but she's still getting the alimony. Plus a fat settlement check. She's definitely not hurting for money."

"She comes from a wealthy family too. The woman will never be broke," I say absently, fixing my gaze on the window to my right, staring at the city. Sylvia is out there somewhere, doing God knows what. "I want a tail on her."

"Are you serious? Why?"

I return my attention to my father. "I don't trust her. She wants to kill my future wife, and I refuse to give her the opportunity to do so. Not on my watch."

"That'll cost you."

"I don't care." Not like I spend my money much anyway.

"How long do you want someone to follow her?"

Till she's dead.

"I don't know. Until I feel like she's no longer a threat." I rise to my feet. "If you won't put it together, I will."

"Calm down. I'll help you. I'll contact the PI right now. I know he's got an entire staff that does surveillance." My father slaps the file shut and hands it over to me. "I'll have them start ASAP."

"Perfect." I take the file from him. "Thanks."

"You're going to a lot of effort over this girl," Dad observes.

"She's the woman I'm going to marry. Someday, she'll be the mother of my children." I can feel my blood pressure rise, and I take a deep breath, refusing to let the old man work me into a froth. "I would destroy this city with my bare hands if it meant I could keep her safe."

He watches me for a moment before he slowly starts to shake his head. "A liability, I tell you."

"I don't care what you think." I slap the file against my chest. "She's not a liability to me."

My father informs me the surveillance is in place, but it doesn't feel like enough.

So I make my way to Sylvia's apartment building, parking out in front of it and lying in wait. I've got the window down, no music playing. Just the noise of the street keeping me company. The occasional siren. The sound of voices talking as people walk by. I barely look at my phone, too focused on the double doors that lead inside, just waiting for Sylvia Lancaster to make her appearance.

With my luck, I'll never see her.

I should be working. Or spending time with Sylvie. Instead, I'm sitting in one of my father's cars, watching the comings and goings of the elite as they enter and exit the building. There are two doormen working the front, both of them elderly. I could take them if I wanted to. Not that I plan on it.

But I do notice there's no actual security standing outside the building. Though nothing this high-end would go without a security detail. There is far too much money in this building to go unprotected.

Not that I'm interested in anyone's money. More like I just want access to Sylvia. Just for a few minutes. I want to give her a piece of my mind, and tell her to stay away from Sylvie for good. I mean fucking business, and she needs to witness it.

"What the fuck are you doing?"

There's a slapping sound, my car rocking, and I nearly jump out of my seat.

Whit is standing there, bracing the window frame of my car, grinning maniacally.

"Jesus." I run a hand down the front of my tie. "You about gave me a heart attack."

"Are you spying out here, Donato? Seriously?" He pushes away from my car and rounds the front of it, opening the passenger side door and slipping inside. "Close the window. It's fucking hot."

"Asshole," I mutter under my breath as I start the car and hit the button to shut the window. I hate that I automatically did his bidding, but it's as if the need to please a Lancaster is bred within me. I've been doing it for years.

Old habits are hard to break.

"What are you doing here?" I ask him as he taps away on his phone. "And who are you texting?"

If he says his mother, I'm going to fucking lose it and start swinging. I don't care if he is my best friend.

"I'm texting my cousin Grant." He taps at the screen for a few seconds more before I hear the telltale swoosh of a text being sent. "The real question is what the hell are you doing here? Lurking outside my mother's building?"

I don't want to answer. I'll sound like I've lost my damn

mind, especially when we already have hired PIs spying on her.

"Come on, Spence. Be real with me. Are you waiting for my mother to magically appear?" I keep sulking, not saying a word, and he eventually scoffs. "Fine. Don't answer me. I already know what you're doing, and I get it. I do. My mother is completely untrustworthy. But hanging out in front of where she lives in the hopes of, I don't know, talking to her, isn't the best move."

"I want to keep her away from Sylvie," I admit.

I can feel Whit's eyes on me as I stare straight ahead, watching as the door opens and an elderly gentleman with a very young woman on his arm come walking out.

"Don't you think the best way to keep her from Sylvie is to be with Sylvie, always?"

He's right. I know he is. But I don't want to be agreeable. I'm pissed. Frustrated. "I can't be with her at all times."

"You could be with her right now," he suggests, sounding so frustratingly logical, I want to punch him in his smug face.

Instead, I scrub my hand across my face. "What are you doing here?"

"Meeting with her. She asked me to come over. I know it's about the baby." He blows out an exaggerated breath. "She's been upset we don't let her spend time with Augie, and now with another baby coming, she's going to whine and try to wheedle her way back into our lives."

"Are you going to let her?"

"No. Summer refuses. Especially since we're having a daughter." He sends me a look. "Now that it's been confirmed what my mother did to Sylvie, Summer is adamant that Grandma dearest doesn't get near our children."

"I don't blame her. But why are you listening to your mother plead her case when you've already made up your mind?"

"I want to hear what she has to say. What kind of lies she'll tell to get me to agree. She's a master of manipulation, but I've been on to her game since I was like…thirteen. I see right through it, unlike some people. Namely, my sister."

"I asked her to marry me," I admit, my voice low.

The surprised look on Whit's face is almost comical. "No shit? What did she tell you?"

"She said yes."

"Well, hell." He grins. "Welcome to the family. You're crazy for wanting to be a part of this."

"I'm in love with her." God, I sound like I'm in pain and maybe I am. I love Sylvie so damn much it hurts. That's why I'm sitting in front of her mother's high-rise, hoping to catch a glimpse of her like a crazy man. What would I do if I saw her?

Shit, I don't know. Confront her? Tell her to back the fuck off? Tell her I'll end her if I catch her near Sylvie?

Threats aren't smart. I know they're not. But that's all I want to do when I think of Sylvia coming near Sylvie.

"I know," Whit says, reaching for the door handle. "I'll mention Sylvie to her too. How she needs to leave her alone."

"She won't listen," I say, knowing I'm telling the truth. "She'll do what she can to try and get her back into her life."

"I'll mention the possibility of a restraining order. Though I will not mention the fact that her future son-in-law is lying in wait for her. That would fuck everything up." He gets out of the car and turns to face me. "Don't do anything stupid."

He shuts the door before I can answer, which is a good thing.

I don't want to make promises I know I can't keep.

CHAPTER THIRTY-THREE

SYLVIE

I arrive at the Newport house late on a Friday morning, excitement rippling through me when I enter the home. The foyer is bathed in warm sunlight, everything clean and sparkling and beautiful. The servants are lined up and waiting to greet me as I walk through the front door like we're in freaking Downton Abbey.

There are so many memories wrapped up in this house. Most of them good. Only a few negative. So many family holidays were spent here. Summers here too, until Mother purchased the Hamptons house and we always ended up going there.

I haven't been to the Hamptons in years. I view that as her territory. She received the house in the divorce and she can have it. There is no desire in me to go to the Hamptons.

None at all.

I greet all of the servants I know with warm hugs and shake the hands of the ones who are newer. A few of them even bow for me, which makes me feel embarrassed. I don't need all the pomp and circumstance like my parents do. Father just expects it, and my mother absolutely demands it.

After all the formal greeting, I escape to my bedroom, collapsing on the giant bed as soon as I shut the door. I stare at the intricate ceiling, the painting in the center circle that dates back to the early nineteen hundreds, and I realize I've never in my life stayed in this house by myself.

It's kind of nice.

Not that I'm alone. There are so many servants, my mother wouldn't dare try anything with me. Not that she knows I'm here but...

She could. She's got spies everywhere.

Spencer is coming out to join me this afternoon. Actually, he should hopefully be here within the hour since he left work early. Traffic wasn't as bad as it usually is when I left the apartment, so I arrived early, which he didn't want to happen. I know he's worried about my mother possibly showing up, but she doesn't know I'm here, and besides, there are plenty of people on the premises.

I'll be fine.

We'll spend the weekend here and head back either late Sunday night or early Monday morning. He also mentioned we're due for a long talk about what he does for his father's business. He swore he would tell me everything, not leaving out a single detail.

"I'll tell you all about it this weekend," he said last night over dinner. "When we're all alone and with no interruptions."

I almost don't want to know. He makes such a big deal out of it, I'm afraid to hear the details. But then again, it might not be a big deal after all. Kind of like when something is overhyped. Everyone raves about that certain movie you've been dying to see and when you finally go to the movie theater, you realize it's not that big of a deal and you're disappointed.

I'm afraid that's what is going to happen with his explanation. It's probably not as bad as he makes it out to be.

My phone rings when I'm about to go downstairs in search of some lunch, and I see Roland's name flashing on the screen.

"Roland! How are you?" is how I greet him.

"Exhausted after chasing that cat all over the property," he grumbles, sounding completely put out, which is his usual mood.

"Did you catch her?"

"I did, but she sure scratched me up." I hear incessant meowing in the background and I can't help but laugh.

"I can hear her complaining to you."

"More like she's complaining about me. She's not happy with me at all. And she probably won't be happy with you either when she gets to the city." He hesitates. "You sure you want to take her in out there? She's kind of wild."

"I'll tame her," I say with confidence.

"It's not that easy. And she's mean as hell." There's more meowing, and I swear she's rattling her cage. "I worry about getting her to you, Miss Lancaster."

"I've already made the arrangements for you. As long as you're still willing to make the drive," I tell him.

I rented a car for Roland to drive across the country with Squirrel, since his old truck probably wouldn't make it. Once he arrives here with the cat, I'll purchase him an airplane ticket— first class—and send him home. It'll take time out of his life, but his schedule is fairly free in the summer, he informed me.

"You'll leave first thing in the morning?" I ask him.

"Yes ma'am. And I hope to get there by Friday. It's going to be a long haul, but I have a leash for the cat. And a nice, comfortable carrier. She'll be in good hands."

"I don't doubt it. I'm excited to see her. And you too."

"You just want your cat."

"It's true," I say with a little laugh.

Spencer was right. I want this, I want that, I want everything. Including him.

Considering how I was raised, I've been indulged my entire life. Money is no object and I'm aware I can be rather demanding.

But when you can pay a retired gentleman with not much going on in his life to transport the wild cat you're drawn to cross country, then why not?

I can't wait for Squirrel to be here with me. I need something soft and cuddly to love on. Though she doesn't sound particularly soft or cuddly.

Oh well. I'll force her to love me. I'm good at that.

Look at Spencer. I pretty much forced my love on him until he didn't have a choice but to love me back.

I took a twenty-minute nap after my light lunch and when I wake up, Spencer still isn't here. I check my phone to see he sent me a text saying that traffic's horrible and he should be there soon.

He better get here soon. I'm already bored without him.

I wander the halls, staring at the portraits of old Lancasters lining the walls. The original Augustus has the most prominent spot at the top of the stairs, where everyone can see him, and every time I look into his eyes, I shiver. They're eerily like mine. Light blue and blazing bright. I wrap my arms around myself as I pass by each portrait, examining them until I end up in front of the photograph of my family. One of the last taken before my parents divorced.

Mother is sitting on a chair in the center, my father standing directly to her right, his hand on her shoulder. Whit looms behind her, tall and thin, his expression dead serious. Carolina stands in front of our father, her hair slicked back in a ballerina's bun, her rosebud lips curled into a barely-there smile.

And then there's me, standing to my mother's left, a sullen-faced girl who looks like she'd rather be anywhere but there. I'm thin and pale and wearing a sweater, though I remember we took the photo in the summer, in the library of this very house. I wore the extra layer so I wouldn't look so frail, but it was no use.

I'm skin and bones and nearly translucent. My mother had reached out at the last moment, right when the camera clicked, catching my hand and holding it so tightly, you can see her fingernails pressing into my skin.

It's a terrible photo, a representation of our family crumbling, yet Mother is clinging to me, as usual. She also made sure to hang it on the wall. An eyesore to remind her husband of the destruction he wielded that summer. By the end of it, she'd discovered he was cheating on her for over a year with Summer's mother.

The next summer, my parents put on a brave front, but by the end of it, they'd split. No more official family portraits taken together ever again. We were irrevocably broken.

And I was left alone with her to help pick up the pieces, something a thirteen-year-old should never have to deal with, yet there I was. My mother's little pet.

"That's one of my favorite photos of us," calls a familiar voice.

Shocked, I whirl around to find my mother standing at the other end of the hall, a faint smile on her altered face. I blink at her, holding my eyes closed for a few beats because surely, I'm hallucinating right now. Being in this house always brings them back, all the memories swarming inside me.

But when I open my eyes, she's still standing there. Even closer now. Her hands are behind her back and she's wearing a chic, flowing summer dress. It's sleeveless and long, a bright floral print that stands out against her lightly tanned skin. Her blonde hair is slicked behind her ears and giant pearls dangle from them, a matching oversized pearl necklace around her neck. She looks as if she just stepped off a yacht and decided to make a surprise visit.

"What are you doing here?" I ask, my voice faint.

Her smile is kind—and a complete lie. "I found out you were here and thought I'd pop in."

Pop in. Like this is a fun little visit that I'm looking forward to. "How did you know I was here?"

The smile turns into a faint smirk and she shrugs her bony shoulders. God, she's the thinnest I've ever seen her. "I have my ways. People who feed me information."

I glance toward the railing, my gaze landing on the empty

foyer below. The house is eerily silent and realization dawns.

One of the servants told her about my arrival. I'm sure she paid the person off for the information.

God, I can't trust anyone.

"I sent everyone away for the weekend. It'll just be the two of us, and we can catch up. Doesn't that sound nice?" Mother smiles, but it doesn't quite reach her eyes.

It sounds horrible. Like my worst nightmare come true.

Mother takes another step toward me, slow and casual. As if she's not a threat. "I've missed you, darling. It's been so long since we've had any alone time together. You're constantly surrounded by people."

"That's on purpose," I remind her, taking a step backward to create distance, but she just keeps creeping closer. "We can't spend time together anymore, Mother. It always ends—badly between us."

For me.

She frowns, her delicate brows drawing together, the only movement on her freshly preserved face. She looks incredibly young. Her features, minus her eye color, remind me of myself, just like Summer told me. "It does not. I've only ever wanted to protect you."

"You've done a terrible job of it." I reach inside my jean shorts pocket, my fingers brushing against the top of my phone. Relief floods me as I whip it out. "Stay away from me. Or I'm calling the police."

Mother bursts out laughing, slowly walking toward me. "Oh, darling, you sound so silly. You can't call the police. I'm your mother. All I want to do is talk. Nothing else." She holds her hands out, palms pointed toward the ceiling. Innocent and nonthreatening—another lie. "I promise."

I take another step backward, my butt bumping against the wall, my head knocking into a portrait of one of my dead relatives and sending it askew. "The problem with your promises is that you can never, ever keep them."

"You think so low of me, don't you?" She makes a tsking noise, shaking her head. "It's such a shame, how badly our relationship has fallen apart."

"Well, you know whose fault it is for that." I brace my other hand on the wall, the phone clutched in my right hand, ready to dial if need be.

"I blame you," she says, her voice serious. "You've pushed me away for years, when all I want is for us to have that special bond we used to share. I don't have it with anyone else, you know. Not your brother, and definitely not Carolina. She treats me with such disdain, as if being in my presence disgusts her. And Whit thinks I'm an imbecile. He has no respect for women, just like your father."

I don't bother correcting her about Whit, because she's wrong. Though she's correct in regards to Carolina. Our mother terrifies her and Carolina keeps her distance. She saw how Mother controlled me, and wanted nothing to do with it.

And I can't hold that against her. She's lucky she got away.

"You're saying this is my fault?" I ask incredulously.

"Of course. If you'd just listened to me, your life would be perfect. Now it's so...messy." She wrinkles her nose, though there's not much movement there.

How much plastic surgery did she get?

"Messy in what way?" If I keep her talking, I'll distract her. And possibly make my way into my bedroom where I can lock her out.

"This relationship with Spencer Donato is not what I envisioned for you. The fact that you're living with him and not even married is—scandalous."

I want to roll my eyes, but I contain myself. This is the same woman who tolerated her husband's multiple affairs throughout their marriage, always turning a blind eye until she couldn't look away any longer.

"Not as scandalous as me marrying a man old enough to be my father, who I barely knew," I point out. "A man who was a closeted homosexual and engaged in questionable relationships during our marriage. I'm sure you'll tell me you didn't know about Earl's preferences."

"I didn't. He came to me with a very specific request—he wanted to marry you."

"And use me as a front."

"You were young and beautiful and wealthy beyond measure. What man wouldn't want you?"

"You never gave me a choice."

"You didn't want one," she stresses. "You don't like making decisions, Sylvie. You've always said that. You want someone in control of your life always."

"That's what *you* wanted for me. You never gave me the choice to decide on my own. You guided my every move, practically my entire life." I clutch the phone tighter in my hand, glancing down when it buzzes. I can tell it's a text, but I can't see who it's from.

"Because you couldn't make a decision on your own. When you're left to your own devices, you make endless mistakes."

"Right, so it's better I let you make all of my life choices."

Her smile freezes in place. "Yes. Exactly."

"So you can decide whether I live or die."

That smile fades, her eyes going wide. "What in the world are you talking about?"

"You know what I'm talking about. You just refuse to see it. Acknowledge it." I glance to my right, my bedroom door so close. "You've been trying to kill me for years. You almost did. That's why I can't be near you any longer, Mother. Can't you see?"

"Well, can't you see how much I love and adore you?" She rushes toward me, until she's standing directly in front of me. Staring at her face is almost like looking in a mirror, her features are so close to mine. Only our eye color is different. Her face shape, her cheekbones, her chin. Her lips, the slope of her nose.

It's all me. I know I resembled her, but I never thought it was this close.

"Amazing, isn't it? How much I resemble you?" Her eyes are sparkling, her smile wide. She's still so attuned to me, it's freaky. "I brought photos of you with me to my consultation. I told him this is who I want to look like."

My vision gets blurry, and my head starts to spin. What she's saying is so…weird. Distressing.

Not normal.

I think I'm going to faint.

"What?" I ask, my voice weak. I sidestep toward my bedroom, not bothering to hide that I'm trying to get away from her, but she moves with me. Like she's never going to let me escape.

"You heard me. I wanted to look like you. I want people to see us and think we're sisters. We have such a bond, you know. We're connected. I know what you're thinking, how you're feeling, what you want to do next. You're my mini me. My special girl. I named you after me. You're mine. And look, now we resemble each other even more. We could totally pass for sisters now."

"I'm not your sister. You're my mother."

"Oh, I know. We just…it's easier to say we're sisters now, don't you think? When you were younger, you were so needy. I might've done some things to you to keep you quiet. What's the big deal? Lots of moms do it."

I blink at her, shocked by her confession.

"I've done some things I'm not proud of, my darling, but that's all in the past. I can't help it if being so worried about you brought me so much attention. Your father was too busy fucking other women to notice me anymore. I had to do something."

Leave it to her to blame my father for this. She still can't take responsibility.

"What you did was wrong, and you know it." I slip my hand behind me when I'm at my bedroom door, reaching for the handle when she lunges toward me, her hand settling over mine.

"Where do you think you're going?"

I say nothing, a trembling breath escaping me when she tightens her grip on my hand. She's standing so close to me, her body brushes against mine, making me want to recoil from her. I lean my head back until it thumps against the door, desperate to get away.

"You can't escape me, Sylvie. No matter how hard you try, I will always find you. I will always be there for you. No matter what." She reaches out with her other hand, gently touching my cheek, and I flinch. Her hand drops away, a frown on her face. "I only want to take care of you. We need each other. Can't you see?"

My breaths come faster, to the point I feel like I'm going to start hyperventilating, and I close my eyes, mentally telling myself to calm down. "Please back up," I tell her when my eyes pop back open. "I can't breathe."

"Oh, darling. Are you having an asthma attack? Come with me." She takes my hand, leading me away from my bedroom door and down the hall. "And give me your phone."

"No." I shove the phone in my shorts pocket before she can grab it. "Let go of me."

I try to pull away, but her grip is like a lock, clamped tightly around my wrist.

"I'm doing this to help you. I have an inhaler in my room. One of your old ones." She keeps walking, never looking back as she drags me behind her. "I'll take care of you, darling. Take deep, calming breaths if you can."

Her words are causing my breaths to come faster, my throat growing tight, as is my chest. I blink hard, my vision going blurry, and I know, without a doubt, I'm having a panic attack.

"Stop," I tell her, my voice soft. Too soft. She doesn't hear me or chooses to ignore me, I'm not sure.

We pass the staircase, heading for the other hallway, where her bedroom is. She stays in the same room she always has, the one she used to share with my father.

That he allows her to stay here is very generous of him. This is a Lancaster residence, and in his eyes, she is no longer a Lancaster. Even though she never changed her name. I doubt she ever will, even if she marries someone else. The Lancaster name just carries far too much prestige for her to willingly give it up.

"What are you doing?" I ask, pausing when I hear the sound of the door opening.

Mother stops, her head whipping to the side, staring at the foyer downstairs. Spencer appears, shutting the door behind him as he slowly glances around.

"Sylvie," he calls. "Where are you?"

I try to speak, the words getting caught in my throat. But as if he can sense me, his head lifts, his gaze landing on mine, and his brows draw together when his gaze shifts.

And settles on my mother.

CHAPTER THIRTY-FOUR

SYLVIE

"Tell him to leave," Mother says to me under her breath, her expression like a deranged mask. Angry and demanding. "Now."

She still believes she has complete control over me. It's baffling, how delusional she is. How utterly strange it is that she tried to make herself look like me. As if she wants to actually become me. I don't understand it.

I don't understand *her*.

"No." I shake my head.

"Do it!" Her words slur together, and I wonder if she's been drinking. Something's not quite right with her. She seems on edge.

Turning away from her, I croak, "Spencer," hating how weak I sound. How weak I feel. I somehow disentangle myself from my mother's grip at the same time Spencer bolts up the stairs, taking two at a time until he's standing at the very top of them. Once I'm free, I'm running toward him, ignoring my mother's shouts.

He grabs hold of my waist when I throw myself at him, my entire body shaking as I wrap my arms around his neck. I hold onto him for dear life, closing my eyes and breathing in his delicious masculine scent.

I'm safe, I think, the relief that floods me nearly rendering me into tears.

He rests his hand at the center of my back, comforting me, though I can tell he's tense. His focus is on my mother and keeping her away from me.

"Back the fuck up," he says, his voice extra deep and sharp. "I mean it, Sylvia. Stay away from her. From us."

"She is my daughter!" The words explode out of her, making me jerk my attention back to her. "Get your filthy hands off of her!"

"Stay behind me," Spencer murmurs, angling me so I'm standing directly behind him. I use him as a shield, cowering, trembling so hard my teeth start to chatter. "I've called the police. They're on their way."

Mother starts to laugh. "They're not going to kick me out of my house, you imbecile. I belong here; whereas, you're just a guest. An interloper. You'll be the one the police are escorting out of here, not me."

"Don't take another step closer." The warning in Spencer's tone is dark. Ominous. I don't dare look at her, afraid of what I might see.

"You can't keep me from my daughter. No one can. I always find her. I will always be in her life, whether she likes it or not."

"Why do you push yourself on her when she doesn't want anything to do with you?"

"I'm her mother."

"The mother who tried to kill her numerous times," Spencer accuses.

The room goes silent, and I wait behind him, my mind awhirl. What is she thinking? What does she look like?

I slowly peer around Spencer's back, noting the way my mother glares at him, her hand at her neck, fingers toying with the giant pearls that lie there.

"You have a lot of nerve, accusing me of such horrible things," she finally says, her voice shaky.

"I'm only repeating what Sylvie has told me." Spencer's voice is calm, which I'm sure frustrates my mother.

"She's a liar." The venom in her words is startling. "She's always lied. Exaggerated the stories to make me look bad. Do you really think I want to kill her? I love her."

"You have a very odd way of showing your love. You always have."

"You don't know me. Or Sylvie. What are you talking about?"

"I'm going to marry her," Spencer says. "And once she officially becomes mine, I'm going to do whatever it takes to keep you away from her for the rest of your life."

"She won't marry you."

"My ring is on her finger. It's happening."

"Sylvie. Sylvie, please listen to me. Don't marry this boy. He'll just drag you down into his sordid world and your reputation will be forever tarnished. Do you want that to happen to you? As you get older, society is all you'll have. Your husband will leave you and your children will abandon you and you'll be all alone. You're just like me, darling. Just like me. That's why we need each other."

"I'm nothing like you," I tell her, my voice stronger. I cling to Spencer's arm, knowing he's got me. He's protecting me from her, and that's the only thing making me feel brave enough to say this. "I will never be anything like you. You're a horrible person who hurts people to gain the attention of others."

Her expression shifts, her eyes narrowing. Lips forming into a thin line. Her cheeks turn red, the flush spreading downward, to her neck. Her chest.

She's furious.

"You're such an idiot," she spits out. "An ungrateful, selfish brat. Always trying to make it about you, when it had nothing to do with you. Nothing!"

Without warning, she comes rushing forward, sidestepping to the right at the last second, headed straight for me. Spencer shoves me backward, and I trip over my own feet, almost falling. With his other hand, he stops my mother from getting any closer to me, bracing it against her shoulder.

"Let go of me!" she shrieks, struggling against Spencer's grip. Somehow, she gets away from him, her hands up, fingers curled into claws when she lunges toward me. "Come here!"

"No!" I scream.

Spencer is between us in an instant, his arms straight out, hands splayed when they make contact with my mother's chest. He shoves with all his might, sending her toppling backward. She stretches her hands to her side as if to brace herself, her mouth open, eyes wide with shock as she pinwheels in the air, her feet slipping from beneath her.

Just before she goes tumbling down the marble staircase.

I'm screaming. It's like I can't stop. Mother rolls down the stairs, landing at the bottom at an awkward angle, her legs going one way, her torso going another. Her eyes are still wide, her mouth hanging open as a pool of crimson blooms beneath her head.

"Fuck," Spencer mutters, running down the stairs and kneeling beside her. He touches her neck with two fingers, then withdraws them, glancing up at me. "There's no pulse."

For a moment, I'm frozen. Scared. I can't breathe.

And then relief trickles through me, flowing through my blood, the same two words on repeat in my mind.

I'm free.

"Is there any staff here?"

I take in the position of her body, how her knee is bent backward beneath her. There's so much blood. It keeps growing beneath her, spreading across the last step and onto the floor.

"Sylvie!" Spencer snaps, when I still haven't answered him, startling me. "Is there any staff here?"

"No." I shake my head. "She sent them all home."

"We need to call the cops."

"O-okay." I nod, wrapping my arms around myself.

"We need to get our stories straight first."

I frown. "What do you mean?"

"This was an accident. I didn't push her." He pauses for a moment. "Right?"

I'm quiet, his words sinking in. If I say he pushed her, he could face charges. Even if it was an accident. And it was, of course. He didn't mean to hurt her.

He didn't mean to kill my mother.

"Right. You didn't push her," I repeat.

"If you say I pushed her, they could arrest me, Sylvie. You understand the implications behind that? I don't want to go to jail."

Panic claws at my insides at the thought of Spencer being arrested for my mother's death. "I don't want you to go to jail either."

"I won't, as long as we agree that it was an accident, which it was. I didn't mean to push her. I didn't mean for her to lose her footing."

Tears are streaming down my face, but I don't bother brushing them away. "I know you didn't mean it, Spence. You were just trying to protect me."

He rises to his feet, pulling his phone out of his pocket. "Here's what we're going to tell them when they arrive. There was an argument between the two of you. I entered the house to find the two of you fighting on the second floor. I ran up the stairs and interrupted the argument, trying to keep you away from her when your mother slipped and fell down the stairs."

"That's exactly what happened," I say with a nod.

"That's what you'll tell them?"

"Yes."

I start to walk down the stairs when Spencer barks out a harsh, "No." Making me pause.

Making me start to cry harder.

"Don't come any closer, Syl. You don't want to see this." Taking a deep breath, I watch as he taps out 9-1-1 on his phone before bringing it to his ear. "Yes, we need an ambulance. There's been an accident..."

The police show up first, their expressions grim when they talk to Spencer. I come down the servants' stairwell that exits in the kitchen, completely avoiding where my mother is lying, so I can talk to the police as well.

They pull me into a small sitting room that's right off the foyer, speaking to me alone. I can't stop crying. I'm a distraught mess and I wish I had Spencer with me, but I know this conversation needs to happen before they'll let me go to him.

"Tell us exactly what happened," the one officer tells me, his voice and expression kind.

Opening my mouth, I let the words flow, explaining the entire situation. I give them the chronological details about her showing up out of nowhere, and that I wasn't expecting her. How our relationship had become strained the last couple of years, especially lately. I don't mention how she tried to kill me before. How I believe she has mental problems. None of those details matter any longer now that she's dead.

"What were you arguing about?" the cop asks when I mention our fight.

"Like I said, we weren't really spending much time together anymore, and I didn't like how she showed up out of nowhere. I didn't expect her to be here, and I didn't want a confrontation with her."

"Was your mother normally confrontational?"

I nod. "We argued a lot. She argues with all of her children."

The officer scribbles something on his notepad before

lifting his gaze to me. "What you're telling me lines up with Mr. Donato's statement. Sounds like it was a terrible accident. I'm so sorry for your loss, Miss Lancaster."

Swallowing hard, I nod, dropping my head, so I can study my clutched hands in my lap. "Thank you. It's terrible, what happened."

The words, *I'll miss her*, stick in my throat, and I swallow them down. I don't want to lie. I won't miss her.

At all.

We leave the room together, Spencer waiting for me in the foyer, and the moment he sees me, he's running toward me, hauling me into his arms and holding me close.

"I love you," he whispers in my ear as he squeezes me tight. "Everything okay?"

"Yes. As okay as it can be," I admit, closing my eyes.

I'll have to tell my siblings. And my father. I don't know how I'm going to say it, but they need to know right away that she's gone.

Sylvia Lancaster is dead.

"I don't want to stay here," I whisper, when I glance up to stare into Spencer's eyes. "I want to go home. Back to the apartment."

"We'll leave soon. They might need to talk to us some more." He glances up, focusing on the stairwell. "The coroner just showed up."

"She's really gone, isn't she?" The hopeful note in my voice is obvious, and that makes me feel like shit.

Spencer slowly nods, smoothing my hair away from my face, his concerned gaze full of love. All for me. "She will never hurt you again."

Thank God.

CHAPTER THIRTY-FIVE

SPENCER

We returned to the city late Friday night, both of us collapsing into bed the moment we entered the apartment. I had fitful sleep, tossing and turning. Dreaming.

So many dreams. Terrible ones involving Sylvia Lancaster and a staircase.

Every time I'd wake up, I realized it wasn't a dream at all. It happened. It was all so damn real.

And there's nothing I can do to change any of it.

Before we left the house, Sylvie called Whit, then Carolina, and finally her father. Whit took over the necessary arrangements immediately, reassuring Sylvie she didn't have to do anything. Carolina had her usual unemotional reaction. Augustus put on a brave front, but I could hear the tremor in his voice. Learning of Sylvia's death shook him.

Knowing I was the one who caused Sylvia's death? Shook me too.

I didn't mean for it to happen. All I could think about was protecting Sylvie. I did what I had to do to ensure her safety. I never thought it would result in Sylvia's death.

I feel terrible. I made Sylvie lie for me, and I lied as well.

Will I ever be able to forgive myself?

Sylvie wakes me up around eight the next morning, shaking my shoulder gently. "Whit is here. He wants to talk to you."

I sit up, running a hand through my hair, my gaze landing on her. She's dressed and put together as if she's been awake for hours, which is shocking. Sylvie isn't one to wake up early. "Tell him I'll be out in a few."

She offers me a sympathetic look, but otherwise says nothing before leaving the room.

Climbing out of bed, I go to the bathroom and take a piss. Brush my teeth. Throw on a T-shirt and a pair of shorts before I make my way out to the living room to find my best friend sitting on the edge of the couch, clad in a three-piece suit, his expression serious.

Sad.

"Whit." He turns his head when he hears my voice, rising to his feet to pull me into a hug. We embrace, clapping our hands on each other's backs like men do before we withdraw. "I'm sorry for your loss."

"Thank you." Whit nods, his face stoic. Only his eyes give him away. They're blazing with an unfamiliar emotion, and I'm pretty sure it's sadness. "I spoke with the detectives who interviewed you both yesterday. They said it was an accident."

"It was," Sylvie says, coming to stand beside me, forming a united front.

Whit studies her for a moment, turning his attention to me. "Was it really?"

I come close to telling him the truth. I open my mouth, ready to spill our secret, when Sylvie takes over.

"Yes, of course. We were arguing. You know how she can get, always trying to tell me what to do. Spencer came upstairs and tried to separate us, and Mom slipped on the floor and fell backward. The bottom of her sandals was very slick, according to the police officer," she explains. "I'm sure they were new."

"The officer mentioned that to me as well," Whit says,

his intense gaze on his sister. "And you're sure that's all that happened?"

"I was there, Whit. That's what happened," she says firmly.

A sigh leaves him, and he collapses back into the chair. "I can't believe she's gone."

"I can't either," Sylvie admits.

I say nothing. Just stand there with my fiancée by my side, praying to God Whit won't figure out our lies.

"I've already started making the funeral arrangements. It will be held Wednesday afternoon," he says.

"They aren't going to do an autopsy?" Sylvie asks.

Whit frowns. "Why would they? It was an accident, right?"

We both answer, "right," at the same time.

The suspicious look he gives us both would make a weaker person spill everything, but not us. We've dealt with him for a long time and know what to do. We stand there with matching blank faces, appearing as if we're in shock.

Which I suppose we are. What we experienced yesterday was nothing short of traumatic.

"Her body has already been sent to the funeral home and preparations have begun. She'll be cremated as per her wishes," Whit says, sounding like he's talking about everyday business, not his mother's death wishes. "After the funeral, there will be a get-together at Father's house. He wants to host it."

"Of course, he does," Sylvie murmurs.

Again, I remain quiet. Nothing I say would add to the conversation.

"How's Summer?" Sylvie asks.

Whit's entire demeanor softens. "She's fine. Uncomfortable. Very, very pregnant. I don't want her attending the funeral, but she insists she wants to be there for me. For us."

"Let her go. She'll be fine," Sylvie says, and I quietly agree.

Summer is one of the strongest women I know.

There's more talk of the funeral. What music should be

played, who should speak. Their pastor will lead the service, and Whit has put a call out to a few of Sylvia's friends, who might want to say something in her honor.

Sylvie doesn't volunteer to speak, thank God. I was worried she might feel obligated, but she didn't put herself into that position. I doubt Whit would let her anyway. He knows what their relationship was like.

How terrible it was.

"Can I speak to you for a moment?" Whit asks me before he's about to leave. Sylvie has already excused herself to call Carolina, leaving us alone.

Unease curls through me, but I nod my agreement, leading him into my home office and closing the door, so we can have total privacy.

"You don't have to tell me what really happened," Whit starts, shaking his head when I try to say something. "I don't need the excuses, or the lies. I have a feeling there's more to this story than what you're telling me."

I clamp my lips shut, saying nothing.

"Maybe it's best. Maybe I don't want to know the truth, but just know this." He takes a step closer, his gaze intense when it locks on mine. "You're like a brother to me, Spencer. And if you're keeping this from me to protect me, and protect Sylvie, then that's—fine. You have my permission. I love my sister, and while I loved my mother too, I hate what she's done to Sylvie. To all of us. She wasn't—right."

"I'm sorry this happened," I tell him sincerely, because I am sorry it turned out this way. But I'm also not offering up any more details about yesterday. "I don't know how this is going to affect Sylvie."

"She seems to be doing all right."

"I believe she's still in shock. I think I am too."

Whit nods, rubbing his chin. "She's free now, you know?"

"Your mother?"

"No. My sister. Our mother can no longer wield her control over her. I know Sylvie was beginning to stand on her own two feet, but I don't know if she would ever be able to do it completely. Not with our mother always around. She couldn't stay out of Sylvie's life, not that she ever tried. Look at how she showed up at the house yesterday." Whit shakes his head.

Her obsession with my fiancée turned into her detriment.

"She was working with the servants. She'd paid one of them off to tell her when Sylvie would arrive," I explain.

"Are you serious? Which one? I'll fire them. All of them," Whit says vehemently.

"I don't know. Sylvie doesn't know either. And you don't need to fire them. Sylvia isn't around any longer to pay them for information."

"Still means we can't trust them, which I won't have. I need to know who did this." He clenches his jaw, seemingly furious. "I'll fire every single one of them if I have to."

"Relax. You don't want to march in there and make wild accusations. Your mother could be very charming when she wanted to be. She probably convinced them they were doing a good thing, helping her. And she most likely made an offer they couldn't refuse."

Whit sighs, rubbing the back of his neck. "We need to break the Lancaster curse."

"And what exactly is the Lancaster curse?"

"The manipulative tactics we use to get what we want. I'm not a good person, Spence. None of us Lancasters are, but we're trying to change. I want to be a better person for my children," Whit says, sounding pained.

"You've changed over the last few years," I tell him, reaching out to give his shoulder a shake. "Thanks to Summer and your son."

"Yeah." He nods, casting his gaze downward. "That's the plan. I want to be a better person for my wife and my children.

I've done some shitty things because I believed the world owed me. My father is the same way. So was my mother."

"Sylvie has changed too," I tell him. "She's much more honest than she used to be."

Whit actually chuckles. "She used to tell some tall tales."

"Unfortunately, most of those tales I think were actually true."

Whit immediately sobers. "Fuck, I hate that." He stands up straighter. "Whatever happened yesterday with my mother, I want you to know that you did the right thing."

"You don't even know what I did," I say, my voice low.

"And I don't need to know. You were protecting the woman you love. My sister. And for that, I thank you."

He pulls me in for another quick embrace, and this time, there's no clapping on the back, no immediate pulling away from each other.

No, we actually hug, clinging to each other for a moment. I love this man like a brother. And, soon enough, he will be my brother through marriage.

And he just basically forgave me for accidentally killing his mother.

"I'll be in touch," Whit says when he withdraws.

I walk him to the front door. "Let me know if you need anything."

"I will."

The moment he's gone, Sylvie emerges from the bedroom. "Did my brother just leave?"

I nod. "Yes."

She practically runs toward me, wrapping her arms around my waist, and I pull her in as close as I can get. "Did he say anything to you?"

"No," I lie, keeping my own secret from her.

It's best. She doesn't need to worry about what her brother knows or thinks. I'll carry that burden for her.

Gladly.

CHAPTER THIRTY-SIX

SYLVIE

The funeral service is beautiful. Elegant.

We're all clad in somber black, my chic Valentino dress something I know my mother would approve of. The blood red diamond Spencer slid onto my finger glimmers and shines in the sunlight that beams through the church's massive stained-glass windows, blinding me every few minutes when I shift and move, restless.

Always restless.

Summer stands next to me in a flowing black dress, her belly huge. She clings to Whit's arm, her gaze only for him, and I'm so grateful she has him, and he has her. He's become a different person since he's committed himself to Summer. A better person.

I'm proud of him.

The pastor drones on, saying nice words about a not-so-nice woman, and I stare at the elaborate floral display. There's no casket—her remains have already been cremated—but there are white flowers everywhere. Sprays of roses and ranunculus flowers. Beautiful arrangements of fragile white orchids and delicate greenery. The entire church smells like a florist shop, heady and sweet, and I find myself clinging to Spencer's arm, overwhelmed by the scent. The moment.

Everything.

My mother is gone, and while there is a hole in my heart that she once occupied, there is also that sense of relief deep within me that grows and grows as every day passes. She's actually gone.

I'm actually free.

Whit hired a harpist, who begins to play a haunting, beautiful song. I don't recognize it at first until the chorus and then realize it's "Candle in the Wind" by Elton John. The song he sang at Princess Diana's funeral.

God, my mother would love that. Such a perfect touch. She always did admire Princess Diana.

Minutes later, we're all walking out of the church. I'm flanked by Spencer and Whit, Summer on the other side of her husband, Carolina walking behind us with our father, their arms linked. Other family members follow, all of the Lancasters turning out for this moment. She may have been divorced from the family, and she wasn't one of their favorites, but by God, the Lancasters always know how to show up and pay their respects.

In this moment, I'm proud to be a part of this family. Prouder than I've been in a long time.

"Are you all right?" Spencer murmurs close to my ear, his hand clasping mine.

I nod, offering him a faint smile. "I'm fine."

"Good." He squeezes my hand, and I squeeze his in return, so grateful for this man I feel like I could burst.

We walk down the stairs, Summer waddling as she carefully takes each step, grimacing when she lands on the last one. She rests her hand on her stomach.

"Oh God," she breathes out.

Whit hovers, his hand covering hers. "What's wrong?"

"Nothing." She flashes a fake smile. "Just a cramp."

"Come straight over to the apartment," Father tells us, Carolina still by his side. I swear to God she flat out doesn't cry. I haven't seen her shed a single tear since Mother passed, and I wish I was as calm as she is. "I've already told everyone. There's food and drink, and an entire staff to serve it. I hired a piano player and everything."

"Mother would love this type of party," I say.

"She would," Whit agrees.

"At least someone is playing the piano in Daddy's apartment," Carolina says with a little shrug.

I study her, taking in her chic black sheath dress, her bright blonde hair slicked into a sophisticated chignon. She's got black Chanel sunglasses on and giant diamond studs twinkle in each ear. She is the epitome of an Upper East Side socialite. The slender ballerina who doesn't walk, but glides.

I envy the way she bottles up her emotions. It's a known family trait, but she's extra good at it. I wish I could be that contained sometimes.

"Carolina," I say.

She glances over at me. "Yes?"

"I love you," I tell her, wondering when I last said those words to her.

I pull her into a hug, holding her to me, and she clings, pressing her lips to my cheek in a soft, sweet kiss. "I love you too."

We load up into sleek black limousines, Spencer and I sharing one with Whit and Summer. The moment we're inside, Summer is hunched over, her hand on her stomach, her eyes closed as she takes a deep breath.

"Summer," Spencer says, his voice full of alarm, "are you in labor?"

"Of course not." She tosses her head back, her long brown hair falling past her shoulders, her eyes still closed. "It's my mother-in-law's funeral. I can't have the baby."

"Jesus, Summer. What if you're having the baby?" Whit gently shoves her hand away from her stomach, pressing his against the side of it. He holds it there, his head tilted as if he's concentrating on what's happening. Like he's some sort of doctor.

"I can actually feel your contraction."

Panic races through me. "We should get her to the hospital."

"Whit can't go to the hospital. We have to go to the gathering." Summer puffs out a breath, her cheeks turning red. "Oh God, it hurts."

"We're going to the hospital," Whit says firmly, reaching out to hit a button to lower the window that separates the driver from us. He instructs him to take us to the closest hospital, and the driver shifts into racecar driver mode, wielding the limousine through the crowded streets with surprising agility.

And at breakneck speed.

I'm clutching Spencer's arm, my heart racing with a mixture of excitement and fear. Whit is the epitome of calm, speaking to Summer in soothing, calm tones, saying all of the right things, and I realize he's an expert at this. He's had a baby before, been there to support her while she labored with sweet little Augie.

Now they're adding another member to their family, and it makes my heart swell with love.

We pull up to the emergency room entrance minutes later, and Spencer and Whit both get out of the car first to help Summer exit the limo. I give her a hug, and then Spencer and I stand by the limo as we watch them walk into the hospital. The moment they disappear from sight, I turn to Spencer, my eyes filling with tears.

"Baby." He reaches for my face, his thumb streaking across my cheek, catching a tear. "Why are you crying?"

"Life is just full circle, you know?" I try to laugh, but it turns into a sob instead. "We've lost my mother and we're going to gain a baby girl today."

"You're right," he says softly, his eyes glowing as he studies me. "It has come full circle."

"My mother would've loved to meet her." My laugh is watery, and I cover my mouth with my hand, my eyes closing tight for a moment. "I wish she wasn't who she was."

"You couldn't change her, no matter how hard you tried." He

cups my face with both of his hands, tilting it up, and I open my eyes to find him looking at me with unmistakable love. "But now you have a sweet little niece coming, and we need to make sure she knows she's loved by her family."

"I can't wait." I frown. "They never did tell me what they want to name her."

"I'm not sure they know themselves." Spencer leans in, brushing his mouth with mine. "I'm proud of you."

"Why?" I whisper.

"You've been so strong. I know this hasn't been easy."

"Is it wrong to admit I'm a little bit...relieved?" I say that last word in the barest whisper.

"No." He shakes his head. "You can admit all of your truths to me."

"All of them?"

He nods.

"Like how I love you more than anyone else on this planet?"

His lips curl into a small smile. "I feel the same way."

"You do?"

"Yes. You know I do." He kisses me again, deeper this time. "I love you, Sylvie Lancaster."

"I love you too, Spencer Donato."

"Shall we go to your father's apartment?"

A sigh leaves me. "I suppose we must make an appearance."

He drops his hands from my face, winding his arm around mine and steering me toward the back of the limo. "It's going to be okay, Syl. She can't hurt you anymore."

Those five words stick with me through the car ride. While we're at my father's apartment, chatting with family, meeting some of my mother's old friends. They were my favorite people to talk to. They knew Sylvia before she changed for the worse. When her negative trait was going after what she wanted, damn the consequences. They tell me story after story, and I laugh until my stomach hurts, grateful for the distraction.

The group text comes to all of us near the end of the afternoon, when the gathering is just winding down. Whit sent it to me, Spencer, Father and Carolina.

Whit: *Seven pounds, four ounces. Twenty inches long. Lungs as loud as her mama's.*

The text is accompanied by a photo of a red-faced, squalling little baby.

All of us share a smile. My father is beaming with pride. Carolina looks pleased. Spencer slips his arm around my shoulders.

Me: *What is her name????*

Carolina: *Yes! We are dying to know!*

Whit takes minutes to respond. To the point that I'm stomping my black Louboutins against my father's marble kitchen floor, frustration rippling through me.

When the text finally comes through, I can't open it fast enough.

Whit: *Her name is Iris.*

"You have a great-grandmother named Iris," Father says, his eyes suspiciously bright after he reads the text.

"I love it," I say with a sigh.

My heart is full.

CHAPTER THIRTY-SEVEN

SPENCER

We're headed back to my—our—apartment after the gathering, Sylvie's head heavy as it rests on my shoulder. She's so tired. The last few days have been a lot, and while I know she's trying to hide the relief she feels about her mother's death to everyone else, she knows she can always be real with me.

Just like I need to be real with her.

"Are you awake?" My voice is soft in the confines of the car, the wall up between us and the driver.

We have complete privacy. I already scoped the vehicle out earlier for any possible bugs. I've been at this too long to let a rookie mistake like that slip past me.

She slowly lifts her head, her gaze searching mine. "Yes. Everything okay?"

"Not really." A ragged sigh leaves me. "I need to tell you something."

"Are you finally going to confess your truths? The ones you keep from me?" Her voice is hopeful. No one else would want to know this kind of shit.

Only Sylvie.

I hang my head, letting my shame wash over me. After everything that's happened with her mother, I haven't been able to tell her about my father, and what I do for him. There are already so many secrets that tie us together.

What's one more?

Taking a deep breath, I lift my head, my gaze finding hers. There's no judgment in her eyes and it's such a relief, the words spill out of me.

"We're in the mafia. Well, we're more on the fringe of it. We work for a family, one that's well-connected."

Her expression doesn't change. "You've already told me that. Well, not the fringe part."

"Right. Yeah." I run a hand through my hair, noting that it's shaking. Fuck, I'm agitated. This isn't easy. "When I was younger, I used to go with the guys and we'd visit the ones who owed us money. Those poor suckers. They'd cry and plead. Beg us not to hurt them or their family."

My chest aches with the confession but she remains quiet, listening. Which is what I need.

"Sometimes things would get—violent." I pause, the words turning over in my brain. "I've hurt people, and I don't like that."

"Oh, Spence." Her voice is the barest whisper, breaking my heart.

"I never killed anyone though. I couldn't muster up the nerve. My father would always tell me it takes time. He didn't make his first kill until he was twenty-six. I had a few years to go." I laugh but there's no humor in the sound.

"Your father…"

"Is decent when he wants to be, but yeah. He's got blood on his hands. So do I."

She touches my hands, bringing one up to her mouth so she can kiss it, and the gesture nearly breaks me.

"I don't do that any longer. I'm an accountant now for the business."

She drops my hand and bursts out laughing, as if what I said was a joke. "You're kidding."

"I'm not." I shake my head.

"An accountant?" Her laughter dies.

"Yeah. We have one set of documents we turn in, and then there's another set." I glance around, like I'm worried there is some sort of spy camera in this place. But I checked it already. My paranoid urges are making me want to search the car again. "You know what I'm referring to."

"I think I do," she says slowly.

"We move drugs, Syl. All kinds. Counterfeit money. Arms." At her frown, I explain. "Guns. Ammo. Anything the family needs us to do, we're doing it. It fucking sucks."

"Then why do you do it?"

"I don't have a choice."

"We always have a choice." She touches my cheek lightly and I lean into her hand, my eyes falling shut for the briefest moment. "Thank you for telling me."

"Thank you for not running away from me."

"As if I would." She smiles.

I smile too. God, this woman.

What did I do to deserve her?

CHAPTER THIRTY-EIGHT

SYLVIE

ONE YEAR LATER

I'm getting married today at our family estate in Long Island, and it's the wedding of my dreams, thanks to the man of my dreams.

Spencer.

The dress I'm wearing is a vivid red, just like the one I saw in the photo all of those years ago. Spencer did a little research and went in search of the designer, who created the wedding gown worn by Paula Yates when she married Bob Geldof. The wedding took place back in the mid-eighties, but the gown is so very timeless.

Jasper Conran designed the gown to look very similar to what Paula wore on her wedding day, who has since passed. She was blonde and wild, and tragically, a drug addict. We are alike in so many ways, and I'm just thankful I realized I couldn't fall down a destructive path with the help of my therapist, who I still see to this day. Spencer helped too, as did the rest of my family.

I'm lucky I have them all. They saved me, though Spencer always reminds me I saved myself too. I'm stronger than I think.

Finally, I believe him. He says I don't give myself enough

credit, and he's right.

So here I am, giving myself a little credit.

Enough time has passed after my mother's accident that I've come to a realization. She controlled every little part of me for so long, I felt lost without her. She was so intricately woven into my life, it was scary not to have her around. When she died, I firmly believed I would miss her terribly. I knew I was free, but I was also terrified to live in a world without her.

The cliché 'can't live with her, can't live without her' was never more accurate.

I'm confident now that I can stand on my own two feet. That I don't miss her. Our relationship was fraught with tension, fear and abuse. What she did to me is unforgivable. Needing her was codependent behavior that she encouraged.

She was a monster, and I'm glad she's gone.

There's a knock on the door, and before I can answer, Carolina enters the room, gorgeous in a cream-colored beaded gown. She stops when she sees me sitting at the vanity, her hand coming up to cover her mouth for a moment as she takes me in.

"You're stunning," she finally says when she drops her hand.

I turn to face her, still sitting on the velvet-tufted bench, a serene smile on my face. I can feel it, the peacefulness that flows through my body. I'm content. It feels so right, to marry Spencer. Like I've been planning this moment my entire life.

"Thank you," I tell her, glad that I kept the wedding gown a surprise until this very moment. I didn't want anyone to see it. Once Spencer found the designer, he let me take over completely, and when I asked for his input, he told me he wanted to be surprised on our wedding day.

This project has been completely my own, something I've been working on for almost a year, and included me flying to London twice for fittings, taking Monty and Cliff with me the second time. They're the only ones who saw the gown, but not the finished product.

"You would have us wearing actual wedding gowns and you're wearing something like that." She waves a hand at me, her bright red lips curved into a fond smile.

She's teasing me, and it's nice. Our relationship has shifted over the last year and I'm so grateful to have her more present in my life. Mother drove everyone, even my family, away from me because she wanted me all to herself.

That hurts, more than I care to admit.

"I like to do things a little differently," I tease. "You know this."

"Very true."

The gown she's wearing has a heavily-beaded bodice and a flowing tulle skirt. She's correct in calling it a wedding gown, for that's exactly what it is. Summer is wearing a matching one, and Monty and Cliff are in full-blown morning suits like the rest of the men in the wedding party. They're all wearing a black tailcoat, black and gray striped pants, a silvery gray vest and matching tie. Monty and Cliff even chose to wear top hats.

Spencer, Whit and his friends are most decidedly not wearing top hats.

"I feel ridiculous in it," Spencer told me last night at the rehearsal dinner. "And I don't want to look at photos from our wedding years from now and remember how ridiculous I felt."

I kissed him because I liked the idea of us looking at photos of our wedding years from now. Possibly sharing them with our children.

"They sent me to come get you," Carolina says, her voice interrupting my dreamy thoughts. "The ceremony is going to start in thirty minutes. Are you ready?"

"Yes." I slowly stand, readjusting the skirt of my gown. The designer and his apprentice left a few minutes ago to grab something to eat and I haven't moved from the vanity since.

"You need help." Carolina rushes toward me, kneeling down to readjust the heavy skirt and train. "The dress is just...exquisite.

It sparkles."

"I know." I sound smug, which I am, so I don't bother trying to hide it. This dress is just magical, and I know it.

It's going to be a magical day, but we deserve nothing less, Spencer and me. We've been through so much, and we've come out on the other side of it all.

Together.

I'm standing with my father, our arms linked, clutching my bouquet in my right hand. It consists of deep red roses and tumbling ivy, matching the arbor where we're to be married, which is laden with red roses, ivy woven throughout. The weather is cool and crisp, the sun shining above. A perfect fall day.

A perfect day to marry the man I love.

"I'm so happy for you today," my father says, resting his hand over where mine rests on his arm. "You're gorgeous in that dress."

"Thank you." I smile at him.

"Your mother wouldn't approve." He can't help but laugh, and my smile doesn't falter. "I probably shouldn't say that."

"No, it's fine. And you're right, she wouldn't approve. She would hate this." My smile grows.

"It's why you chose it, then?" He lifts his brows.

"She had nothing to do with it. I saw a photo years ago and was inspired," I explain. But maybe she did have something to do with it. One last bit of rebellion on my part.

Maybe I'll always be rebellious. It could be the Lancaster in me, or this is just…me.

The middle child. The wild one. The one who always needs attention.

"All right, places everyone!" Miranda, the wedding planner, is like a dictator, clapping her hands at us, getting everyone in the wedding party lined up. Spencer is already standing in place with his best man—Whit—and the groomsmen. "The ceremony is about to start!"

As the eldest Lancaster cousin, Grant is participating in the ceremony by escorting Spencer's mother to her seat. Cliff walks down the aisle first, Monty following close after him. Then it's Summer, beautiful and voluptuous, her curves more pronounced since having Iris.

Carolina is next, gliding down the aisle as if her feet never touch the ground. She's moves so effortlessly, so gracefully. Must be the dancer in her.

The children are the last to walk before the bride. Augie clutches his sister's hand as she toddles down the aisle, wearing a red dress that's similar to mine, a ring of red roses sitting atop her head. Downy whisps of blonde hair curl about her face, and when she spots her grandma sitting in the crowd, she becomes completely distracted.

Summer passes her bouquet to Carolina before she comes rushing forward, picking up Iris and handing her off to her mother before she takes Augie's hand and leads him to the altar. He stands in front of his father, adorable in his matching morning suit, though he's not wearing a top hat either.

Typical Lancaster child, doing what he wants.

Finally, the music changes, and my father and I step forward in unison. "At Last" by Etta James begins to play, and once the intro is finished and Etta starts singing, we begin our descent down the aisle.

The red veil floats behind me, nearly as long as the train of my gown, and the roses and ivy sitting atop my head are heavy. I smile at everyone as we slowly walk toward the altar, my gaze locking on the group of people we invited. Our wedding is small. Intimate. Not nearly as big as Whit and Summer's, which is fine with me. We only wanted our closest friends and family to celebrate this day with us.

Every step forward takes me to my almost-husband. I finally look at him when the lyrics say, "A dream I can call my own," our gazes locking, and tears immediately spring to my eyes because it's true.

He is my dream. The boy I crushed on. The boy I imagined being with and teased and taunted and tortured. The man I've always, without a doubt, loved with my entire heart.

The song fades when we stop in front of Spencer, and when he smiles at me, all of the earlier nerves and worry and anxiousness float away. As if it never existed.

"Who gives this woman to be married to this man?" the minister asks.

"I do," my father says, squeezing my arm before he lets go of me...

And Spencer takes my hand.

A wedding ceremony is symbolic of so many things that I never noticed before. The passing of me from my father to my husband. The ones we love who are standing up for us, my niece and nephew playing a part too. The words the minister says, binding us together for all eternity, and the way Spencer looks at me, as if I'm the most beautiful woman in the entire world.

I let the tears flow, though there aren't many. And they're all tears of happiness, because why else would I cry when marrying this man? He is my love. My future. My entire world.

"...I now pronounce you husband and wife. You may kiss the bride," the minister finally says, after we've repeated our vows to each other.

Spencer settles his hands on my waist, pulling me gently toward him and pressing his mouth to mine. The kiss is soft and sweet, with the faintest tease of his tongue, and when he pulls away, everyone begins to applaud.

"Introducing Mr. and Mrs. Spencer and Sylvie Donato!"

We beam at everyone as the applause grows before we head back down the aisle, followed by the rest of our wedding party.

Spencer clutches my hand in his, our fingers interlocked, and I'm laughing. This is just the best day.

And the party is only just beginning.

"Let's get you positioned for photos!" the wedding planner demands, but Spencer ignores her.

"Give me a few minutes of privacy with my bride," he says, escorting me back into the lower level of the house.

He pulls me into a small room, shutting the door behind us, and I want to laugh at how much room my dress takes up. There is red silk everywhere, bunched all around me, covered in red tulle, and when Spencer wraps his arms around my waist and tugs me closer, I go to him willingly.

"You're stunning," he murmurs before he kisses me.

I break the kiss seconds later, already breathless. "So are you."

"I love you." He kisses me again, even deeper this time, and when he groans, I definitely break away first.

"We have photos to take," I remind him.

He exhales, nuzzling my cheek with his. "Do we have to?"

"Yes." I press my hand against his shoulder, stopping him. "You can maul me later."

"I plan on it." He cups my cheek, tilting my face toward his. "I just wanted a moment alone with you."

"I like our stolen moments alone. I always have." I smile just before he kisses me again, savoring the sensation of his lush mouth on mine.

"I like them too," he admits when he pulls away. "We'll have plenty more, Mrs. Donato. Uninterrupted ones for once."

"I hope so. As long as Squirrel isn't around."

He laughs. Roland and the cat arrived days after my mother's funeral, and it became my mission to tame the cat and make her mine. With a lot of patience—and tolerating a lot of scratches and yowling in protest—Squirrel has become my cat.

She follows me everywhere, scratching at my ankles and feet.

Sitting in my lap. Sleeping between us on the bed at night. She's the sweetest thing.

"Feisty but lovable," Spencer said to me one night when she was curled up behind his legs and purring loudly. "Much like you."

Maybe that's why Squirrel and I are such kindred spirits.

There's a heavy knock on the door, followed by a familiar voice.

"The wedding planner is going to stroke out if you two don't come out here right now," Whit calls.

A sigh leaves me and I stand up straighter, glancing over at Spencer. "Are you ready?"

He smiles. "As I'll ever be. Let's go, Mrs. Donato."

Well, I could definitely get used to that.

I love the sound of my new name.

CHAPTER THIRTY-NINE

SPENCER

We decided to honeymoon in Italy, on the coast.

We're staying at a hotel in Capri, the interior white and clean, a view from every room. Sylvie booked the biggest suite they had, of course, with the best views of the ocean. The weather is still warm, and she's currently out on the balcony of our suite, tanned from the sun and clad in a white bikini.

Topless.

I remain inside, staring at her through the glass door, contemplating what I should do. I'd planned on going down to the massive pool and relaxing on a lounger for an hour or two before we explore and find somewhere to eat lunch.

Seeing my wife's breasts on blatant display has changed my plans.

Giving in to my urges, I open the sliding glass door and step outside. She's on a lounger, her knees bent, a giant straw hat on her head, shading her face. She cracks open her eyes when she hears the door, a faint smile on her face.

"Care to join me?"

"I was going down to the pool."

"Maybe you should go down on me instead." She laughs when I say nothing. "I think the Italian air is making me horny."

"I like your idea better." I sit on the edge of her lounger, settling my hand on her knee. Her skin glistens from whatever she rubbed all over it, and fuck, I'm tempted.

"I can't sit topless by the pool," she says, sounding logical. "That's why I'm doing it here." She closes her eyes, looking every inch the rich socialite that she is. Thin gold chains around her neck, and gold bracelets on her wrists. My ring on her finger, accompanied by a slender band of diamonds.

"You're wearing sunscreen?"

"Yes," she says, her lips curling. "With a low SPF, though."

"Syl." I sigh.

"Spence." She sighs in response.

I run my hand up her leg, my fingers drifting across her thigh. "You're having fun?"

Her eyes pop open. "This has been the best vacation of my life."

"I agree." It's been nothing but sun and water and sex and food. We can't keep our hands off each other. I agree that there's something in the Italian air.

I always want her. Just like I always have.

After our honeymoon, we're going to the house in California and spending a few weeks there. The renovation is almost complete. Sylvie's been going out there at least once a month to check on the progress, taking her damn cat with her. Squirrel actually likes the leash Sylvie keeps on her, or so her owner says.

I see the look in Squirrel's eyes sometimes. I think she barely tolerates Sylvie and that leash, which is kind of amusing.

I'm slowly pulling out of my father's business, and he's letting me. We haven't really talked about it, but I know he's going to let me walk. Sylvie's words, saying we all have a choice, gave me strength, because she's right.

And she is my choice. My wife, and our new life is what I want to focus on. Nothing else matters.

Just her.

Scooting closer to Sylvie, I toy with the strings at her hips, slowly undoing one. The fabric parts, and with a brush of my fingers, she's exposed, the bikini bottom hanging off one hip.

"What are you doing?" Her voice is a low murmur, her eyes closed once more, and I shift to the other side, undoing the tie there before I pull the bikini bottom back, exposing her completely.

"What's it look like I'm doing?"

She lifts her hips and I yank the bikini from underneath her, letting it drop onto the warm terracotta tile. "People can probably see us."

I glance down at the pool, to the many people sitting around and swimming in it. "No one is paying attention to us."

"That's too bad. I'm sure we could put on quite a show." She removes the hat from her head, letting it fall onto the tile, and I quietly take her in.

Lush and beautiful and completely naked on the lounger. My wife is incredibly sexy since she's become so comfortable in her own skin.

Not that she wasn't sexy before. More like she's become even sexier. And it's almost to my detriment.

I never want to be away from her. She's constantly on my mind, even more so now than ever before. I'm a man obsessed.

And she loves every minute of it.

She spreads her legs, showing me everything she's got, and without hesitation, I touch her there, my fingers gently stroking. "Wet," I murmur.

"Mmm, hmm." Those eyes fall closed yet again, her head tilted back, her face shining in the sun. "Make me come like this, Spence."

I continue searching her, sliding one finger inside her. Then another, the wet sounds of my fingers slipping in and out of her getting louder and louder. Leaning in, I draw a perfect, hard pink nipple into my mouth, sucking and licking and biting. Making her hiss in a breath. Making her moan low in her throat.

I make her come with just my mouth on her breasts and my fingers inside her wet, welcoming body, that soft "oh" she emits just before her body is consumed with shudders the only indication that she's coming. When the orgasm eases, I pull my fingers from within her body and stand, taking off my shirt. Shucking my swim trunks until I'm as naked as she is, and desperately hard for her.

"Get up," I demand, and she does as I say without protest, knowing she's going to benefit. I sit on the lounger and encourage her to sit down on top of me, which she does eagerly. Within minutes, we're readjusted, my cock embedded inside her body, her tits in my face, her arms wound around my neck.

"I like this," she murmurs with a faint smile before she delivers a tongue-filled kiss.

I kiss her in return, shifting my hips, thrusting inside. She rides me, clinging to me, her mouth fused to mine, her pussy clenching tight around my cock until I feel like I might explode. The warm air brushes against our bare skin, making me break out in goosebumps, and I shiver when she draws her fingernails down my spine.

"I love you," she whispers against my lips, just as another orgasm ripples through her. Her inner walls squeeze and torment, ringing my own orgasm straight out of me.

I come with a surprised shout, not giving a damn if I disturbed someone or caught the attention of a complete stranger. The orgasm came so quickly, but I'm too far gone to care.

"That was fast," she says once our breaths have calmed and our heart rates have slowed.

I squeeze her close, dropping a kiss on the top of her breasts. "Felt good."

"It always feels good with you," she says with the utmost sincerity.

I smile at her, brushing the stray blonde hairs away from her face. "I love you."

"I love you too." She kisses me, shifting her hips, my cock still inside her. She keeps moving like that, I'm going to start fucking her again. "We don't need to go down to the pool. Not yet."

I raise my brows. "What do you want to do then?"

"I want you to keep fucking me. Just like this." She surges forward, her hot pussy pressing against my lower stomach, and I'm instantly hard again. "Slow. Like we have all the time in the world."

"We do." I thrust forward, sending myself deeper. "We have the rest of our lives, remember."

"You promise?" Her smile is small. Her laughter, sweet.

"Yes." I kiss her, murmuring against her lips, "I promise."

We do have the rest of our lives. Together.

That has a nice ring to it.

EXCLUSIVE

BONUS

CONTENT

SYLVIE

I stare at the little screen on the test, disbelief coursing through me as I read what it says again and again.

No. No way. It can't be true.

But the single word flashes at me on the test stick almost mockingly.

Pregnant.

I drop the stick into the sink, the clatter when it hits the marble somehow extra loud, and I jump, my heart racing.

I'm...pregnant?

Pregnant.

Oh no.

Leaning against the edge of the bathroom counter, I cover my face with my hands and close my eyes, trying to take deep, cleansing breaths. My thoughts are spiraling and my heart is racing and this is just...unbelievable. Oh, and this definitely wasn't a part of our plan. When Spencer and I first got married, I told him I didn't believe I was capable of being a mother. My own messed me up so badly, I was scared of what I might do if I ever had a child. I'm not maternal.

Not even close.

He nodded and said he understood, because of course he did. Spencer loves me more than any human being on this planet, and I know it. I appreciate it.

I appreciate him.

My husband has never pressured me to have a baby or to start a family. He never even brings it up. I'm the one who has to say something every once in a while. As if I need to reassure myself that everything is okay between us and he's not resentful of me choosing not to get pregnant.

He never is. He just accepts me for who I am.

I'm lucky. I know I am.

I love being an aunt. I overindulge all of my nieces and nephews, and I enjoy spending time with them every chance I can get. I can be trusted around children—not like my mother—but I just didn't like the idea of having children. Couldn't imagine it.

Well, sometimes I did. I'd secretly watch my handsome husband and wonder what it would be like, having a baby with him. A baby who looked just like him. Dark-haired and dark-eyed and not a lick of Lancaster in his features. Just the way I preferred my imaginary baby.

Always a son. Never a daughter. I didn't want a mini me. I wanted a mini him.

A mini Spencer.

Dropping my hands from my face, I rest my right hand over my still-flat stomach, trying to calculate how far along I might possibly be. Over two months, I'm guessing. I've never really had regular periods and was even told at one point that I have a lazy ovary. That my chances of getting pregnant are lower than other women and as I get older, it'll only get worse.

I stopped taking birth control because I didn't like how it made me feel, though at least I was regular then. I suppose Spencer and I got careless. Even though we're married. We've been together for years. What's wrong with having unprotected sex? Not like I ever got pregnant before.

But I am now.

A knock on the bathroom door startles me, and I drop my hand from my stomach, whirling around to stare at the closed door.

"You okay, Syl? You've been in there for a while."

My loving husband, always making sure I'm all right. This man.

Clearing my throat, I call out, "I'm fine. I'll be done in a minute."

"Okay." He moves away from the door, and I turn to the sink, grabbing the pregnancy test and giving it a quick rinse before I set it on the counter and wash my hands.

Within minutes, I'm exiting our bathroom, stopping when I find Spencer pacing. He sees me and comes to a halt, his expression agonizing as he studies me.

"What's wrong with you?"

I blink at him, shocked by his question. Surprised even more by the fear I hear in his deep voice.

"Nothing's wrong with me," I say slowly, my hands behind my back, clutching the pregnancy test.

"You've been acting weird the last couple of weeks. Not sleeping. Tossing and turning all night long. You're not eating—"

"I am too," I say, interrupting him. "I just haven't been that hungry."

"If you are eating, you're sneaking away to the bathroom to throw up." He comes to me, frowning when he realizes my hands are behind my back. "Are you hiding something from me?"

He's too perceptive. He pays attention to every little detail when it comes to me, and I'm suddenly nervous to tell him. Will he be happy? Does he want to have a baby with me? Or is he worried I'll be a terrible mother?

I'm worried I'll be a bad mom. What do I know about babies? Nothing.

"Maybe," I admit, pressing my lips together. I feel like I'm going to burst. "Just...will you sit down, please?"

He glances backward before he falls onto the edge of the mattress, staring up at me with distress filling his gaze. "Say it, Sylvie. What's wrong?"

"There's nothing wrong." I shake my head, swallowing hard. It feels like my heart is pounding in my throat. "I have some news."

"What is it?" The fear in his voice becomes even more obvious, and I feel terrible.

"I'm... We're going to..." My voice drifts, and he shakes his head.

"Tell me, damn it."

"I'm pregnant." I hold the pregnancy test out to him. "We're going to have a baby."

He blinks at me, his gaze dropping to the stick in my hand. He reads the little screen, his lips parting, and I stare at the top of his head. His thick, dark hair that I love to run my fingers through. I love this man so much.

"Sylvie..." He leaps to his feet, tossing the pregnancy test onto the bed. Reaching for me so he can cradle my face in his hands. "A baby?"

I nod, tears filling my eyes. "Are you okay with that?"

"I didn't realize..."

"That we were even trying?" I shrug, a soft laugh escaping me. "I didn't, either."

His gaze roams over my face, his lips curling into the faintest smile. "This is... This is great news."

"You think so?" I ask hopefully.

His hands drop from my face, and he pulls me in close, hugging me tightly. "It's the best news I've ever heard."

I cling to him, the relief that floods me making me weak. "You think we'll be all right?"

"What do you mean?"

"I know you're going to be a perfect father." There's no doubt in my mind that he'll be amazing. Attentive. Doting. He'll spoil our child completely. "But what about...me?"

He pulls away slightly so he can look into my eyes, his hands shifting up to cup my cheeks again. "You're going to be an amazing mother."

I want to believe him. It's just...

"Are you sure?" The doubt rises within me, filling me with fear. "My mother—"

"You're nothing like your mother," he says vehemently, cutting me off. "You're you, Syl. And while you didn't have the best example growing up, look at you now. You're the best woman I know."

I smile at him, tears pricking at the corners of my eyes. "You really think so?"

"I know so," he says, his voice firm. "You're going to make a terrific mother. And I'm going to be a dad."

He grins, his eyes sparkling, and I swear I'm witnessing the realization sink into his brain.

"A dad." Spencer leans forward, pressing his forehead to mine. "And a mom."

"That's us." I laugh, the tears slipping down my cheeks. "Can you believe it?"

"I can," he whispers just before he kisses me. "I love you, Sylvie."

"I love you, too." I return his kiss, losing myself in it for a while, until I feel him smile against my lips.

"We're going to be parents."

"I know." I laugh. So does he.

Thank goodness we're in this together.

• • •

Spencer and Sylvie Donato are excited to
announce the birth of their son
Christopher Thayer
On August 14th
8 pounds, 4 ounces
20 inches

ACKNOWLEDGMENTS

I was supposed to write this book last winter. I was gearing up for it, and then someone else started whispering in my ear, insisting he get his book first.

His name is Crew Lancaster.

So I shelved Sylvie and focused on the other Lancasters, including Charlotte. Her books were planned last fall as well and had a delivery schedule, so Sylvie had to wait. Impatiently, I might add. Once Crew was out of my head (he was very loud), she started speaking to me, but I was swamped with personal things. Like my baby graduating high school, going to Book Bonanza, getting sick afterward, moving my son into his college dorm…the list goes on. I snuck Sylvie in where I could and I just felt so…distant from the story. Is it any good? Did I redeem her? Poor Spencer, tolerating her for so long!

I sent it off to edits, crossed my fingers it was okay and when I got it back and read it again, I realized hey, I'm proud of this book! I feel like I gave Sylvie enough reason for her to act the way she did, and I think (I hope) she redeemed herself. It was so much fun having Whit and Summer play such a big part in the story, and including the other Lancasters too.

Y'all go on about what a great gift giver Crew is (and yes, he's amazing), but Spencer gave Sylvie the ultimate gift at the end of this book. He gave her back her freedom. And for that, she is forever grateful. Sylvie really touched my heart. She's been through a lot, most of it at the hands of her mother. I do love writing a villain, but Sylvia Lancaster is one of the worst.

I hope you enjoy this book. I put a lot of pressure on myself, writing the follow up to Crew and Wren, and I just want you to love Spencer and Sylvie. Their story is different, but I love them just the same.

Okay, now it's time for me to thank everyone! To the readers - you've made a huge difference in my career this year thanks to your love for A Million Kisses, and I'm forever grateful to you. I always say this but it's true: I can't do this job without you. Thank you.

I also want to thank everyone at Valentine PR for taking care of me - Nina, Kim, Valentine, Daisy, Kelley - you ladies are the best! Nina, thank you as always for your insight. As usual, you made this book that much better and I love you.

Thank you to my editor Rebecca and proofreader Sarah for all that you do. Jan, thank you for reading and being one of my biggest cheerleaders. Emily Wittig, thank you for your stellar design skills, and for being so easy to work with. And thank you for keeping tabs on my books and letting me know when AMK is in a bookstore or back on the charts. I appreciate you!

p.s. - If you enjoyed PROMISES WE MEANT TO KEEP, it would mean the world to me if you left a review on the retailer site you bought it from, or on Goodreads. Thank you so much!

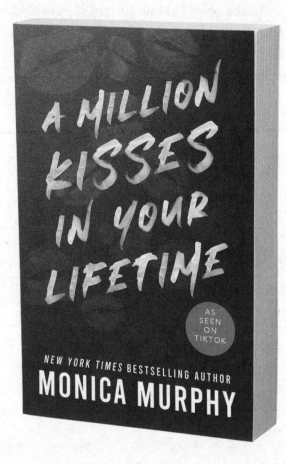

Promises We Meant to Keep is a second chance dark romance with old money vibes. However, the story includes elements that might not be suitable for all readers. Parental verbal and physical abuse, violence and death of a parent are mentioned/shown/discussed in the novel. Readers who may be sensitive to these elements, please take note.

AMARA
an imprint of Entangled Publishing LLC